Hot Stew

Fiona Mozley

JOHN MURRAY

First published in Great Britain in 2021 by John Murray (Publishers)
An Hachette UK company

1

Copyright © Fiona Mozley 2021

A CIP catalogue record for this title is available from the British Library

Hardback ISBN 9781529327205
Trade Paperback ISBN 9781529327212
eBook ISBN 9781529327304

Typeset in Sabon by Palimpsest Book Production Limited,
Falkirk, Stirlingshire

Printed and bound in Great Britain by Clays Ltd, Elcograf S.p.A.

John Murray policy is to use papers that are natural, renewable and
recyclable products and made from wood grown in sustainable forests.
The logging and manufacturing processes are expected to conform
to the environmental regulations of the country of origin.

John Murray (Publishers)
Carmelite House
50 Victoria Embankment
London EC4Y 0DZ

www.johnmurraypress.co.uk

For my sister, Olivia

Midsummer's Day

Common Snail

On the corner of the street, there is an old French restaurant with red-and-white chequered tablecloths. Des Sables has been there for decades and has changed very little in that time. It has served the same dishes, with ingredients sourced from the same suppliers, and wines from the same vineyards. The bottles are stacked on the same shelves, and when they are pulled out and dusted off, the silky liquid is poured into the same set of glasses, or ones of a similar style, bought sporadically to replace those that have smashed. The plates are the same: small, round, porcelain.

When the weather is good, tables are placed outside. There is a space between the public thoroughfare and the exterior wall, and the tables are set tightly, with two chairs tucked beneath. One of the tables wobbles. Over the years, thousands of napkins have been folded and placed under the offending leg, hundreds of customers have complained and moved to alternatives, and thousands more have quietly put up with the inconvenience. They have spilled glasses of wine, grumbled, and considered asking to move, before deciding against it.

The restaurant serves escargots. The restaurant has served escargots since it opened. Hundreds, thousands, maybe even millions of snails. They have been thrown into boiling water, and their carcasses scooped out and served with garlic butter. The chewy pellets have been picked with forks and fingers, and the curled shells discarded.

It is lunchtime in midsummer. A box of snails has been taken from the fridge and placed on the side, its contents ready to be immersed and scalded. It is left unsupervised as chefs bustle around the kitchen with sharp knives, pots and pans, bunches of parsley and stalks of celery. A single snail, on the small side, wakes from its chilly slumber and climbs over the edge of the box, down the side, and on to the stainless-steel counter. Slowly, it descends to the floor, then to the back of the kitchen, where there is a door to the street. After about twenty minutes, the little snail finds itself in the alley behind the restaurant, feasting on the discarded outer leaves of a savoy cabbage. Once sated it continues its journey. It begins to climb the wall, flexing and releasing.

The building stands in Soho, in the middle of London. The foundations were constructed in the seventeenth century, during the Interregnum, in the space between a father and a son; the ampersand between The King is Dead & Long Live the King. Bricks and plaster overlaid on to a now-crooked timber frame. There are wormholes in the timber and snail licks on the bricks.

The district was once a suburb. London was enclosed by a wall, and to the north there was a moor. There were deer and boar and hare. North-west of London; north-east of Westminster. Men and women galloped out from the two cities to hunt, and their cries gave this place its name: So! Ho! So! Ho!

The stone came. Bricks and mortar replaced trees; people replaced deer; sticky grey grime replaced sticky brown dirt. Paths carved by the tread of animals were set in stone, widened, edged with walls and gates. Mansions were built for high society. There was dancing, gambling, sex. Music was played and plays were staged. Bargains were struck, sedition was plotted, betrayals were planned, secrets were kept.

New people arrived. Émigrés from France came to escape revolution, guillotine, war. Mansions were divided and subdivided. Drawing rooms became workshops; parlours became coffee shops. Whole families lived in single rooms, and disease spread. Syphilis erupted in sores on the skin and delusions in the mind. Cholera hid in the water, crept through the drains, came out of pumps and down human throats.

Books were written, ripped up, rewritten. Karl Marx dreamed of utopia while his wife cooked dinner and scrubbed the floor. His friends met on Great Windmill Street where wind was once the means of production.

When the bombs fell on London, Soho took a few. Dark lesions appeared in the lines of Georgian townhouses and people sheltered beneath ground.

After the war, the concrete came, and parallel lines, and precise angles that connected earth to sky. Houses were rebuilt, shops were rebuilt, and new paving stones were laid. The dead were buried. The past was buried. There were new kinds of men and new kinds of women. There was art and music and miniskirts and sharp haircuts to match the skyline. Films were made; records were cut. Soho came to be filled with the apparatus of sound and vision. Electric currents ran through cables and magnets and copper coils and pushed rhythmic air into dark rooms where people danced in new ways, and drank and smoked, and ingested new drugs imported from old places. And they spoke again of revolution.

And they spoke until the winds changed. Trade and commerce and common sense and common decency prevailed, and men and women availed themselves of all opportunities. New roads were laid; office blocks shot up. And luxury flats stood on crumbling slums like shining false teeth on rotten gums.

At the top of the building, whose ground floor is occupied by the restaurant, there is a secret garden. It was planted by the two women who share the garret, where the ceilings are slanted and dormer windows jut out. Outside the windows is a ledge, where the roof meets the exterior wall. The windows are large enough to climb through and it is possible to stand on the ledge. The woman called Tabitha discovered this. She is an intermittent smoker and the other woman, Precious, won't allow her to smoke inside. Tabitha found that, along the ledge, there are steps and, if you climb the short flight, you come to a flat terrace, sheltered by the adjacent slanting roofs but exposed enough to trap the midday sun.

Precious and Tabitha have filled the space with life. It began with a cheap chilli plant Precious picked up from the supermarket. The chillies did better than expected and Precious bought others, then the generic herbs of a kitchen garden: parsley, rosemary, chives. She bought a rose and ornamental grasses. When the weather is good and Precious and Tabitha have free time, they sit out together.

'Do you know what I find really quite rank?'

'What do you find really quite rank, Tabitha?'

'The fact that you put crushed snail shells around your plants to stop snails eating them.'

'What's wrong with that?'

'It's weird. Don't people use eggshells?'

'Yeah, but I get the used snail shells from the restaurant downstairs. They also give me mussel, and clam and cockle shells. It's what's available.'

'I get that. I'm just saying: I don't like it. It would be like someone building a fence to keep out people, and instead of using wire or wood, they built it out of human bones. Do you know what I mean?'

'Not really.'

Tabitha has a cigarette in one hand and an e-cigarette in the other, holding both as if they are glasses of expensive wine and she is sampling each in turn. She takes a drag from the real cigarette, holds the smoke between her cheeks, makes a whirling motion with her pursed lips, and exhales, then repeats the process with the e-cigarette. She frowns and pouts, deep in concentration.

'It's not the same,' she says.

'It's never going to be. The question isn't whether you can tell the difference but whether you think you could make the switch.'

'Well, no, then. The answer is no.'

'For god's sake, could you at least give it a proper try?'

'I have done!'

'For longer than, like, five seconds.'

'I don't like the way it feels in my mouth. It feels artificial. Like detergent.'

'Because the others are one hundred per cent natural, organic carcinogens.'

'It's real tobacco, at least. Plant-based.'

'Give those to me.' Precious snatches the packet of cigarettes from the table next to the older woman. She looks down at the grim warnings and harrowing images printed on the side of the carton, pulls back her throwing arm and pelts the cigarettes off the roof. The little box tumbles in a graceful arc over the side of the building and out of sight.

Tabitha's eyes widen, incredulous. 'That could seriously injure someone.'

'There was hardly anything in it. The most it will give someone is a paper cut.'

'Paper cuts can hurt,' Tabitha points out. She returns to the lit cigarette still in her hand, and takes a long, ostentatious drag. She blows the smoke towards her friend. 'What's it to you, anyway? Me smoking.'

'I don't want you to die?'

'Would you miss me?'

'Funerals are expensive.'

'Just chuck my corpse in the river.'

'It'd scare the tourists. They'd be chugging down the Thames on a sightseeing cruise then see your ugly mug bobbing around in the shallows.'

'Simple solution: weigh me down with bricks.'

'It might be easier to give up the cigs.'

'For you, maybe.'

'Well, at least don't do it next to my rose. She doesn't want your exhaust fumes.'

'Oh, for god's sake. Not allowed to smoke inside. Not allowed to smoke outside. Is this a totalitarian regime?'

A phone rings. It's a landline but with a cordless receiver which Tabitha has brought outside. She puts down the e-cigarette and picks up the receiver and continues to smoke the real cigarette as she talks. She says 'yeah' and 'uh huh' a couple of times and nods as if her gestures can be seen by the person she's speaking to.

Tabitha hangs up and puts down the receiver. 'John,' she says simply.

Precious is bent over the flowerpot pulling out weeds. She straightens her back and peels off her gardening gloves. She digs the trowel into the soil and throws the dirty gloves on to one of the folding chairs. She sticks a leg over the side of the building and, clutching the railings, lowers herself down the ladder then squeezes through the open window into the flat.

Down on the pavement, a woman and a man sit at the wobbly table. Having sat here before, the woman has placed a paper napkin beneath the offending leg. The furniture is now still, but the chequered cloth moves with the breeze. There is a bottle of red Bordeaux, two glasses, a bowl of green olives, and another for discarded pits.

'You must be joking,' says the woman. Her name is Agatha Howard. She is in her mid twenties, dressed elegantly but in the style of an older woman – a politician or a business executive. She is wearing a linen trouser suit, the jacket removed and folded on the back of her chair, and a white blouse buttoned to her neck. There are jewels around her wrist and hanging from each earlobe but these – rubies set in gold – age her. She holds a small photograph loosely between a thumb and forefinger. The photograph is of a piece of fabric. The fabric may once have been a handkerchief but it is now old and shapeless, and ragged at the edges. It is mostly grey, but at one corner there is a dark brown stain.

'I am not joking,' the man replies. He is an antique dealer. 'Hand me that letter of verification.'

The man hands the woman a letter of verification pertaining

to the square of fabric. It is typed on headed paper, and signed. Agatha reads to the end, frowns, then looks closely at the signature. 'I haven't heard of this historian,' she says.

'He's at Durham. He is young but very well regarded.'

'If he were well regarded, I would have heard of him.'

Agatha looks again at the letter, then again at the photograph of the rag. It was supposedly dipped in blood at the foot of the guillotine, taken as a keepsake of the dying order.

'It's the kind of money I would expect to pay for a relic of the Bourbons, not for a minor member of the nobility.'

'Not a minor noble. A descendant of the Valois kings through the female line.'

Agatha considers. She studies the photograph again, and then the man. She sits back in her chair and looks out to the street, then up at hanging baskets of red geraniums. Inside one, there is a discarded packet of cigarettes. The box is lying among the dark green foliage, and one of the cigarettes has become caught between the soil and the metal wire of the basket.

People these days have such a fundamental lack of respect.

She looks back at the man.

'No,' she says.

'What?'

'I said no.'

'Would you like to come in and see the original?'

'I'm not interested.'

He has dealt with her before, so knows she is serious.

'Fine,' he says. 'Keep the photo in case you change your mind.' He seems neither affronted nor disappointed. He shouldn't be – Agatha has spent huge amounts of money at his dealership.

'I have to go,' she tells him.

'You're not staying to eat?'

'I can't, but you should. This place won't be here for much longer. I'm redeveloping most of the street. Restaurants like this are quaint, but they aren't profitable.'

9

The man looks at her as a disappointed teacher might look at a wayward pupil. He asks her what he should order.

'The escargots are excellent.'

She gets up, knocking the wobbly table. She says goodbye and makes her way to the end of the street where her driver is waiting for her in a blue Rolls Royce.

Just along from the French restaurant, there is a grate in the pavement, and along from the grate there is a hatch. Beneath the hatch, which opens and shuts on rusty hinges, there is a dark cellar, and inside the dark cellar there are a number of people. Two of the people come out of the hatch, and race each other down the street. They are making their way to an old pub: the Aphra Behn.

The Aphra Behn

Paul Daniels and Debbie McGee walk into a bar. The man they call Paul Daniels and the woman they call Debbie McGee walk into the Aphra Behn of Soho. They enter through an open back door then stand in a hot, poorly lit kitchen. On the counter, there is a second-hand feast: a plate of chips; a ramekin of tartare sauce; a gravy-sodden pie crust; an unfinished Greek salad with feta and pomegranate seeds.

The man they call Paul Daniels and the woman they call Debbie McGee pass through the kitchen without touching the food, and enter the main public room. The bartender looks up from his phone to see them pour the remaining liquid from discarded drinks into an empty plastic bottle. Gin, tonic water, lager, rum, cola, sparkling wine, Pimm's, a strawberry, a slice of cucumber and a novelty cocktail umbrella. Paul Daniels screws the lid on to the bottle and hides it in his coat, which he wears even on hot days. The mixture is an insurance policy. He will consume it later if something better cannot be begged or stolen.

The bartender returns to his phone. He swipes right on all the pictures of women, 18 to 35, who have placed their profiles online for his perusal. He stopped following his employers' instructions to keep the riffraff at bay several weeks ago, when he decided bar work wasn't for him.

They call the man Paul Daniels because he performs magic tricks for tips and the woman Debbie McGee because she is always by his side, but unlike their glamorous namesakes, they have neither expertise, talent, wealth, nor much of an audience.

Paul Daniels is making his rounds of the tables and standing patrons. He inserts thin, purpled fingers into his pockets and pulls out a cup and three red sponge balls. They are lighter than their size should allow; a small-scale optical illusion. They stick to his fingers like marshmallows. He begins at the first table with the Three Cup Trick, even though in this he rarely succeeds. He knows how it should be done but loses concentration and forgets where he's put the ball. The man in front of him correctly guesses its location, and flips the cup with a satisfied smile.

'There you go, mate,' he says. He is wearing a baby-pink polo shirt with a logo embroidered on the chest. 'Now pay up.' He holds out a hand.

It is well known in the Aphra Behn that Paul Daniels is not allowed to lose. For all the occasions on which grubby playing cards slip from the frayed sleeves of his coat, or silk handkerchiefs reveal their secrets too soon, the loyal patrons of the Aphra Behn feign astonishment and hand over their pennies willingly.

The man in the polo shirt insists on collecting his winnings. He is not a regular at the pub but a tourist. He intends to spend the evening watching women with silicon breast implants and the hair of Russian prisoners (severed, imported, bleached, glued to the new scalp) remove their clothes and dance for him while he slips crisp twenty-pound notes into their garters. He is a man who knows the price of everything. He likes to win and on this occasion he has won. He wants his 40p: 20p for his stake and 20p for his winnings.

Paul Daniels is unwilling to part with his cash. He hesitates.

'What's your game?' the man asks the magician. 'If you win you take the money and if you lose you take the money? That's no way to run a business. Who's going to play your cup game if it's not properly competitive?'

Paul Daniels's hands tremble as he searches for copper coins. His ribcage convulses with incoherent apologies.

The woman they call Debbie McGee remains calm. It's a calmness derived from rehearsed apathy.

Nobody in the Aphra Behn can remember anything ever provoking emotion from Debbie McGee. There was once a time when she took pleasure in many things: a compelling film, a well-taken photograph of family and friends, late-night karaoke, an Indian takeaway. There was once a time when she was saddened by other things: a break-up, news of hurricanes, the sight of her baby sister leaving the house for the last time. There was also a period of her life when nothing but heroin made her happy or sad. She was happy when she had it; she was sad when she didn't. That time also passed. For the woman they call Debbie McGee, there is nothing left to feel.

She remains silent throughout the exchange. Her eyes return to the man behind the bar. He has set aside his phone to follow the dispute.

Some of the pub's regulars shift on their bar stools. One of them is quietly celebrating his sixty-fourth birthday. Although Robert Kerr has been drinking beer with his friend, Lorenzo, he hasn't told him it's a special day. He is content with his daily routine and doesn't want to disrupt it, and besides, Lorenzo is much younger than him, young enough to be his son, and he probably wouldn't be interested in the birthday celebrations of his long-time neighbour and drinking companion.

Robert turns to watch along with the rest of the pub. He had hoped it would be quickly resolved. With a deep sigh, Robert raises himself from the bar stool. The leather padding has settled to the shape of his buttocks after several hours of stasis. He takes the four or five steps to the scene of the altercation. 'Do you know what you are, mate?' he asks. The tourist is nearly thirty years younger than him. He doesn't reply. 'You're a cunt,' Robert tells him.

Fights are now rare in this part of London. When Robert first came to the area they were common. In those days, assailants carried knuckledusters and switch-blade knives.

The tourist at the table stares up into the face of the older, burlier man. He notes the gold chain around the thick neck and the nose that's been broken and clumsily repaired several times. He sees the scar on his forehead, which is large and perfectly square, the sort that cannot be caused by mishap.

Robert reaches into the pocket of his jeans and pulls out a fifty pence piece. He drops it into the man's gin and tonic. 'With interest.' The greasy hexagon meets the acid of the lime and fizzes against the sides of the glass. The man makes no attempt to fish it out.

Robert's friend Lorenzo has been sitting with him all afternoon. They're regular drinking companions. As Robert made his intervention, Lorenzo subtly lifted himself from his own bar stool – likewise customised to the curve of his arse – and slipped out the front door of the pub to the street, where the bouncer stands.

The bouncer is a middle-aged woman called Sheila. She is around five feet tall. Her hair is bleached blonde over grey. Every morning she rubs wax on to the palms of her hands then runs her hands through her hair, creating little spikes and curls. Sheila's employed to marshal patrons and gently reinforce the pub's rules. She makes sure people leave the building to smoke and that they keep behind the white line that's been drawn on to the pavement to demarcate the acceptable smoking-and-drinking area. She greets patrons who enter the pub and she calls taxis at the end of the night for customers who are too drunk to find their own way home. She also deals with disturbances, although these are a rarity these days or else the managers of the Behn would have employed a brawnier bouncer to do the work.

Lorenzo beckons Sheila inside and points to Robert. The other man has still said nothing.

Meanwhile, Paul Daniels looks about the premises, searching for a convenient escape.

Debbie McGee is at the bar, finishing a row of drinks that have been left by a group of middle-aged women, now unsure of their choice of venue and keen to hurry on to a nearby theatre and its production of *Julius Caesar*.

14

Sheila faces a conundrum. She is fond of Lorenzo, and he has brought her inside to eject the tourist. She likes Robert too but he appears to be the aggressor. The man they call Paul Daniels is hopping around the pub despite the instructions she has given him to stay away. Sheila has no objection in principle to this desperate man and woman coming into the pub each day for a short amount of time to ply their trade, but she is also the sort of woman who takes her job seriously.

Robert spots Sheila's entrance and goes out on to the street, pushing the door open with a strong left arm then allowing it to swing shut behind him. It used to be second nature for him to come outside like this and smoke. He quit a few years ago, but he still feels the compulsion to interrupt his drinking to stand on the pavement and breathe the fresh air. And he wants to give that dickhead a chance to leave by the other exit.

Paul Daniels also spares Sheila the awkwardness of an altercation. He scoops his belongings from the table and stashes them in his coat. As a parting gesture, he takes hold of the glass of gin and tonic and, as the man in the pink polo shirt watches, incredulous, he pours it down his ulcerated throat in a hollow gulp, coin and all. He hops towards the front door then rushes out. Debbie McGee notes without expression the departure of her beloved, and quietly follows.

Robert Kerr has known the woman some people call Debbie McGee for many years. He knew her before she came to be called Debbie McGee, when she was known by her real name. He knew her before she met the man with whom she now walks the streets, before her bones dried and fractured and were set in casts by concerned nurses, before her skin withered, before she pierced it with blunted needles, before she slept curled up between strange men. Robert looks at her now and sees all the many changing seasons that have passed. He sees rain and wind. He sees months of creeping sickness. He sees moments of giddy health. He sees poverty and fortune.

He sees terror and hunger and pain and hope. He sees time as she stands still.

In the same pocket of his jeans from which he plucked the fifty pence piece, Robert finds a twenty-pound note. He unpicks the folds with the care of a pastry chef for fine filo and holds it out. It flutters in the breeze like a handkerchief at a passing train.

'Don't spend it all on smack,' he says to her. 'Get yourself some chips or something. And a decent place to sleep.'

The woman they call Debbie McGee does not meet the old man's eyes but focuses instead on the note. She takes it in her right hand and tucks it into the sleeve of her T-shirt, too tight even for her slight frame.

Across the road, Paul Daniels weeps and swears and stamps. He throws up his arms and screams at the sky. Phlegm and spit fly from his mouth. He pays no attention to the location of his companion, nor does he look behind to see if she follows as he zigzags down the street, pushing pedestrians out of his way, causing black cabs to swerve and stop.

Debbie McGee does follow. She keeps to the sides of the pavements where the tall buildings cast shade, and where chewing gum and half-eaten burgers, and the butts of cigarettes are thrown, and where dogs and drunks defecate and piss.

The woman they call Debbie McGee keeps pace with her beloved. Robert Kerr watches her go.

Familiar Streets

Robert doesn't return inside to finish his pint. It is a hot day and he and Lorenzo have been drinking cold lager, which will now be warm. He looks into the pub and sees his pal speaking animatedly with the bartender, presumably about what has just happened. Robert hopes he hasn't embarrassed him. He did what needed doing but didn't mean to cause a scene.

Sheila begins to sweep the pavement with a coarse wooden-handled brush. Robert feels sure he must have annoyed her, but as she shuffles towards him she smiles. He thinks then, as he often does whenever he sees Sheila or any woman he considers good and kind and honest but for whom he feels no sexual desire, that he ought to marry her. But the moment passes, as it always does, and he thinks anyway she is probably in a relationship with the other lady bouncer at the lesbian bar around the corner.

Robert walks south. He glances at his watch: six o'clock. He wonders if it is late enough to visit the other place at which he is considered a regular. It will be open, but it might be too early for that kind of thing. He slows, and looks in at some of the shops and restaurants along the route. He passes private members' clubs with grand old doors leading to dark corners and deep armchairs. He passes restaurants and cafes and shops that sell oysters and noodles and sashimi and frozen yoghurt. On the corner, a sex shop displays lurid butt plugs and leather thongs. In the window, the management have hung an A1-size poster of two men kissing. Their bodies are tanned and waxed and lightly oiled. They are both wearing tight fluorescent swimming trunks. One of the men is clean shaven but the other has a neatly groomed beard. This confuses Robert. He knows from Lorenzo that these sorts of men would generally be described as 'Hunks', owing to their height and tight muscles. However, the presence of the beard indicates the category 'Bear', to which Lorenzo enjoys informing Robert that he, Robert, would belong if he were a gay man. The man on the poster muddles these categories. Robert walks on past the sex shop pondering, from the information he's been given, how Lorenzo might be defined. But Robert can't remember. Lorenzo is just Lorenzo.

Robert passes Des Sables and turns left. The shaded alley down which he slides brims with birds. Pigeons pluck the crumbs of Cornish pasties from between the slats of cast-iron grates and mutter to each other as they apportion scraps. A hen pigeon drags a gammy foot as she is pursued by two cocks. They hock flattering remarks but she remains uninterested and continues to hop. She tears her malnourished body into the air with lean but powerful wings and settles on a windowsill, squeezing easily behind the contra-avian spikes. The cock pigeons coo to one another as if disputing whether to pursue, then collectively decide to sate their hunger rather than their lust and return to the business of pecking. Further down the alley, there is a pigeon so white it is almost a dove. Its snowy wings are marred only by an irregular flight feather of dust and coral that hangs aslant as if aware of its own deviance. Beyond the pigeons, a flock of sparrows. Too few, too few. When Robert first came to London, nearly fifty years ago, sparrows smudged the skies and dotted every pavement. In those first decades, they were common, and he fed them from his bare, outstretched hands.

Robert steps into the brothel. Old Scarlet sits behind the little desk. Karl leans against the wall, flicking through a glossy magazine. Both look up. Old Scarlet's eyelids are painted with shimmering cyan that illuminates her brown eyes, tired from thirty years of late nights and dark rooms. Her lips are tinted the colour of her namesake. She greets Robert warmly. Karl is even larger than him and has even less hair on his head. He wears nothing but black: a black shirt and a pair of black jeans tightened with a black leather belt. He notes Robert's presence then returns to his literature. He hardly ever speaks.

'How are we today?' Old Scarlet asks.

Robert answers that he is well and asks how she is.

'Oh, you know,' she says. 'Sciatica. We're not as young as we used to be.'

'We're not.'

She opens the ledger. The only computer in the brothel is attached to the webcam upstairs. Old Scarlet runs the business with pencil and paper.

'Tiffany and Giselle and Precious are free now, or we've got Young Scarlet in half an hour, or Crystal an hour after that. It's Candy's day off.'

Robert raises his hands in indecision. 'I'll go with whoever will have me. To an old thug like me they're all absolutely lovely.'

'Precious, then. You and her get on well.'

Old Scarlet makes a mark in the ledger and instructs Robert to take a seat in the showroom. 'I'll tell Precious you're coming. Help yourself to a drink.'

Robert wraps his knuckles on the wooden desk by way of thanks and turns from Old Scarlet and Karl. He takes the swing door to the left of the admissions desk and steadies it shut before proceeding. A long and familiar hallway stretches before him. The walls are coated with a red fabric like velvet but with longer strands, like the coat of a shaggy dog. It gives the walls the texture of something organic, something that has grown from the plaster. Robert stretches out both hands, as he always does when he walks through this familiar passage. He allows his hands to glide across the fabric. He enjoys the soft tickle. The carpet is likewise red and it is padded with a kind of satin towelling. Robert's shoes sink into it. The lighting is dim and rose-pink. Long tendrils of silken cord, this the deepest red of any of the fabrics, have been stitched into the padded ceiling and hang to approximately the height of Robert's waist. The silk tendrils are the red of bull's blood. They are the red of sow's blood. They hang as if dripping.

Robert walks through the web of cloth. It strokes and caresses his face and he carves a path through it as if parting a sea. The light from the pink bulbs shines on the red fabric of the walls and the floor and against the crimson tendrils. The hall is steeped in a spectrum of red, and the red is alive with movement.

Robert is colour blind. For Robert, red is green and green is red and there's nothing in between. When he takes this short walk between the foyer and the waiting area, he does not think of the heat and clamour of the busy street behind nor of the pleasures beyond. He finds himself in a forest that he knows of old, in a wood so thick and fecund he can see no more than an arm's length ahead and an arm's length behind. He feels the fabrics as foliate, like the tender needles of young firs. He seeks a path through the branches to the room beyond, and when he comes to it he blinks, though the light here is hardly dialled brighter.

The far wall presents a familiar brass drinks trolley, with glass and crystal decanters holding brown and gold and burgundy liquids. He pours himself a whisky and waits. After a minute or so Old Scarlet comes rushing in from the reception.

'I forgot to ask,' she says. 'What can I tell her you're after?'

'Full service,' replies Robert. 'It's my birthday.'

The Trickle Down

In another part of the city, Bastian Elton watches his girlfriend preen. There are parts of her routine he's permitted to see and parts he isn't. She goes inside the bathroom to wax, to shave and to pluck, but stands in front of the living room mirror to apply her make-up. Rebecca keeps her catalogue of accoutrements in a metal box with compartments that fold in and out like the doors of an aeroplane. It is highly technical. There are boxes within boxes, and pastes and gels and brushes. She selects a white tube and squeezes a precise amount of clear gel on to her forefinger. She uses the fingertips on both hands to rub it over her face, then pulls out a small plastic tub, unscrews it, and balances the lid on the mantelpiece. The tub contains a fine powder resembling ground skin.

Bastian is sitting on the sofa with his legs slightly apart. His hands are between them, holding the jacket of a suit that has just been delivered. The clothes Bastian used to buy came from expensive high street shops, but when his grandfather discovered this, he set up an account for Bastian at a tailor's shop on Savile Row and took him for a fitting.

Bastian continues to watch Rebecca. She touches the dust with a long brush with bristles that fan out like the tail of a peacock then bounces it across her face until the powder becomes invisible. Next, she attends to her eyes. She clicks open a disc containing powders of varying hues, divided into sections. She applies some of the beige powder then two shades of brown. She puts the items back into the box then pulls out a pencil and a long thin tube that Bastian recognises as mascara. She traces the tip of the pencil around her eyes to create a dark rim then sets about touching the tip of the black mascara brush against her eyelashes while she stares into the mirror with her lips parted. She finishes this process and sneezes. Bastian has previously noticed her sneezing after touching her eyelashes with the mascara brush. It makes him smile. It reminds him of the family cat he had when he was growing up: a fluffy pedigree named Purrsia. Purrsia used to sneeze when she was excited. She would stop, stand still, steady herself, and shut her eyes. When the sneeze came, she would hardly make a sound. Rebecca's sneezes are also strangely silent. She scrunches up her face and draws her shoulders up to her ears to brace herself against the minor, internal explosion. She looks very cute when she does this.

Rebecca is a highly measured person. Bastian is frequently astonished by her levels of self-control. She keeps a rigid routine; Bastian has never known her to be late. She eats healthily and exercises regularly, and is tidy in her appearance and domestic habits. She thinks before she speaks. Her sneezes are a minor aberration; a stray note in an otherwise perfect symphony.

It took Rebecca a long time to allow Bastian to see this part of her routine. They met at Cambridge, during the first week of their first term, and were in a relationship by Christmas. For three years, before they graduated and moved into this flat, Bastian saw neither her un-made-up face nor her un-straightened hair. She brought her make-up box when staying over in his room and, in the morning, she locked herself in the bathroom and emerged as a pristine facsimile of herself from the day before. When they moved in together, she relaxed her regimen but only slightly. She began to come out of the bathroom with wet hair wrapped in a towel, wearing no make-up. Now, she stands in front of him while getting ready.

There is still a lot Rebecca doesn't let Bastian see, but he finds evidence in the flat. He sees her tweezers lying on a shelf in the bathroom cabinet, and her razor on the side of the bath with spikes of dark hair tucked between the blades. He has opened the lidded basket she placed by the toilet for paraphernalia to deal with her periods. He smells traces of her too. He sometimes smells the odour of menstruation, and the singed keratin of her straightened hair.

Rebecca has moved on to her hair. She feeds strips of her dark brown locks between the hot tongs and irons out any kinks or inconsistencies. Next, she stands back from the mirror and considers her reflection. She flicks a couple of stray hairs into place.

Bastian rises and pats out the creases in his jacket. He swings it around his shoulders and slips his arms into the sleeves. He moves towards the mirror and checks his own appearance. He looks more or less how he wishes to look or, at least, he has come to terms with how he looks.

His face is on the feminine side, perhaps. He thinks he is reasonably good-looking, but he isn't one of those men who has a large, square jaw and an assured brow.

The suit fits him well. He turns to the right then to the left as he did when he first tried it on. It is nipped in at the shoulders and at the waist. He was told the cut would show off his slender upper body.

Bastian places a gentle hand on Rebecca's waist then leans in to kiss her cheek.

'You'll smudge me.' She moves away.

Bastian backs off, frustrated rather than hurt, and moves to the sideboard. He collects his keys and wallet and puts them in a trouser pocket.

They take a black cab to Soho as the wait for an Uber is too long. The driver is from the East End and speaks to Bastian briefly about West Ham football club, before realising his passenger has no idea what he's talking about. Then he tells them a story about a restaurant he went to where he ate a seaweed soufflé. 'Seaweed! A soufflé made out of seaweed!' Then he turns on the radio.

As they cross the Thames, the sun is low over the Palace

of Westminster. It carves wobbling halos around the gothic turrets, each a flaming torch. Bastian reaches for his phone to take a photo. The cab slows for the line of traffic caught on the bridge. He sees a bevy of swans in the shadows by the north bank, the largest he has ever seen in the city. There must be at least thirty, bobbing on the water, perhaps a whole extended family of cygnets who never left their parents and grew up, found partners and raised cygnets of their own.

Bastian nudges his girlfriend. She leans over him to look out through the glass and her eyes follow the direction of his pointing finger to the river. She recoils.

'Oh god, Bastian, you know I have a phobia of birds.'

'Sorry.' Bastian turns back to look out at the family group. They bob contentedly on the current.

Rebecca doesn't have a phobia of birds, she just dislikes them: the way they move when walking or flying; the sounds they make and the parts of the city they inhabit. She considers them to be unclean. She uses the word 'phobia' because it lends more gravity to her distaste.

The cab pulls off the bridge and follows a series of back streets, a route known only to the drivers of black cabs and cycle couriers. They pass grand Georgian terraces that have been converted into flats and offices. They filter through tight streets lined with shops and restaurants. They feel affluence and poverty beneath the wheels of the car as they roll over smooth tarmac and pristine paving stones, then stretches of road that are potholed and warped. These paths take them through the few blocks of council flats that still linger like boorish relations at the end of a party.

'In the Middle Ages, swans signified sex,' Bastian says, not to anyone in particular. 'Pictures of swans hung above the doorways of secret brothels.'

Rebecca looks at him. 'Wasn't everything a symbol of sex in the Middle Ages?'

Bastian keeps his gaze fixed to doors and bricks and signs and pedestrians that flash past the window of the cab.

'No,' he says simply. 'Not everything.'

The cab stops just outside a club. Bastian takes out his wallet and gives the driver two twenty-pound notes and waves away the change. He doesn't like to carry coins. They make his wallet bulge, which ruins the line of his jacket pocket. And tipping generously gives Bastian a pleasant feeling of his own largesse. Wealth, after all, is meant to trickle down.

Hot Bath

Precious allows Robert Kerr to kiss her goodbye. She is fond of the man, in a way, and sees no harm in indulging him.

'Until we meet again,' he says, in an affectation of a 1950s music-hall comedian. He laughs at his joke. Precious laughs too. She is good at her job. She sits on the bed, pulls the loose silk robe over her thighs and breasts and allows her patron to kiss her again before he lets himself out.

Tabitha enters from a door behind the bed. She carries a stack of fresh towels. She sets these down by a copper bath at one side of the room, turns the hot tap, and water gushes into the bath. The copper hums as it is struck, a softening musical note as the water pools and rises. The steam has a metallic scent, but as lavender oil is added this becomes the dominant aroma.

Tabitha has called herself Tabitha since she was in the trade.

As well as the women who work with their bodies, the building contains other personnel. Each woman has a maid, who is older and previously worked in the trade herself. The maids help with the women's day-to-day life. They cook and clean and increase the safety of the work: they can hear from the next room if something is going badly wrong. When necessary, they phone downstairs for assistance from one of the security guards, like Karl. Many of these are ex-military, and are paid from a mutual fund. They come when they are called and, when required, they pull men out of the beds of women and throw them on to the street and make sure they never return. The mutual fund also pays Old Scarlet's wages. Like the maids, she was once a sex worker herself. She sits at the front desk and manages the girls' appointments.

Now Tabitha is a maid, and she takes good care of her charge. She tests the temperature of the water, then turns the cold tap until it is on full.

'No!' Precious insists. 'Hot! I want it hot! Hot, hot, hot! None of your cold tap today!'

'It'll scald you!'

'Nonsense,' Precious replies. She rises from the bed and lets her dressing gown slip to the floor. She lifts one leg up to the edge of the bath, points her toes like a small child pretending to be a ballerina, and holds them there with practised poise. She looks at Tabitha and narrows her eyes. Tabitha holds her gaze and mirrors the expression. Then Precious plunges the pointed toes along with the foot and leg into the steaming water.

Precious doesn't flinch. Tabitha recoils and shields her eyes, as if it is her own skin being boiled. Precious cackles and reaches out to pull the older woman towards the spectacle. She throws back her head and howls. It is not the meek, flirtatious laugh she performs for clients. This is a roar. She shifts her weight on to her bathing leg then drops her whole body into the lavender water.

'You're horrible, you are,' Tabitha observes.

'Charming.'

Tabitha smiles despite herself and takes the smile with her into the kitchen. She comes back with two flutes of sparkling white wine.

'Prosecco?'

'Don't mind if I do,' says Precious, taking the glass. Condensation has settled on its surface, pooling to droplets where it meets her warm fingers.

Tabitha returns to the kitchen to prepare dinner. She stoops as she walks. Her legs are bowed and her hips well worn.

Precious lies back in the bath with her wine-bearing hand quivering on a loose wrist over the rim. She relaxes all muscles she is conscious of and allows her body to bob on top of the cushion of compacted water. She aches. It has been a long day and hers is not an easy job.

Her legs come up through the surface of the water and jut over the end of the roll-top tub. Water pools and trickles to the floor, tapping on the mahogany-effect laminate.

Precious washes herself with a simple bar of soap, not the bottles of expensive bath and shower creams that sit in her cupboard. There is a nostalgia to the new block, wrapped in paper. She stands and strokes the bar across her skin: around the back of her neck, between her legs. She divests herself of grime, the thin film of soot that has accrued from the fumes of exhaust from the city outside; the fingerprints of five men; the semen and saliva and sweat of the same men, and the grease from her own pores. The soap eases these substances from her body into the steaming water. She lifts her body from the tub and reaches for one of the fresh towels. It feels cold and crisp. She rubs it over herself and gouges the remaining dirt and dead cells from her skin, then puts on another, more comfortable dressing gown.

Tabitha emerges from the kitchen carrying two plates of steak and kidney pudding.

'Have you made that meat and gravy spongey thing again?' Precious asks.

Tabitha lays the plates on the coffee table and returns to the kitchen for the peas and oven chips.

They eat together. Precious squashes her steak and kidney pudding with the back of her fork then mixes her peas into the concoction before scooping it into her mouth. Tabitha says her table manners are disgusting. They drink more of the wine and discuss the possibility of new furnishings in the flat. Tabitha pulls out a general knowledge crossword from the middle of her newspaper. Some of the letters have been filled in pencil.

'Greek god of wine,' says Tabitha. 'Eight letters.'

'Dionysus.'

'How're you spelling that?'

Precious spells it out.

'Nah, it's got to have an "m" in it. Third letter's an "m".'

'Then you've got the other answer wrong,' Precious replies. She pulls the paper towards her and traces the list of clues with her forefinger. 'There you go,' she says. 'Fifteen down isn't McCorory, it's Ohuruogu.' Precious picks up the pencil, rubs out the mistake and makes the alteration. Her friend snatches back the paper, with a look of reluctant gratitude.

They continue with the crossword until supper is finished. Tabitha takes the plates back into the kitchen. From the other room, she says, 'We got another letter from Howard Holdings.'

Tabitha said it so casually that Precious has not heard. She repeats, more loudly, 'We got another letter from Howard Holdings.'

'Where is it?' Precious replies, immediately this time. She gets up from the table and begins to cast around the flat, lifting towels and strewn clothes. 'What are those bastards up to now?'

'It's in the drawer beneath the keys.'

Precious goes over to the cabinet and finds the letter, returned to its envelope, mixed in with other post. 'When did you open it?'

'This morning. I didn't tell you because I knew you'd get angry. Like this.'

'Damn right.'

Precious pulls the letter from the envelope and unfolds it. As she does, Tabitha relates its contents, 'It's basically exactly what you predicted.'

'They're trying to tip us over the edge.'

'Probably.'

'They want us out.'

'Maybe. Could be they're just trying to squeeze out more money.'

'No way,' says Precious. 'I've dealt with people like this before. And I've been watching it happen all over the neighbourhood.'

Precious reads the letter a couple of times, then she tightens the strings of her dressing gown and lets herself out the flat, leaving the door open behind her. She walks along the corridor. Some of the doors have signs to indicate that their occupants are busy with a client, others don't. She knocks on a couple of the doors and stands back to allow their owners time to answer.

A door is pulled open and a face peers out. Seeing Precious, the woman pulls the door wider, and steps into the threshold and leans against the frame. She is wearing a full pink track-suit, which tells Precious she is taking a day off. Her long hair is dyed a reddish purple and tied in a tight ponytail. 'I thought I'd be seeing you this evening,' says Candy.

'Read the letter?'

'Yep.'

'What do you think?'

'You were right and I was wrong. They won't stop until we're out. Did I tell you I spoke to some of the girls from Brewer Street and they're actually facing proper evictions now. Sorry, not evictions. Tenancy terminations. Contract non-renewal, or whatever.'

Precious crosses her arms. She is still holding the letter in her right hand and it crumples in the crook of her left elbow. 'I can't even,' she says. This is what she says when she is too angry to construct a proper sentence.

'I know, love,' Candy replies.

'It's not even the money. It's not really even the prospect of moving, though obviously I don't want to. It's just the fact that these bastards think they can treat us like this. It's the lack of respect.'

'I know, love,' says Candy again.

'Look, have the other girls got letters too?'

'I assume so.' Candy walks across the hall and hammers on another door. Shouting comes from within, first a man's voice then a woman's. There are footsteps and the door opens a crack, steadied by the safety chain.

'What is it?' whispers Young Scarlet between her teeth.

'What the fuck?' shouts the man from within. 'I hope this'll be coming off my bill.'

Young Scarlet turns back to her client and puts on a voice that is sweet and pliable, a voice she reserves for men. 'Just a minute.' She turns back to Precious and Candy and her voice returns to its normal pitch. 'This better be good.'

'Did you get this letter?' Candy asks. She indicates towards the letter in Precious's hand.

'Does it look like I'm in here reading?' Young Scarlet replies.

'It's from the landlords,' says Precious.

'Oh fuck. Is it curtains?'

'Not yet. Just a rent increase, only it's not a small one this time.'

'For fuck's sake. If I wanted to lose eighty per cent of my income each month I'd still have a fucking pimp.'

The man's voice comes from within. 'I'm in here losing eighty per cent of my erection.'

Candy cannot help but laugh.

'Don't laugh at that,' says Young Scarlet, 'he's funny but he's a total twat. Listen, I'll just finish him up quickly and come and find you. Get the other girls, yeah?'

'My place as soon as you're free. I'll get Tabitha to boil the kettle.'

'Bugger tea. Tell her to open a bottle or two. And none of that rubbish from the corner shop. We all know what you two have got hidden away from your France trip.'

Après nous

'It would be easier for everyone if they left of their own volition.'

'Clearly, but Roster tells me the ratio of rent to custom is too good, even with the increases we're enacting. The level of footfall, the Soho address, the circumstances of their lease. These things are all too advantageous to expect a voluntary departure. But if we raise the rent enough – as much as we're allowed to – and make life inconvenient for them in other respects, when we ask them to leave they won't make as much fuss as they otherwise might. They will just move somewhere new – to a part of London more in keeping with their profession.'

Agatha Howard holds the phone flush against her ear. The voice of her long-time lawyer, Tobias Elton, is an irritation. She has told him her intentions on so many occasions she is almost reciting from a script.

'It does seem like an awful lot of bother,' says the lawyer.

Agatha tries to stifle her irritation. 'It will be difficult work for all of us but the benefits will be substantial. We need to get them out, Tobias.'

Tobias waits on the line. Agatha can tell he's thinking of another question. He finds it difficult to construct thoughts and turn them into sentences, but Agatha doesn't want this to become a protracted conversation. After years of enlisting his legal services, she knows it's best to keep the conversations frequent and brief.

'We'll talk again tomorrow,' she says curtly. 'Goodbye.' She has spoken with him too many times to bother waiting for a response. She places her phone on the large, walnut desk and slides her hand to the furry head resting between her legs. She takes one of the silken ears and threads it between her fingers, rubbing the soft tip with her thumb. He is a pedigree borzoi: the size and shape of a greyhound, with long white fur and a pointed face.

Fedor opens his eyes. His irises are as black as his pupils, and in the dim light they almost look recessed. He pulls his jaws into a wide, prolonged yawn, revealing thin canines, broad and jagged molars, and a pink, colubrine tongue with short, coarse bristles. Agatha takes hold of Fedor's head with both hands, and when he closes his mouth and settles his jaws together, she draws her palms towards her, along the length of his nose, then back again towards the flopping ears.

The dog fidgets. He sniffs at her lap then begins to whine. He wants up. His hind legs are tensed and he bobs on the spot several times, asking for permission. Agatha pushes her chair back to give the pup room to emerge, and Fedor springs to her lap. He places his bony hips on her knees and his front paws on the tops of her thighs. Spindle claws dig deep. She will have red indentations later.

Agatha's study is on the second floor of her Georgian townhouse, in Mayfair. It is where she spends most of her day and is one of the finest rooms in the house, with an intricate parquet floor, high ceilings framed with Roman cornicing, and three tall sash and case windows along one side. Through the windows she can see the street which is wide, clean, and lined with plane trees and expensive cars.

Her desk is littered with documents. There are tenancy contracts and outlines of planning permissions. There is a letter from one of her sisters. It reads: Give us our fucking money, you fucking Russian slag. This is on top of a pile of documents she was readying for the forthcoming arbitration. Beneath a newspaper, she finds the photograph the antique dealer showed her earlier in the day. It shows a white handkerchief marred by a small, somewhat faded bloodstain. According to the letter of verification, the handkerchief is

French, dates from the 1790s, and the blood came from the foot of the guillotine. During the Great Terror, when notable individuals were decapitated, spectators used to rush forward and collect souvenirs: blood, hair, items of clothing. The morbid mementos are still collected: the more famous the decapitated party, the higher the price.

Agatha has been fascinated by the Revolution since childhood and has accumulated items from the period ever since she has had the money to do so. She used to spend the summer school holidays with her mother in Monaco. She was alone much of the time. She sat and read by the hotel pool, or in the restaurant between meals while the staff were clearing breakfast and preparing for lunch. Sometimes she wandered down to the beach by herself and read her books on the sands while watching leathery old ladies in bikinis arrange and rearrange diamond necklaces on their sagging chests. She covered herself head to toe in factor-50 sun cream and propped herself up with a couple of towels and her school rucksack. In the evenings, her mother went to parties and Agatha was left in the hotel room. She ordered room service and was later told off for drawing attention to her neglect.

One morning at breakfast, Agatha's mother, Anastasia, told her that the King of France had arrived in town. She said she would be going to a party with him that night.

'But there is no King of France,' Agatha pointed out.

'He is some kind of pretender,' Anastasia explained. 'He's descended from the old kings and queens. The ones who were overthrown and slaughtered by the guillotine.'

'So he isn't really the king.'

'He would be the king if they hadn't been deposed. If there had been no revolution and no Napoleon.'

'But there was a revolution and Napoleon.'

'But apparently lots of people in France would rather there hadn't been, and they see him as the rightful king.'

During this exchange Anastasia had avoided making eye contact with her daughter. Agatha was sceptical, and Anastasia quietly agreed with her, and Agatha knew her mother agreed with her.

Later, when Agatha returned to school, she went to the library and got out all the books she could find on the French Revolution, the ancien régime and the Bourbon succession. She read about their descent into decadence, their lavish lifestyles, their fashions, their affairs, their huge gambling debts, their war debts, their parties, their illegitimate children. Then she read about their demise. The trials. The executions. She read about all the chances they were given by the revolutionaries to save themselves, and about how they squandered those chances. She read about their unquenchable belief in their own rights, their total ignorance of or refusal to believe what was happening right in front of their eyes.

The fragility of law and order is never far from Agatha's thoughts. News had recently come in of a revolution in South America. She kept checking the news on her phone, and scrolling through sets of images. There were crowds of people running through tear gas to storm government buildings. Flags were torn down, and documents were torn up. Statues were tipped on their sides and kicked and spat on.

Nobody but Agatha seems at all concerned about the prospect of revolution in this country. Everyone walks around in a state of extreme presentism, as if the world has always been the same and always will be the same. She feels alone in her concerns, as if she is alive in 1913, with a unique foresight of what is to come, or at Versailles in 1788. What did Madame de Pompadour say when she left the palace? *Après nous, le déluge.*

Agatha pushes Fedor down, and stands. The room is unlit. She has been sitting at her desk all evening and the long dusk has burned low. There's something about the night in this city that is brighter than the day. The spread of muddy phosphor illuminates dark corners. The emphasis of shapes that sunshine melts. The drawn, bending, sonorous beams of buses loping from stop to stop.

Fedor trots across the large, oblong room and scratches the panelled door with his front paw. Bare wood shows through the paintwork from prior expressions of impatience.

Agatha follows him and pulls at the handle. The lights in the landing are dim but she can just about see the shadow of a man standing to the right of the doorway.

'Have you been there the whole time?' she asks.

'Yes,' Roster replies.

The dog begins to lick the man's wrinkled hands feverishly. Agatha notes again the discrepancy between the affection Fedor shows to her and to Roster.

'You spoke to Elton,' Roster says.

'I did,' she replies. 'Were you listening?'

'It's difficult to hear properly through these doors but I caught the gist. You're taking my advice.'

'I told him what you said.'

Roster nods.

The dog whines.

'There's fresh water in his bowl,' says the old man. 'I'll take him out for his evening business.'

He lopes down the stairs, hunched like a locust. The borzoi trots behind without being called, all legs and bones and white feathers: an albino vulture.

Tremors

Debbie McGee feels the ground beneath her quake and grind. The vibrations catch the cracked skin on the soles of her feet. They pulse up through her legs, into her pelvis and up through her organs. The tremors unsettle thin blood in loose veins. The residue of cartilage that still resides between her bones drags and creaks. The liquid around her brain trembles and the coarse strands of her hair quiver. Her eyes are no longer instruments of vision but instruments of vibration. They are now tactile. Touch becomes her only sense. Light and colour fade, and the scent of the cellar diminishes.

Debbie stoops and bends her knees until they touch the ground. She holds out her arms and turns both palms away from her body and places them on the ground. She holds herself on four points like a half-spider awaiting prey then lowers her right ear. The compacted sun-starved bare earth is cool against her face.

The trembling stops. She presses her cheek deeper but feels nothing. She stretches out her limbs and lies on her front, listening. She hears vermin in the walls and feels the cold and damp.

She remains in that position for nearly half an hour, until Paul Daniels comes to find her.

'What are you doing?'

'Listening to the earth.'

He leaves, and pulls back the curtain across the opening that leads to that part of the cellar.

Debbie listens for a while more, then turns her head to try the other ear. After twenty minutes in this position she rolls on to her back and falls asleep.

Grubs and worms, awakened by the tremors, begin to settle again within the tunnels they have mined. They have followed the quaking rocks and dug deeper than ever before. Now the clamour from below has quietened, they are left with the familiar shuffle of the city above: the pulsing of human footsteps, rubber wheels scuffing tarmac, pencils being dropped, hammers striking nails, knives and cleavers landing on chopping boards, mugs of hot coffee clunking on tables, bums on seats, bodies on beds.

Woodlice dwell in the cracks between the bricks of the cellar wall, in the places where Victorian mortar has worn away. When night falls and the little light that refracts through the squares of glass between the cellar and the pavement fade to an amber glow, they creep from the cracks and scuttle around and over the sleeping woman and gather any fabric or flakes of skin that still hold sustenance.

Dark Room

The room is dark but still a place for looking around. Three women watch Bastian as he and Rebecca pass. Two of the women return to their conversation but the third stirs her cocktail and keeps her eyes fixed on the back of Bastian's head, his shoulders, his long back, the way his auburn hair catches the dim reddish haze and shines like dull tarnished copper, the colour of a well-worn penny. She looks away only when Rebecca, at Bastian's side, turns and catches her eye.

The club is decorated in varnished wood and glass. Mirrors hang in strategic locations to create the impression of infinity held by four walls. Light speaks to light. There is a bar at the back and a collection of dark leather armchairs.

A barman pours measures of gin then tips them into a cocktail shaker and adds measures of vermouth. He seals the lid and shakes then pours the liquid into tall martini glasses.

Bastian watches him work then orders two gins and tonic. The waiter sets the glasses on the bar and fills them with the liquids over crushed ice. Bastian pays with a crisp twenty-pound note and refuses change. The waiter thanks him. Rebecca stretches her lips over her teeth to form a smile. There is something mocking in the expression.

They sip in unison. Rebecca stands back to allow Bastian to lead the way to a table. He finds one with two deep leather armchairs and looks back at his girlfriend to see if the selection is acceptable.

'Not there. I always sink into those kinds of chairs. They're too deep. How about the high stools?'

Bastian picks up his drink, which he had tentatively placed on the table, and leads Rebecca to the high stools.

Rebecca checks her phone. 'They're running two minutes late,' she says.

Bastian nods. He isn't sure he has ever bothered to text someone about a two-minute delay. He sips his drink. It is too cold, and his molars begin to ache.

They are waiting for Rebecca's work colleagues. She has a new job helping to value and market East Asian ceramics at one of the big auction houses. The people she has met so far move in similar social circles: it turns out they have mutual friends from school and university. Bastian hasn't met them yet but has heard stories from Rebecca. A couple are bringing boyfriends, and one who, for some reason, is already married, is going to bring her husband.

'So you'll have someone to talk to,' Rebecca said when she told him who would be there. Bastian wasn't sure whether she meant the husband in particular or the men in general, but he felt uneasy either way.

The group of seven arrive together from a work event which Rebecca was too junior to attend. Bastian shakes hands with the men and kisses the women's cheeks.

The women gather around Rebecca and relate tales from the party: news of eccentric colleagues, descriptions of the canapés and the venue, professions of how little they enjoyed the evening and how much they would have rather been here with her. The men ask Bastian about his work and then about his university and his school. The husband, Dave, remains largely silent.

The conversation continues beyond the first set of drinks and Bastian offers to fetch a round. The women order complex cocktails. The men order lager. Bastian has another gin and tonic. One of the women – the one who is married – comes over to Bastian to stroke his soft linen suit. 'He's lovely,' she says to Rebecca with a performative wink at her husband. 'Can we swap?'

The women laugh. So do most of the men. The husband, Bastian notes with some discomfort, does not see the funny side, though his wife ignores him and has already returned to a conversation about vintage fabrics. Dave fixes Bastian with a threatening stare. Not wishing to cause a scene to satisfy any latent machismo, Bastian turns away and begins a conversation with someone else.

Half an hour and another round of drinks later, Bastian quietly makes his excuses and scouts for the loo. He has not been here before and is confused by the layout of the building. He searches the various rooms, first downstairs then upstairs, but sees neither signposting nor staff to ask. His search takes him along a dimly lit upstairs corridor, then through a heavy fire door.

He steps into a room. The squalor is vivid. There is a small coffee table, the kind that can be found in dentists' waiting rooms, surrounded by chairs of a similar theme. The table is covered with boxes and cartons from pizzas and other sorts of delivered food. There are a couple of empty, scrunched cans and stacks of plastic glasses, sticky with multiple shades of sugar. Beyond the coffee table and armchairs there's a space that looks like a makeshift campsite. There are four or five mattresses laid out across the floor with less than a foot between each of them. On the mattresses, there is a jumble of sheets and sleeping bags and a couple of blankets and pillows. Clothes hang on a rail at the back of the room and on the walls there are pictures, some photographs of people, some postcards showing white beaches, blue seas and skies.

Bastian notes that one of the mattresses is neater than the others. Its owner has pulled the sheets up to the top and tucked the corners beneath. He or she has then folded the blankets into squares and placed them on top of the pillow. Clothes and other belongings are stored in a green fabric suitcase in perfect alignment with the end of the rectangular mattress. This, Bastian guesses, is the occupant responsible for the small stack of plates and mugs that have been washed in the sink then placed on the plastic drying rack.

'Excuse me.'

Bastian turns to see a small woman, not more than five feet tall.

She studies him as he fumbles for words then looks past him into the room. She exhibits no surprise at the camp beds.

'Excuse me,' she says again.

'I'm sorry,' he says.

The woman is wearing an apron and a pair of marigolds. There's a bucket of dirty soap water at her feet, which is still swilling from having been set down a moment before.

'I was just trying to find the loo. It's not clearly signposted.'

'Excuse me.'

'I didn't mean to intrude. I'm sorry. I'll go now.'

Bastian walks around the woman. She doesn't come up to his shoulder. He hurries along the corridor, finds the loo, uses it quickly, washes his hands and makes his way back downstairs. As he takes the last few stairs he sees someone he knows. He speaks before thinking. 'Glenda?'

Glenda stops on the first step so she's the same height as Bastian, though he is now on the floor.

'How are you doing?'

He's not totally sure the recognition has been mutual. Glenda seems confused by his presence. Maybe she doesn't remember him.

'Oh, you know, all right,' she says. Then, after a pause, 'How are you?'

'Yeah, good thanks. Really good.' Glenda doesn't seem to have much more to say, so Bastian continues. 'I haven't seen you for ages. When did you move to London?'

'I've been here for a couple of years now.'

'Wow, I had no idea. Where are you living?'

'Right here in Soho, actually,' she says.

'I didn't think anybody lived in Soho.'

'Yeah, well, they do. But I'm here through a kind of . . . series of events, I guess. A friend set it up for me. I'm living above the Aphra Behn near Soho Square. Do you know it?'

Bastian shakes his head. He pauses for a moment in his

own questioning, wondering whether he could ask her to have a drink with him, whether he could persuade her to come and join his group, and how Rebecca would respond to that.

'What are you doing with yourself?' he asks.

'You mean in terms of work?'

'Yeah, well, maybe, yeah.'

'Various stuff. I did an internship with this talent agency for a while. You know, working with actors and that. Setting them up in roles. That was quite fun. And now I'm working at a kind of estate agents.'

'Oh right,' says Bastian.

'Yeah,' says Glenda. 'It's just a short-term thing, though. To make a bit of money. I work at the branch here in Soho, and obviously houses and flats go for loads in central London and you can make a lot on commission.'

'Oh right,' says Bastian. 'I suppose you can.'

'Yeah. I wouldn't be doing it otherwise. I mean, I don't want to stay working there for long. I'm saving up so I can do a qualification in Theatre Directing.'

'In London?'

Glenda shrugs. 'No. Probably not. Probably somewhere else. Maybe Bristol, or Manchester or Glasgow. London's too expensive.'

'But you'd have to give up your flat in Soho.'

'It's not really a flat,' she says. 'More of a room. And I don't know how much longer I'll be allowed to live there at the rent I'm paying. It's all a bit dodgy.'

'Oh. Well, never mind then.'

Glenda looks down at her shoes, which appear too small for her feet, and are scuffed at the toe. 'Yeah,' she says. 'Anyway, what are you up to?'

'Not much,' he says. He isn't sure he wants to tell her where he's working. She's the kind of person who might be judgemental about him walking into a well-paid job at his dad's company. 'I'm thinking about going into the law. I'm doing an internship at the moment at a kind of property-law place.'

Glenda smiles. 'Cool,' she says. 'Anyway, I've got to go. I really need the loo. Nice to bump into you.'

Glenda begins to ascend the staircase. Bastian watches her climb. When she's at the top he calls after her.

'Hey! How's Laura?'

Glenda turns and smiles at him knowingly. It's the first time she's smiled since the beginning of the conversation. He notices, as he had not before, how sad her overall demeanour is, and has been for the whole time they've been talking.

'Oh,' offers Glenda. 'Laura's doing really well. You should get back in touch.'

Blank Slating

The long and elegant index finger of Lorenzo Mendis carves shapes in the condensation lining his glass of cold lager. He draws ovals and triangles and oblongs and swirls. The moisture warms and collects at his fingertips then drips the length of the tall glass.

Lorenzo is waiting for a friend. He spent most of the afternoon in the Aphra Behn with Robert but has now moved to an exclusive club down the road, and propped himself against the bar. He thought he saw her arrive, but the Glenda-shaped person who came in through the door has disappeared off somewhere. Glenda is often late, even more now than she used to be; her girlfriend split up with her a few months ago and she has quietly fallen apart.

Glenda and Catherine shared a flat in Walthamstow, which Catherine, being a fair bit older, owned. Glenda had to move out quickly, and Lorenzo found a room for her above the Aphra Behn. The owners couldn't advertise the room and get a real tenant with a real, legally binding tenancy agreement as they didn't have the correct permits, and it didn't meet the legal requirements. The building stood on this street when Samuel Pepys walked along it. Or, if not Samuel Pepys, then never-bored Samuel Johnson. The floors are warped from years of use, so dropped pencils roll from one side to the other. The door frames are tilted, and, rather than having been mended or propped up, the doors have been shaved and sanded to the new shape. The windows are single glazed and the wooden window frames are chipped and draughty. In winter, wind sneaks through. In summer, people stand on the pavements and drink and smoke, and there is a jagged torrent of noise until morning. Nobody would choose to live there, but the room is in central London and costs a quarter of what it would have cost were it safe, legal and habitable.

Lorenzo met Glenda when she did a six-month internship at the talent agency he works for part-time. This is one of two part-time jobs he does to earn money between roles. His acting career once held so much promise, but the last few years have been lean. He was involved with theatre at university, then secured a place at a prestigious drama school and was later given a short-term contract with the Royal Shakespeare Company. Then the auditions began to fizzle out. He was short on cash and started doing more supplementary work to pay his rent, but the work was tiring and required more of his time than he anticipated. He took the job of personal assistant to film star Yolanda Crimp. It was meant to be a temporary situation, but he's been working for her ever since. He spends three afternoons a week at her house, organising her affairs. He books appointments, arranges holidays, goes to the shops to pick up outfits for her to try on and dismiss. When the nanny calls in sick he plays with Yolanda's children. He attends her parties and meets relevant people but none of them can see him as anything other than Yolanda's PA. They hand him empty wine glasses and make cutting remarks under a guise of good humour.

Lorenzo feels someone tapping his elbow, and turns to see his friend. He is pleased she has arrived but less pleased that she has put no effort into her appearance. When Glenda and Lorenzo worked together she was far from immaculate but had, at least, brushed her hair, ironed her clothes and polished her shoes. Now she does none of these things.

'You look nice,' he says. He leans forward to kiss her on the cheek.

'Sorry,' she replies. 'I didn't have time to organise myself properly this week. Again. So, I'm my usual scruffy self.'

He didn't mean for his insincerity to be detected.

Lorenzo quickly finishes his pint and they both order cocktails. Lorenzo's is tall and sleek, while Glenda's comes in a squat tumbler stuffed with layers of ice and citrus. Lorenzo gets up from his bar stool and they find a table together at the back.

'I thought I saw you go past the Behn on your way home from work,' Lorenzo says.

'I live above the pub,' Glenda replies. 'It would be difficult to avoid.'

'Why didn't you pop in and say hello? Did you see me in there?'

'Yeah.' Glenda fiddles with a paper napkin. She tears off little pieces and piles them up like a cairn on top of a hill. 'I saw your old man friend too.'

'Robert?'

'I don't think he likes me.'

'He's just a little afraid of you.'

'Because I'm a woman?'

'Because you're a particular kind of woman.'

'Gay?'

'No, he isn't homophobic.'

'Just a misogynist.'

'Not a misogynist as such, just a bit scared of women.'

'Isn't that where misogyny comes from?'

'Well, yeah, but, I don't know. I'm not trying to justify it.' He isn't trying to justify it, although he realises that's how it seems.

'Sorry, I'm not trying to have a go. I just don't get it. Well, I do get it. But I also don't get it.'

Lorenzo feels a bit awkward. He has got the impression previously that his friendship with Robert was a sticking point between him and Glenda, but they have never had a conversation about it.

Glenda continues: 'I can absolutely appreciate that he can have issues and still be a decent person in other respects, but a general, difficult-to-define, non-specific fear of women – that he may or may not have – just isn't something I have the energy to put up with.'

'I understand that.'

'But hey, you go ahead with your outreach thing.'

He is annoyed now. 'Yes, he's older and rough round the edges, but I also think he's a good man. I'm not saying it's okay he's not comfortable around you, but he's able to be friends with me, so deserves at least six out of ten on the Absolute Caveman to Enlightened Metrosexual scale.'

Glenda starts to giggle.

'What?' Lorenzo asks.

'It's just I haven't heard the word metrosexual for years. It's very noughties.'

Lorenzo smiles, and relaxes. 'Sorry,' he says. 'I suppose I'm defensive about him because I do recognise what you're saying, and I know we seem like odd drinking companions, but I've known him my whole life, and it is what it is.'

'It is,' Glenda agrees. 'And also . . .'

She doesn't finish the sentence but hovers on the last syllable and raises her eyebrows to indicate there's something she's holding back.

'Don't say it,' urges Lorenzo.

'Daddy issues,' Glenda finishes.

'Yep. Fine. You've got me there.'

He playfully flicks at the pile of paper napkin pieces Glenda has arranged, and they flutter in her direction.

It is true that Lorenzo has a bad relationship with his father, and the links between this and his tendency to form surprising friendships with older, straight, working-class men isn't lost on him. He just doesn't think it's the only reason he's friends with Robert.

Glenda looks at Lorenzo sheepishly from behind her glasses. There are greasy fingerprints on the lenses, which Lorenzo notices for the second time. He has the urge to take them from her and polish the glass with his cotton shirt.

'Sorry,' she says.

'No, don't be silly.'

'I think we have both said "sorry" to each other about five times now.'

'Something like that.' He looks again at her dirty glasses. 'Changing the subject, do you know what I saw on the Tube the other day?' He doesn't wait for her to guess. 'I was alone in a carriage on the Bakerloo Line going up to Yolanda's, and the only other person there was this middle-aged woman sitting opposite me. She looked totally normal. Totally respectable. And do you know what she was doing? She was watching pornography on her phone. I saw it reflected in her glasses. Can you believe that?'

'Oh my god.'

'On the Tube. What the actual fuck?'

'What kind of pornography was it?'

'God knows. I looked away pretty rapidly. I just had enough time to see some naked arses, and that was about it.'

'Maybe it was an arthouse film.'

'It could have been, but that's still a weird thing to watch on the Tube. She was only on between Oxford Circus and Marylebone.'

After this, Lorenzo asks Glenda about her work. She is now employed by a major firm of estate agents. Lorenzo is fond of houses: their interiors and exteriors, the domestic routines they contain, their place in the economy, and their potential to make or break fortunes. He does not think that it is the right job for Glenda in the long-term, however. She is too sensitive for a sales role, or any kind of highly pressured business environment. She is too much of an introvert, and going out of her way to talk to strangers and persuade them to buy or sell expensive property couldn't really be more antithetical to her character. But Lorenzo understands she needs the money. Glenda wants to be a theatre director (which, if Lorenzo is being honest, is also a bit unrealistic), and to pursue this, she needs to have enough money saved either to do a course or unpaid internship.

Last week, Glenda's company started work on a new project. They are collaborating with a development firm that owns a significant amount of property in central London, much of which is not currently *Achieving its Full Potential*, which Glenda and Lorenzo agreed sounded like something they would have both received in their end-of-year school reports. The flats and retail spaces which the firm – Howard Holdings – owns are currently occupied and let, but at a far lower rate than they could be. The strategy was to increase the yield either through renegotiating contracts with existing tenants or by 'blank-slating' them. 'Blank-slating', Glenda informed Lorenzo, was the term her employers had adopted to describe evicting people from their homes or businesses, gutting the buildings and employing a fashionable architect to redesign them from the inside-out. Once this had been achieved, the estate agency for which Glenda works stepped in to do the flogging.

Glenda is charged with this operation. She wears a uniform made up of a black pencil skirt, a white fitted shirt and a little rayon scarf in the colours of the company tied at her neck like an air stewardess. She sits behind a little desk next to the large, inviting windows at the front of the shop, where dreams of extravagance and domestic bliss are displayed on glossy placards.

'It's going okay,' Glenda says, when Lorenzo asks. 'I mean, I'm obviously completely incompetent, but the project itself seems to be progressing. And progress is a good thing, right? We're looking to blank-slate some properties in Soho at the moment, actually. The architect's already done the sketches.' She shows Lorenzo a picture on her phone.

They finish their drinks and Lorenzo buys another round. He pays for everything when they go out, being older and, when they met, her senior colleague. When he returns to the table, she asks him if he's got any auditions coming up. Glenda is relatively new to the world of theatre and has not learned that, for an actor, this is quite an annoying question.

'Ah, no,' replies Lorenzo reluctantly. He lowers his head and grasps the two little paper cocktail straws between his lips and pulls some of the liquid into his mouth.

'Have you spoken to Joanne about it?' Joanne is the managing director of the talent agency for which Lorenzo works part-time and is also Lorenzo's agent. 'Have you been in contact with Tamzin Chapworth? What has Yolanda said?'

'Oh, um, no, and nothing much.'

Glenda fixes Lorenzo with a patronising look that, in Lorenzo's view, is not appropriate for a younger and less experienced person to fix on an older and more experienced person.

'I did speak to Joanne about making more of an effort with TV work,' Lorenzo offers.

'That's good. I don't know why you were so reluctant before.'

Glenda means well but doesn't understand his situation as well as she thinks she does. His reasons for being ambivalent about TV work are complex. A few years ago, he was on an episode of a popular spy drama. He played a Radical Islamist. On another occasion, he was on a long-running police procedural and played a Radical Islamist. Lorenzo's dad came from Sri Lanka and his mum came from Italy, and both were Catholics, but casting directors overlooked these subtleties. It wouldn't have felt much better to be cast in these roles repeatedly had his heritage been Pakistani Muslim, but somehow the obliviousness of TV executives to who he was and the particularities of his background were especially galling.

'Joanne did suggest a TV thing to me last week, actually, but I told her I wasn't interested.'

'Why would you do that?'

'The show sounded awful. Like, really awful. Not my kind of thing at all.'

She asks him how he knows this without having yet been to the audition.

'I just know.' Lorenzo hopes this will be the end of the interrogation.

'You're so principled,' she says.

'Is that a compliment or a criticism, I can't tell.'

'In general it's a compliment, I've heard.' Her demeanour becomes more serious. 'Really though, I admire you for it. I think it's very noble. But it's frustrating seeing all sorts of talentless people on the telly while you sit here with me drinking. I mean, I love that I get to spend time with you in person rather than watching you on a screen, but also there're lots of great things getting made that I think you should be a part of.'

'This isn't going to be one of them, believe me.'

'But it might lead to further work. It'll help you make connections.'

'That's possible. It would be painful, but possible.'

She keeps on at him until he promises to attend the audition. The prospect makes him feel queasy. He used to think the constant rejection associated with his chosen career would get easier as he got older. He's now thirty-three and it's harder than ever.

The Archbishop

Debbie McGee wakes. She creeps from the secluded corner of the damp cellar to the wider room, where her companions sit in an unstructured semi-circle; a parody of a mutual-help group. They sit with their backs against the stone walls or slumped forward with heads on knees. They sit on repurposed palettes, rancid mattresses or on the hard floor. Syringes lie around in degrees of decay, rust on their needles and filthy fingerprints on their pistons. Clear acetate bags that were once suppositories can be seen discarded and shit-stained beneath sheets of newspaper and chip-shop wrapping. Silver spoons with scorched bellies glitter in the dust.

'Blessed be the ground,' says the man they call the Archbishop. 'Blessed be the ground beneath our feet. Blessed be the soil that scuffs our skin. Blessed be the earth that holds our fathers' bones and feeds the worms and bees.'

'Bees don't eat earth!' snaps the man they call Paul Daniels.

'Blessed be the rocks that hold our cities in place. Blessed be the stones that aid the rocks. Blessed be the iron ore. Blessed be the tin. Blessed be the—'

'What about the magma?' asks Paul Daniels. 'There's magma beneath the rocks and stones, right in the centre of the earth. What about blessing the magma?'

'Blessed be the rivers that cut through the earth. Blessed be the underground lakes and seas. Blessed be the fossils. The ammonites. The Devil's Toenails. Blessed be the sleeping dragons that wait beneath this land.'

The man they call the Archbishop continues in this vein as Debbie McGee crawls across the room and takes her place by her partner. As the Archbishop cants, Paul Daniels continues to mutter about bees and magma, then finds new faults with the Archbishop's taxonomies and offers his adjustments and interpretations as they arise.

The Archbishop blesses further elements and compounds, below the ground and above it. He spits as he speaks. He rocks and closes his eyes and turns his head to the ceiling.

For the first twenty-five years he roamed the streets of Soho, they called him Vicar. His fervent brand of spiritual ejaculation held nothing of the established Church of England but he dressed in black and spoke like the master of a public school. He preached to untold generations of forlorn vagrants. His flock came and went. They entered the city and found succour in its fetid core. Some came for sex. Some came for drugs. Some came for pints and packets of crisps. Some came for jobs. The fortunates came in the evening and left before the dawn. The unfortunates stayed for longer. He preached to them all. But it was the men and women who loitered and lingered, and who were more touched by the sex and the drugs and the liquor and the desperation for vocation, whose attention he drew. He collected these vagabonds. They came to squat with him in his underground palace like dozens had before them. Most who stayed were addicted to something, or half mad, like him. Many remained for years, some for decades, but none stayed as long as him. 'You'll outlive us all, Vicar,' they said.

After a quarter century of service to his delinquent parishioners he was promoted in their vernacular to the episcopate. His elevation came after his hair and beard, once a living sponge of golden curls, had turned grizzled white. They altered his title to 'Bishop' as befitted a man of his age. Nobody could remember whose idea it was.

The Archbishop had welcomed the change. He was nothing if not vain. He had ridden the wave of adulation and preached more vehemently still. He had donned purple like others of his kind. He had revelled in his false position even more assuredly than before and lauded his status over the residents of his squat.

It was not eighteen months since his flock had taken the step to add the prefix to his already illustrious title. Paul Daniels had been the one to instigate this latest alteration. The addition had initially been delivered with more than a hint of sarcasm. 'Arrrrch-bishop!' Paul Daniels had spat one morning when the ramblings of the old man had come between him and his first fix of the day. After that the epithet had slowly taken hold, and now it was ingrained. Now it was just his name, as if his own mother had bestowed it upon him.

The woman whose mother didn't christen her Debbie McGee leans against the shoulder of her beloved and turns her head towards him so that her mouth is adjacent to his ear.

'The ground's moving. It's shaking. Truly it is. Maybe the Archbishop felt it too. Maybe that's why he's blessing the earth tonight.'

Paul Daniels is riffling through a pack of playing cards. It's a defective pack, discarded and thrown into a dustbin from which Paul Daniels retrieved it. Their backs bear the logo of a Soho sex shop and their fronts, in small rectangles bordered by the specific number and suit of each card, bear a picture of a different naked woman being fucked by a different dog. A busty brunette is being mounted by a Weimaraner. A blonde receives the graces of a ferocious-looking pit bull. The Ace of Clubs presents another being humped by a pack of chihuahuas. Although there were a number of slightly defective packs of pornographic playing cards in the bin round the back of the sex shop, Paul Daniels laughed and snorted when he saw this particular set and stuffed it into one of his pockets.

'Shush,' he says, and he continues to shuffle. He's testing his handiwork on a new trick. He divides the pack of cards into two with the thumbs and middle fingers of each hand, and uses the nail of his index fingers to press each half-pack into a crescent so the cards can be released and allowed to tumble back together.

'It was rumbling,' continues Debbie McGee. 'I felt it right

through my skin and bones. Like it was an earthquake or something.'

'No earthquakes in London. Never have been,' said Paul Daniels. 'Isn't that right, Archbishop?'

The Archbishop enjoys a direct question if it presupposes his superior intellect, and he generally pauses from his sermons to answer it.

'What you asking?' says the Archbishop.

'Earthquakes in London. There've never been any earthquakes in London, have there?'

The Archbishop narrows his eyes. 'Earth quaking in London?' He struggles over each consonant. His gums are soft. 'No earth quaking in London for a thousand years. A thousand years or more. The earth hasn't quaked since the dragons last woke. Since the red and the white dragons came from the mouth of the river and swept up over the city. But now it quakes again. We can all feel it.'

'What the fuck are you talking about?' asks Paul Daniels.

'Tremors, my boy. Tremors. The ground is alive once more. The earth is riddled with beasties.' He stretches back to gaze momentarily at the ceiling then rocks forward to consider the floor upon which he sits. His hips creak.

It cannot be said that the Archbishop doesn't look his age because nobody knows his age. But he does not look any age, any age that is possible. He appears past the count of years, past any numerical measure. His spine is pronounced and it curves crooked. Vertebrae seem to protrude through his skin like the plates of a stegosaurus. The hairs that grow from his head and his chin haven't thinned but are so old they look gnarled. The soft tissue beneath his eyes droops and tugs his lower lids to reveal a thick line of blood at the base of his eyeballs and when he walks he rolls on the balls of his feet like a strange bipedal spinning top.

Debbie McGee rarely looks at the Archbishop, so hideous is his image. But tonight she gazes at him intently as he riddles and reasons.

'Where did you feel them, my child?' The Archbishop addresses Debbie directly. This was not usual. 'Where did you feel the tremors?'

Debbie McGee is a quiet person. She only rarely uses her voice, and sometimes when she opens her mouth and sets her tongue in motion to form words, her breath doesn't come as it should, and no sound is made. This happens now.

'Speak up!'

'I felt it in the ground when I was sleeping through there.' She gestures to the other side of the large cellar. 'And I thought I felt it earlier in the day, when we were out and about.'

'Where?' The Archbishop is insistent. She's not used to him paying her any attention.

'I, um, felt it over by the cranes. I felt it in the soles of my feet when we were standing there on the pavement.'

The old man turns his attention to Paul Daniels. 'Did you feel it too?'

'Nah. I didn't feel nothing. And I wouldn't listen to this mad cow, neither.' He's referring to his lover. 'She's bat-shit crazy, this one.'

'You do not believe.'

'No, I do not believe! I'm not having any of it.'

The Archbishop believes, and others in the group follow his lead. He pulls himself into an upright position, and others get up too. Soon afterwards, they set off to find the epicentre of the mysterious vibrations. The Archbishop leads his flock around his archdiocese and as they walk he tells stories of the past.

'It's named for the sound the men and the animals made when there was hunting afoot,' the Archbishop states. 'A so and a ho from man and beast. A so ho, a so ho. That's what they shrieked when they got on their horses and chased deer through the forest. Before there were bricks and windows and sewers, there were grasses and roots and trees and deer. Deer deer deer that brought the men out of the city on horses with a so and a ho.'

Paul Daniels initiates his own line of conversation. He pulls on the arm of Debbie McGee's jumper and whispers into her ear. 'We need new tricks,' he says. 'That business at the pub this afternoon can't happen again. These days any old sod with a mobile phone can go on the internet and discover our secrets. I've heard there are actually magicians out there who video themselves doing tricks, and then they put them up on the internet and then they explain how they performed the trick! Can you believe it? They give away our secrets! Whatever happened to the Magic Circle? Whatever happened to our code of honour? How can an honest performer make a living if his punters can all look up the routine on the YouTube? No, no. It can't happen again, my lovely. We need new tricks.'

Debbie McGee makes no response.

'We need to carve out a patch for ourselves, like them in Covent Garden do. They set up an arena with a little rope on the ground and everyone gathers round and they've got themselves a captive audience for their whole routine. I've seen people put tenners in their pot at the end. Do you hear me? Ten-pound notes! We'll set up in Soho Square or something and we'll perform a full routine. We'll do proper tricks. None of these cards and cups shit for me any more. I'll get one of them boxes you can fit a person into. And I'll put you in it, my lovely. And then. And then, I'll make you disappear. Bam.'

The woman they call Debbie McGee makes no sign she's heard anything her companion has been saying.

'What the fuck are you on about now?' says someone from behind. Richard Scarcroft is an army veteran. He joined the Archbishop's flock reluctantly after falling out with the managers of the local shelter and finding himself in need of somewhere else to sleep. He doesn't hold with the Archbishop's nonsense, and still less with the nonsense propelled by this shady man everyone keeps referring to as Paul Daniels.

'Do you know how much skill that kind of thing requires?'

says Richard. 'I've seen the tricks you do, and they're shite. Absolute shite. As if you could pull off anything on that scale. Not to mention the equipment you'd need. How on earth would you afford all that? With the pennies you make from your cards and cups? What a load of shite.'

'Who asked you? Shut your face.'

Richard Scarcroft turns away. It's not important enough for him to start an argument. He's said his piece.

The group follows the Archbishop around a corner and comes to a building site. It's quiet now, after hours, but for security reasons it's illuminated from above by powerful flood-lights. Long, sharp shadows are cast by heavy machinery. Winches and pulleys hang from cranes and sway in the breeze. There's a criss-cross of girders and scaffolding; sheets of tarpaulin flap and smack their tethers. Debbie McGee notices the shadows and thinks that if this were the only bit of the scene you could see, like if your vision couldn't take in light, only shade, you could just about make out a forest in this tangle. She keeps this thought to herself.

A King Among Dogs

Agatha lies in bed waiting for Fedor to come back from his walk. Her best ideas come to her when she's just settled down for the night. It used to be one of the few times of day she could relax and be herself, by herself. Now she's alone much of the time, but the habit of spending this window in quiet reflection has stayed with her.

When she was at school she was never alone, but had often been lonely. Her school was like that. There was a constant clamour of people, routine and activity, but unless you were the kind of person who slipped naturally into friendship, there was little charity.

Agatha did not require much attention. Her classmates were bland and she preferred her own company. Hers was the kind of school where all the pupils had titles and connections and country houses. They lorded it over her, even though in just a few years, come her twenty-first birthday, she would be able to buy and sell them all ten times over. Possibly they knew this.

When they went out riding they would enquire whether Agatha would be coming along too. Asking was not a kindness. They knew she would decline, once again, because she had no horse and could not ride. They came to ask her in their jodhpurs and riding boots, clutching helmets and crops, and after she had said no she heard them running along the corridors towards the stable, sniggering. When they came back following the afternoon hack they feigned astonishment that Agatha had not been out too. Then she found their dirty riding clothes crumpled up with her clean school uniform and she spent the night scrubbing and ironing it. They knew she only had two sets: one to wear and one to wash.

She told them she was only poor temporarily, because her father died before she was born and his money was in trust somewhere for her and she couldn't access it until her twenty-first birthday. But when you are thirteen, your twenty-first birthday is far off, and the only salient fact was that she, Agatha, looked poor and dressed like she was poor and acted as if she was poor, and what was more, she literally had no money.

Everything Agatha and her mother had during these first twenty-one years came from Anastasia's boyfriends. They gave her clothes and jewellery and other expensive trinkets and Anastasia retained what she needed to look the part of a trophy girlfriend and sold the rest to pay for her daughter's boarding school fees.

'You must receive the best education that it is possible to receive,' her mother said to her. 'You must live now the life you will later live,' Anastasia insisted. 'There will be people always who will question your right to own all that you will own. But you must not let them question it. You must make them see how much you are worth.'

Anastasia grew up in poor circumstances in a small village between Moscow and St Petersburg. She never mentions its name, nor talks about her early life much at all. Agatha knows that her mother's childhood was difficult, that her mother's mother was drunk and her mother's father was violent, and that there were lots of siblings, and that Anastasia was the eldest and was expected to look after them. In 1990, when she was fourteen, she ran away to the capital.

In Moscow, Anastasia found a city caught between fat beginnings and slim endings; an empire decaying and regenerating all at once. The wall in far-off Berlin had crumbled, its rubble repurposed as paperweights and ornaments on bourgeois mantelpieces. All those subservient countries between Russia and the West had sidled away, and while the satellites and space stations continued to orbit the Earth, nobody much cared. There was no food in the shops and whole families had to live off a bag of flour and little else for weeks.

Anastasia attached herself to a gang led by a former tank commander in the Red Army. He and his men had seized various military assets as the state fractured, and they were in the process of moving their profits from Moscow to London. Anastasia went with them. She was passed around, but they treated her well enough otherwise. Better than her father had. They clothed her and fed her and some of them chatted to her and made her laugh.

Anastasia met Agatha's father in Soho in the early 1990s, in a nightclub he owned. He was seventy-three. She was sixteen. His name was Donald Howard. His associates called him Donnie. She called him Donski.

Agatha turns on to her side then on to her back then on to her side. The sheets are soft and slip against her skin. She begins to fall away into sleep but is then awake. This is a common pattern. She's not sure what manner of insomnia it is. It is not that she cannot fall asleep, but that she cannot stay asleep. She flicks on and off like a faulty generator.

Fedor still hasn't come upstairs, though it is likely he and Roster have returned from their night-time walk. She rises from the bed and tucks the sheets behind her. She slips a wool blanket around her shoulders, walks across the bedroom and pulls open the heavy doors. Across the wide landing from her bedroom there's a gaudy life-size portrait of her father. She never met the man but here he is, illuminated from below by the dim nightlights. The portrait once hung in the entrance hall, looking down at anybody who entered. After staring at it every time she came into the house for years, she decided to assert her presence in the building and remove anything she didn't want. That included most reminders of her father. Instead of following her instructions, Roster has evidently simply decided to move the picture upstairs.

It is indicative of something, Agatha supposes, that the

painting survived at all. Her elder sisters were grown up by the time of her conception. After they heard of the death of their father and the fact that his entire estate was left to an unborn child of a new Russian mistress, they did what they could to loot the movables, coming into the house and lifting everything that wasn't nailed down. But not this portrait. Nobody wanted it. It hung in the entrance hall looking down at the women and their husbands as they squabbled over its subject's possessions, pored over the jewels, the crockery, the wine cellar, and after they dragged the white baby-grand piano through the front door on its side, peeling off the lacquer on the stone steps. Not one of them glanced up to look at the man to whom they owed their wealth, diminished as it admittedly was by his last will and testament. This proud man with grizzled sideburns and a forehead like a marble plinth. This gilded patriarch with the frame of a gladiator and the brow of an emperor.

Agatha descends. Roster lives on the lower-ground floor, next to the kitchen. He has a couple of rooms which have refused any of the technological or aesthetic developments of the last four decades. When Agatha renovated the house, he insisted on no alteration to his small portion of it. He cooks his own drab meals not in the glossy kitchen, which Agatha's chef uses, but on his own gas stove. His utensils are Bakelite. His electricity is tungsten. His carpets and curtains and wallpaper are stained with cigarette smoke and spilt whisky and tea.

She is constantly telling Roster to clean his flat. She enjoys telling him about people she knows who have entirely redeveloped the basements of their townhouses. It has become fashionable for wealthy Londoners to dig deep into the ground and build an underground warren of swimming pools, games rooms and home cinemas. Some have built panic rooms or underground bunkers in case of emergency. It was not unheard of for very wealthy individuals such as her to be the target of kidnapping, armed robbery or extortion. And when

London rioted a few years ago, a crowd of looters actually ran down her street wearing black balaclavas, whirling golf clubs and cricket bats.

Agatha knocks. She hears the old man rise from his wing-back armchair. She hears Fedor scuffle and slip on the linoleum floor then leap to the door and sniff its base. Roster pulls it by the handle and Agatha sees him in the smoky gloom. Fedor lifts himself on to his hind legs and places his forepaws on Agatha's chest.

'You were only supposed to take him out,' she says. 'You're not supposed to keep him down here with you in this dirt.'

'He's a dog. Dirt is his domain.'

'Nonsense. He is a pedigree borzoi. His ancestors slept on the beds of Russian Tsars. His ancestors were kings among dogs.'

Roster looks down at Agatha. His cool grey eyes are dulled by the light. 'And yours were thieves and whores.'

The Stews of Southwark

Tabitha places a copper penny on the bedside table. She and Precious stand and look at it. Tabitha holds her hands above it. Her eyes and mouth are wide in anticipation. Precious frowns.

'What am I supposed to be looking at?'

'It did it before,' says Tabitha.

Precious leans towards the penny, as if heightened concentration will alter its state.

'It was vibrating,' Tabitha insists. 'It moved across the table.'

'Well, it's not moving now.'

They wait for a few seconds. Precious feels like an idiot. Then the penny does begin to shake. It jingles across the surface of the table like a bell being rung, then settles, still and silent.

'What do you think it means?'

'Probably nothing.'

'Why is it doing that?'

'Maybe you have magical powers.'

'Do you think it's an earthquake?'

Precious concedes London does experience small earthquakes. She picks up the penny and puts it into her purse, then goes to the sofa to sit down.

They are waiting for the rest of the girls to arrive. Precious and Tabitha's flat is the best place to meet as it's the biggest, and has access to the roof garden.

Only some of the other women connected to the walk-up live in flats in the building. Others live elsewhere and hire rooms by the hour. For the most part, they get on, but it's no utopia. Young Scarlet once called Cynthia a basic bitch and now the two women barely speak. Precious, however, is liked by everyone.

Everyone assumes 'Precious' is the name she adopted on entering the trade, just as most of the other girls adopted new names. But it was the name her mother gave her at birth. Her childhood was spent between Lagos and London: most of the year in Nigeria, then long summers in the UK, visiting family. Her stepfather spent time between the two cities. He was the pastor of the strict, evangelical church in which Precious was raised, and he had travelled extensively for work, going between the UK and Nigeria and America and Canada, on preaching tours.

A clear path of marriage and domesticity lay ahead of Precious. Sex was for reproduction. She began a midwifery qualification in Lagos and then spent a year with a scheme her church ran which offered medical assistance to women in poorer parts of the country. She toured villages in the north of Nigeria to administer ante-natal and post-natal care to mothers, as well as assisting the midwives with births. She saw many things. She touched bodies. She learned not to be squeamish. Although part of an evangelising programme, this year gave Precious a taste for independence. She lived away from her family, made friends and went out in the evenings. She danced and laughed and sometimes was propositioned by men. Sometimes she accepted these proposals and went on dates, and sometimes she had sex. Sometimes the sex was wonderful. Sometimes the sex was disappointing. But she always felt in control.

She became serious with one of the men and ran away with him to London. The relationship seemed like a good idea at the time. Michael had lofty aspirations and a desire to see the world. In these things, Precious saw similarities with herself. Michael found work in a local business without too much difficulty but Precious spent longer looking for something. She gave up on midwifery and retrained as a beautician.

She got a job at a beauty parlour in Highgate. At that point they were living in Peckham so every day she took the 63 bus to Elephant and Castle and afterwards the Northern Line. She massaged bodies and used special scrubs and muds and oils to exfoliate naked skin. She waxed and shaved and threaded body hair. Sometimes she inserted plastic tubes into anuses and flushed the customer's insides of food they had eaten and half-digested.

Precious and Michael had a son, Marcus, then things began to fall apart. There were arguments about money, childcare and domestic arrangements. There were arguments that started quietly then grew. There were arguments about arguments. Most of all, there were arguments about the fact that Precious still worked. Michael had expected her to work for a couple of years but thought she would then give up her job and concentrate on raising a family. Precious disagreed. She liked working, though the employment in Highgate was not as fulfilling as the employment she had had in Nigeria. Michael left suddenly, a month before the birth of their second son.

Precious, Tabitha, Hazel, Candy, Young Scarlet, and a few others spend the evening drinking wine. They speak about the letter from the landlord: what could be done to combat the changes, and what they would do if nothing could be done. Later, the conversation turns to Scarlet's website. She operates online as well as taking 'walk-up' clients, and reckons she'll be fine if they have to leave Soho.

'It's all done with subscriptions,' Scarlet explains. 'There are different levels of subscription depending on how much you want to pay and how much access you want.'

'Does it start with the I Don't Normally Do This Kind of Thing membership and go all the way up to Absolute Bloody Pervert?' asks Candy.

Precious and Tabitha laugh but Young Scarlet scowls.

'The tiers are actually Bronze, Silver, Gold and Platinum,' she continues, as if Candy hadn't said anything, and isn't sitting on the sofa next to her. Then she turns to her friend. 'It's actually a very classy website, Candida, unlike your cum-shot extravaganza.'

Precious and Tabitha continue to laugh. Young Scarlet and Candy throw each other venomous looks.

Scarlet goes on to explain what the various tiers mean, and what services she provides to her members, and about how some of her online customers go on to visit her in real life, or IRL, as she calls it. 'But then on the other hand,' she says, 'I've never met some of my biggest fans. They couldn't be more enthusiastic about my tits but they've never actually come over and touched them I-R-L.'

Precious is wary of the internet. Some of the other girls think Precious is reluctant to take her business online because she is old-fashioned. They teased her for operating as a kind of vintage prostitute, contacted by telephone (landline!).

'You're like a retro hooker,' says one.

'An artisanal, hand-crafted hooker,' says another.

'Honestly, Precious,' says Scarlet. 'You're missing out on a major source of revenue. These days I'm making almost as much from my website as I am from my walk-up. And on top of that there's the money I earn from selling the data to this big research company that predicts what kind of car someone is likely to buy based on what kind of porn they watch.'

Precious shakes her head. She doesn't trust technology, as she has told Scarlet before. 'You totally lose control,' she says. 'As soon as you film yourself or take photos and put them online, they could literally be anywhere. Anyone could be looking at them or passing them on.'

'No, no, no,' says Scarlet. 'I have control.'

'You don't though,' says Precious.

'Well, I don't care. I'm not as fussed about that kind of thing as you are. I'd rather have money than control.'

Scarlet says nothing more for a bit. It is possible Precious went too far. Everyone has different levels of comfort, different boundaries. It isn't for her to tell Scarlet what she can and cannot do. She only meant she wouldn't be comfortable with it herself. She doesn't like the idea of her digital image being out there in the world for all to see, but then obviously not all women are comfortable with having sex for money.

Precious sometimes likes to think of herself as being like a valuable painting. She is worth the money she is worth because she is unique, exclusive, difficult to access. If she allowed her image to be replicated again and again and again, she would be worthless. How could she charge clients as much as she charges them if they could just log on to her website and have a wank?

She voices this thought to the room and the others just look at her as if she is insane. Candy says something about pieces of art that are just piles of literal crap on a table in the middle of a fancy gallery, and everyone laughs, and Precious returns to her wine.

After the other girls leave, Precious and Tabitha clear up together then get ready for bed. They share a double. They are as close as two people can be, though their relationship is not romantic. They are in love but they are not lovers.

The bed isn't the large, ornate bed in the front room where Precious conducts her business, but is at the back of the flat, in a small bedroom. It is an expensive ergonomic bed with a special mattress because Tabitha suffers from intermittent, shooting back pain. Precious bought it from John Lewis. Precious also bought the bed sheets from John Lewis, in the sale. They were a fine cotton and soft on Tabitha's sensitive skin. Precious sleeps with one pillow and Tabitha sleeps with five.

Tabitha likes to read in bed before falling asleep, which Precious finds frustrating because she is tired and wants the light to be switched off immediately. However, she is used to the set-up and it would be unreasonable to stop her friend reading before bed.

Tabitha is reading a book about Elizabethan London. She

is into the Tudors in general, and Elizabeth I, in particular. Precious was taught the history of Nigeria at school, and the history of the African diaspora, so did not know who the Tudors (or simply 'Tudors' as she calls them) were when she first met Tabitha. Tabitha found this very strange.

'Henrytheeighth,' she said, as if this was explanation enough. 'Henrytheeighth and the six wives of.'

Precious later deduced Tudors were kings and queens from a while ago, but she cannot grasp the fascination. Tabitha once gave her a book on the history of the British monarchy, and Precious was more interested in the Civil War period, in which the monarchy was briefly deposed.

Precious has turned on to her side and is dozing off when Tabitha says, 'Did you know in Paris in the Middle Ages a bunch of prostitutes banded together and tried to offer some money for the construction of a stained-glass window in the Notre-Dame cathedral?'

'No, I did not know that. Is that what it says in your book?'

'No, this book is about Elizabethan London not medieval Paris. I read it in another book ages ago and just remembered it.'

'Right,' says Precious.

'Did you know in Tudor times all the brothels were south of the river in Southwark and it was only much later that they moved up this way to Soho. Stews, they were called then.'

'Yes, you have told me that before.'

Precious shuffles her body to shift some of the duvet over to her side of the bed. Tabitha has a habit of hogging it.

Minutes pass and Precious is again on the cusp of sleep.

'Elizabeth I was dead into the occult. It's unbelievable when you think about it,' says Tabitha.

Precious tries for a couple of minutes to sleep, then realises it is impossible while Tabitha is reading. There is a constant threat of interruption. She turns over to face her friend. 'What do you think the modern-day equivalent of the cathedral thing would be? All us doing a fun run and collecting donations for Children in Need or something.'

'Yeah, or donate a day's takings to the RSPB. Birds4Birds.'

Precious giggles into her pillow. Unable to sleep, she pulls herself up to a sitting position and leans back against the cushioned headboard. She lifts a gossip magazine from the drawer of the bedside table. She turns the pages with the tip of her index finger and stares at photographs of minor royals in front of large fireplaces and luxury cars. Britain is weird, she thinks, not for the first time.

'If we do have to leave here, will you come with me?'

Tabitha closes her book but she leaves her thumb between the pages to mark her place. 'I suppose that depends on where you go. Have you had any thoughts about that?'

'Not really,' says Precious. 'I've not had a proper think. Maybe back to Peckham to be near Marcus and Ashley.'

Tabitha creases her face. 'I don't fancy Peckham. I'm in my sixties. It's not exactly an enticing retirement destination.'

'I like Peckham.'

'So do I, in a way, but I always thought I'd end up in a pretty cottage in the countryside.'

'What work would I get in the countryside? We set up in Chipping Norton so I can service the local Conservative Club?'

'Why not? That's the way it's all moving, I hear. You rent an Airbnb in the country for a month or so and advertise your services online. Then you move locations before the police start sniffing. Pop-up brothels. It opens up your business to a whole new market.'

'Like that organic pop-up farm they're setting up in Soho Square?'

'I suppose so. Move the pigs into Soho and put the tarts out to pasture.'

'You know those countryside brothels are all trafficked girls,' says Precious.

Tabitha re-opens her book.

Neither of them like to talk about sex trafficking. It is only possible to speak casually about such things if they are many steps removed. If there is only a translucent membrane between your own world and its hellish simulacrum, it is better to look the other way.

'I'd miss all the bright lights,' says Tabitha, returning the conversation to their own situation. 'Wherever we go that's not here, I'd miss all the noise, and the sense of being at the centre of things. I like that it's busy. I've always liked it. If we go anywhere else, it will seem so quiet.'

Steam

Bastian stops on the pavement outside the club and puts in his earphones. He scrolls on his phone for some music and returns the device to his inside jacket pocket. The earphones fit snugly; the plastic beads like tiny snails curled in their shells. The music dampens the city and makes him feel as if he could be anywhere, doing anything.

He walks to the Tube. Bastian is making his way home alone. Rebecca wanted to stay out and go dancing with her friends. He could read her well enough to know she wasn't completely happy about his early departure, but she didn't make a fuss. He told her he had a headache, which was partly true, as in, he could feel a kind of discomfort in his head, even if it wasn't physical pain.

After bumping into Glenda on the stairs, he returned to the table and told Rebecca who he had just seen.

'Am I supposed to know who that is?'

'We were at uni with her.'

'I have literally no memory of that name. What does she look like?'

Bastian described Glenda's appearance as best he could.

'That could be about five hundred different people.' The conversation was taking place in front of the group, and Bastian could tell Rebecca was enjoying the performance.

Bastian tried again with some more descriptive material, then mentioned a couple of events and anecdotes about Glenda that might jog Rebecca's memory. The trouble was, Bastian hadn't known Glenda well either. He knew her friend Laura, whom he was emphatically not mentioning to Rebecca, but there were very few defining incidents involving Glenda that he could call to mind.

'I think she was on the committee for that Syrian refugee fundraiser thing.'

'I see. She was political.' Rebecca turned to her friends, with an expression that implied this last word was the only explanation they needed.

Bastian wasn't sure raising money for refugees counted as being political in the way Rebecca meant, but he didn't press the point. Rebecca was emphatically apolitical, which meant she liked things the way they were. She voted in general elections, like any respectable person, but she didn't believe in campaigning for good causes, and found anyone who did deeply irritating.

She turned again to her work friends and explained, 'Our college was full of Social Justice Warriors who were constantly in the bar trying to get you to sign petitions for god knows what. They all had, you know, dreadlocks.'

Her friends laughed obligingly. Bastian didn't join in. He tended to agree with Rebecca about student politics but was, at this moment, too unsettled by the encounter with Glenda and the mention of Laura. Rebecca, however, was on a roll. 'Bastian used to give this fantastic analysis about all those people,' she continued. 'What was it you used to say? When boys are young, they all want to be good at sport. Football or rugby or whatever. That's how they sort out the social hierarchy. Then if they discover they're not very good at sport, they get into music. They become, you know, those boys who set up bands and things, because that's the only way they can get laid. And then if that doesn't work – if they're not very good at music – they go off to university and get into student politics.'

The women laughed. Some of the men looked uneasy. By this point, Bastian felt the need to intervene. 'Yes, I did say that once, but I'm not totally sure it's true. I mean, it's true that some of the student politics that went on when we were at uni was kind of annoying, but I think on balance those people did a lot of good. I mean, I'm glad they raised that money for the refugees?'

After he said this, Bastian remembered the scene upstairs. The camp beds, the postcards, the woman with the mop and bucket. He thought about telling Rebecca but the conversation had moved on and, for some reason, he felt uneasy about mentioning it to her, or to anyone. It was as if he had transgressed by walking into that room and seeing what he had seen. Describing the scene would also be a transgression, as if talking about it made him complicit in some sort of crime. It would be easier to forget it, but he suspected that if he did nothing, it would become one of those thoughts that wriggles around and slowly corrodes, like woodworms in an old church. He made a mental note to talk to his dad about it in the morning. Bastian has just started working for his dad's business, which represents a woman who owns a lot of the property in the area. The club might even be one of hers.

Bastian gets to the underground station and swipes himself through the barriers. A long escalator takes him to the lower levels. He can hear someone playing jazz standards on a tenor sax. The music jars with what he's listening to, and he pops his earphones out and pays attention to the live performance. The notes bounce against the tiles, back and forth on the curved walls, through the long tunnels. He gets to the bottom and sees the saxophonist clutching his instrument and crooning into it with his eyes shut. There is a collection tin at the saxophonist's feet, but Bastian has no loose change, so he picks up his pace and makes his way to the platform.

Bastian plays the double bass, but compared to this guy he's a total amateur. He hardly ever plays in public, but Laura did once manage to get him to perform for her. He played part of a contemporary concerto, and then put down his bow and plucked a couple of walking jazz bass lines, which she found hilarious. He knew she was messing with him, and she said she'd actually really enjoyed it, but he was too shy to play for her again.

Bastian had met Laura in the last few weeks of his degree. Exams were finished and finalists were waiting to graduate. Those weeks were filled with garden parties and balls. Everybody drank a lot of Pimm's and champagne and ate smoked salmon blinis and cocktail sausages. They punted and fell into the River Cam and lay on freshly mown lawns.

Bastian and Rebecca had fallen out. The pressures of finals got to them both, and they were 'on a break', like Ross and Rachel from *Friends*. They were no longer seeing each other but there had been no official end to their relationship. They decided to reconvene once exams were over, only Bastian's exams finished several weeks before Rebecca's and he was left alone in the summer celebrations.

Bastian met Laura Blind at a late-afternoon cocktail event in the garden of one of the colleges that backed on to the river. He had seen her around, and knew they were in the same year, but they had never spoken to each other. They did different subjects and had very different sets of friends, with almost no overlap.

The party had a carnival theme. There were people dressed as strongmen and mime artists, jugglers and magicians. A stand in one corner advertised a 'Freak Show' which, for reasons of good taste, mainly consisted of plastic figurines and misshapen vegetables. In another corner, there was a hall of mirrors, and a little tent with a fortune teller inside. Bastian hadn't been in, but apparently there was a woman dressed up as a soothsayer, who did tarot and palm readings, and had a crystal ball.

Bastian saw Laura standing by the strawberry stand picking out the reddest and juiciest looking specimens then placing them into her cardboard bowl. He watched as she moved over to the jug of cream and poured it over the fruit as liberally as if she were pouring milk on to breakfast cereal.

She didn't appear to be with anybody but stood alone by

the stand with her bowl and spoon and she ate without looking up. She took the bowl of cream, stained pink from the juice of the berries, with both hands, and brought it up to her mouth and drank from it until it was empty.

Bastian approached and saw that some of this pink cream had lingered on her lips, highlighting their curve. He doesn't know why he walked towards her. He didn't know at the time. He doesn't know now.

Laura didn't notice his approach until he was standing directly in front of her.

'Nice strawberries,' said Bastian, unaware of what he was saying until the words had come out of his mouth.

'What?'

She must have thought he was a total prat.

He thought it best to continue in the same vein. 'They go very well with cream, don't they?'

More idiocy.

'Um, yeah.'

Laura began to look over Bastian's shoulder to spot a friend or someone else to whom she could escape.

Feeling the need to atone, he asked her if she wanted a glass of Prosecco. It was a shallow offer. All the drinks at the event were free. However, she said yes, and Bastian went off to get a bottle. He pulled one from a nearby bucket and opened it. He was glad of the task: it broke the awkwardness.

Laura smiled uncertainly as she took a glass from him. It was a smile that said 'thank you' but also 'go away now'. But he didn't go away. Instead, Bastian held out his right hand with his palm upturned. He looked at Laura very deliberately and said, 'What's my fortune?'

Laura had just drawn a large gulp of Prosecco into her mouth and she was holding it there on her tongue to savour the sweetness and let the bubbles dissolve. After Bastian spoke she held the liquid there a little while longer and considered his words, looking repeatedly between his face and the palm of his hand.

She swallowed and said: 'Yours will be a life of adventure and intrigue, so long as you follow your love line rather than your fortune line.' He relaxed his arm.

After that, there was talking and listening. They laughed a lot; Laura made Bastian laugh. They left the event together and headed to a pub and ordered a bottle of the cheapest, nastiest house wine, which they sipped from scratched glasses. Afterwards, they went back to Laura's room. It was at the top of a dark, winding Victorian staircase, and had a slanted ceiling and a window looking out over the market. On the far side of the room, there was a single bed. Laura kicked off her shoes and headed towards it, leading Bastian by the hand. Then she turned and kissed him. Her lips were stained blood blue by the wine. He realised his must be the same colour.

They were only together for a month, but of that month they spent every day and every night in each other's company until, one morning, the relationship ended abruptly. Bastian still can't get his head around what happened. Soon afterwards, Bastian and Rebecca got back together. He and Rebecca made more sense, he decided. They had more in common. They had known each other for a long time. He promised Rebecca he wouldn't contact Laura ever again, and it was a promise he kept.

Back in the flat, Bastian goes to the narrow kitchen and prises open the freezer. Inside, there's a bottle of vodka encrusted with frost. An upturned glass lies on the draining board. He rights it, pours in some of the gloopy liquid and takes a drink. He just about swallows the mouthful and feels it burn the length of his gullet, into his stomach. He fills the rest of the glass with water from the tap, then drains the glass in one go. He repeats both actions. By the time Rebecca returns, Bastian is drunk.

She didn't go dancing after all, and is back earlier than expected. She lets herself in, and comes through to the sitting room. Bastian is lying on the sofa. He has replaced his earphones with a set of expensive headphones, which are plugged into an elaborate hi-fi system. A record is spinning on a turntable. Bastian's eyes are shut.

Rebecca nudges him. He starts, and then, seeing who it is, he pulls the headphones down to hang around his neck.

'I've worked it out,' Rebecca says. She hasn't put her bag down yet.

'Worked what out?'

'Who Glenda was. She was that lesbian who hung around with Laura Blind.'

Bastian feels himself redden. He should never have brought it up.

'Are you two back in touch?' she continues.

Bastian pulls himself up, so he is sitting on the sofa with a straight back. 'No,' he insists. 'God, no. I haven't spoken to her in two years.'

Rebecca looks at him for a while longer, without saying anything.

Bastian can hear the music coming out of the headphones around his neck. It sounds tinny, like cutlery scratching an empty plate.

He takes a couple of deep breaths. So does Rebecca.

'Because if you did get back in touch, that would be us over.'

'Yeah, I know that.'

Rebecca pulls at her lower lip. Her lipstick has rubbed off. She turns away from him, walks into their bedroom and shuts the door. He can hear her going into the ensuite bathroom and turning on the shower.

Bastian switches off the music and tidies away the headphones and cables. He is beginning to sober up. He is feeling like a complete dickhead. When he thinks about the time he spent with Laura, he is usually able to construct a network of explanations and excuses that align in his favour: Rebecca had made it clear she didn't want to see him; Rebecca could have done something similar if she had wanted to (for all he knows, she did); there was never any certainty that he and Rebecca would get back together. And when they did get back together, Rebecca was so businesslike about it, he was never forced to consider her feelings.

Sometimes it seems to Bastian that Rebecca views their relationship as a sound investment. They are from similarly wealthy backgrounds; they are likely to have similarly successful careers. They are both good-looking and intelligent.

He knows she likes being in a relationship with him, but he doesn't know if she likes spending time with him.

He likes spending time with her. He likes seeing her holding forth in front of company, or making people laugh, even when she's mean. He likes going out to restaurants with her and eating new and exciting food. He likes it when she tells him stories about her day at work, and he especially likes it when she tells him about the ceramics she has been working with. Bastian knows nothing about ceramics, or art more generally, or indeed East Asia, but it seems to be a subject Rebecca is genuinely enthusiastic about. It is her passion, something she actually likes, not just something she thinks she should like.

Bastian stands outside the door of the ensuite bathroom and knocks. She tells him to come in. Her voice sounds formal and distant through the door, as if she's making a service announcement on a train.

The bathroom is filled with steam. The clear glass shower screen is thick with condensation and Bastian can see the shapes of Rebecca but none of her details. She looks like a template of herself. He moves towards the screen, reaches out, and places his palm on the glass.

'I'm not going to have sex with you.'

Bastian reels. 'That's not why I came in here.'

'Well, I'm just letting you know.'

'That's not why I'm fucking here. For fuck's sake. I just came in to see if you were okay. I wanted to, I don't know, stand here and have a fucking chat with you.'

'There's no need to lose your temper.'

'I'm not losing my temper,' he insists. He steadies himself, and takes a couple of deep breaths. 'I'm sorry for losing my temper. It's just, I hadn't come in here to make a move on you, I just wanted to say hi.'

'Hi,' she says.

Bastian allows his hand to fall, painting the gesture in the condensation like a cockerel's plume. He goes back to the living room. He assumes that Rebecca gets out of the shower and goes to bed. He wouldn't know. He falls asleep on the sofa.

Archaeology

The group spreads out across the building site like a dropped handful of sand. Each finds a dark corner with its own heap of detritus. 'You never know what you might find,' the Archbishop reminds them, frequently. They look for discarded metals, power tools, wood that can be salvaged and repurposed, anything to turn a profit.

Paul Daniels finds a stack of wooden crates and begins to sort through them. Somebody else makes his way towards the skip, piled high with discarded timber, building rubble, wooden planks with rusted nails stuck through them, broken drill bits, snapped broom handles, chipped bricks, valuable masonry discarded because of minor imperfections.

The woman they call Debbie McGee wanders among her friends. She has not forgotten the tremors. She walks among the rubble, taking care to step gently, allowing the soles of her feet to move over the ground and feel any vibrations that the earth might throw up. She moves like a metal detectorist over an ancient battlefield, working as methodically as her patchy short-term memory will allow, treating the building site as a grid, walking in the straightest lines she can, turning at right angles.

She walks to the furthest corner of the building site. She steps with her left foot then her right. When she tries to step again with her left foot, she trips. She hits the dirt, putting hands out in front of her body to break her fall, grazing her left elbow.

Winded, she tries to pull her foot loose but she is snagged. She twists her body around to see what has caught her. Reaching out, she grabs what appears to be a thick, metal hoop. It is cold to the touch and covered with clods of mud. It is half-wedged in the ground. It must have been exposed when the builders removed the topsoil. Once she has freed her foot, she stands and takes hold of the thick metal hoop with both hands. She pulls and pulls and jiggles the hoop and slowly the earth relinquishes its tight grip on the object. She stumbles backwards, clutching the treasure.

The commotion attracts attention. A couple of the others start trotting towards her. After they see the object she is holding, they beckon others over too. The arrivals peer at the shiny hoop. They are amazed.

Some of them reach out to touch it. Debbie McGee moves the object towards a beam of light shining from high up on a crane, and the object begins to sparkle through the layers of dirt. There is a glint of gold, and other colours too, translucent and opaque, flickering, catching the light then falling back into shadow.

The man they call the Archbishop and the man they call Paul Daniels are the last to arrive, but they do so with the most audacity. Paul Daniels pushes through the crowd, shoving others aside. He sees his woman at the centre of the circle. He looks first at her face, captivated by something she is holding. He sees that she is gazing at the thing with more wonder and awe than she has ever expressed in his direction, and he reaches out and snatches the metal hoop easily from her hands.

Debbie McGee does not resist. As soon as the treasure has been removed from her grip, she recoils, drawing her arms into her body like a flower retracting its petals when the sun disappears. She steps back. She herself is no longer illuminated by the bright white light from the crane. She slinks back into the collective, engulfed by the little crowd of vagabonds, absolved of any protagonism.

The group turns towards Paul Daniels, who is now at their centre, holding the object. He does not fill this role for long. Soon the Archbishop arrives, and plucks the metal hoop from the hands of the man they call Paul Daniels, and focus resolves instead on him.

'Bring water!'

The Archbishop snaps this instruction at nobody in particular, and one of his lackeys runs off and returns with a bucket of water that had been standing by the cement mixer.

The Archbishop dips the object into the bucket and cups water with his hand to dowse it, as if baptising an infant.

The crust of dirt slowly dissolves and when the Archbishop pulls the hoop from the water he reveals a golden crown, set with bright gems: blue, red, green, yellow.

'Oh,' they say. 'Ah,' they say.

He raises it with both hands, holding it up to examine the stones. The harsh floodlights reflect and refract. The jewels dazzle; their colours true. The Archbishop lifts the crown higher still, then slowly, with liturgical solemnity, lowers it on to his head.

The Death of Debbie McGee

Robert gets up from his bar stool, falters, steadies himself, then pushes through the heavy wooden door and stumbles on to the pavement. He left the company of Precious several hours ago feeling worse rather than better. He hoped spending money on sex would stop him spending money on drink. Sex is better for his health if not his bank balance, and usually it improves his mood.

This evening, it didn't make him feel better, and he still had enough spare change to continue drinking. He didn't want to go back to the Behn and explain his absence to Lorenzo, so he went to a different pub and sat alone at the bar, hunched, and ordered a double measure of blended whisky.

Robert Kerr has fucked for fifty years. He first fucked when he was fourteen. Back in Glasgow, Rangers lost to Celtic catastrophically. A die-hard fan, he got in with a group of supporters who took their love of the club to its murky extremities. Club and country. God Save Rangers; God Save the Queen.

After the game, Robert left the Ibrox with this crowd and found a pub off the Paisley Road. By rights, he was too young to drink and smoke with these hard men but he was big for his age and eager to keep up. They found some girls around the corner and brought them into the back rooms.

One of the girls marked out Robert for herself. She had wide hips, large, white breasts and hair the colour of Irn-Bru. She sat on his lap and allowed him to caress the inside of her bare thigh with his fingertips then reach up beneath her dress. An older man saw the beginnings of the assignation. 'You taking that hen upstairs?'

Robert did. The rooms above the pub were still drenched in wartime ruin. There were blackout blinds but no curtains; holes in the walls where cast-iron light fittings had been removed. The sheets on the bed hadn't been changed between occupants.

It was in this setting that Robert Kerr first kissed a woman's lips, first kissed a woman's nipples, first felt a hand that was not his own grip his dick, first felt a mouth and tongue there. Though young, he knew instinctively what to do. He took the lead.

He fell in love as assuredly as any fourteen-year-old boy in his position would. For him, the red-headed woman who might have been more than twice his age, was the most beautiful thing to have ever walked the banks of the Clyde. At the end of their encounter, he paid the going rate.

That evening, Robert fucked Precious for fifty minutes. He worked up a sweat. Precious wriggled beneath him. She is good at her job but not so good that she could feign interest for almost an hour without letting up. She did her best, Robert could tell, not to look actively bored, but the manufactured excitement and engagement of the first twenty minutes dissipated. Robert felt a stab of guilt. Guilt for taking so long, guilt for being so old and ugly and for inflicting his body upon this beautiful woman, guilt for going out whoring at all.

After Robert left the walk-up, he was followed by the bouncer, Karl. Robert got to the end of the street and turned a corner, then felt a hand on his shoulder.

'What do you want?' Robert asked.

'To let you know that place is finished,' Karl replied.

'Finished how?'

'The landlords have been trying to chuck them out for months. They're fighting it but they've got no chance of winning. They'll be out soon enough. I've already got another job lined up. There's a bunch of guys down in Surrey who've got a place going. All Russian or Eastern European or something and they need blokes like me. And, well, obviously they're looking for customers.'

Karl reached into the inside pocket of his black leather jacket. He pulled out what looked like a business card, only it had nothing printed on it. He then took out a pencil and wrote a mobile phone number. 'If you're looking for a new place when this one packs up, give me a call.'

Robert took the card and watched Karl as he walked back to his sentry duty.

Surrey. Robert knows of those kinds of places: unlikely looking detached houses on the outskirts of insignificant towns. Boarded up windows. Girls drugged and thrown on beds. Johns handing their cash over to men like Karl. Idiots like Robert picked up by black cars with tinted windows, dropped off again when it was done. It isn't for him. Maybe it is inevitable, as Karl said it was, but Robert can't stand those places. He's seen a few, to his shame, but only for work.

Bugger Karl for lining a job up with those Eastern Europeans while he's still working for the girls. The girls are paying him good money to look after them. People have no sense of loyalty any more.

Robert veers across the pavement and trips on to the road, steadying himself with a hand on the tarmac. Revellers edge around him. A group of young women on the other side of the street turn away. He tries hard to keep a straight course. He manages perhaps twenty steps before stopping to rest.

The spot is next to an alleyway that leads to a large area enclosed by plywood boards, emblazoned with the lettering and logo of a well-known building contractor. Behind the boards, there is a noisy building site. It has been there for several years and keeps changing shape and enveloping then releasing new tracts of land. Nobody Robert knows has seen what is being built behind the boards, but he probably could have found out easily.

If he read newspapers, listened to the radio or watched

television other than football, he would know that a deep hole is being dug. A new underground line is being built, deep below the earth. The plywood boards mask huge machines. Diggers loosen the topsoil and move piles of earth, before shifting it on to trucks and out of the city. Vast drills bite into the bedrock. They swirl and cut and push debris to the surface. There are pumps to pour water to cool the drill as the friction rises. The machines rumble. The rock and soil and buildings around them rumble too. As the hole gets bigger, the machines go deeper. The rumblings get deeper too.

Robert leans against the wall, steadies himself and catches his breath. As he waits, he sees a figure approach, slowly. The streetlight is reflected on her pale skin and her synthetic clothing. She looks herself like a slit of light, a single ray, the crack between a door and its frame. She continues to wander towards him and he blinks several times to clear his vision. He tries to steady his focus so he can see the figure as single and crisp, not double and frayed.

'Oh,' he says as she gets near enough to be feet and legs and arms and body and a head with hair and a face. 'It's you.'

She slinks forward and joins him in the shadows. He looks at her eyes and sees the blood within them and the lines beneath them, as he did earlier in the day. He sees the cracks in her skin around her nose and mouth and scars where previous cracks opened, healed, opened, healed.

'What are you doing here?'

Her reply is whispered. 'Archbishop sent us out looking for the tremors what I felt. They've gone home, but I've stayed. I know this is where it'll start again.'

The reply means little to Robert. He's too far gone to listen.

He nods all the same, and grasps Cheryl's arm; Cheryl, who is known to most people in this part of the city as Debbie McGee.

Robert leans in and says to her: 'You take care of yourself, now. Promise me you will.'

She promises in fragile whispers.

'You take care of yourself and if you get in any bother – any bother at all, mind – come straight to me and I'll sort it out. You hear. Straight to me.'

A fragile nod.

Robert pushes himself off from the wall against which he's been leaning, and shunts himself down the road towards home.

Cheryl, the woman they call Debbie McGee, remains. She returns to the building site. She finds the opening of the huge crater, and a ladder leading down. She descends. She does not return.

The End of September

Suburbs

The city is far too clean. All the good dirt – the earth, the soil, the compost, the organic matter – has been cleared away, shunted along tarmacked streets and out to the suburbs. It sits in gardens and parks, and at the centre of roundabouts and the sides of motorways. Surfaces are wipeable. Windows are washed, carpets are hoovered, countertops are disinfected. Even the streets are cleaned, cleared of dust, dead pigeons, fallen leaves. There is no time for good dirt. No time to let it settle, dissolve, disintegrate, rub along with the dirt that's already there, then re-emerge as something new and beautiful: a flower, a tree, a decorative fungus. Instead, there is grime: the residue of noxious solvents, a thin film of condensed smog on buildings, soot that seeps into nostrils and the pores of skin.

In the suburbs, Jackie Rose sits on her garden bench. Jackie likes her garden and she likes to garden. She has lived in this house for thirty years. She and Keith have raised three sons here. All three are tall, athletic, intelligent and kind. Jackie and Keith couldn't be more proud. The eldest is at university but still lives at home. He gets the train to Queen Mary and studies engineering. His name is Harry. They named him after Prince Harry. Jackie cried when Diana died. The second son is an apprentice carpenter. Andy is probably the most handsome: girls stare at him in the street. Jackie takes a strange, vicarious pleasure in it. Yes, she thinks: this is my son. I made him. The youngest is Mark. He is studying for his GCSEs. He's got a girlfriend but Jackie and Keith think he might be gay.

Jackie sees the garden as hers. Everything else belongs to her and Keith together: the house, the cars, the motorhome, the furniture. But the garden is hers alone. 'My garden,' she says. 'What have you done to my garden?' when the boys hack through the tulips with a football. 'We'll get that for my garden,' when she and Keith spot an attractive planter at the garden centre. 'How's my garden looking?' when she's away from home, working on a case.

She plants, prunes, mows, puts up wire for the climbing roses, and bamboo poles for sweet peas. She digs holes for the bulbs then tops them over with compost. She trudges and tramples and squelches in green wellies after they've had rain and the ground is good for turning. Now it is autumn, she sweeps fallen leaves that have shrivelled, browned and crisped.

There are also weeds: unwanted, interlopers. There are dandelions, daisies, clover, moss. They infiltrate the pristine lawn Jackie and Keith set down when they bought the house: strips of turf rolled up like sacred scrolls, laid side by side to stitch themselves together over that first summer.

Jackie wages war on weeds. She wages war with a miniature pitchfork, secateurs and chemical weapons. She hoes, she scarifies, she pulls weeds from between the patio stones with clenched fists before they have time to settle. She rips, tears, snips, swears.

It's a Tuesday morning in late September. It is the equinox. The day is as long as the night and the night is as long as the day. The temperature is moderate. There is dew on the grass and a thin covering of mist. It's 6 a.m. Keith brings Jackie a cup of instant coffee with milk and sugar. Jackie is holding an arch-top folder and flicking through some of the documents held within.

Soon afterwards, she heads off to work, at a police station in central London. She goes to the office of her commanding officer for a quarterly review. She brings with her the notes and cases she wants to discuss and the details of the resources she thinks her team needs.

Michael Warbeck is sitting behind his desk, leaning back in his chair, looking at his phone and tapping on its screen with his two thumbs. He looks up briefly as Jackie walks in and then he says, 'I'll be right with you, Rose.' He continues to tap.

Jackie settles herself in the chair in front of his desk and places her bundle of documents on her knees. She begins to riffle through them and pulls to the top the ones that are most worthy of discussion.

'Right with you,' he says again. 'I just need to . . .'

He trails off.

'You writing a novel?' Jackie asks. It's rude but she's too old to care. She can retire in just three years.

Warbeck chuckles in a hollow sort of way. She can tell that he's affronted, but not enough to cause her any bother.

'Sorry,' he says with a toothy smile. 'What can I do for you today?'

'It's my review,' says Jackie.

'God, is it? That's come around quickly.'

'Every three months.'

'Goodness me. It feels like you were here yesterday. You've obviously loomed large in my thoughts these last few months.'

'Sir, I've printed out some graphics to help you better understand the situation the department is now facing.'

Jackie finds that Michael Warbeck responds better to images than to words. Bullet points are also useful as they arrange the words into shapes, if words are needed at all. Since his promotion above her eighteen months ago, Jackie has become an expert in concision. She can now fit three months of her department's work on to a single side of A4 paper.

She pushes the document across the desk. He picks it up, casts his eyes over it, then puts it down.

'I know,' he says. 'Why don't you set it all out to me here and now. Speak to me, Jackie.'

Jackie smiles. She expected this. She pulls some more notes from her folder.

'Sir, things are getting much worse. If there were a disease that made people disappear, we'd say we had an epidemic on our hands. Vulnerable young people are being reported as missing at a rate I've never seen before. Men and women.

The men we suspect as suicides – that's what the evidence points to, and on that score I'm not sure it's something we as the police can do much about. The women, on the other hand, well, the evidence my team have collected points to sexual exploitation and trafficking. These are women from difficult backgrounds; many are first- or second-generation immigrants, some illegal immigrants; many have been on our radar before, either us the police, or social services; many grew up in foster care, and then they just disappear, and there's no one around to do all that much about it.'

'It doesn't sound like it's been a very productive few months. Any success stories? Found anyone?'

'Sir, I'm afraid the people we find are people who would probably turn up anyway. I can't say we've had much luck in uncovering the whereabouts of these individuals I'm talking about. What we need is better strategies for identifying these vulnerable people in the first place, and we also need to be working more closely with other teams within Serious Crimes – the Sexual Exploitation framework – so that we can do more to prevent grooming and trafficking.'

'Jackie, Jackie, stop there for a second.' Michael Warbeck holds out a hand. 'I know that's where you wanted to be. We all know that. You had your heart set on Sexual Exploitation. But it just didn't work out with the arrangement of personnel we had available. We needed you on Missing Persons. I'm sorry, but that's just the way it is. Now, I hope you're not using this as an opportunity to segue into that line of work.'

'No, sir. My priority is to find people who are reported to us as missing, it's simply that better links with other teams would help us achieve that. Let me give you an example.' She riffles through her papers and brings out a case file. 'This is Cheryl Lavery, sir, a.k.a. Debbie McGee.'

'As in the wife of Paul Daniels? The one from *Strictly Come Dancing*?'

'Yes, sir. That's her nickname. She and her man were known

to go around Soho performing magic tricks. Hence the names. He's Paul Daniels.'

'I see.'

'One way or another, Cheryl Lavery has been known to social services and the police for a while. She's a drug user, she's spent a long time without a fixed address, she has been convicted for shoplifting, public indecency and solicitation. Finally, she was reported missing about three months ago. Now, we don't know for sure, but we suspect she has fallen victim to a pimping ring. They take vulnerable people like her, who may have been working regularly or occasionally on the streets, and they set them up in a brothel somewhere and work them around the clock.'

'Well, in that case, that's a job for a different unit.'

'But if we worked together. If we sent a small team on secondment.'

'Jackie, I'm not sure we've got the budget for secondments.'

Jackie steadies herself. 'Absolutely, sir. It's just, I can't help but feel frustrated when we encounter the case files of all these people who've gone missing, who could have been helped. Who could still be helped.'

Michael Warbeck nods sympathetically. 'It's a difficult one,' he says. 'It's one of the most difficult things we have to come to terms with as police officers. It's very easy to become emotionally involved in our case work.'

'It's not that, sir. It's a case of productivity.'

'Jackie,' he says again, getting up from his chair. 'I'll tell you what, we can reconvene later. I'm afraid I've got meetings at Whitehall I should be preparing for. I'll tell you what though, I'll have a read of your report, and there might be something in it that I can raise with the Minister. How about that?' He holds out his hand for the papers.

Jackie understands that she's being dismissed. She collates some of the key documents along with her summary and longer report, and hands the bundle to her commanding officer, certain that they will have very little further contact until her next quarterly review.

Hunting

Agatha takes the dog out early to avoid the kinds of people who walk their dogs after 9 a.m. She would like to avoid all other dog walkers but, in London, this is impossible, and she read that puppies need to be socialised, so it's a good idea to allow Fedor to meet others of his kind. If he is to encounter dogs, she must encounter dog walkers. In her experience, the ones who emerge before 9 a.m. are preferable to the ones who emerge after 9 a.m. The former are the kinds of people who get up early and get on with their days, and have things to do – jobs, etc. They're hard-working, disciplined people and their approach to their dogs is similar. People who walk their dogs after 9 a.m. are slovenly. They're not likely to have jobs or commitments, and they're likewise lax in their approach to their animals. Whenever Fedor gets into scraps with other dogs, it is after 9 a.m. Agatha has decided this is no coincidence.

This morning she slept in and is out later than she intended. She holds Fedor's lead while Roster follows, carrying the dog's coat – in case the weather changes – and other items of dog-walking paraphernalia.

'What's that one?' Agatha asks Roster. She points to a dog in the distance, running between trees and sniffing the leaf litter.

'A pointer,' Roster replies.

'Wrong,' says Agatha. 'It's a Vizsla.'

'A Vizsla is a type of pointer.'

'From Hungary, yes. But you can't just say pointer. If you say pointer without any qualification then I'll think you just mean a standard pointer, not a Vizsla. Imagine if you pointed at a Clumber spaniel and just said spaniel.'

'Imagine,' says Roster.

They continue to walk along a gravel path beneath a canopy of trees. Beech masts are strewn across the grass with the first fall of umber leaves. Fedor strains at his harness. Agatha looks around for hazards, then leans down and unclips the lead.

He has grown significantly in the last three months. He has now reached his full, adult height, although his torso hasn't yet filled out – his growth has been channelled through length rather than weight. His shoulders jut out and his spine is visible through his fur, from neck to hip. Each connected vertebra is distinct, undulating like cursive handwriting on a page.

Fedor speeds away and buries his long dart of a nose in the lively aroma. Agatha is struck by the extent to which dogs use their noses to navigate the world, and how their experiences of the world must be so different from those of humans, led by their eyes. Dogs scoop from the air the fabric of the earth. When Fedor presses his face into the leaf litter, he breathes morsels of the rotting leaves, and particles of fungi from the soil beneath. He breathes the urine and the faeces of mice and voles, or he might detect the owl that flew overhead the night before, swooping silently to capture its supper. Through its nose, a dog deals with history.

Agatha's senses only decipher the present. To access the past, she must rely on the testimony of others.

She was the sixth daughter of Donald Howard. He fathered no sons. The first pregnancy occurred unexpectedly. In 1934, aged fourteen, Donald knocked up a girl from his village. Marry her, everyone said. He didn't marry her. He fled. He moved to the capital and found work as a butcher's apprentice in its East End, near the marshes. He sectioned hogs and swept their blood and excrement from the slaughter-house floor. He became a skilled handler of sharp blades.

His second daughter was also the granddaughter of the butcher, his employer. When the pregnancy was discovered, the butcher came at him with a cleaver but Donald was faster and ducked and swayed and caught the old man in the belly with a carving knife. He swept up the butcher's blood and dumped him in the canal with a dumbbell fastened to his ankle. Local gangs, everyone said. It was known the butcher had failed to comply with the demands of the hard men who ran the neighbourhood. Donald went along with the story, and this time he did marry the girl. Together they became figureheads for the backlash against these gangs, and the result was a new gang, with Donald at the helm. The gang was built upon the premise of seeking revenge for the slaughtered butcher but it became more violent and detached from its original purpose. Donald rallied local lads and they drove the previous gangs east, and they took control of much of the gangland business. They ran brothels and backstreet casinos and smuggled cigarettes and alcohol.

By the time the war came, and with it conscription, Donald had already suffered two separate knife wounds to his left thigh and had begun to walk with a limp. He avoided military service but other men of his age did not. Donald worked this to his advantage. His influence spread. So did his reputation. It was around this time that his first wife left him, and with her went his second daughter. He's changed, she said. He's changed, everyone said.

After the war, Donald bought property in central London. Prices had slumped and much of it was in disrepair through wartime poverty or outright bomb damage. It was going cheap. A few years previously, Donald Howard had gone to see a motion picture in full technicolour at the Leicester Square Trocadero. Its name was *Gone with the Wind*. Land, it's the only thing that matters, Mr O'Hara had said to his daughter. Donald had taken these words to heart. He bought and he bought. All the money he earned from his illicit activities was poured into property in Soho. He ran more brothels, and strip clubs, and underground gay bars, and he became achingly, blindingly rich. Another wife. This one was significantly more glamorous than the last: she had aspirations in musical theatre and smoked cigarettes using a long, red cigarette-holder. Three more daughters, five in total. He and his glamorous wife named these daughters after London landmarks: Angel, Chelsea and Victoria.

By the time Donald met Agatha's mother, Anastasia, he was already old. *Donsky, darling, it's a boy. I know it's a boy.* The young and beautiful Anastasia told him this again and again. Donald wanted desperately to believe her, and in the last months of his life, which he spent with his Russian wife, he changed his will, so the estate would be left to his youngest child, as yet unborn. Donald Howard died shortly afterwards. When the baby arrived, she was a girl.

Agatha has scheduled a day of meetings. She is looking forward to none of them. She enjoys the parts of the business that involve designing and building, working with architects and engineers, and taking a derelict, useless wreck and turning it into something beautiful and productive, but lately, so many of her plans have been stymied by the situation at the brothel, and the ongoing legal disputes with her sisters. Her first meeting is with a police officer, who she hopes can deal with the former issue, and the second meeting is with her lawyer, who has news regarding the latter.

She spots another dog and its owner coming in their direction. The dog is very small, and as it gets closer she makes out the face and features of a Yorkshire terrier, a pink ribbon tied into a bow between its ears. The dog's owner is a man of about 5 foot 5 with strong arms, a round belly and a shaved head. His face is round and reddish.

Fedor is still off lead but close by. He hasn't noticed the other dog.

Agatha and Roster continue to walk and so does the man with his Yorkshire terrier. They are now perhaps ten metres apart. The approaching man begins to smile at them. He looks as though he is going to speak. Neither Agatha nor Roster returns his smile and his face begins to fall.

Fedor catches the scent. He stands to attention. His ears

are pricked; his eyes are wide; his lips are closed but ready, quivering. The man has not noticed the sighthound's stance; neither has Roster. Agatha has noticed Fedor's posture but thinks little of it.

The Yorkshire terrier lets out a short, high-pitched bark. Triggered by the frequency, the borzoi lurches forwards. His hind legs are released like the arm of a catapult. He is immediately upon the small creature.

Nobody understands what has happened. All three of the humans look, Agatha frowning slightly, Roster a couple of steps behind. The man who owns the Yorkshire terrier continues to hold the end of the lead, the other end of which is attached to the small dog, which is in the mouth of the large dog.

Even the little terrier hasn't realised what is happening. She hangs limply, and makes no sound.

Then the Yorkshire terrier's owner panics, and he begins to shout. He has a thick accent from a part of the country Agatha hasn't visited, and she can't make out what he is saying. She has never been shouted at by a complete stranger before. She has very little interaction with what she would call 'members of the public', and she has still less experience of this manner of incident. She recoils a little but is otherwise immobile.

The large dog is still holding the smaller dog in its jaws. The smaller dog is now quivering and making a high-pitched whimpering noise. Roster is trying to explain to the shouting man that this is only making matters worse; that the borzoi is simply responding to his very sensitive prey drive; that the borzoi believes the Yorkshire terrier to be a rabbit or some other traditional prey animal.

It takes nearly ten minutes for Fedor to be persuaded to drop the other dog. By this point, the man is in tears.

Happy Go Lucky

Lorenzo begins the day with an audition for a role in a new television series. He's doing it for Glenda, he tells himself, but also he could do with the money. The production company is American though filming will be done in the north of England with a largely British cast. This is to give the programme an 'Old World' feel. Though set in a fantasy land, it's supposed to be a kind of medieval fantasy, and it's felt British accents will be more authentic.

Lorenzo's agent put him forward for one role but the production company came back and offered him an audition for another. Because the show is to have a big budget, there's a lot of secrecy surrounding it, and the details of the part he's auditioning for aren't clear. He was told that he'd find out more when he got to the studio.

Lorenzo enters the large, high-ceilinged foyer through rotating glass doors. He's ushered to the waiting area by a young woman. She takes his photograph on a small digital camera clipped to the back of her computer for this purpose, and soon afterwards hands him a day pass with a fresh image of his face on it. He's joined in the waiting area by two other men of a similar age. Following the laws of courtesy, the three men sit as far apart from each other as is possible and, after a cursory smile and nod, they each do everything they can to avoid further interaction.

Lorenzo picks up a left-leaning periodical from the coffee table. Someone has written an article about being 'Second Generation Working Class'. Lorenzo didn't realise that was a thing.

Sure, I was brought up in a nice house and went to school

in a decent catchment area, but my parents were both raised on a bootstrap and didn't eat pasta until they were at university.

Lorenzo reads another line.

When chatting to friends about opera or art, I just don't have the same shorthand, the same inherited cultural cache.

And then,

I've never been skiing.

Lorenzo throws the periodical back on to the table. He tries to steady his thoughts. He recites in his head some lines from the piece he prepared. They might not even ask him to perform it. The thought makes him feel both better and worse.

He is summoned to the audition room last. The other two contenders were either shown out of the building through a different exit after their auditions or else they've been murdered and chopped up and flushed down a toilet, because Lorenzo doesn't see them again. He's led upstairs into a room with a wooden floor and tall windows along one side. There are mirrors along the wall facing the windows. The room has the look of a dance studio.

He is greeted by a lanky man with thinning grey hair, wearing a black, merino-wool jumper.

'Lorenzo?' The man holds out a hand.

'Hi. Yes,' says Lorenzo. He meets the man's hand and shakes it. The man doesn't follow with his own name. He must have forgotten that particular rule of social engagement.

'Great, let's get going,' says the man. He turns away and goes to sit down behind a table, where a woman and another man are already sitting.

Lorenzo remains standing in the middle of the room. He bounces on his toes a couple of times and wonders if he should have done some of his old drama-school warm-ups. Probably. It's too late now.

'What do you know about the role?' the lanky man asks.

'Very little,' Lorenzo replies. 'I knew a little bit about the role I was put forward for, but I know almost nothing about this one.'

'Sure, yeah, that's fine. We didn't expect you to know anything. It's all been hush hush.'

The man picks up a sheet of paper and leans across the table to hand it to Lorenzo. Lorenzo walks forward to take it.

'Take a seat,' says the woman.

'Oh yeah, take a seat,' says the man. 'Sorry. Where are my manners?'

Lorenzo sits down, holding the sheet of paper.

'So yeah. Huge, huge, sweeping fantasy drama,' says the man. 'Loads of episodes.'

'We hope,' interjects the woman.

"We hope,' says the man. 'We hope loads of episodes, and filming mainly here in the UK.'

'In the north,' says the woman.

'Yeah, in the north.' The man puts on a bad Yorkshire accent: 'Up North! There's a great little studio there and lots of beautiful, gorgeous rugged landscape, which is just what we need. Hills and cliffs and waterfalls, and lots of moody black clouds. That sort of vibe. And, hopefully, other locations around the world. Nice, exotic places. You okay with that?'

'Sure,' says Lorenzo. 'Sounds fantastic.'

He's beginning to feel more optimistic about his foray into television work. They're speaking to him as if trying to sell the part to him.

The man continues: 'The role itself is really fun. You know, it's the kind of role the right actor could really make a lot of. There's a lot of creativity; a lot of light and shade.'

'Great writing as well,' says the woman.

'Yes,' agrees the lanky man. 'Great writing. We've got some real talent on board.'

'Well, that's always a good sign,' says Lorenzo. He doesn't want to appear to have nothing interesting to say. 'Good writing's often the most important thing, isn't it? Good writing can improve an average performance, but a good performance can't mask average writing.'

'Right, yeah,' says the man. 'I'd never thought of it in that way.'

'Actually I disagree totally with that statement,' says the woman. 'In fact, I couldn't disagree more. I think that is completely wrong.'

'Um,' says Lorenzo, weakly. It was such a strong response, Lorenzo wonders for a moment if she's testing him. It had been an idle comment. He isn't sure whether or not even he agrees with what he just said.

The woman doesn't seem to require a reply, thankfully, but also she doesn't seem to be joking. The lanky man continues as if he hasn't heard what the woman said. The third panellist – the other man – has spent the whole conversation staring at a piece of paper on the table.

'So you'd be a pimp,' says the lanky man, bringing the conversation back to the casting.

'Right,' says Lorenzo.

'But a really fun pimp,' says the lanky man. 'You know, a really exotic one. The feel we want to go for is of a kind of happy-go-lucky, cheeky chappy, who sells things here and there and who's done this and that with his life and been around the block a bit, but who's now found himself at the head of a really luxurious high-end brothel in the kind of economic and political centre of this world. How does that sound?'

'Well, yeah, fine. I guess I'd have to see the script to get into the role, but in theory that sounds fine.'

'We've seen a reel of some of the comedy you've done. But also the Shakespeare stuff. You can do that thing where you're happy and jolly and likeable one minute and then really lethal and menacing the next. Do you know what I mean?'

'Um, yeah. I guess I can do both.'

'And you've got the look.' The lanky man turns to his colleagues. 'He's got the look, hasn't he?'

The woman nods. The third man looks up from the piece of paper on the table and considers, then also nods.

Lorenzo wonders what 'the look' means in this context.

The three panellists mutter under their breath, behind their hands. The lanky man says: 'Okay, fantastic. We'd love to see you in a few situations. I think we've got a measure of you as an individual performer from what we've seen of your reel, but we'd like to test you out with another performer.'

'Okay,' says Lorenzo. 'That sounds good.'

'Fantastic,' says the man. He gets up. Lorenzo becomes aware of how tall the man is. Some thin people look taller than they are because of their proportions. This man isn't one of those: he's both thin and genuinely tall. He walks to the far end of the room to an open door. 'Kim,' he calls. 'Kim?'

There's a scuffle within, and a person who is presumably called Kim comes to the entrance then into the room.

'This is Kim,' says the man.

'Hi, Kim,' says Lorenzo. 'I'm Lorenzo.'

'Hi Lorenzo,' says Kim. She holds out her hand and Lorenzo shakes it in the way that's just one person brushing their fingers against another person's palm.

Kim is a standard actress, as defined by any description of an actress provided by a big studio casting call. She's 5'3" with long, fair hair. She is pretty, maybe beautiful, but not scene-stealingly so. She would upstage nobody. She could be as old as thirty or as young as eighteen.

'Great,' says the man as he comes out from around his desk once again with some papers in his hand. 'So Lorenzo, we'd like you to run through this scene with Kim. Is that okay? She's been through it already with a couple of the guys we've auditioned already for the part. I mean, I don't mind telling you that we're auditioning other people.' He laughs. Lorenzo laughs too. The man hands the papers to Lorenzo and Kim. 'I'll give you a couple of minutes to familiarise yourself with the material. Then we'll give it a go. Is that okay?'

'Fine,' says Lorenzo. He looks down at the script.

OMATIO: Spread your legs, you fucking whore!

WHORE 1: Please, sir, please. Not again.

OMATIO: You think this is a game? You think this is a fucking game? You think I brought you all the way over here so you could keep me company? So you could tell me stories about your fucking home country?

WHORE 1: Please, sir. I didn't know. I didn't know.

OMATIO: Because let me tell you, whore. I don't want to hear them. I don't give a shit about that fucking shithole. Do you hear me? Now we've got paying customers out there right now, and every minute you're sitting in here with your legs closed is a golden floren I've lost.

[Kvist, a patron, enters wearing fine clothes]

OMATIO: Good sir! But a moment! Has one of my men poured you a glass of our finest wine? We have every good vintage. We shall bring you your selection in just a moment.

KVIST: I heard a commotion.

OMATIO: It was nothing. It was nothing, sir.

KVIST: Is that girl crying?

OMATIO: Tears of laughter, only! She was just now entertaining me with tales of her people. You know the Sand Dwellers of Amon K' Tur? She is one of those. Did you know that they cover their bodies in a mixture of sand and piss to protect themselves from the sun? And one time a traveller came through and was so aroused by the aroma he bottled it and sold it for luxury perfume at the market in Temorry for fifty golden florens a case!

[Kvist laughs]

[Omatio laughs]

[Whore 1 continues to weep]

The scene continues in this vein for several pages. Lorenzo reads it over a couple of times then performs it with Kim as

Whore 1 and the lanky man as Kvist. At the end of the piece he's required to slap Kim across the face. Lorenzo gained extensive fight training at drama school so is able to do this without causing any physical harm. After the audition, he shakes everyone's hand and leaves the building feeling ill. He did a good job. He hates himself for having done a good job.

A Full English

Following the unpleasant incident with the Yorkshire terrier, Roster and Agatha loop back on themselves and head towards the car. The senior police officer Agatha has arranged to meet is Michael Warbeck. She's heard he's one of the brightest stars in the service. His career in the force commenced with a graduate scheme for talented young people and he's been promoted quickly and frequently. It is rumoured that Michael Warbeck has political ambitions, and that he will shortly leave the police force and announce his candidacy for Mayor of London. It is all very secret, however. Because of his position, he is entirely debarred from any political activity, and must make any preparations covertly until he has quit his job.

They meet at a cafe near Agatha's house. Roster parks the car outside and waits. The cafe has white linen tablecloths and silver coffee pots. There are several types of smoked salmon and caviar on the menu, as well as pastries and cooked breakfasts. Michael Warbeck arrives late and orders a cappuccino and a Full English.

'Do you mind?' he asks as he orders.

'Not at all,' Agatha replies.

There are a few minutes of small talk then Agatha guides the conversation to a topic that ensures he's aware of the full extent of her wealth and reach. Next, they speak guardedly about the current Mayor of London, then briefly about the coffee in their cups and their respective breakfasts, then Agatha finds an opportunity to bring up the subject about which she's most keen to speak.

'The thing that I think is really preventing this city progressing as quickly as it could, is that there is still so much inequality.'

Michael nods. His cheeks are stuffed with baked beans.

'And particularly when it comes to housing,' she continues, 'as recent events have made apparent.'

Michael nods again, still with a mouthful of fry-up, but this time his expression is appropriately graver, in response to the grisly event to which she's alluding.

'It's atrocious, really,' she says. She pauses, allowing him to chew and swallow his food. She doesn't want to hector. The ideas she's trying to elicit will be much more effective if he thinks they are his own.

'The situation is shocking. We see it on the ground all the time. We in the police force, I mean.'

'I'm sure.'

'You know, there's less integration between communities now than when I joined up. We used to talk about ghetto-isation as if it were a totally American phenomenon, but we're seeing it here now as well.'

'That's terrible.'

'It is.'

Michael returns to his breakfast. Agatha wants to make sure the conversation remains on this topic rather than deviating, so while he cuts up his sausage, she says: 'Even I've noticed it. I am, of course, a person of great privilege, but first and foremost I'm a Londoner. That's how I see myself. And I have certainly noticed that there is huge variation between neighbourhoods. It can't be healthy.'

'Well, exactly.'

He's being frustratingly monosyllabic, so Agatha continues on her own. Perhaps she should have suggested a meeting place that didn't involve food. 'You know, it's something I've actually been thinking about more and more. And about what I as a developer can do about it. Some of the properties that my father owned are so run down, and since I've taken control of the business I've been doing what I can to renovate them. But it can be difficult, you know.'

'It's interesting to hear you say that. A lot of property

owners aren't so concerned by these issues, if you can believe that. Tell me, from your perspective. I mean from the perspective of a developer—'

'And a Londoner,' she interrupts.

'And a Londoner,' he adds. 'From your perspective, what can be done? What's the number one issue?'

'Well, I'm not sure about what the solution is. I suppose that's for other people to decide. But I know what I see as the number one issue. Safety. Safety is a big issue. It's important that people can feel as safe in one part of the city as they do in any other. Particularly women. A woman should be able to feel as comfortable walking down the street in Croydon as she does in Highgate. Or in Soho,' she adds casually. 'But, well, Soho is a whole other issue. There you find all sorts of dangers, as a woman.'

'Oh really?'

'Oh yes,' she says. 'A large amount of my property is in that area and we – my colleagues and employees and I – encounter all sorts of unsavoury scenarios. Of course, traditionally, it's the seat of the London sex trade, some of which is, naturally, legal. But there is also the intersection between what is legal and what is not. Sometimes we see situations or set-ups in the properties we run that we question. But, obviously, there's little we can do about it. More often than not, the tenants in these properties have extraordinarily long leases. And we can't evict them, of course, for no reason, as is right. But nor, it seems, can we evict them when we have serious concerns about what manner of activity is occurring within those properties.'

'What kind of activity?'

'Well, we wonder about drug taking. And more particularly, from my perspective, as a woman concerned about the safety of other women, I wonder about trafficking. Sex trafficking.'

Michael Warbeck sits up in his chair and, having finished eating, places his knife and fork together on his empty plate, pulls the white linen napkin from his lap and uses it to dab the corners of his mouth.

'Sex trafficking is really big right now,' he says. He places the crumpled napkin on the table next to his plate. 'I mean, sex trafficking is currently a major concern in the UK.'

'As it should be,' says Agatha.

'It's something that is still woefully under-resourced. And it's a ticking time-bomb. We half-know about activity all over the place, but we're not doing anything because we don't have the resources to discover any specifics. Communities don't talk to us any more because there aren't enough officers on the beat.'

'That's dreadful.'

'It is dreadful,' he agrees. He runs his fingers through his cropped hair, then says, 'You know, if someone were to run for Mayor who really cared about these issues, a huge amount could be achieved.'

'I'm sure it could.'

He starts to fiddle with his napkin. 'And, in general, I think it's important for any policing to be informed by the community, by particular individuals who have certain experiences or insights to offer. Citizens-in-the-know, as I like to call them. People like you. You have experience of business, and of property development, and your experience in those areas means that you see situations as they are on the ground. You really understand what's going on at street level.'

'Absolutely.'

'Without people like you, how can we as police officers operate? This uniform can create a real barrier between us and the community, you know. The police are more detached from real life than you might think.'

Michael Warbeck has ordered another cappuccino. When it arrives, he takes hold of the silver spoon that rests on the saucer and stirs the frothed milk into the dark coffee. He then picks up the cup and sips, and makes a face that suggests the liquid is either too hot or too bitter. Agatha doesn't touch her own coffee but she does look down at it, catching her own outline in its silky, black surface.

*

Later that morning, Jackie Rose is called in again to see her commanding officer. This time he gets up from behind his desk and comes to the door to greet her, ushering her into the room with a directorial arm. She sits in the same chair but Warbeck, instead of reassuming his position behind the desk, perches on its edge. His crotch is approximately at her eye-level.

'Thanks for popping in again,' he says, like she's doing him a favour rather than following a command.

'No problem. I was desk-bound today anyway.'

He smiles weakly and makes an ambiguous noise in his throat, then his manner becomes more serious. 'Listen, Jackie, we've had something come in. You know that Debbie McGee case?'

'Cheryl Lavery?'

'Yes. I'd like it to be your priority.'

It's such a sudden change of direction, Jackie isn't sure how to respond.

'There's no catch,' he continues. He stretches out his arms in a sort of reconciliatory gesture. 'I've been thinking about what you were saying. About the safety of women on our streets. It should be our number-one priority. And this particular case is a good one to take a stand with.'

'That's great,' says Jackie. 'Obviously, I couldn't agree more.'

'Yes,' he says. 'So I'm allocating you some more resources. I want you to take a team out – begin today, if possible – and start asking questions. We'll print some posters, featuring Cheryl, start an online campaign. And I'll be doing a press conference later. You're welcome to speak at that as well if you like, but dealing with those awful people – journalists, I mean – is just such a hassle. You don't need distractions like that.'

'I don't mind either way,' says Jackie, 'but in general I'd rather be out on the street, chatting to people, collecting information.'

'That's where your talents lie. You're one of the best, in fact. You always have been.'

Soon afterwards, Jackie leaves the police station and heads out on to the streets.

114

Luxury Flats

Bastian rolls over in bed. He stretches his arm out to the warm dip in the sheets. There was someone beside him and they have left an indentation like a dimple in a smiling face.

He dreamt of Laura again.

Before he bumped into Glenda in the club he'd not thought of Laura or that short period of his life in a long time. When he and Rebecca got back together, it was as if the memory of Laura was repressed to cope with the absence. Now he finds himself thinking about her all the time, and the memories don't come in stages but all at once. They shoot through him like an X-ray, revealing that which is tender.

As Bastian wakes, the details fall away like water off a body stepping out of a swimming pool. He remembers the sound of her laughter and the shape of her breasts.

He blinks as bright sunshine streams through a crack in the curtains, and he smells fresh coffee. The curtains are pulled aside and the coffee is on his bedside table and Rebecca is standing above him. Bastian feels guilty for the dreams and half-dreams.

Rebecca looks stressed. Bastian has started to appreciate what a deeply anxious person she is. She worries about everything: about work, whether or not she is working hard enough, whether she is doing well, whether the people at her work like her really or whether they are only pretending to like her. When Bastian probes her on this, she can't give a reason why they might be pretending, although she did once confess that she pretends to like people all the time when she actually doesn't, so it is only logical to assume that other people do the same.

He thanks her for the coffee and reaches across to take hold of it, cradling the hot mug between his hands until it is cool enough to sip. He watches her get dressed. Rebecca skips back and forth between the bedroom and the ensuite bathroom then the living room to the kitchen. Bastian hears the toaster ping and Rebecca comes through to the bedroom with a piece of buttery toast clasped between her teeth and she holds it there while standing on one foot and slipping the other into a pair of black tights.

Bastian thinks that tights are strange and he tells Rebecca as much. Then he says, 'Isn't it weird that men and women wear different clothes.'

'Weird how?'

'Just strange. Like, it's one of those things that you become so used to, you don't ever think to question it, but then sometimes, for instance, just now watching you put on those tights, you realise it's kind of bizarre.'

'You could say that about anything,' Rebecca replies. It is sometimes difficult to read her expression and tell whether she finds something humorous or exasperating. On this occasion, he suspects both. 'Would you like to wear women's clothes, Bastian?'

'Not especially. They seem kind of uncomfortable. Especially tights. It's just that it's strange that I'm not allowed to. Or, rather, I am *allowed* to, but it would be perceived as a dramatic statement about my identity when actually, when you think about it, why should anyone care?'

'How radical of you.' This time, she is making fun of him, but he thinks it's in a friendly way. She goes back to the kitchen and Bastian hears her pour some coffee from the cafetière into her thermos flask and screw on the lid.

Rebecca tries to get to work at 8 a.m. every morning whereas Bastian doesn't start until nine, so she gets up earlier and has usually left before he's dressed. She brings him a cup of coffee and he sits in the bed they share for a while as he slowly sips.

'Do you fancy the cinema tonight?' he calls through to the next room.

Rebecca doesn't answer immediately but pokes her head around the bedroom door and says, 'I would love to, but I have to work late again.'

Bastian nods.

'Sorry,' she says. 'But you know how busy I am.'

'Yeah, no problem.'

She goes to the sitting room to gather her things. Bastian returns to his coffee, looks down into his cup, now almost empty save for a layer of earthy liquid and some stray granules.

Rebecca has been working hard lately. The auction house has a big sale coming up and they have to get everything ready to exhibit the antiques – they have to take high-resolution photographs and write accurate descriptions of the items. If they get anything wrong they could be sued, so they must check and double check every sentence.

Rebecca leaves soon afterwards. She calls out to him from the hall to tell him she's leaving and to say goodbye, but she doesn't come through to see him. He thinks about getting up to wave her off but doesn't. Then he gets out his phone. He considers checking if Milo or Alexander are free, but then he thinks of Glenda.

Bastian and Glenda have seen each other a number of times over the last few months. They were never really friends at uni, only knowing each other a little through Laura, but after bumping into Glenda in the club, Bastian had got back in touch. After exchanging a few messages, and realising they worked a couple of streets away from each other, they decided to get dinner together one night at a pizza place that had recently opened.

The restaurant had been busy and the waiter grimaced when they said they hadn't booked, but he managed to squeeze them in at the back.

Early on in the night, Glenda asked Bastian about Rebecca,

and he felt himself blush. Glenda looked confused. Bastian tried to say something non-committal to move the conversation on. He told her Rebecca was well and then mentioned that she'd been busy at work, and was having to stay late several evenings a week.

'Where does she work?'

Bastian told her, and Glenda seemed interested. 'Oh yeah, I know someone else who works there. They say the auctions can be really exciting, even though they don't personally have any stake in it. As in, they're not the ones doing the buying, and they're only tangentially doing the selling, but they get really swept up in it all. Like, you've just dropped a cool mil on a two-hundred-year-old bookcase. Bam.' She smacked the table with her hand.

'I don't think Rebecca has much involvement in the auctions. She mainly works with clients to verify what they've got. To check if it's real or fake.'

The pizza arrived, and the waiter fussed a bit with black pepper and Glenda wanted chilli oil in addition to jalapenos. The waiter raised his eyebrows but did as she asked. There were a few minutes of silence as they concentrated on their food and then Glenda said, 'You two must have been together for quite a while now. Apart from the gap in the middle.'

Bastian finished chewing his mouthful of pizza and swallowed. He placed his knife and fork on his plate and used the paper napkin to wipe his mouth. He needed to achieve a level of composure before having this conversation with Glenda.

'Speaking of the gap in the middle,' she continued, 'I was chatting to Laura the other day.'

'Really?' Bastian had tried to sound casual.

'Yeah, you didn't come up though.' She said this as if he had asked, which he hadn't.

'I didn't think I would have come up.'

'You would have done about a year ago, though.'

'Really?' This time he couldn't sound casual.

'Oh yeah. She took a bit of time to get over you.'

Glenda looked up from her plate and watched for Bastian's reaction. He had no idea how his face looked to her, but he could feel his heartrate quicken, and he became aware that he was blinking more than usual. He hadn't expected Laura to have taken any time at all to get over him. He had no idea that, on her part, there had been anything to get over. He was only partially, and latterly, aware that his own feelings for her had been strong, and that still wasn't a fact he felt able to think about for longer than five seconds, let alone articulate. He had always thought of her as almost impervious to any kind of vulnerability.

He thought about confiding in Glenda. He thought about revealing that he had been thinking about her friend a lot. He considered trying to explain to her the various ways in which aspects of Laura had been creeping into his daily routine. When he brushed his teeth he thought about how she had stood next to him and brushed hers. He thought about the peculiar intensity of her expression as she scrubbed. He still owned a white cotton T-shirt she had worn a couple of times, plain except for a small black logo on the right sleeve. He could remember her in it, sitting by his open window on hot afternoons. It hadn't been a problem before, but since the evening he'd bumped into Glenda, he couldn't look at it without being reminded of Laura. He had to ball it up and stuff it at the bottom of his wardrobe, as if hiding contraband.

In lieu of any explicit statement about the time he spent with her, or the time he's spent thinking about her since, he had asked Glenda how Laura was doing.

'She's well. She hates her job though.'

'Where does she work?'

'At some kind of charity. They treat her like shit but are constantly going on about how grateful she should be for working in such a friendly environment, and how they're doing a really good thing by paying her a salary rather than getting her to give her time for free. She wants to leave as soon as she can.'

'What does she want to do?'

'I don't think she's fussy. I think in an ideal world she'd be working for some great political campaign with someone amazing she really believes in. But how on earth is she going to find one of those? And, you know, how many people actually get to do a job they like?'

'But isn't working for a charity a bit like that? I mean, isn't she already working for a good cause.'

Glenda looked at him as if he'd just vomited.

'Not really,' she explained quietly, as if so embarrassed by what he had just said she didn't want anyone at the neighbouring tables to hear her set him right. 'Charity is inherently reactionary, isn't it? It puts the onus on individuals rather than the collective. It relies on certain individuals having large amounts of disposable income. I think Laura would rather pursue political solutions to the world's problems rather than charitable ones.'

'Oh right,' Bastian replied.

'Are you happy with Rebecca?'

'What?' Bastian began to wonder if Glenda was drunk.

'I was just wondering why you contacted me? I thought maybe you wanted a way of getting back in touch with Laura.'

'No,' he said quickly. 'Not at all. I'm really happy with Rebecca. It's not perfect but what relationship is? We understand each other, Rebecca and I. We have a lot in common.'

'You come from the same background,' said Glenda.

'Do we? She's from Berkshire.'

'No, but, I mean, the same sort of level. Social and economic.'

'Oh, right.' He felt his face redden again.

'I always thought you were a lot more interesting than the rest of them, though. I mean, I was still quite surprised when you and Laura had your thing but, like, not as surprised as I would have been if it had been Milo Chelmsford or Alexander Garnick. Are you still in touch with that lot?'

'Sort of. Yeah, a bit. We go for drinks now and then. Why?'

'No reason.' She prodded at her pizza crusts with a serrated knife. 'Do you remember that party for Milo's twenty-first birthday?'

'Yeah, I do. Why? I didn't know you were there?'

'I was on the catering team.'

'Right,' said Bastian. He didn't know what else to say.

She smiled weakly, almost sarcastically, without exposing any teeth. Bastian couldn't quite make out her motives and found her company a little unsettling. She was very direct but managed to deliver her cutting remarks with enough good humour that it was difficult to tell whether or not she was serious. Bastian topped up both their wine glasses and then their water glasses, then returned to his pizza. After a few more glasses of wine they found some topics of conversation that didn't put Bastian on edge, and they started to have quite a good time.

They had got on better than Bastian was expecting, and ended up seeing each other again, and then quite regularly. He never lies to Rebecca about this, as such. He tells her he has been having a quick drink with 'work people' which is tangentially true, but he never elaborates. There is nothing really wrong with going for a drink with Glenda, but for some reason he isn't sure Rebecca will see it that way. Rebecca has quite a jealous nature and he tells himself that he doesn't want to cause her any unnecessary anxiety. If he was being more honest with himself, he might have realised that he simply didn't want to cause himself any unnecessary difficulties. Life with Rebecca was easy and for the most part satisfactory. He thinks about Laura, yes, but he manages to convince himself that this is no different from just thinking about hot women in general, which is obviously something that is natural and normal but not something to be discussed with Rebecca. He is sure Rebecca thinks about hot men too. In fact, he hopes that she does.

*

Bastian finishes his coffee and gets out of bed. He takes the empty cup through to the kitchen and places it on the top shelf of the dishwasher. Then he showers, dresses, and heads to work.

He meets his dad at the office.

'I've ordered a car,' Tobias tells him, when he arrives.

'It's a fifteen-minute walk, if that. Can we go on foot?'

Tobias agrees, and Bastian watches as he takes out his phone and presses an uncertain thumb on the car-service app Bastian recently downloaded for him. He taps the screen a few times, trying to cancel the vehicle he's booked, and when the app doesn't respond, he taps at it more forcefully.

'Damn thing,' he says.

Bastian takes the phone and does it for him, then hands back the device. He checks his own phone to make doubly sure of the best route, and notes that it's an estimated twenty-four-minute walk, though he won't tell his dad it's further than he said. Tobias Elton eats too much red meat and drinks too much red wine, and he never does any exercise. Bastian worries about his health.

They set out, Bastian walking more slowly than he usually would.

'Have you given any more thought to the GDL?' Tobias asks. Bastian had been thinking vaguely about studying the law.

'A bit,' Bastian replies. 'I definitely don't want to start this coming round, but maybe the year after.'

The two men revert to silence for a bit, then Tobias says, 'You know, you don't have to do it at all. There are other roles you can take in the business, and I really don't mind if you just use this job as a stepping stone. You can gain experience in a few different areas then move on somewhere else.'

'Yeah,' says Bastian. 'I don't know. I quite enjoy the strategy stuff. I like thinking about where and what to develop. I do like the legal bits as well, though, but it's all quite detailed and repetitive.'

'Were you thinking of something more creative? Your mum's the person to speak to about that.'

'Maybe. She did invite me to stay with them in New York, to see if I wanted to do something out there, but I don't want to live with her and Jerome.'

'No,' agrees Tobias. 'I can understand why you wouldn't want that. And you're settled in Rebecca's flat.'

Bastian doesn't reply to that.

Tobias continues. 'I am still planning on setting you up with a property of your own, you know. When this latest batch of Soho flats is finished, Agatha Howard says she will sell me one at a favourable rate. If I put it in your name, you and Rebecca can rent it out or you can move in and rent out her place. With the income from that, and the interest from your grandfather's trust, you should have enough stability to take some risks.'

Bastian thanks his dad. Then he says, 'Is that what we're meeting Agatha for today?'

'What? Oh, no, no. It's all this awful business with her sisters. You see, you think I'm a glorified conveyancer, but really it's probate I've had to specialise in.'

Bastian knows that Agatha Howard's sisters have been contesting their father's will, and suing her about various things, for years. Tobias rarely discusses the details of the dispute but he does speak about some of the people involved, particularly the three sisters: Angel, Chelsea and Victoria.

'I do want to introduce you to Agatha, though. If you do want to stay on, you should meet her at some point.'

Bastian realises that he knows all sorts of information about Agatha Howard's business and her legal disputes, but he has never heard his father speak about her as a person.

'What's she like?' he asks.

'In what sense?'

'In the sense of her personality.'

Tobias laughs.

'What?'

'You'll see.'

'What do you mean?'

'She tries very hard,' Tobias says. Then he laughs again.

Bastian begins to laugh too, prompted by his father's bizarre response. Bastian asks his dad what he's getting at.

'She thinks she's very sophisticated, much more sophisticated than her sisters. But really, they're not so different.' Tobias glances at his son and detects that he is still confused. 'They're very showy. All of them.'

'Okay,' says Bastian, still unsure. 'I'll wait and see.'

The walk takes them through Soho, along Old Compton Street. Bastian hadn't thought this through when he suggested they walk. There are sex shops and gay bars, and men sitting outside cafes with their arms around each other, watching passers-by. He feels suddenly alarmed that people might think he and his dad are a couple, and he momentarily tries to work out how best to outwardly present a filial relationship, before telling himself not to be so ridiculous.

Then they pass the club, and Bastian remembers the room he found upstairs with the camp beds. Bastian told his dad about what he saw that night. Bastian had expected his dad – or anyone he told – to think he'd been hallucinating, and for this reason he was reluctant to mention the incident at all. At first he just tried to forget about it. But the memory didn't lie still, or slowly diminish. It began to breathe within him and reach around for other memories to attach itself to, like ivy between a line of trees. Bastian found the memory in unexpected places or, rather, it appeared while he was thinking about all sorts of other, unconnected things. He was in the corner shop and saw a box of rubber cleaning gloves, and he thought of the pair of marigolds the woman wore. He went shopping for camping gear and remembered the mattresses, arranged side by side. Even takeaway boxes, or a certain kind of industrial-looking carpet. And whenever he read anything on the internet about displaced people, or illegal migrants, he thought about that room.

In the end, Bastian did tell his dad. It was a couple of months ago now, and Tobias responded strangely.

'When was this?' he asked.

Bastian searched his mind for the precise date. 'End of June,' he said. 'I can't be more precise than that without looking back through my texts, which I can do if you need me to.'

'No, no, I was just curious.'

'I mentioned it because I thought Agatha Howard might own the building.'

'She does.'

'And it was really weird. Do you have any idea what was going on?'

'It sounds to me like a gang of domestic staff had been put up there.'

'Right. Well, erm, that's not usual, is it?'

'I don't know how usual it is, but it's certainly illegal.'

'Yeah, it didn't seem quite right to me.'

'I'll speak to Agatha about it when I see her next.'

That's where the conversation ended. Bastian wonders whether that's what his dad will be discussing with Agatha Howard today. Either way, he has a strong sense that he has discharged himself of any duty he might have had to report what he had seen, whatever it was that he had seen.

They cross over Regent Street into Mayfair, and arrive at the club before Agatha. Bastian waits in the lobby while his dad finds an appropriate table at which to greet his guest. Bastian settles himself on an uncomfortable, creaking antique chair, and gets out his phone. Glenda has messaged back.

Not free but would be lovely to see you! Going for dinner with my mate Lorenzo (you've met him briefly, I think) and he says he's happy for you to come too. Meet at the Behn for a drink first and we'll go over to the restaurant together. It is called Feast and sounds . . . intriguing . . .

She has sent him a couple of reviews and Bastian reads them. It sounds bizarre. Feast comprises one long table situated in a disused Soho theatre. Everyone who comes sits on benches and eats cuts of meat from one animal that has been slow-cooked for hours. Where you sit at the table affects both the price and the cut of meat you get served. It is meant to mimic some historical custom, where your social rank determined what portion of the animal you got, and when. Instead of the determining factor being social rank, you simply pay a different price. It meant you could choose to pay a lot and sit at the top of the table and eat fillet steaks, or you could pay very little and sit at the lowest end of the table and eat the cheaper cuts. The 'social enterprise' part of the concept was that right at the very end, homeless people or people who used food banks can come in for a free meaty broth made from the bones.

In the Sight of God

Precious waits. There are five women in front of her in the queue for the self-service checkout machines. Two are wearing headphones, swaying to private melodies. One is reading a glossy magazine. She casts through pages of fashion tips and candid photographs of startled celebrities. Two are looking at their phones, eyes drawn by bright lights and moving images. There has been a mass shooting in America and one of the women is checking a live news feed. There are embedded videos of weeping parents and a blank-looking NRA spokesman.

Precious is holding a shopping basket laden with tooth-brushes, toothpaste, soaps and fizzy bath bombs. It is her day off. She is running errands – first this, then a visit to the GP, then some downtime. Later, there will be a demonstration on the street outside the walk-up, and after that she is meeting a photojournalist who got in touch. It is the second protest they've staged, and the culmination of months of campaigning. Precious has doubts about the effectiveness of such activities, but they have to do something.

A group of teenagers loiters nearby. They are telling lewd jokes competitively. One of the teenagers is clearly uncom-fortable with the behaviour of his peers, and shuffles nervously. He throws anxious glances at Precious, as if concerned she will immediately telephone his mother. She must look like the type of person to be easily offended.

The queue progresses and Precious makes her way to a self-service machine. She scans her items one by one and places them to the side while the self-service machine calcu-lates how much money she owes. She decides there are too many disparate items to carry safely so takes a plastic bag. The machine asks for £7.28. Precious shoves a handful of loose change into the slot without counting it, and the machine spits out the overpayment.

Outside, a cool wind skips along the street. It kicks up litter and tips out pools of the night's rainfall from shopfront awnings. Precious unties the arms of her thin sweatshirt from around her waist and puts it on. She draws the fabric close around her body and hunches her shoulders. Summer wore itself out.

The clinic is on the next street. Precious has an appointment to see the nurse for a routine mammogram. It's a task she resents more than she can explain, but she's at that age, apparently. She'll be 42 in December.

The waiting room is full, and there is a shortage of chairs. Precious has one at first then gives it to an elderly man and goes to lean against a wall next to a noticeboard displaying images of common ailments. The old man now sitting in her chair winks at her. He has spilled part of his breakfast down his shirt. Precious can see a crust of milk and dried porridge oats. He winks again. She looks the other way.

There are women with children. One young mother is trying to distract her toddler from his stomach ache with a set of wooden farmyard creatures. The cow and the sheep provide no help. The pig does a little better but the boy soon tires of the creature's curly tail and toothy grin and his wailing resumes.

Precious recognises a woman in the corner, but can't place her. Her clothes are understated and elegant. She is wearing a neat, natural linen dress and a number of diamonds are positioned on her fingers, on one of her wrists, and around her neck. They are cut roughly, in the way that is currently fashionable, as if they are not diamonds at all but pieces of weathered glass found on the beach and sold at auction for thousands of pounds.

Precious is called in to see the nurse. Her name sounds rusty through the tannoy. The P pops and the 'shus' rustles.

Her surname is swallowed. She makes her way to the end of the waiting room and pushes through a set of heavy swing doors then follows a narrow corridor illuminated by murky skylights. The door Precious needs is the last on the right. She knocks gently then enters.

'Good morning.'

'Good morning.'

The nurse reads Precious's full name from her computer screen.

'Yep, that's me.'

The room is both musty and caustic: a mixture of cleaning detergent and whatever odour the detergent was meant to expel. It smells like a wet swimming costume left overnight in a sports bag.

Precious takes off her sweatshirt, her T-shirt, her bra, and folds them on the chair. The nurse conducts the examination. Her hands are cold. She prods methodically then guides Precious towards the mammogram machine and helps her place her breasts into the opening. The process is awkward and uncomfortable.

The nurse is short with her and refuses to make eye contact. She must have read Precious's records and made some inferences, most of which are probably accurate. There is a small, silver crucifix around her neck.

Precious used to be a Christian. She was raised within a church that was strictly evangelical, led by her stepfather, though Precious was obliged to refer to him as 'Pastor'. He drove a Rolls Royce and owned a collection of Rolex watches. When Precious was little she confused the names of these luxury brands and referred to the man's shiny gold car as a Rolex Royce. For Pastor, luxury was next to godliness. It was the rich who would inherit the earth, and entrance to heaven was something to be bought and sold. He encouraged his congregation to take as great an interest in worldly advancement as they did in matters of the immortal soul, and he promised aid in exchange for substantial donations to the church. As Precious grew up she slowly became disillusioned, although the rest of her family were well and truly duped. They fell out about it.

When the procedure is over, Precious puts her clothes back on and steps into the bright sunshine. On the way out, she sees the winking old man. It turns out he has a twitch, and was not trying to flirt at all. He has emerged from the doctor with a patch and looks considerably more distinguished.

Precious stops at the street market. There are stalls selling clothes, second-hand vinyl, cheese and chutney, and a couple of fruit and veg stalls that have been there since Precious can remember. She goes to one of them and considers buying a fresh pineapple. It would be nice to have it in the flat even if she never gets around to eating it. People buy flowers to decorate their homes, so why not fruit? She picks a pineapple from the crate and inspects it for bruises, turning it this way then that, lifting it to her nose. It smells of honey and moss. Satisfied, she passes it to the grocer. As he folds the pineapple inside the brown paper bag, she plans her lunch. She will make a curry and use the pineapple. She asks the man to wait, and she assembles more fresh ingredients: broccoli, onions, ginger, chillies. She has some specialist pastes in her fridge and spices in jars. She wants something hot. Something that will raise her heart rate and make her eyelids tingle. Something that will get her in the mood for a fight and keep her on her feet all afternoon.

She hands over each additional item, and he wraps them in brown paper bags. She pays and walks from the market to her house with two full bags of shopping in each hand. The straps draw red grooves in her fingers, and she can feel the weight pulling her elbows and wrists. Sometimes, she notices her spine curling to a slouch and corrects her posture. The action reminds her of the remonstrance of a mother, far off, and a grandmother, far off, possibly deceased.

The prospect of the protest later makes her feel uneasy. The first one, a month ago, attracted a large crowd and press attention, but Precious is worried the novelty of their cause will have worn off. For the last few days, she has checked the weather forecast regularly. She can't imagine many people will want to come along if it rains. The Met Office has predicted sunshine with intermittent cloud cover, and the possibility of a deluge at three o'clock. The protest begins at two.

Precious looks at the sky. It is currently a bright blue, but there are storm clouds in the distance, sitting somewhere over south-west London. Hopefully there will be enough time to gather, have a bit of a shout, get the message across, and hand out flyers before the heavens open. Most of the organisation for the event was done by some enthusiastic activists who have become involved, but she still feels responsible for its success. She feels as if she has organised a party, and must now wait, done up in her best clothes, to see if anyone will come, dance, eat the finger food.

In the last few months, the question of the brothel has attracted an unexpected amount of attention. Not one but several feminist groups have taken up their cause, either in support of the sex workers or in support of the 'prostituted women'. The former assortment of well-wishers campaigns in favour of them remaining in their homes and continuing to practise their trade. The latter view them as the victims of pimps, johns and, on a larger scale, the patriarchy itself, in which they and their bodies are unwittingly commodified. They tried to persuade Precious and the others not to be prostitutes and they also colluded with the police. Tabitha went and told this lot to fuck off.

Some religious groups also tried to get involved. Although they looked different from the feminists and used different words, their aims were more or less the same: Precious and the others needed to be rescued and they were the only ones who could do it. There was also much discussion of daughters. They were all 'daughters', 'our daughters', 'somebody's daughter', 'imagine it was your daughter'. Precious has no daughters so presumably can't pass comment.

For Precious, the situation has become tedious. She was grateful for the support at first, but she doesn't like having to justify her existence and pretty much all of her life choices to several people every day. Precious isn't oblivious to these competing views, but she tries to ignore them. For her, it is just a job. She does it for the money. She doesn't much like it or enjoy it but she didn't much enjoy her previous employment either, and at least in her current occupation she has no boss, she keeps all the money she earns, she can take days off whenever she likes, and she has no commute.

Precious thinks her life is okay. She doesn't mind the work. It's only sex, for fuck's sake. She doesn't get what the big deal is. She never has. It is a thing you do with bits of your body. It sometimes feels good. It sometimes feels a bit uncomfortable.

When she worked in the beauty parlour in Highgate, she once accidentally dripped a tiny amount of hot wax on to the leg of an important customer and, despite admitting her mistake, and apologising, the client slapped her across the face. She complained to her boss but the boss sided with the client, and docked her a week's pay. In her current line of work, when a punter gets aggy, Tabitha phones downstairs and the bouncers come and take the man away and kick the shit out of him.

Precious knows this set-up is unusual, and she is unique within the brothel for having only experienced this arrangement. Tabitha has lived in different circumstances. Before coming to Soho and retiring from sex, she worked in every type of horrible situation. She used to live in Chapeltown, a district of Leeds. She was pimped, she walked the streets, she was passed between venues, she slept rough, she lost a friend to the Yorkshire Ripper, and another to a man who'd beaten a couple of prostitutes to death but not so many of them as to become a household name. Precious can't bear to think of the things her friend has been through. It's a million miles from her own experience.

About a week after they received the eviction notice in the summer, the residents of the brothel gathered in the Aphra Behn to discuss progress. Some of the customers recognised them but pretended not to. The women returned the favour. Other customers recognised them but were unfazed and greeted them as friends.

Tabitha bought a round of drinks. Precious waited patiently for everyone to arrive, for the preliminary gossip to be told and heard, for handbags to be placed on the floor and jackets to be slung over the backs of chairs.

She began, 'We are gathered here today.'

'In the sight of god.'

Laughter.

Precious ignored the heckling. 'We're here today to discuss some very important things. We are here to work out how we are going to protect both our homes and our livelihoods. Because both are right now under attack. If we cannot remain here in Soho, what will we do?'

'No fucking pimps. That's the main point.'

'So it is, Scarlet. Thank you.'

'So far we have sought some legal advice and through the lawyers written some letters to the landlords. But we have also been complying with the changes.'

'Temporarily.'

'Most of us have been paying the increased rent rates in the hope that it'll be refunded if we win the legal proceedings.'

'But I can't afford it any more. I'm not making enough money to get by. I may as well go get myself a job in Tesco,' says Young Scarlet.

There was a murmur of assent.

'What would you have to offer Tesco?' another woman asked. 'A blow-job counter?'

There was more laughter.

The woman continued, 'Pick up your eggs and bacon and go round the back of the pasta aisle for a quickie.'

More laughter.

Another woman joined in. 'You'd be all right with the cold meats section, eh? Salami specialist, eh, eh?'

This prompted less laughter.

'Anyway,' interrupted Precious. 'We need to have a rethink. We all agree that we can no longer afford the rates, and none of us want a protracted legal battle.'

'Too right,' said another woman.

'So what's to be done?'

There was silence. The women all looked around at each other but nobody spoke.

Then one woman said, 'I've got a john who's an MP. I could ask him what to do.'

'Yeah, right.'

'What?'

'Love, I don't think he's going to want to get involved, do you?'

She shrugged.

'What, raise the issue in Parliament? 'Ere, your honours, my hooker's in a bit of bother, let's get the army in.'

'Maybe. Not the army, but something.'

'Are you joking? No, love, we're on our own. It's not a glamorous cause. We're hardly going to get Bob Geldof and Bono fighting our corner.'

'Look, stop,' said Precious. 'Let's be serious for just a minute.'

'Sorry, Precious.'

'Sorry, Precious.'

'I had a think. And also, I was sort of approached by someone – a journalist. A photojournalist, really. And she wants to do a piece about us. Why our job is better than what other women have, and that. And she wanted to print it in a big newspaper. I don't know, I guess because she'll be on our side, it might do us some favours. She reckons her piece about rogue landlords in Glasgow made a bunch of them back off. It might be all we need.'

'I don't know, Precious.'

'Yeah, and I don't really want to be in the paper, to be honest. Not all my family know what I'm doing over here in London.'

'No, of course. I said that to this woman – Mona is her name – and she said she expected that, and was happy for us to have our faces concealed. And that the photos would be really good. Tasteful, but also capture us as our true selves.'

'Might actually be good for business. Free advertising.'

'Well, possibly,' said Precious. 'Look, I'm not saying I'm totally behind it, but I think it's an option we could explore.'

There were some murmurs of agreement and murmurs of dissent, but in the end what all the other women did agree on was that if Precious thought it was a good idea then she should do it.

The photographer is going to come along to the protest today. This is another reason why Precious is anxious. She and the others will be wearing masks – for their safety as much as anything else – but she is still nervous about having her photo taken and put in the public domain. The photographer is going to come up to the flat and talk to her and Tabitha, and take some photos of where they live. Precious wants to show people that they're no different from anyone else.

Precious arrives at the flat. There's a back entrance for personal use, so the women don't have to go through the front door and bump into customers. It is accessed through the alley the local restaurants use to store their bins. When the chefs forget to lock the lids at night, tramps and foxes fish through the black plastic bags looking for leftover food. The result is messy. A box of a dozen eggs has been dropped, and split yolks and whites have created a network of sticky fjords. There are cabbage leaves and potato peelings. A couple of snails are crawling over the rim of one of the large containers and wasps are swarming around a discarded lemon tart.

Precious pushes open the back door, which should, by rights, be a fire escape. It is heavy and blue. Someone has scrawled their initials on it in black marker, and someone else has crossed them out and added their own. Inside, there is a dark vestibule and a damp flight of concrete stairs with a rusted iron bannister fitted to the wall with iron pegs. Precious takes the first flight of stairs two at a time, then slows for the rest of the ascent.

She heaves her bags through the door and sees Tabitha in the sitting room with her feet up, reading the newspaper. When Precious left earlier this morning, Tabitha was cleaning.

'Oh good,' Tabitha says when she sees Precious. 'I was just about to get up and pop the kettle on, but now you can do it.'

'Charming.'

Precious goes through to the kitchen with her bags. She unpacks the items, first on to the counter and then into the cupboard and the fridge, setting aside the ingredients for the curry. She puts the kettle on, takes Tabitha's favourite cup from the cupboard, and throws in a black teabag.

'Do you want to help me cook?' Precious calls from the kitchen.

'Not really,' replies Tabitha, but soon afterwards she pops her head around the door, then comes in and leans against the countertop.

Precious is peeling the pineapple. The handle of a squat knife rests in her hand. The blade teases apart the spines and thick, woody rind from the golden flesh, and juice oozes all along the knife, on to her hand, on to the chopping board below.

'You know they eat you as you eat them?'

'Excuse me?'

'Pineapples digest you as you digest them. Only more slowly, so you win. When you put a piece of pineapple in your mouth it starts to digest your tongue and cheeks and gums. It'll even take the enamel off your teeth. It's got some sort of chemical or enzyme in or something. And then when it's in your stomach it starts to digest your stomach too, only the acid in your stomach is stronger so works faster than the pineapple does. And you win.'

Precious does not look up. 'A sobering tale.'

Precious and Tabitha eat their lunch at the table in the kitchen, while watching a daytime cookery competition on the small television fitted to the wall. They argue about which of them would do better if they were contestants on the show.

'I hate to say it, Tab, but your presentation would let you down. I love your food, you know that. You're a great cook, but on this show you need to be all fancy.'

'No, no,' replies Tabitha. 'All the fancy stuff develops gradually. At first I'd wow them with big, bold flavours and then I'd later learn how to do all the fiddly bits. They'd love me. You, on the other hand, you're too inconsistent. No offence. I mean, sometimes your food is absolute knock-out – loads better than mine. Then at other times, I don't know, you just lose concentration or something and bam, you've overcooked the veg and burnt the fish. Now don't argue with me – you know what I mean.'

'Oh really? Enjoying your lunch, are you?'

'It's absolutely delicious. Thank you very much for making it.'

Precious flutters her eyelashes and tucks into her rice.

After a while Precious hears a scuffling sound coming from the bathroom. 'Is someone in there?' she asks Tabitha. She gets up to go and look.

'Now, Precious, love, before you get angry . . .'

'Oh, it's not . . .'

'Well, it might be.'

'Oh, you didn't!'

'I might have.'

Precious swings open the bathroom door.

'Oh, for god's sake,' she says.

Inside, there is a man on his hands and knees, scrubbing

the floor with a bright blue toothbrush. He stops work when Precious opens the door and he looks up, eagerly, hungrily.

'Miles!' Precious exclaims, exasperated.

'I'm sorry,' says Miles from his position on the floor. 'I'm so sorry.'

'You've got nothing to be sorry about, love. It's this one who should be sorry.' Precious waves an arm in Tabitha's direction.

'He was begging me to let him,' Tabitha explains. 'And, well, it needed doing so I thought, why not? It allowed me to get on with some other stuff.'

Miles is still on his hands and knees, apologising, spraying detergent, scrubbing the bathroom tiles with the toothbrush.

'If you're worried it's exploitative, I've asked around and everyone I spoke to said if it's what he wants then there's nothing wrong with it.'

'It's not that,' Precious replies. 'I couldn't care less if we're exploiting him, it's just it's my day off.'

'But that's the beauty of it, you see. You don't have to do anything at all. You can just sit around and Miles is paying us and the flat is getting cleaned at the same time.'

'But I can't relax knowing there's a client . . .'

'But he's not a client, though.'

'But there's still some bloke through there doing god knows what.'

'He's just cleaning,' says Tabitha.

'Yeah but if he gets off on it, what else is he doing?'

'I've told him: any hanky-panky and he can fuck off.'

'I bet he loved that.'

'He did actually.'

In Disguise

Lorenzo returns home from the audition to find Robert sitting on the step that marks the entrance to their block of flats. Robert holds his head in his hands, which are marked with uneven cuts, thick with clotted blood and mild infection. There are two empty cans of lager next to him. One is crumpled and partially ripped, exposing a sharp metallic edge. The other holds its shape but lies on its side and slides back and forth as the breeze funnels inside it and pulls it this way and that.

'Where the hell have you been?' Lorenzo asks Robert. 'I've not seen you in weeks.'

Robert looks up at his friend then returns his head to his hands.

'Jesus Christ,' says Lorenzo. He looks at the empty cans again. 'You've started early,' he observes.

Lorenzo leans down and takes hold of Robert's upper arms and tries to ease him into a standing position. Robert is a much bigger man than he is, and he is unable to lift him.

'I'll get up if you take me to the pub,' says Robert.

'I'm not sure that's a good idea. How about we go up to mine and have a cup of tea. I'll make you a bacon sandwich.'

'Nope,' says Robert. 'I'd rather stay here. Pub or nothing.'

Lorenzo checks his watch. The Aphra Behn will only just be open. He knows it's not the best plan, but he hates it when busybodies withhold alcohol from drunks just because they are drunk. What's more, Lorenzo also fancies a pint.

'Fine,' Lorenzo says. 'But you can get yourself up, you swine.'

Robert lifts himself with a rasping groan and shakes his

body like a dog out of water. Lorenzo smells the beer on his clothes, and something harder on his breath. The two men walk together down the street, then take a cut-through filled with stacked wooden crates and uncollected refuse. The pub is on the corner. Apart from the staff, they are the first to arrive. Lorenzo steers Robert away from their usual seats at the bar towards a table in the corner of the room which has two armed oak chairs set against it and a stack of cardboard brewery coasters on top. Lorenzo goes to the bar and orders two pints. The thought of not buying an alcoholic drink for Robert, after having chosen the pub as a venue, does occur to him, but only briefly.

Lorenzo carries over the beers and sits. 'What's up?'

Robert wipes his face with his sleeve as if he's wiping away tears, but there are no tears, nor have there ever been tears. 'Nothing,' he says. 'I'm right as rain.' Robert takes hold of one of the pint glasses with his cut hand and pulls it towards his mouth. Froth remains on his upper lip after he drinks, and he takes his sleeve up to wipe his face again.

'Well there's obviously something wrong. I've not seen you for weeks. That's an unprecedented amount of time for you to be away from the pub. So what is it?'

Robert says nothing. He looks at his friend then down at his pint glass then back to his friend.

'I'll rephrase the question,' says Lorenzo. 'What have you been doing? Where have you been?'

Robert's clever enough to recognise that this is still a question about his feelings, but in disguise. 'I'm fine,' he says. 'Honestly, I'm fine.'

Robert has another sip of beer and sits up straight in his chair, so that Lorenzo feels suddenly, fleetingly diminished. He sees himself as a child, and Robert as a grown man, and a brute. He thinks, what am I doing being friends with this man? What the hell am I, a Sri Lankan Catholic faggot, doing sitting here drinking a beer with this thug? What do I know about him, really? What things has he done in his life? What things has he seen? In a different world, or not even that different, just a different era, a different decade, a few years ago, he might have stabbed me in the street, or punched my face in, or set me on fire.

The feeling is fleeting, and as soon as he looks again, he sees a friend, and feels at ease. He waits for an answer. He hopes the silence will encourage Robert to speak.

'Bugger it,' says Robert. He rubs his face with his hands. 'I'm a bad man, Lorenzo. I've done bad things. Have you heard of a man called Donald Howard?'

'Of course,' Lorenzo replies.

'I used to work for him.'

'In what capacity?'

Robert doesn't answer, but Lorenzo thinks he can probably guess. Donald Howard was infamous in these parts. Lorenzo's mum and aunt used to speak about him and his gang in hushed tones, even though he was dead years before Lorenzo heard the stories. He owned flats in the same building as theirs and they remembered his men going around collecting rents. Later, someone at school told Lorenzo that when Donald Howard's gang executed someone they would make a death mask of his face. As a child, Lorenzo had a vivid imagination and this story gave him nightmares for months.

'Do you know how I got this?' Robert asks, moving on. He points to a scar on his forehead, between his eyebrows.

Lorenzo indicates that he doesn't know.

'I had a tattoo there I got removed,' explains Robert. 'Do you know what the tattoo was?'

Lorenzo shakes his head.

'It was a swastika,' says Robert. 'I had a swastika tattooed to my forehead.'

Lorenzo looks at his friend but says nothing. Then Robert asks directly, 'What do you say to that?'

'Please don't ask me to respond directly to that, Robert. Obviously I had my suspicions but now that I know for certain, please don't ask me to pass comment. Let's just . . .'

'I did bad things,' says Robert.

'I'm sure,' says Lorenzo. 'It goes with the territory, I guess.' He picks up his glass and takes a long drink to give him an excuse not to have to say anything more for at least five seconds.

'I'm not . . . any more,' says Robert. 'And I never really was, you know, into it. Politically. It was just the people I was mixed up with at the time, when I came down to London. The firms and that.'

Lorenzo nods. 'I once voted Liberal Democrat.'

'Eh?'

'Nothing,' says Lorenzo.

'You know Cheryl's gone missing?'

'Who's Cheryl?'

'You know, Debbie McGee. She goes round with that magician cunt.'

'Paul Daniels and Debbie McGee?'

'Aye. Cheryl is her real name. She's gone missing.'

'I didn't know that. I haven't seen her for a while, I suppose. I didn't really think anything of it.'

'Most people wouldn't.'

At that moment, the barwoman comes to their part of the pub and busies herself arranging chairs and beermats and wiping the sticky parts of tables that have been missed by whoever was meant to be cleaning them the night before.

'I think she's my daughter.'

'What, her?' Lorenzo beckons to the barwoman.

'No! Fucking hell. Debbie McGee. Cheryl, I mean. Cheryl's my daughter.'

'Oh my god,' Lorenzo says, simply.

'I think,' says Robert. 'I mean, I'm almost completely sure. I know it. I know it, here,' he says, gesturing to the place within his ribcage where his heart might be stored.

The two men meet each other's eyes then look away. Robert rubs his face with his hands. Lorenzo glances out of the greasy window, notices that the sun's reappeared.

Lorenzo doesn't say anything more but looks closely at this strange friend, strange because of the fact of their friendship.

'I never did anything for her,' Robert says. 'Not really. I never did anything for her or her mother. I told myself I did. I'd slip them bits of money here and there, sometimes do some odd jobs. I hung around a bit. But I never really did anything. Gloria – Cheryl's mum – she was a girl I used to go to back in the day. I mean, lots of men did, she was a stunner. But when she got knocked up I knew it was mine. I knew it even if she didn't. But did I do anything about it? Did I do anything to help? Did I fuck. I cared about her, that Gloria. I mean I cared about her as much as I've ever cared about a girl. You'd probably use the word "love" but, well, what does it matter now? And I did fuck all for her. And after she passed away I did fuck all for her daughter. For our daughter. And now she's fucking gone.'

'I'm sorry,' says Lorenzo.

'There's no need to be sorry,' says Robert. 'And there's no call for me being sorry. It's high time I fucking did something about it. Only I haven't got a clue what I can do. And I've just spent the last three months sitting on my arse drinking myself half to death like the fucking useless waste of space I am.'

'Excuse me?' There's a woman sitting at the table at the other side of the pub. Neither Lorenzo nor Robert saw her arrive nor take up her seat nor purchase the cup of black coffee on the table in front of her.

Lorenzo's first thought: coffee in a pub? Robert's first thought: fucking hell, I wouldn't have sworn so much if I'd known there was a lady present.

'Excuse me?' The woman speaks again.

'Er, yes?' replies Lorenzo.

'Hi, my name is Mona. I'm a photographer.' She pulls out an expensive-looking camera. 'Would you mind if I took your photo?' She's speaking to Robert.

'My photo? Why my photo? He's the star!' Robert points

to Lorenzo who waves away his friend's finger, embarrassed. 'He's a big-time actor, you know. He was in that show.'

'Stop, Rab.'

The photographer speaks again to Robert. 'I just couldn't help overhearing part of your conversation,' she said. 'Can I take your photo? You know, of the tattoo.'

Robert stops smiling. 'Oh, right. Well, that wasn't the main point of the conversation. I'm not involved with any of that any more. I had the tattoo removed. I don't like to talk about it.'

The photographer, Mona, has already lifted the camera to her face and is taking pictures. The shutter clicks several times.

'No,' Robert insists. 'I don't want people to know about that.' There's dismay in his voice and across his face. At least, Lorenzo knows it to be dismay. Another person might read it as anger. Robert has the sort of face that seems to project every emotion as a kind of anger.

Mona the photographer stops clicking. 'Oh, I'm sorry, I didn't realise. No problem, I'll just delete those. It just sounded like an interesting story, that's all. And you have such a fascinating face.' She turns the camera over in her hands and presses some buttons on the back. Lorenzo and Robert hear a beeping sound and assume the photos have been deleted.

Robert says, 'That's okay, love. No harm done.'

Mona leaves the pub. Her coffee remains on the table, undrunk.

Lorenzo tells Robert he's going outside for a smoke, even though Lorenzo quit years ago and Robert probably knows this. Robert nods, and tells him he'll have another round waiting when he gets back. Lorenzo picks up his coat and puts it on. He swings open the door, closes it behind him and stands just beyond the threshold. Through the window he can see Robert moving towards the bar. He turns to face the street. Soho is busy but not unbearably so. Weekday business is different from weekend business. Pedestrians have clear destinations. They walk quickly in straight lines. Bikes and motor vehicles likewise move with purpose.

Lorenzo has known Robert all his life. He has never asked him much about his past, thinking it better to remain ignorant. His mum and aunts sometimes made comments about their neighbour, but must have thought he was safe enough latterly, otherwise they wouldn't have let Lorenzo hang around with him. He guessed he was a bit dodgy and had done shady things. He knew he'd been to prison, years ago. But this.

Lorenzo has always given a certain type of man the benefit of the doubt. It is a type of man that, he now realises, he is fundamentally terrified of, and always has been. And yet it is also a type of man that he finds himself bending over backwards to make excuses for.

Perhaps he is like that man in the Herzog film who went to live with grizzly bears in the Alaskan wilderness for several months each year, believing them to be good-natured, amicable, tame, or thinking they loved him enough to set aside their nature. He thought he was special to them; that they had a unique bond. But then, one day, they ate him.

Lorenzo looks back into the pub. Robert is sitting back down at the table, with a pint for himself and another for Lorenzo. Lorenzo turns away and heads down the street.

Nothing Like Harry Potter

The man they call Paul Daniels is sitting in the dark cellar with his back against the wall. He is slightly apart from the rest of the group. Shadows obscure his features, his expression and the direction of his gaze. If the others could see him clearly, or if they cared to look, they would see that he is scowling with intent, towards the Archbishop. The Archbishop is in his usual place – a chair, a throne, almost, constructed from wooden pallets set with ragged blankets and stained cushions. The Archbishop is asleep, and the crown on his head is aslant but firmly in position, as if it has been shoved down over his brow, down to his ears, with two forceful hands.

The Archbishop snores loudly as he snoozes. His leathery lips vibrate like a horse's with each exhalation, and a mist of saliva falls on to the front of his dressing gown. Occasionally he twitches in response to an enervating dream and, more rarely, he calls out, sometimes something childish, sometimes nonsensical, sometimes obscene.

To those of the group sitting far from Paul Daniels, Paul Daniels would seem silent, static, but if any were to get any closer they would detect a low, almost but not quite imperceptible, muttering. He watches the Archbishop sleep, and he mutters to himself. The subject of Paul Daniels's mutterings are the sleeping prelate and the crown upon his head.

When the crown was found, it was encrusted with dirt and, in places, rusted. It is now a little less dirty, having been rinsed in a bucket and worn, but it is far from immaculate.

Paul Daniels feels that if the crown were in his possession it would now be gleaming. He would take care of it properly, he would wear it properly and he would take it down to the jewellers in Piccadilly Arcade and obtain a correct valuation for it.

No. Not the poxy jewellery shop. Perhaps it would be better to take it to an antiquarian on the streets of Bloomsbury near the big museum. But they might be rascals too. More likely than not they are rascals. They wouldn't give him a fair valuation. They would underestimate the value in the hope of driving the price down. They would want to buy it from him for well below what it was worth. They would take one look at him and think they could pull a fast one. They'd try and take it off him for a fraction of its real worth and sell it on at auction to some Russian oligarch or African warlord or Arab prince and they'd make millions – billions, probably – and Paul Daniels would never see any of it.

Bugger the antiquarians. He'll take it directly to the museum. They will want it. They have all sorts in there. He'd been in once, years ago. They had statues and paintings and jewels and tombs and relics and swords and suits of armour. He especially liked the swords and suits of armour and imagined himself in them, riding off into battle and cutting off people's heads.

He would take the crown to the museum and they'd be beside themselves. They'd fall about each other singing its praises and singing his praises for being the clever person who found it. And they would pay him millions – maybe billions – of pounds for it, and they would lock it up in a glass cabinet in pride of place.

Except, no. Something wasn't right about that. The man they call Paul Daniels wasn't sure he'd ever heard of a museum paying someone – anyone – billions of pounds for something.

And besides, if he went down those sorts of official channels, who was to say there wouldn't be inconvenient legal obstacles? Who was to say there wouldn't be some busybody old bag asking rude questions about where he found the crown, and when, and then there might be even more prying questions about who he was with and who owned the land where he found it. As far as Paul Daniels is concerned: Finders Keepers.

Paul Daniels will take it to someone in the know who can get it out of the country directly, to an Arab Prince or African Warlord or Russian Oligarch or South American Kingpin. Or better still, he'll do it himself. He'll scout for suitable buyers. All he needs to do now is take possession of the actual crown, but it is unfortunately still very firmly planted on another man's head. The Archbishop has taken to wearing the crown wherever he goes, day or night.

'Damn you, Archbishop! God damn you!'

Paul Daniels is on his feet, shouting. He points a finger at the old man. 'God damn you all the way to hell!'

The old man wakes with a start. He sees Paul Daniels standing over him, and instinctively raises a hand to the crown. Then he shows Paul Daniels his teeth and lets out a low growl.

Escalation is prevented by a knock at the door. Nobody ever knocks at the door. Either people live here, so they just come straight in, or they don't have any reason or inclination to come here at all. Either way, there's no knocking.

Someone gets up and climbs on a chair so they can peer through the grate between the cellar and the pavement. They look back to the Archbishop, stricken. 'Police.'

'Fuck that,' says Paul Daniels. He collects his scant belongings and hurries away into the next room, or rather behind the old theatrical curtain that has been hung to divide the space into rooms.

The Archbishop slowly rises, the crown still on his head. He goes to the ladder that leads up to the hatch they call a door, opens it, and rises to the pavement, where he comes face to face with two policewomen.

They are looking for the man who has hidden himself behind the curtain.

'He's not slept here for weeks,' the Archbishop offers. 'If he comes back I'll tell him you called.'

148

'It's about the disappearance of Cheryl Lavery.'

'Yes, yes, we all know about that. That's why he's been away. Don't you lot know anything?'

'What do you mean?'

'He's gone searching for her, hasn't he?'

'With any success?'

The Archbishop shrugs cartoonishly.

'According to our records, the absence was reported by a Richard Scarcroft who gave this as his address. Is he here?'

'Never heard of the man.'

As Policewoman Rose and Policewoman Granger leave the building they're accosted by a man of medium build with long hair and a shaggy beard.

He introduces himself as Richard Scarcroft, then asks, 'Is it about the woman? The Debbie McGee woman?'

'Cheryl Lavery. That's right.'

'It's taken you long enough. She's been missing for months.'

'Additional resources have been allocated to the case. Can we ask you a few questions?'

'Yeah, but not here. Any excuse to get out of this dump.'

They take him to a police station, show him into an interview room and bring him some water and a cup of tea.

'I hardly knew her, to be honest with you. I try to keep myself to myself at that place. I'm only there because I've got no choice. They're all nutters and follow that Archbishop round like he's some sort of cult leader. And that Paul Daniels is the worst of the lot. Anyway, when his bird went missing nobody reported it or nothing, so I thought I would, even though I don't think I ever spoke to her. It's not right though, is it? Just because she's a smackhead doesn't mean it doesn't matter, does it? The poor girl's had nobody to look out for her. Her fella's gone mental since she's been gone but hasn't done nothing proper. He's just gone round shouting blue murder. You got a cigarette?'

'I'm afraid you can't smoke in here.'

'Are you serious?'

'Yes, Mr Scarcroft, I'm sorry. Tell me, did you notice anything suspicious in the days or weeks leading up to her disappearance? Did you see her speaking to anyone new? Did she have any visitors?'

'Like I say, I didn't know her. I honestly can't recall ever speaking to her. But in terms of contact with weirdos, well, they don't come much weirder than that magician bloke. He's a proper fruit loop. And well, that's who she spent all her time with, isn't it? If something bad has happened to her, he's your man. Perhaps he was short on change. Honestly, that geezer would sell his own grandmother, let alone his bird.'

'Sell her how?'

'You know what I mean. It's Soho, for Christ's sake.'

'You mean Paul Daniels, sorry, Kevin Metcalfe, was her pimp?'

'Probably. There was blokes coming round all the time.'

'Tell me, of these men who were coming round, were there any who were particularly regular? Or were there any who stood out for any reason?'

'Not really,' he says. 'Although, hmm, let me think . . .'

He gulps the last of the brown liquid, allows that which spills at the sides of his mouth to drip down his chin and through his beard. 'Got any more tea? And some biscuits?'

They bring more tea and a tin of biscuits. He selects a couple of jammy dodgers and a custard cream and places them on the table in a pile next to his mug.

'There was only one that would come regular enough, like. And I remember him because he seemed like a decent bloke – not totally barking anyway – and he clearly had a fixed address and everything so I remember him because I always thought it was weird that he was coming to see her, know what I mean? She was proper manky. Maybe some fellas are into that. Takes all sorts.'

'Do you remember his name?'

'Nope. Never knew it. Like I said, I share a cellar with that lot but I don't stop to chat any more than I can help.'

'I understand. But do you remember what he looked like? Have you any idea where we might find him?'

'Try the pub around the corner. The Aphra Behn. Used to see him in there a lot. As for appearance: I don't know. Mid-sixties. Big bloke, but strong, you know, not fat. He just looks like he could handle himself. No hair. And he had a weird scar on his forehead. Like Harry Potter. Only, nothing like Harry Potter.'

A short while later, two police officers turn up at the Aphra Behn. They find a man who fits the description sitting at the bar. It's easy to convince him he needs to come to the police station. It's as if part of him was expecting them to arrive. On the way out the door, he begins to confess.

'It's my fault, it's my fault,' he wails. Once inside the police station, his misery turns to anger. 'It's my fault, it's my fault,' he yells, though what is his fault he won't say. He overturns a table and is wrestled to the ground by three constables, then arrested, and put into a cell to sober up.

Jackie does background research into the man they've picked up. It's easy enough to extract a name. Robert Kerr. Aggravated Assault. Grievous Bodily Harm. Robbery. Five years in Wormwood Scrubs. Nothing on his record since he'd been out of prison, and that was thirty years ago, but there's enough to work with.

Paper Thin

Agatha doesn't know why she agrees to meet her lawyer in the tepid dregs of British imperial power. Tobias has invited her to his club, which is an organisation for men of his class. He chooses these locations to humiliate her; in all other respects he is required to be subservient to the point of obsequious.

Agatha considers Tobias Elton to be an idiot and often tells him so, but there's nobody else who knows so much about her holdings, or who's so personally invested in her interests. Except Roster.

Donald Howard's fortune was placed in trust for Agatha until her twenty-first birthday. The trust was administered by his lawyer, Tobias Elton, and it was through the efforts of Tobias Elton that the fortune remained intact, despite the legal and sub-legal activities of three of Agatha's sisters; those who were the product of his second, and lengthiest marriage, and who were already grown up by the time he died.

During these disputes, Elton defended Agatha's interest, acting alongside Roster and her mother to make sure the trust was protected. He derived a large part of his income from this work and guessed correctly that if he ingratiated himself with the child and her mother, he could stand to gain much more.

The rhythms and routines of Agatha's life are directed by that last will. The document is her blueprint, her star chart, her DNA. Its contents laid out for her a life radically removed from anything her ancestors knew. It informed her geography and her geology. Wealth does not simply determine the external: the life the document set out for Agatha built her from the inside out. The opulence she was to inherit nourished her from the day she was born until the day she claimed it.

Agatha spends much of her time contemplating that piece of paper and its hold on her. Had it not been written, her mother might not have kept her in the country, or kept her at all. She might have stuck a pin in her before she was born, or left her on the doorstep of an Orthodox church.

Agatha wonders if they would have returned to Russia. It's unlikely: Anastasia has never shown any interest in going back, even to visit, but what else would she have done? Agatha has met friends of her mother's who've not been so fortunate. They likewise attached themselves to rich men but didn't manage to stick around. Women like her mother but not her mother tended to wash up in brothels in dark houses on council estates. Their children too were forced to grow up far too young. If it wasn't for that piece of paper she might have been thrown into a life of poverty, alcohol and narcotics.

Roster stops the car outside the front entrance of the club and gets out of the driver's seat to open the door for Agatha. Fedor is with her. When she steps on to the street he shows no signs of wanting to follow, but remains sprawled across the comfortable back seat, tucked up in a blanket.

'I'll park the car and take the boy out for another run,' says Roster.

'If he lets you,' replies Agatha. 'He'll want to sleep.'

'We'll see.'

Agatha pushes through the heavy doors into the foyer. She's met by a porter who looks at her trousers and opens his mouth as if wanting to say something about them. Female guests are required to wear skirts. He hesitates. Most of the staff in the club are from Eastern Europe and are likely to speak a little Russian as well as English. She says to him in Russian: 'Does it matter?'

He looks up at her, startled by the choice of language, and replies, also in Russian. 'Not to me, but if we don't at least try to enforce the rules, we suffer for it.'

'I'm not going home to change my clothes,' she says in Russian. 'So you'll have to suffer.'

The porter's face begins to redden. He looks down at his clipboard but does nothing to counter her barb. In English, he asks for the name of her host.

'Tobias Elton. He'll be in the Trafalgar Room.'

Each time Agatha comes to this club, she is struck by its shabbiness. It fills a townhouse on one of the most expensive squares in the capital, but its interior is decrepit. The aesthetic is so pronounced, it must be deliberate. Expensive carpets are worn thin and antique furniture is scuffed, because what does it matter to these men, presumably? Renovation is a bourgeois concern.

The porter opens the door of the Trafalgar Room and stands back so Agatha can go in, then closes the door behind her. On the walls, there are portraits of British men who may once have been notable but have since been forgotten. Tobias is sitting in a deep leather armchair by one of the tall bay windows. As Agatha approaches, he doesn't get up, she notes. He does, however, pour milk into a cup followed by tea from a silver pot, then slides it in her direction. She sits down opposite him and crosses her arms and legs.

In recent weeks, there have only been two topics to discuss: the evictions in Soho, and Agatha's sisters. Agatha gets on well with her eldest sister, Valerie, who was born when her father was a teenager, is now elderly, and still lives in the village in which she grew up. The next three, Chelsea, Angel and Victoria, are an active and continuous nuisance. Not one of them seems to have anything to do outside harassing her, and they are still making claims on her money.

When Agatha was a child, her sisters tried to have their father's will overturned on the grounds of diminished capacity, but the argument didn't stick. It was possible he wasn't in his right mind when he had the will drawn up but, then again, he may *never* have been in his right mind. Not having met the man, Agatha's understanding of his character is borrowed, constructed piecemeal from offhand remarks, overheard conversations and – from those seeking to ingratiate themselves with her – hagiographies. The impression she has is crude but it is of a man who was darkly charismatic and often unhinged. She has heard stories of violent outbursts, of petty revenge. She remembers sitting in the back seat of a car when she was very young, pretending to listen to her portable cassette player while eavesdropping on the adults' conversation. Roster was in the front speaking with another man she didn't recognise. They mentioned a room behind her father's Soho office full of waxwork statues, like those found at Madame Tussauds on Marylebone Road. They said that when her father didn't like somebody, or when they did something that angered him, he showed them the waxworks. Agatha hadn't fully understood the story, the significance of the statues or why her father's adversaries would be so frightened by them, and as the years passed the details she remembered became detached from those she had actually heard. But the image stayed with her. When she was older, she looked for the room but didn't find anything, and when she asked Roster he claimed not to know what she was talking about.

The trouble for Chelsea, Angel and Victoria was that they needed to navigate legal channels to wrestle from their sister a fortune that was earned illegally. After failing to overturn the will, their approach has been incendiary rather than incisive. Now, their aim seems not to be to take control of the business but to destroy it, along with Agatha. They believe that the threat of this will force her to offer them some kind of cash settlement.

'In reality, it amounts to little more than blackmail,' says Elton. 'They have evidence your father's wealth was gained by illegal means.'

'It was gained by illegal means,' Agatha replies. 'Everyone knows that.'

'Yes and no. His cash riches came from, well, who knows

where? That was never any of my business. But his property was purchased in plain sight of the law, albeit with that same cash. The property is, now, far and away the most valuable asset. He had the foresight to buy exactly when and where he did. But your sisters say they have evidence connecting him directly to the Soho sex trade, to pimping and indeed to trafficking, evidence that suggests he was more than just an oblivious landlord to the brothels, but rather involved in soliciting and in taking a direct cut from the earnings of the prostitutes, which was and is illegal. And moreover, they claim that this involvement is in fact continuing. They say they have evidence that could connect the Trust to pimping and by association evidence that could connect you to these activities.'

'I have never had anything to do with any of that,' says Agatha.

'I know, but there are aspects of some of the long-term rental agreements you have with these establishments that could connect your income more directly to the activities of your tenants than you might like.'

She perches at the front of the deep armchair. It's designed for a man's hips, back and shoulders, and has been sat in and settled by such men. She looks about at the room, at the paintings she just a moment before so easily dismissed, at the other leather armchairs in the large empty room which have, like hers, been worn down by and made to fit a shape that isn't hers. The men of this room have traded in skin for hundreds of years. They built their fortunes on the sweat of others, but if she so much as touches the business of bodies, she might be ruined.

'Those bitches,' she spits. 'They know they'll never get the settlement they want in court but they would rather everything he built was seized by the government than allow me to have it in peace.'

'Quite. The thing is, they already seem to have copies of certain documents.'

'What documents? Have you seen them?'

'No, but our first step might be to arrange a meeting. To see what they actually have.'

'Good. You can see to that.'

'Yes. But they have stipulated that any meeting to negotiate must involve you directly. They want to sit down with you face to face.'

'I would rather not,' says Agatha.

'I realise you have managed to avoid them thus far, but a face to face meeting is coming.'

Tobias takes a sip of his tea. It's clear he has more to say, but Agatha steps in: 'We need to accelerate the evictions. We've been too tolerant. They've had their fun with these little protests. They have a big one planned this afternoon, I am told. But now they need to leave. The whole thing is frankly embarrassing. For them particularly, but also for us.'

'You've been establishing useful connections with the Met?'

'Just this morning,' says Agatha. 'He seemed receptive. He's running for mayor, you know, the rumours are true. All hush hush, until he resigns his job in the police force, of course, but clearly he is already interested in the prospect of my support, and will act accordingly while he is still wearing the badge.'

'Good,' says Mr Elton. 'That ought to put some fear into these girls. If the Met gets involved they won't want to take the whole thing much further.'

'Perhaps,' says Agatha again. She sits back in her chair, feeling utterly depressed. The protests have been getting more attention, not less, and they have been spreading like inflammation in a sick body. London feels angry, and ill-prepared for large-scale unrest. There is so much hubris here.

They know about revolutions in Paris. There, rioters prised cobbles from the street and threw them. They dragged carts into the lanes to block them. When Napoleon III rebuilt the city, he made sure the streets were wider than the length of a cart, and paved with something heavier than cobble. Then in 1968, disaffected students overturned double decker buses and used those to block the streets instead.

The grander parts of London are wide and bright and difficult for dissidents to take by force. In Soho, the streets are narrow, and the lanes are dark. And it has always been a place of sedition.

Agatha has made preparations for a worst-case scenario. As well as her Mayfair townhouse, she has a manor house in the north of England, and with it land and tenanted cottages. The property was bought by her father at some point in the later stages of his life. If she reads the warning signs correctly, there should be time to collect her things and get out of the city before it becomes dangerous. If the action is restricted to the capital, that is. If unrest is more widespread, she will need to leave the country altogether.

She keeps a yacht, named *Versailles*, moored on the Thames, fully provisioned, manned by a permanent crew. It is expensive but worth it. Her mother is for ever asking her if she can take the yacht on little jaunts to the Med, but notwithstanding the trips they go on together in the summer, Agatha invariably says no. When she is in London, the yacht will always be moored on the Thames.

The advantage of a yacht over, say, an aeroplane, is that it is easier to access. Airports and airfields would potentially be flooded with people, and there would be security checks and delays. In a boat, she could just sail down to the Medway and out into the Channel and then she'd be away.

Nobody else knows about these contingency plans. Just her and Roster. If she told anyone they would think she was deranged, like all those people who live in bunkers in New Mexico pickling cucumbers and canning roadkill in preparation for apocalypse.

Elton has already moved on to other topics. He is telling her about his son. Agatha's mind is elsewhere, but the son comes in and she meets him. He is better looking than she expected – his looks must have come from his mother, as they can't have come from his dad. Then she remembers Elton used to have an unexpectedly bohemian wife who left him in sordid circumstances, and she smiles to herself at the thought of this.

Soon afterwards, Agatha calls Roster and leaves the club to find him outside, standing next to the car. Fedor gazes from the back seat. Agatha takes her place beside him and places a hand on his silken ribcage. Roster climbs into the driver's seat and turns the key in the ignition. The car rolls into gear and the old man steers it slowly through the Georgian streets, lined with fallen autumn leaves.

'What did the fancy man have to say to you today?' Roster asks.

Agatha tells him.

'He has his own methods, but you know I have mine. If you should ever need them, I wouldn't hesitate.'

'Your methods are exactly what we're trying to leave behind. You might have served my father in that way but that cannot be how you serve me. The business has moved on. The world has moved on.'

Roster turns the car down a back street to park it by a small cafe run by an Italian family that has been there for decades. It's his sort of place rather than hers: a relic of a bygone era. It serves greasy fry-ups to hungry builders and steak and kidney pies with gravy, mushy peas and chips. Plastic chairs are attached to plastic tables, each with a complement of salt, pepper, vinegar, tomato ketchup and brown sauce. It's not the sort of place that Agatha visits regularly, but she has a soft spot for it, and comes with Roster every now and then, as she has been doing since she was a little girl and spent time in London with him and her mother.

Roster puts on the handbrake and turns off the engine. He speaks from the front seat without turning his head.

'The business might be taking a new direction, but the world is much the same as it ever was.'

Worms and Thunder

Precious holds a carnival mask she bought in Venice. It is embossed with rhinestones and framed with feathers which are black beneath clouds but iridescent beneath sunshine, like an oil slick. The vendor overstated its quality. In the golden light of a Venetian spring, the glimmer appeared authentic. In the copper light of a London autumn, it looks tacky.

She puts it to her face and tucks the elastic strap at the nape of her neck, then spots herself in the mirror. The mask covers her forehead and the area around her eyes, but her mouth and chin are exposed. If someone saw her they might be able to recognise her just from this. It would depend how well they knew her. Close friends, perhaps. Her sons.

She is holding a placard by her side. There is a wooden post in her hand, and the attached sign rests on the floor. Some of the other girls made their own with cut-up cardboard boxes stuck to the ends of broom handles, and slogans scrawled with permanent markers. Precious wanted something more durable, so commissioned a sign from a printers.

'You want it to say what?' the saleswoman asked, aghast.

'You heard,' Precious replied, in no mood to pander. She contemplated a number of slogans, before settling on this one. Others went for jokey signs but Precious didn't.

'It's a serious issue,' she told Crystal when she saw hers. 'People will be lined up to dismiss us because of who we are. We don't want to give them even more reason to think we're thick.'

'Do you think a thicko could come up with this? I don't think so. The whole point is to attract people's attention.

You're not going entice anyone with SAY NO TO EVICTION OF SOHO PROSTITUTES. It's dry.'

'It sums up our aims, unlike OCCUPY MY VAGINA.'

Precious is in her front room, while Tabitha is still in the bedroom getting ready. If she peers out the window she can see the street below. A crowd has begun to gather. She spots some of the girls from her building, and friends from Brewer Street. There are even some women from Chinatown. She registers both Scarlets, Young and Old, standing together, looking cold and bored. Precious didn't expect mother or daughter to be punctual, but here they are. She sees more signs. The one Giselle is holding reads NO TO BANKING | YES TO BONKING. Precious shuts her eyes and breathes deeply, then opens them again and turns back into the room.

The event isn't due to begin for another half hour, but it is good people are arriving early. Some have come from the women's groups they've been in touch with, wearing second-hand clothes, scruffy shoes, angular haircuts and over-sized glasses.

Tabitha emerges from the bedroom. She is wearing black jeans, a black fleece, comfortable leather pumps and a Darth Vader helmet.

'It's all I could find,' she explains apologetically. The helmet has a built-in voice modulator to make her sound like a Sith lord. She looks and sounds completely ridiculous.

'Right,' says Precious, taking a deep breath. 'Let's go.'

They pick up handbags and placards and make their way downstairs to the street. The crowd has swollen, absorbing newcomers. They spot Candy, Young Scarlet, Old Scarlet, Hazel and Crystal and push through groups of people to get to them. Candy and Hazel have placards too. Hazel's carries a statement about her body and her choices, written in pink and blue felt tip pen. Candy's sign is facing away from Precious. She swivels the pole, and Precious sees her own masked reflection in a shiny piece of silver cardboard.

'What's that?' Precious asks.

'A mirror to society,' Candy replies, as if this were obvious.

Precious just nods. Go with the flow, Precious, she says to herself, wondering not for the first time why she is putting so much effort into maintaining a living situation that keeps her in everyday proximity with these people.

The crowd sways like the crew of a tall ship, and heaves out some half-hearted chants. They haven't warmed up yet. Precious spots Cynthia loitering on the opposite pavement and beckons for her to join them. Young Scarlet lets out a performative sigh and rolls her eyes ostentatiously. Young Scarlet and Cynthia hate each other.

Cynthia makes a fortune from her work; significantly more than any of the other women. There is a clear reason for this, which everyone apart from Young Scarlet understands and accepts. Cynthia has the largest arse in the United Kingdom. She even won a competition. There's a trophy in a cabinet in the room in which she works. If a person has a particular thing about big arses, they will travel hundreds – sometimes thousands – of miles to visit her, and they will pay the necessary premium. This seems perfectly reasonable to everyone else, but Young Scarlet can't get her head round it.

'She's a fat bastard,' Scarlet said when she first discovered the discrepancy in their revenue. Tabitha seriously chastised her for the comment, and Young Scarlet half-heartedly apologised, but later expressed amazement that anyone would want to shag 'that lard arse'.

Young Scarlet considers herself to be the most attractive woman in the brothel, although nobody else agrees. She is one of the youngest, and her looks most readily align with a prevailing type. She is around 5'4", she has a slim build but large breasts, she has long blonde hair and a face that can be described as cute rather than beautiful. She keeps herself looking neat and tidy, and she wears a lot of expensive make-up. Everything she sees in films and on TV and reads about online and in magazines has taught her that she is desirable. And she is. But it's the kind of desirability that is common, while the desire that flourishes in this part of the city is varied. Those whose bodies command the highest prices are those whose bodies are more unusual. Within her own field, lard-arse Cynthia has a monopoly.

Cynthia sees Precious waving to her and she easily barges through the groups of people with her record-breaking hips. She hugs Precious, Candy and Hazel, and after Precious explains who is lurking beneath the Darth Vader mask, she hugs Darth Vader too.

As well as friends, there are unfamiliar faces. Looking at the crowd, Precious is struck by how big the city is, and how many people there are here who she doesn't know.

The sun has gone and the day is overcast.

A group of people have brought drums. The drums are held at their waists by colourful holsters, and they are beating them with their hands, or large batons. The rhythm becomes more and more ferocious. Someone else has brought some kind of horn, which lets out a sporadic, single note. It is obnoxiously loud and comes at unexpected intervals. Tabitha is standing next to Precious and jumps every time the horn is blown, knocking against Precious and once standing on her toe.

Another group of protesters has brought circus paraphernalia. A man is juggling multi-coloured clubs and another is tossing an object into the air with two sticks and a string. Someone else is walking around on stilts.

'Who invited the hippies?' asks Young Scarlet. 'Isn't it possible to go to a protest and also brush your hair?'

As a rule, Precious tries to be less judgemental about other people than Young Scarlet, so throws her colleague a disapproving look, while secretly agreeing. The overall tone of the crowd is now one of scruffiness, and in Precious's view, one of their main objectives is to present themselves as respectable and responsible. So many of the people have come along expecting to have a good time, as if they've turned up for a carnival or music festival.

The sun keeps popping out from behind the clouds, and catching on Candy's mirror. Whenever this happens she holds it aloft and sweeps the reflection across the crowd. The other members of the protest don't seem to be entirely happy about this, especially when one of them gets the full sunbeam right in the eye. Candy, however, is having a great time. 'I'm like the Eye of Sauron,' she says.

Precious has been standing for a while now, and the balls of her feet and her calf muscles are beginning to ache. She shifts her weight on to one side and another, then repeats the movement.

The gathering has little direction. There are some chants, but nobody is leading them. People are milling around in little groups. Then some people, who look as if they go to a lot of protests, begin to make announcements. Precious doesn't recognise any of them, though someone says something about them being from an anti-gentrification movement or some political organisation. Someone says something about the government. She worries that the real reason for the gathering is falling away from them, and she's letting it fall.

Precious feels someone nudge her hard in the back and Cynthia leans in and whispers, 'What are they talking about? It should be you up there.'

Precious shakes her head. She's never spoken in front of a crowd.

Tabitha agrees with Cynthia that it should be Precious up on the steps with the loudspeaker, but Precious again refuses.

She wouldn't know what to say. When she thinks about how being forced out of Soho makes her feel, she is overcome. She wouldn't know how to explain her feelings without getting it wrong and being misunderstood. It's such a delicate situation, and so important to her; it isn't something she wants to muddle up in front of a huge crowd.

In a way, it is funny that Precious has become so attached to the place. In Soho, there is dirt, pollution and so much that is vicious. There are people here who would sell their own mothers, or eat you alive. If society fell apart because of global warming, or nuclear war, this is the last place she would want to be. It wouldn't take long for the food to disappear, and all the water to be drunk. Then people would start eating rats, then cats and dogs, then they would begin to feast on each other. Precious has heard human flesh tastes like pork.

But she also sees compassion, and different people rubbing along together. People come here to drink and take drugs and have a quick shag, and people come here to laugh, and hear music, and dance, and to eat sticky sweet cakes and dumplings, or snails cooked in garlic butter, and drink chocolatey coffee and red Bordeaux, and watch plays, and hear music.

And it's home. She doesn't totally know what a home is but she guesses it's got something to do with friends and family and also something to do with being in a place that you feel has left its mark on you, for better or worse, and also being in a place that you've left your own mark upon, for better or worse. A place that remembers you've been there, that bears your imprint, like a squashy chair you've sat in a bunch of times.

When Precious thinks about it, she realises that is what it means to her, and why she doesn't want to leave. She is pushed on to the steps by Tabitha and Candy. Someone hands her a conical loudspeaker and shows her which button to press. She grips it in her right hand, curls her fingers around the handle, puts her forefinger against the trigger. When she pulls there is a click, and any words she chooses to speak will be shot through the air.

'Hello,' she says. Her words are loud, but they sound strange, as if she's shouting into a cardboard box. It takes her a couple of seconds to realise she doesn't need to raise her voice as the device will do the work for her. Tabitha and Candy and Young Scarlet and the others are looking up at her expectantly. Tabitha has taken off her Darth Vader helmet and is smiling up at Precious like an encouraging parent watching their child in a school play. Precious doesn't know whether the sight of her friends makes her feel better or worse. Would she rather embarrass herself in front of a group of strangers or in front of people she knows? She isn't sure.

'Thank you all for coming. It means a lot to us all. When we started fighting this battle we had no idea anyone would notice. We thought we were completely alone. And if today does anything, then it shows us that people – some people at least – care about us. And that, well, that's always a nice thing. I haven't got a speech planned, or anything, but I'd just like to ask a question. What will Soho be without people like us? Whatever it is we are. There will still be plays about us, and musicals. There are even operas about women like us over in Covent Garden, where all those fancy people sit with their champagne and their little binoculars. People will go to Piccadilly Circus or Leicester Square to see shows and films where people like us sing and dance, where people like us get naked and have sex or where we get murdered or die of tuberculosis, or fall in love with some twat who wants to rescue us. But if these evictions go ahead, we won't be here any more, real people with real lives. And some people might think: big deal. Get them out. Clean up the neighbourhood. But the thing is, where will we go? Look, it's not easy to talk about this stuff without painting everything like it's black and white. I'm not saying that it's the perfect job, or the job we all dreamed of doing when we were little. But that's life. Most of us end up a long way off from where we started out. But what we have going here is a good situation. Not everyone is as fortunate as us. If we get kicked out our work will be more dangerous, not less. And I'm just fed up with the hypocrisy. People have sex for loads of different reasons. And, well, we have sex for money.'

A cheer goes up. Candy is whooping. Cynthia has her hands raised above her head, and she's clapping them together like she's at a rock concert.

Then Precious sees the men. They are wearing dark

uniforms, stab vests, black lace-up boots. She looks down a thin alley connecting this street to the next, and she sees them jogging in a line, parallel to the crowd. They are clutching shields and batons. Precious panics and spins around to see if there are any more coming. She sees a van pull up in the distance. The doors slide open and more masked men jump out and begin to rush in their direction. Precious turns again and sees another group of masked men at the other end of the street. They are already nearing the crowd and are walking slowly towards the assembly of protesters. The drumming stops. Its rhythm is replaced with that of steel-capped boots on hard tarmac, tapping against the ground like a set of chattering teeth.

'It's a kettle!'

Precious doesn't know what a kettle is in this context. She looks around desperately. Other people, apparently, do know what a kettle is, and it doesn't seem good. She sees people beginning to run away. It doesn't occur to Precious to run away. She loses sight of Tabitha and tries to find her, but the crowd has become a tangle of frightened faces, and she can't for the moment see anyone she knows.

The police close in around them, and form a blockade. They are trapped. Nobody is allowed in or out. Minutes pass, maybe twenty, maybe more. Precious begins to tire. The police will keep them here until they are told by their superiors to release them. Everyone around her becomes fractious. Even the police officers become fractious. She can feel the anger behind their shields and masks.

Precious can feel an elbow digging into her lower back. Her face is pressed against a policeman's shield. The clear acrylic is heavily scratched, from years of use. Her left cheek and eye are squashed against it, and through the hazy glass she can see the riot police, standing shoulder to shoulder, with shields and batons, and more behind to hold the line.

She remembers her sons standing on the other side of a plate-glass door, between the kitchen and hall in her old flat.

They used to press their faces against it while she was cooking, squashing their lips and cheeks into the glass to make her laugh.

Someone is standing on her foot. She tries to shift it.

She can hear Candy squaring up to another policeman. She does her best to twist her body in the direction of the sound.

The man Candy is shouting at is exceptionally large. In his boots, he is nearly a foot taller than she is. He is wearing a helmet, so Precious can't see his face clearly, and his hands are covered by thick, dark gloves.

Candy tells him he's a bastard. She tells him he should be ashamed of himself. Then she changes tack. 'I piss on men like you every day,' she says. 'I piss on men professionally. I piss on their faces. I piss on their cocks.'

His response is shrouded by the balaclava and his heavy helmet with its visor. He doesn't look down at Candy, but up over the crowd.

Candy continues to shout. 'I've pissed on police officers. I've pissed on judges. I've pissed on politicians.' She is getting angrier and angrier. The policeman ignores her, but his colleagues are now watching. One policewoman looks furious. Another scared.

Then Candy stops shouting. Her face becomes calm. She looks like she is trying to reach something on the ground, but the weight of people around is forcing her to remain standing. She lowers herself slightly, so she is just out of sight, and then she comes back up. Precious tries to push back against the person standing behind her so she can get a better look, but she doesn't need to see. She can soon feel it underfoot. Urine.

The large policeman is now looking down at her and she is smiling up at him. And then he jumps. He has felt what she is doing. He moves like a spooked bull in a cattle chute. He is pinned to his position by the crowd of protesters in front and the line of police to the back, but his movement is involuntary, and explosive. He swings his arms wildly. People around him are knocked to the ground. Candy is knocked down, and Precious too. Precious manages to crawl away, but she watches as Hazel and some of the others are wrestled to the ground by police officers, then dragged kicking and screaming and shouting into the backs of police vans and driven away.

Then the rain comes. Clouds were building all afternoon, but now they fall, as if clouds are what happens when the world begins to daydream, and rain comes when it is revived. At first the water falls as thick drops, slowly then suddenly very quickly, then as ice. The hail shatters against tarmac and concrete and brick, casting shards into the gutters and drains.

The Past

Robert often sees a ghost. The ghost walks at night with a ghostly dog. He isn't as tall as he used to be, his bones having fallen into one another with age like kindling licked by flame, but Robert still recognises the outline: his gait, his long nose, the way he looks over his shoulder after he changes direction. The dog is new, but suits him, tall and thin like a greyhound, but with long, white silky fur. It trots at his heel. They come from Mayfair, cross Regent Street, then walk the backstreets of Soho. Robert thinks about calling out to the man, or going over and tapping him on the shoulder, but he doesn't.

Robert moved from Glasgow to London in his twenties. During an Old Firm fight he bottled the son of someone important and was advised to disappear. He travelled to London with a small piece of paper in his pocket, with the address of someone who could help him get work scrawled in pen, and a name Robert couldn't make out. He followed directions from Euston Station into Soho and knocked on a door at street level, then was led upstairs to an office. When Roster was a young man he was exceptionally handsome. Even Robert remembers being impressed. Reginald Roster was five, maybe ten years older than Robert, and he looked after him, in a sense. Roster was the boss's driver, but also much more. The boss had all his most important conversations in the back of his car, and Roster heard them. He sorted everything out for him, and he gathered men like Robert to help him do it.

Robert sits alone in a holding cell. He was brought in for a chat, then he got rough and was put in the cell to cool off. He has a phone call. When he used to get in trouble, back in the day, he would call Roster, and Roster would come with the lawyer. It must be thirty years, but that phone number is still as clear to him as ever. Robert has no idea if it is still in use. He isn't sure where it was connected to, at the time; either to a line in the Soho office, or maybe to a line at the Mayfair townhouse.

Robert thinks about calling Lorenzo, but he's already regretting everything he told him. Lorenzo left the pub without saying goodbye, and Robert sat there for a bit drinking until it was clear he wasn't coming back. The lad had looked at him like he was some kind of monster. Perhaps he is some kind of monster. Only, that's not how he feels. He feels like a person with memories of a bad past and hope for a better future.

Robert saw Lorenzo grow up. He remembers him going off to school in the mornings then coming back in the afternoons and sitting out on the balcony doing his homework on hot summer days. He always worked so hard. Robert thought the lad would be a doctor or lawyer or businessman. When he got the place to study at Cambridge, his mum and aunt organised a party and Robert chipped in with a case of champagne (which he stole from a strip club he did security for). It seemed right to mark the news with something fancy. 'You'll have to get used to this sort of thing,' he told Lorenzo. 'You'll have to stop drinking lager and start drinking champagne, and you'll have to learn what all the little knives and forks are for. When you come back at Christmas we won't recognise you.' Robert meant it as a joke, but the lad looked upset. He peered down at his drink then up at Robert. 'Sorry,' Lorenzo said. This wasn't what Robert had intended. He put down his own drink and placed a hand on each of the boy's shoulders.

'Never apologise for having an education,' he said. 'Never apologise for being clever and working hard and doing well. I'm proud of you.'

It was a surprise when Lorenzo announced he was going

to be an actor. His family were anxious about his prospects. His dad was especially loud about it, though Robert suspected Jimi wasn't so much anxious as ashamed. It was clear by that point Lorenzo wasn't going to be the type of man Jimi wanted him to be.

Lorenzo's dad was hardly around when he was a boy, and the lad was raised by his mum and aunts, who all worked at an Italian restaurant. Jimi was in the merchant navy. He was from Sri Lanka and met Maria when he was docked in the Medway and had come up the Thames to enjoy the city. In Robert's opinion, Jimi was a pure cunt. He was away for much of the year, which would have been fine if he sent his wages home to his family as he should have. Instead, he spent them in foreign ports. He was a looker and a charmer, and Robert wouldn't have been surprised if the man had other families in other cities. It was a dishonest way to carry on. Robert knows all about lust, but he doesn't lie and cheat. Though perhaps that's because he's never had anyone to lie to; anyone to cheat on.

He is led out of his cell, down the corridor to the phone. His fingers find the old number. He hears the dial tone, and then the sound of ringing at the other end of the line. After seven or eight rings, he feels sure nobody will answer, but reckons he might as well stay on the line while he figures out who else to call. Then someone does answer. He hears the man's voice, familiar but distant. He explains who he is and what has happened. Roster says very little. Robert doesn't know if the man has remembered him.

Then he returns to his cell and waits. He watches through the open grate of the door as girls with placards are dragged past. He recognises a few. He's fucked more than one, though he hasn't visited the walk-up in months. He has lacked desire. It seeped out of him as the seasons turned. He feels cold and hollow and brittle, and his body is strange to him, as if he is a stranger within it.

One of the girls is put in a cell near his. He recognises her voice as she shouts obscenities at the duty officer.

'Candy?' he whispers.

'Who's that?' Candy asks.

'It's Robert.'

'Robert who?'

'Robert Kerr.'

'Who's that?'

'I'm one of your regulars.'

Silence. Then, 'Are you the big tough-looking bloke with the scar on his head.'

'That's me.'

'The one who likes to do the husband-and-wife role play?'

'You what?'

'You know: under the covers, missionary position. Classic, no-nonsense sex.'

'Well, what else would I do?'

'Look, never mind. What you doing here?'

'Just some bollocks. You?'

'Got picked up after the protest. A bunch of us did.'

Robert heard about the protest. He also remembers what Karl said to him that time about the evictions. Then he says, 'I don't know what I'd do if you lot had to leave.'

'For god's sake, I'm sure you'd live. It's not really about you, is it?'

'No. Sorry. It's not about me.'

Then she says, 'Listen, do you know any good lawyers?'

Robert thinks about giving her the number he's just called. 'No,' he replies. 'But they'll fix you up with someone.' He means the police.

Roster arrives with Tobias Elton. The lawyer sits with Robert as he is questioned in an interview room by a police-woman called Jackie Rose. She asks him about Cheryl Lavery – how he knew her, when it was he last saw her. At first he can't understand the line of questioning, and then it becomes clear she suspects he was involved in Cheryl's disappearance.

Robert loses his shit. Elton tells him to shut up and sit down. Robert does what he's told.

The police ask Robert if he kidnapped her. They ask if he was put up to it by someone. They say they're investigating a ring of traffickers. *Did you drug her? Did you send her off somewhere? We know you're in and out of the walk-ups. We know the kinds of people you used to work for. Working for them again?*

Elton tells him to keep quiet, so he does. Afterwards, Roster pays the bail, like he always used to. Then Robert and Roster go for a drink at the Behn and the lawyer disappears back to wherever it is lawyers go.

'How long's it been?' Roster asks as they sit down on low stools either side of a small, round table. 'Twenty-five years? Thirty?'

'About that,' Robert replies. 'Or a couple of weeks, depending on how you look at it – I see you around now and again, though I don't come over.' There are two pints of beer on the table, and Robert has put down his brown leather wallet too. 'But, yes, over twenty-five years since we last spoke.'

'One or two things have changed since then.'

'So they have.'

Roster wraps a hand around the pint glass. Robert notices a set of knuckles not unlike his own. 'I'm working for Don's daughter now,' Roster tells him. 'The youngest.'

'The one he got from the wee Russian?'

'That's the one.'

'Does she look like her ma or her da?'

'A bit of both. She takes after her dad in temperament.'

'Stubborn?'

'You could say that. Clever. Serious. She can be ruthless like him, but in a different way. Different times, she reckons.' Roster tells Robert about some of the changes Agatha Howard is making to the area.

'Aye, I've heard all about that from the lassies. They're not best pleased.'

174

'Maybe not, but they can't win.'

'How's that?'

'Come on, Rab.'

Robert nods grimly and takes a sip of his beer. Of course they can't win.

Roster then reinforces the point: 'When a terrier's got his teeth to a rat, there's no letting go.'

'Aye.'

'And it'd be best for them if they didn't wriggle around so much.'

'You can't blame them for wanting to fight it. Some of those girls have been there for years.'

'Can't blame them, no, but I would tell them to stop it if I were a friend of theirs.'

Roster places a fist on the table, then sticks out the index finger in Robert's direction and taps it on the wood. Robert gets the point.

'I don't think they see me as a friend,' he replies quietly.

'They should know you have their best interests in mind.'

'Maybe.' Robert doesn't want to say anything decisive.

Roster changes the subject, though only in the way a hawk shifts direction after a missed catch to loop back and try again. 'You still in that flat in the new tower block?'

'I am, but the tower block hasn't been new for at least sixty years.'

'I suppose not. It was a nice deal you got there.'

'I earned it, right enough.'

'Did Donald give you the flat outright, or was it just a long lease?'

Robert has never seen himself as a clever man, but even he can tell Roster is reminding him of the debt he owes.

'I think you probably know.'

'Yes, I do. It was a long lease. It would be difficult to get you out but not impossible.'

'To put it bluntly,' says Robert, trying to keep his voice light.

'To put it bluntly,' agrees Roster sharply. Then he sits up

on his stool and puts his hand on his knee. 'Agatha hopes the police will take care of the walk-ups for her, but I'm not so sure their involvement is a good idea. I've been making plans of my own – gathering a few of the old crowd. We just need to take back the building. Rough them up. Scare them off. That'll take the fight out of them.'

Roster doesn't stay much longer. He takes Robert's most recent phone number, and double checks his address. Then he reminds him again of the favour he's just done for him up at the police station and heads back towards Mayfair.

Robert finishes his pint and decides to go home. He walks back from the Behn full of booze and memories; drunk on both. It's like that old man, who Robert thought he would never speak to again, has stepped up, taken him by the hand, dragged him to a local graveyard and started digging. He feels as if he's standing in front of an abyss he's been running from for twenty-five years, only to discover he's been running in circles and that here he is, after all this time, standing in front of it again with nowhere else to go.

He passes Des Sables on his way back to the flat. It's still in business but only just. Nobody is sitting outside even though the evening is mild, as Robert sees it. Inside there looks to be only waiters. Above Des Sables, there are the flats the girls live in. Precious, Candy, and all those. He thinks about going up now and telling them about the conversation he's just had with Roster, but isn't sure what good it would do. They know there are folk out to get them and it's not like Roster told him anything that would help.

Below the restaurant is the Archbishop's basement. He thinks again of Cheryl. He feels like falling to his knees, taking his head in his hands and staying that way until he turns to stone.

Rapunzel, Rapunzel

'We're right at the top. And we don't have a lift, just these stairs. Would you like a hand with your equipment?'

'If you don't mind.'

The photographer passes Precious a black canvas bag with a long leather strap. Precious hoists it over her shoulder. It is heavier than she expected. Mona picks up the remaining bags and a folded metal tripod and she, Precious and Tabitha begin to climb the stairs.

'I would help too,' Tabitha begins apologetically, 'only I've got weak ligaments in both shoulders and I'm not allowed to do load bearing. I'm on a waiting list for an operation. Keyhole surgery, but they'll still knock me out.'

'Right at the top?' Mona asks.

'I'm afraid so.'

'Like the princesses.'

'Which princesses?'

'All of them. They always live at the top of high towers waiting for Prince Charming to come and get them. Like Sleeping Beauty. Wasn't she in a tower?'

'Forest,' Tabitha corrects her.

'Rapunzel.'

'Was he the dwarf who tricked the lady and wanted her to guess his name, then got caught out by dancing around a fire while shouting it?'

'No.'

The trio get to the top and pause for breath before continuing down the hall to the flat.

They go inside. Mona doesn't wait to be shown around but immediately walks to the centre of the room and begins to set up. 'I thought I could take photographs of you in various locations around the flat, like here on the bed and over there on the couch. I want to see how you two live. You know, make it about you as people – your lives, etcetera – not just prostitute – sorry, sex worker – in underwear on bed, you know?'

'You want me to be in my underwear?' Precious asks.

'Not for all of it. Just a couple of shots, for context.'

Precious exchanges a look with Tabitha. She should have been clearer with Mona when they first spoke on the phone. 'I don't do that kind of thing. Sorry, I know to you it must seem all the same – like, I suck cocks for a living so why would I have a problem with some smutty photos, but it's just not something I personally am comfortable with. You never know with photos these days, where they will end up.'

Mona stops fiddling with her tripod and listens. She remains kneeling but straightens her back. She looks at Precious seriously. Her eyes were bright when they met outside but Tabitha has just switched on their red light, and what was previously green now has no colour at all. They are completely black – more black than black – as if Precious is being gazed at by some revenant from a horror film.

'I completely understand,' Mona says. 'It's my fault. I should have talked to you more about my intentions. I definitely don't want any of the photos to be smutty. Listen, let me talk you through what I'm aiming for, and let me tell you about some of the equipment I use.' She leans over to the bag Precious carried up the stairs and unzips it. Then she pulls out a large, expensive-looking camera and holds it up. 'This is my digital camera,' she explains. 'It's big and shiny and new and has lots of buttons. When I take photos with this, they become digital files, and can be uploaded on to a computer and, as you quite rightly say, anything can happen to them. Once they're on the internet, that's it. They could go anywhere. Believe me, as someone who takes photos to make a living, this bugs me too. However, with you, I'm going to use something different.'

Mona puts the digital camera back in the bag and zips it away. Next to the bag, there is a wooden box. She unclips the latch and slowly unfolds a very old, very large camera. Precious has never seen anything like it in real life – only in the period dramas Tabitha makes her watch.

'Wow,' says Tabitha, leaning against the doorframe, having been wandering back and forth to the kitchen waiting for the kettle to boil.

'I use a photographic technique called palladium glass printing.' Mona pulls from another box a rectangle of glass like a single pane from a sash window. She passes it to Precious who instinctively holds it by the edges, as she would a photograph. 'I take glass plates and coat them in a photo-sensitive substance. Where light hits it, it darkens, so when light is directed on to it in a controlled manner, by a lens, the brightest parts are black and the darkest parts remain clear. And a negative image of the scene is produced. Then I project the image on to the photosensitive paper, then develop and fix it with other chemicals. When you use this technique, the result is so detailed and beautiful, Precious, everything about you will be captured, but it won't be harsh like modern cameras can be. It will be soft, and skin tones will be rendered in shades of silver. You'll sparkle. It won't look anything like porn. And it won't be digital so it can't get on the internet. Yes, for a few shots, you might be in your underwear, but I'll also focus on details of your life, on the flat. I want to see you in your environment. Have you heard of a photographer called Diane Arbus?'

Precious says that she hasn't.

'I have,' Tabitha interjects.

'Have you?' Precious swivels around to look at Tabitha. She strongly suspects Tabitha is lying to impress their guest.

'Of course,' she insists.

Mona explains, 'She was an incredible photographer,

famous for her environmental portraits; those that situated her subject within their surroundings. Let me see if I can find an example.' Mona takes out her phone, types, then scrolls. She turns the phone round and shows Precious a photograph of three identical girls – triplets – sitting on a bed. They are wearing matching white shirts and dark skirts and their dark hair – all cut the same length – is held back with matching hairbands.

Tabitha comes closer to look, and leans over Precious's shoulder. The cups of tea she was making have been forgotten. The kettle boiled and switched itself off some time ago. 'God, triplets are freaky, aren't they? Twins are bad enough but triplets are even worse.'

'Well exactly,' Mona agrees. 'Arbus is playing with us. The girls are identical, yet there is no symmetry in the image. A lesser photographer would have lined them up perfectly and stood at the end of the bed and the photograph would have been an exercise in precision. But Arbus subverts our expectations. Nothing is lined up. Everything is out of kilter. And so cramped. You can see the girls' other two beds on either side. The curtains and the wallpaper are very fussy. It's all too much. It's claustrophobic. We're invited to think about the lives the girls lead, what it's like to be one of three. You can tell as much about a person from a photo of their bedroom as you can from a photo of their face.'

'More,' agrees Tabitha, sycophantically.

Not to be outdone, Precious contributes too. 'We know that better than anyone.'

'I bet.' Mona nods towards the bed Precious, and now Tabitha, are sitting on. 'Is this where you sleep?' She directs the question to Precious but Tabitha answers.

'God no. That would be like sleeping at the office. This is where Precious does her thing. We've got a little bedroom out the back. The bed's actually much more comfy than this one though. We've got a memory foam mattress.'

'You say "we". Are you a couple?'

Precious and Tabitha exchange a knowing look. 'You see, Mona, that's a good question with an answer that is, for some people, very easy to understand, and for other people extremely difficult to understand,' Tabitha says.

'I'm very open minded.'

'I'm sure you are, Mona. The thing is, when I met Precious she was in her mid-twenties and I was in my mid-thirties.'

'You were forty.'

'Whatever. I was a working girl, booking a room in this building in shifts. That's how some of the girls here work; not all of us live here, and I didn't back then. Anyway, I was wanting to wind down, move towards the maid side of things, see if there was someone younger who could use my help.'

'Excuse me, but what do you mean by maid? Are you her cleaner?'

'I do cleaning and laundry. But it's more than that. A maid looks after her girl, helps her out, is there to watch out for her when she's got a dodgy client. Anyway, about ten years ago now—'

'Closer to twenty.'

'I met our Precious. Back then she was working at a beauty treatment place up in north London. It was dead fancy. Lots of rich clients, and celebrities and that. I could tell she hated it, and obviously saw she was gorgeous so could make a packet in my line of work. And I made the suggestion.'

'And you became a prostitute, Precious? Just like that?'

Precious shrugs. 'The money was better and the people were nicer.'

'At first it was occasional. She was living down Peckham way bringing up the boys. She came up here every now and then. When they were teenagers they went to live with their dad's mum in Crystal Palace, and me and Precious moved into the flat together. We knew each other really well by that point. An intimacy develops, you know, when you do our work. Like a lot of maids and their girls, we share a room.' Tabitha goes on with her story. Precious knows she's enjoying it. 'Are me and Precious a couple? Well, let's see. I love her more than I love anyone else in the world. I live with her. I share my finances with her. I go on holiday with her. I sleep in the same bed as her. I cook for her and she cooks for me. She looks after me when I'm under the weather. I run hot baths for her after she's had a hard day at work.'

'You knit hats and scarves for my sons and granddaughter.'

'I knit hats and scarves for her sons and granddaughter.'

Tabitha stands back and puts her hands on her hips as if she's proved some kind of point. 'Sounds like a couple, doesn't it? But what's missing?'

'The obvious thing. Are you romantically involved or just friends? Do you have sex?'

Tabitha throws her hands into the air and smiles at Mona enigmatically. She says nothing more.

After a brief pause, Mona asks, 'Well, do you?'

Tabitha laughs. So does Precious. Tabitha loves bringing people to this point.

'With all due respect, love, that's none of your fucking business.'

She winks mischievously and potters into the kitchen.

After she has gone, Mona whispers to Precious, 'I'm sorry, I didn't mean to cause offence.'

'Absolutely none taken. She's messing with you.'

Precious follows Tabitha into the kitchen to collect their tea.

Mona disappears beneath a black cape that she has brought with her. Precious hears some clinking and rustling and then Mona asks her to undress to her underwear and to sit on the bed. Precious does so. She removes the blazer she was wearing to make herself look respectable and sophisticated for the protest. Then she takes off her top and the neat skirt she selected. She is wearing a bra and knicker set in ivory silk and lace. The colour suits her. She is confident in this get up.

Mona tells Precious to make herself comfortable but Precious doesn't need telling. She sits at the edge of the bed with her legs crossed and the toes of her left foot just about touching the floor. She stretches her arms out behind her and rests her palms on the bedspread, fingers outstretched and turned away from her. She tucks her tummy in a little, not because she is self-conscious at all, but she is having her photograph taken so clearly wants to look her best. She wears a broad smile.

'Say when,' she says.

'It'll be a little while yet. I've got a bit more faffing to do.'

Mona seems to take a long time to get the camera sorted, and even after it appears as if it is sorted, she continues to fiddle with it for many minutes. As she turns knobs and tightens screws, she chats to Precious as she said she was going to. They talk about lots of different things. Precious tells her about her childhood, her family, her life in Nigeria. She tells her about moving to London, about her ex-husband, about how she felt when her granddaughter was born, about the first time she fell in love.

After a while, Precious herself becomes curious, and asks Mona a question. 'Why do you do what you do?' she asks. 'What do you get out of it?'

Mona looks her in the eye. Her expression is blank; she gives nothing away. 'I seek fame and fortune through the beautiful rendition of other people's pathetic lives.'

Precious falters. Her face falls. She panics. Mona takes the photograph.

The Devil's Reward

After her meeting with Tobias Elton, Agatha tells Roster she'll see him at home, then she walks to a nearby gallery.

There is an exhibition of religious art from the Spanish Golden Age she has been meaning to see. Paintings have been imported from all over the world.

She pays the small entrance fee and buys a programme to read as she walks. There are lots of virgins. Virgins with child, Virgins in ascension. Virgins as no-longer virgins but mothers weeping over dead sons. Lots of Baptists. Baptists pointing at lambs; Baptists with conches; Baptists in itchy camel clothing; Baptists with no heads; Baptists with no bodies; Salome with her silver platter; Herodias looking on. Apostles, evangelists. Sinners damned. Bodies engulfed. The gaping mouth of hell. There's a room at the end devoted to contemporary photography from Iberia and Latin America. The photographs are posed, and reflect the compositions of the earlier paintings. One photographer has gone into a woman's prison and taken photographs of the inmates as the various incarnations of Maria. Maria the virgin; Maria the mother; Maria the demigod. The women in the photographs are tattooed. Some bear obvious scars of childbirth, violence, drug use, and these scars are emphasised.

Agatha considers this half of the exhibition to be bland, predictable. The themes illuminated by the photographs draw upon standard modes of leftist disaffection. The usual moaning. Perhaps these people think they're being very clever, but as far as Agatha is concerned, the work is derivative. She returns to one of the earlier rooms to look again at an El Greco.

184

A nearby infant wails and won't stop. Agatha tells the mother to take the infant outside, but the mother refuses and becomes angry. There's a dispute, which Agatha wins by remaining calm while the mother becomes hysterical, drawing the attentions of the gallery attendant and subsequently the security team.

Agatha returns home to hear laughter rattling around in the basement. One of the voices belongs to Roster. The other is female, though just as familiar. Agatha descends and pushes open the door to Roster's rooms. She doesn't knock. She sees Roster sitting back on his grubby old armchair and her mother, Anastasia, lounging on his lap. Roster is wearing his usual black suit. Anastasia is wearing a fitted minidress. They both hold large glasses of brandy that tip dangerously as they cackle. Anastasia's hand has found its way between the buttons of Roster's shirt. His necktie is askew.

Agatha is unsurprised by the tableau. 'You don't have to sit down here. You can sit in the upstairs rooms.'

'But I wanted to see my Reggie. Lovely Reggie.'

She means Roster. Anastasia always uses his first name.

'Take him upstairs as well. For goodness sake, why would you choose to sit down here?'

Agatha turns her back on the pair and goes to the stairs. As she ascends, Anastasia rushes up behind her.

'Are you happy to see me, my darling?' She says this in Russian. 'Will you kiss me?'

Agatha turns and brushes her lips gracefully against her mother's cheek. She continues up the stairs and into the main reception room at the front of the house. It has a view of the park. Her mother follows and so does Roster, who doesn't sit with the women but instead stands by the door. He has buttoned up and tucked in his shirt, and straightened his tie.

'Come here and sit with me, Reggie, sweetie.'

'He won't,' says Agatha.

'He won't if you remain so cold to him. Why are you so cold to him? He's family.'

'He just won't. When he comes upstairs he's working. It's nothing to do with me. I just know that he won't sit with us.'

'Come here, Reggie.'

'A man must have structure in his life. I am now at work.'

'Bollocks to that. Come and cuddle me. Come over here with that ox's cock.' Anastasia turns to her daughter. 'Did you know that our man here is hung like an ox? The devil blessed him with a big one as reward for all the sins he would commit.'

Anastasia laughs at her own joke.

Agatha does not look at Roster. She asks her mother why she has come to visit.

'What a welcome! Perhaps one day you will at least pretend to be happy to see me.'

'I didn't say I wasn't happy to see you. I just wondered what, in particular, prompted the visit.'

'Reggie phoned me. He tells me you're having more trouble with those bitch sisters. And with a pack of whores that won't budge.'

Agatha looks at her driver, who's still standing stiffly by the door, like a gallery attendant.

'I talk to your mother on the phone every now and then,' he says, 'and it happened to come up during our last conversation.'

'So I came immediately,' interrupts Anastasia. 'You are too weak with these people, Agy. You let them get the better of you.'

'I do no such thing. I am dealing with both situations.'

When they sat down, Agatha chose the sofa opposite her mother. Now Anastasia gets up and squeezes herself into the small space between her daughter and the armrest, moving one of the cushions on to the floor to make room, sitting with her feet up and drawn into her body.

Agatha begins to shift over but Anastasia wraps her arms around her and puts her head on her shoulder.

'Do you have a boyfriend, Agy? Or a girlfriend? I wouldn't mind. It would be a bit more difficult to have children, but only a little. It would just require additional planning.'

Agatha's posture stiffens. She tells her mother she has no boyfriend, but that it would be a boyfriend if there were anyone.

Anastasia takes hold of a lock of her daughter's long blonde hair and runs it through her fingers. 'Is it wrong of me to want grandchildren? I know that not every woman wants to be a mother, but I know for certain that every mother wants to be a grandmother. If you had had a child at the same age I was when I had you, I could almost be a great-grandmother.'

'You're not even fifty yet,' Agatha points out.

Anastasia makes a little noise at the mention of her age. 'If Roster had started as young as I did, he could have a whole clan by now. He would be like Genghis Khan, with his genes spread across a vast continent.'

'Maybe I did start as young as you,' says Roster quietly.

Agatha gets up and goes over to Fedor's bed in the corner of the room. She picks up one of his toys and squeezes it to make it squeak. The hound's soft footsteps can be heard on the stairs, and then his long nose seen pushing against the door. He trots over to Agatha and takes the toy from her hands, then shakes it.

'Darling, let's go out,' says Anastasia.

'I've just got in,' replies Agatha.

'But you've not been out properly. You've been working or doing something boring. Let's go into Soho. We'll get some drinks, maybe some dinner, then go dancing. You might meet someone.'

'I don't want to meet anyone in Soho.'

'We'll dance, then. I haven't danced in so long. It feels like years.'

'I'm sure you danced in Cannes.'

'A bit, maybe. But it isn't the same. There isn't anywhere to dance like in Soho.'

'Sleazy, you mean.'

'Well, maybe. Is that so bad?'

'I suppose it depends on your perspective.'

'I want to feel someone grinding against me in the dark.'

'That's where we differ. You wish to be molested by a total stranger. I can't think of anything worse.'

Anastasia slumps back on the sofa, pouting. Agatha is struck by how childlike her mother looks in this posture. Anastasia spends her summers in the sun, and her skin is bronzed and, despite the application of expensive creams, beginning to sag and wrinkle. But her aspect is young. She has the mannerisms of a teenager. She sighs and pouts and shrugs and sulks, and she laughs at juvenile jokes and makes crass remarks.

Agatha is conscious that she may have been a little unkind. 'Perhaps we could go out for dinner,' she says. Her mother sits up. Her face brightens. 'I'll need to have a shower and change my clothes. Let's leave in an hour.'

Anastasia becomes very excited by the prospect of getting ready for a night out with her daughter, and starts talking about hair and make-up. Agatha smiles and plays along, and after her shower she allows Anastasia to blow-dry and straighten her long hair, and she even allows her mother to do her eyeliner and mascara. She doesn't take on board any of Anastasia's clothing suggestions, but her mother is so happy to be allowed the physical contact with her only daughter that she doesn't argue too much.

She and Anastasia decide to walk into Soho. Anastasia tells her daughter that a short walk before entering a bar does more for a woman's face than a thousand pounds' worth of cosmetic treatments; and that if she wears high heels, it'll do even more for her arse. Anastasia is full of this kind of advice.

As they walk, Agatha asks her mother how she has been since she saw her in the summer. 'How is Mohammed?' she asks.

'He's depressed.'

'I'm sorry to hear that,' replies Agatha, startled. Mohammed seemed well last time she saw him.

'It's because I split up with him. I broke his heart and now he is depressed.'

'I'm sorry to hear that too.'

'He became so boring. I had to end it. He wanted to put me up in an apartment and come and visit me and have little family dinners with me like I was his wife. I told him not to. I'm not your wife, I said to him. I said, I don't want to be your wife, stop trying to treat me like a wife. And then he said he was sorry and that he was in love with me or something and then he said he wanted to spend all his time with me and that he wouldn't be able to get divorced from his actual wife, because of his children and his job, but he already saw me as the most important person in his life. And I told him, that's not what this is. Meet me in a hotel, yes. Take me out for dinner, yes. Buy me diamonds, handbags, a car, yes please. But don't expect me to sit in a little house baking stupid cakes and waiting for your flight to get in. No thanks.'

'I liked Mohammed.'

'Well, he didn't like you. He thought you treated me with a very little amount of respect. He had no idea why I put up with it.'

'Okay,' says Agatha. There isn't much more she can add to that.

They are walking down a street Agatha doesn't recognise. She doesn't come this way much. Her mother takes hold of her arm, perhaps in reconciliation after her unnecessary barbs, and they find their steps falling into time. They are the same height, and their legs and feet are the same length and size, although Anastasia's heels are much higher so she has to stoop to hold her daughter's arm.

The streets are crowded and the bars and pubs are overflowing. Men in suits stand on the pavement with pints of beer, jostling for space by the window so they can place their glasses or elbows on the sill. A big man takes a step back without looking around, and both Anastasia and Agatha are pushed into the road. Anastasia swears at him but the street is busy and the hubbub from the bar is loud so he doesn't notice.

They come to the French restaurant, Des Sables. Agatha hadn't realised this is where they were heading. She hadn't paid attention as her mum had led her through Soho.

'Not here,' she says.

'I love this place. Your father used to bring me here when we were first dating. He knew how to treat a girl. I never had eaten food like this. Snails. And garlic. He used to order all the most delicious foods for me and all the most expensive wines. I thought I was getting fat, but it turned out I was pregnant.' She raises a hand to Agatha's cheek tenderly.

Agatha rarely hears her mother speak affectionately about her father. Conversations about him, in whatever context, tend to centre on his money. On another occasion, she might want to coax more out of Anastasia, but she is too flustered by the sight of the restaurant. 'But it's on the way out. We've already given them notice.'

'Even more reason to make the most of it.'

'Mum, they know who I am.'

'Why do you care? They wouldn't dare say anything. They need all the business they can get.'

'I don't care, particularly. I just think we can do better elsewhere. Leave places like this behind.'

Anastasia concedes. They head elsewhere and debate the merits of different European cuisines before settling on an Italian restaurant that serves tasty but generic Tuscan fare to an exclusive clientele.

The Shortest Day | The Longest Night

Debbie McGee Redux

Debbie McGee is not dead. On the day she felt the tremors she walked into the building site at the centre of Soho. She found the mouth of a vast hole, like a crater gouged by a mortar at the Somme. She found a ladder and steps. Through the dark, she felt her way. Her hands gripped the cool metal rail, and her feet found the rungs. She took her time. If she slipped, she steadied herself, waited, then continued. She climbed down, deep into the earth. She found tunnels, and walked along them, back and forth, up and down.

The tunnels led in every direction. There were tall tunnels that were big enough for trains to pass through. There were smaller tunnels, corridors that a person could walk along. There were tunnels that were narrower still, that she would have to stoop to pass through, or crawl along on her hands and knees. There were tiny chambers, capillary-like, that spooled out from the main arteries, for rats, moles and other small mammals. And there were the seams big enough only for insects. Debbie McGee found tunnels that were fresh and new and lined with concrete; others that were old and worn out, held in place by rotting timbers and chipped bricks; walls of bare earth or cut from the bedrock. She felt the roots of trees, some alive, some dead. There were grubs and worms and other things she did not have names for. She walked for what felt like days. She drank the water that dripped. She did not eat. She lost herself in the darkness, feeling her way, seeing nothing.

And then, far off, she saw a light, and walked towards it. The light became larger and brighter. Its shape changed from ill-defined blur to a rectangle with horizontal lines. She reached with her arms into the light and moved as if to push against it. Her outstretched hands pressed a cool metal grate. She felt it shift in its holster, felt it give way, slip, disappear into the room with the light. She heard it clatter against a hard surface and the sound of the clatter ringing through the hole in the wall and bouncing around the dark tunnel, giving texture to the space. She placed her hands on the edge of the grate, pulled her featherweight body up and slipped through the hole. She blinked. She saw an expanse of rippling turquoise. A fevered Hollywood dream, a Kodachrome test-strip. It was a swimming pool, lit from below, lit from above. The swimming pool was lined with tiles in shades of blue. The walls from floor to ceiling were a photograph of a beach front, white sand, gently breaking waves, sun. The sides of the swimming pool were lined with tropical plants. Palms with leaves the size of parasols, long thin tendrils in a static, green explosion, and flowers as large as a baby's cradle. Pinks, yellows, lilacs, reds. There were UV lamps, the like of which she had seen in marijuana factories. The plants, too, were fed hydroponically. It was an underground eco-system, a subterranean oasis, a chlorine and halogen haven, a garden with walls on six sides. She walked around the pool three times, reaching out to stroke the plants, bending and crouching to smell the flowers. She stood on the edge of the clear water. She peeled off her sooty and ragged clothes, folded them and placed them in a neat pile. She stood naked and stretched her arms into the air. She could hear the calls of birds and the scratches of insects, parrots chattering, cicadas rubbing their legs together. Were there loudspeakers hidden among the plants? Did they broadcast the recorded sounds of the rainforest? Or was it that she saw the water and the plants, and smelt the flowers and the leaves, and felt the UV rays on her skin and had imagined these sounds to fit the scene? She crouched, then lowered herself into the water. She pushed out and began a breaststroke, remembering her childhood swimming lessons, paid for by a man she couldn't quite recall:

armbands and earplugs and swimming caps and Lucozade and KitKat afterwards. She took deep breaths, filled her lungs with the ersatz tropical air and dipped her head beneath the surface. She held open her eyes despite the sting of chlorine. The water swept through her loose hair and teased out strands of soot and oil. She surfaced, renewed.

She discovered an underground complex. In the room adjacent to the pool there was a lounge with a kitchenette, a large, gently humming fridge, and rows of expensive champagne. In the cupboards, she found pretzels, crisps, nuts, jars of caviar, globe artichokes, stuffed jalapenos, green and black olives, foie gras. She ate and drank as much as she could. The food in the cupboards was non-perishable but had been there a while. She opened a sealed packet of crackers that crumbled in her hands as she took them out. She found a jar of dill pickles that had mould growing around the lid. Some of the frankfurters she bit into were hard.

In the first few weeks she was sick. She didn't know whether it was the food or the withdrawal. She lay on the sofa wrapped in blankets and vomited until she could only retch. She sweated and shook and turned off all the lights she could find. She couldn't stand the brightness. She couldn't stand to catch her reflection in the mirror, or in the aluminium of the fridge or the glass of the oven door, or in the bright water of the swimming pool or the concave in the back of spoons, convex in the stainless-steel sink.

After the drugs left her system she slept, for what felt like days, weeks. She tucked herself up, wrapping herself in all the blankets she could find, then piling sheets from the linen cupboard on top. She cocooned herself.

She didn't put her old clothes back on, but left them by the pool. She found a towelled dressing gown in the cupboard by the sauna and wore that along with a pair of slippers. She moped around the complex like this. If there had been anyone else there to see her they might have thought her a customer at an upmarket spa.

She worked out how to use the sauna, and sat in the warm cubicle and picked dead skin from the soles of her feet and scraped dirt from her pores before coming out, rinsing off, drying herself and coating her body with shea butter from a tub she found in a cupboard and initially mistook for food. She did this every day. She used tubs of the stuff. Her skin began to heal. She used to have cuts, sores, bruises, but these began to recede until all that could be seen was a smattering of scars.

She started to turn the lights back on, using the dimmer switch to illuminate and darken the rooms, admiring the fresh tone and texture of her skin in different gradients of light. She began to enjoy looking down at her own arms and legs and hands and feet and watching as the flesh and muscle beneath the skin began to return. This new flesh. She pressed her fingers into it and watched it recess then bounce up and back into place. Her skin didn't do this before. Before, when she pinched, it stayed in position like whipped egg whites.

In one room, there was a small cinema with folding red theatre chairs. She sat in the dark and watched moving images projected on to a screen. She watched for so long, the faces and stories swirled with her own memories and became indistinguishable one from the other. Was she Cheryl Lavery or Debbie McGee? Or Scarlett O'Hara or Vivien Leigh? In another room, there was a bowling alley. The lanes were pristine, and finely polished. There were no scuff marks or chips in the wood laminate. Many of the balls had not been taken out of the cardboard boxes in which they had arrived, so sat like ballast in the hull of a ship, as if to hold the building in place. She pulled balls from their boxes and threw them down the lanes at skittles. She practised and practised. She perfected her technique. She found locked doors and searched for the keys, and when she couldn't find the keys she picked the locks with a bent paperclip. In one of the locked rooms, she found expensive fitness equipment, including dumbbells and rowing machines and yoga mats. She lifted the dumbbells and had a go on the rowing machine, and contorted her body into yoga postures she found outlined in a book. In another room, she found boxes of foreign currency and, behind the boxes, bars of gold bullion from floor to ceiling. She took these from their shelves, held them in her hands, gazed at them then replaced them carefully and closed the door. There was a library. She read novels, and travel books, and books about history, and self-help books. She learnt how to motivate herself. She learnt about being a productive member of society. She learnt how to be happy.

She began to count everything. Measure everything. She counted the number of books she read, and how quickly she read them. She compared the number of pages, the number of words on each page, the number of letters in each word. She counted the films she watched, and everything within them. How many times does that character say 'yes'? How many times does this character say 'no'? She counted the number of lengths she swam and the speed with which she swam them. She counted what she ate, not just the packets, but the individual crisps, peanuts, noodles. She wrote all the numbers down in a little book and carried it with her wherever she went, as if this collection of numbers held something of value.

She has now been in the basement for six months. The supplies are running low. She has emptied the cupboards and the fridge and the storeroom filled with boxes she discovered in her fourth week. The boxes are mostly gone, and Cheryl is getting tired of caviar and stuffed olives. She has read all the books and out-of-date periodicals and she has watched all the films. She has swum 8,266 lengths of the pool. She has used up the soap and shampoo in the pool-side shower. She has tired of the jacuzzi.

The tropical plants in the pool room have little labels stuck into the soil, announcing their Latin names. She has learned all of these and has also given the plants pet names of her own. Besides her, the plants are the only living creatures in the basement, unless you count bacteria or the mould on blue cheese (which she doesn't). She has paced, and picked her nose, and masturbated. She has slept in a bed with a duvet and pillows, and soft linen sheets. She is fit and healthy. Her diet in this bunker, though strange, has been more nutritious than ever in her life before. She has exercised extensively every day. She has massaged expensive moisturiser into her skin. It is no longer dry, brittle, cracked, bruised. It is soft and elastic and tanned from the UV lights.

She is ready. She goes through the pool room, says goodbye to her botanical friends, gently brushes her hands against petals and leaves. She lifts herself out through the grate by which she entered and begins to march back through the tunnels. In the last six months, the only thing she has failed to count accurately are the days. When she descended, it was midsummer, the solstice, the longest day, the shortest night. The day she chooses to ascend, it is midwinter: the shortest day, the longest night. She descended as the earth's tilt took the northern hemisphere away from the sun. She ascends as the light begins to return.

Oxbridge Escorts

Glenda and Bastian sit opposite each other on the train. Both look out the window. Glenda follows the scene outside as it rushes from behind. Bastian watches as it rushes from ahead. They speak very little. The soft skin around Glenda's eyes is pink. Elsewhere, she is pale – even paler than when he found her the night before. Every now and then Bastian offers a smile. Sometimes she returns it. At other times, she just sits and watches her friend.

'Thank you, Bastian,' says Glenda. 'I don't want to get too sincere on you, but you're a good mate for doing what you did.' She turns away from him towards the window again. They streak past fields and copses and outbuildings and beaten-up farm equipment.

There is no need for him to respond. He leans his head against the glass, creating a smudge with the natural grease of his hair. Then he rummages in his bag for a book.

It is still early. The train is full of business types heading to meetings in northern cities. They sit with teas and coffees and complex spreadsheets.

The night before, Bastian worked late, into the small hours. He has been put in charge of communications at Howards Holdings, and has been inundated with freedom-of-information requests and enquiries from news platforms. He had to put together a statement to send out in the morning.

He got a taxi home. When he arrived, he noticed from the street that the lights were on. It was 2 a.m. He entered the building, took the lift up to the fourth floor and let himself in.

Bastian placed his keys in the bowl by the front door. He

dropped his messenger bag beneath the coat hooks and slipped off his shoes. He walked from the hall into the living room in his socks. Rebecca was sitting on their sofa with her arms and legs crossed.

'Where the fuck have you been?'

'I've been at work. Didn't you get my text?'

'You expect me to believe that you were at work?'

This sounded to Bastian like a line from a soap opera and he couldn't help but smile, although he did so while his head was turned away from Rebecca.

'Why wouldn't you believe that?' he asked.

'Your little friend came round here this evening. Hammering on our door in the middle of the night.'

'Which little friend?'

'You've got more than one, have you?'

'Rebecca, I'm sorry, but I haven't got a clue what you're talking about.'

'The hell you don't.'

Bastian chose not to respond to this. He was too tired and it was all too confusing. He went into the kitchen and poured himself a glass of water from the tap. He came back in and said to her, 'I've obviously done something that's upset you but I genuinely don't know what it is.'

'Your friend Glenda.'

'Glenda came here?'

'Blind drunk. Stumbling all over the place. Crying and wailing. Cuts all over her hands. Hammering on the door. I mean, what the fuck?'

'Oh my god, is she okay?'

'How should I know? I didn't let her in. She was in an awful state. She was asking for you. I should've known you were carrying on with that Laura again. You've been so shifty lately.'

'Where did she go?'

'My god, the way she was carrying on. What a mess.'

'Yes, but where is she now?'

'That's what you're worried about? God, do I mean so little to you that you're not even going to try to salvage this relationship?'

'Rebecca, I don't know what you think I've been doing, but to be honest that discussion can wait. Glenda's vulnerable – she's had a rough time lately and has been really struggling. And frankly, I can't believe you didn't let her in.'

'Why should I? I'm not about to let random drunk people into the flat.'

'But she's not a random drunk person, is she? She was at our college. You may never have spoken to her but you know who she is.'

Bastian took his phone from his bag and called Glenda but her phone went straight to voicemail. He put his shoes back on and went out into the night in search of her, all the while Rebecca shouting and screaming that it was over, that if he went out that front door he could forget coming back in.

'I'm fucking my personal trainer,' she had yelled as a parting shot.

'Dave? Your friend's husband?'

'That's right. We've been fucking for months.'

Then she had slammed the door after him.

Bastian walked the streets around his flat, searched at the bus stops near the Tube station. He clambered over the fence of the park – now shut – and searched on the benches and by the pond. He walked all the way to the banks of the River Thames. Swans hid their heads beneath their wings. The water lapped the shore.

All the time, he thought: how can she care so little? Glenda's a person who obviously needed her help; our help. And she turned her away.

Bastian found Glenda on the bridge between Embankment Tube station and the Royal Festival Hall, looking out over the Thames. She wasn't wearing a coat and she was shivering. There were tears in her eyes.

He convinced her to go with him and they went to sit in

the McDonald's on the Strand which is open twenty-four hours a day. Bastian bought Glenda a cup of hot tea and a Big Mac, and he bought for himself a Filet-O-Fish meal with Fanta because he'd never had a McDonald's before and he didn't know what to order, and thought the name sounded funny.

Glenda had returned home the previous evening to discover that she had been evicted from her room.

'It was all dodgy anyway,' she said, 'and I knew it would all come to an end sooner or later. I just didn't think it would be so abrupt.'

'Isn't it illegal to just kick you out like that?'

'Well, it was illegal that I was there in the first place, so I guess there's not much I can do.'

'There must be. It wasn't you who was breaking the law; it was them. Do you have any lawyer friends?'

'Must do.'

'If not, my dad's one.'

'You don't have to ask your dad for help, it's okay.'

'It's not okay. You don't look okay. I mean, are you literally homeless now?'

'No, don't worry. I've got a job and a safety net. I'm lucky. I'll never be homeless. I'll just move in with my aunt in Barkingside or back up north to my parents. It's not like it's working out here anyway.'

'Maybe it's a good idea to get out of London for a bit,' he said. 'You could go and stay with your mum and dad. You don't like your job anyway.'

Glenda shrugged then agreed, then thanked him.

They sit on the train together. Bastian recognised some of the landmarks on their way out of the city: a football stadium, a university, a block of flats where he'd once been to a New Year's Eve party. Now they are in the countryside, and the landscape is new. There are low hills, and gnarly copses, and empty fields. The train bisects them, splitting the scene into neat sections that fill the window frames. When they pass beneath a bridge, or slice through a short tunnel, there is a flicker of darkness followed by a flash of bright colour.

After a while, Glenda starts talking.

'The thing is though, I can see how ridiculous it all is. It's like I have these constant multiple out of body experiences. I'm me, feeling all these things, and then I'm also outside myself looking in, aware of how lucky I am in the grand scheme of things or whatever. And then beyond that there's the realisation that everything actually is pointless, and that if I fundamentally don't enjoy my life there really is no point in living. And then of course, there's the thing that actually keeps me alive: the awareness of how much pain I would cause to my family and friends by ending my own life. So I'm just stuck here, I guess. Stuck here feeling shit but unable to do anything about it. Like, I've never completed a single project I've started and that includes suicide.'

All this is said very quietly so as not to alarm the other passengers.

'What would it take for you to begin enjoying your life? I mean, I know that's a really difficult question, but—'

'It's not a difficult question. It's a really easy question with some really easy answers. I'd like to find a person to love who loves me in return. I'd like to find somewhere to live with her. Nothing fancy, but it would be lovely if it had a little garden. And yeah, in terms of a job, I just want to have a job that pays a modest amount and lets me bumble around and achieve some tasks and then go home and be with the person I love; whoever that person is. I don't need loads of money and success; I don't need lovely clothes and luxurious holidays. I don't want to run fucking marathons for charity. I just want simple things. They just seem so unbelievably out of reach. They seem so far from achievable it's like I can't even see the path towards them.'

'Is there a chance of you meeting someone?'

Glenda gives him a look that's something like a grimace.

'Is that really such an awful suggestion?' he asks.

'No, it's just. Look, do you really want to chat about this stuff? I feel like such an over-sharing twat.'

'Yes, I actually want to chat about this stuff.'

As soon as Bastian says this, however, he wonders if he might come to regret the statement.

'I feel like I should re-establish my personhood or whatever before I try to meet someone new. I hope it can happen eventually, but the thought of intimacy with another human being isn't really something I can contemplate right now.'

The train trundles along. The conductor comes around and checks tickets. Glenda continues, 'It would probably be easier if I put myself in lots of dangerous situations and just died from a natural disaster. Like, maybe I should take up mountaineering, which would greatly increase my chance of dying in an avalanche. That would be a glamorous way to go. Nobody would be like – Oh, that Glenda's died of an overdose what a loser, they'd be like, Oh, that Glenda died in a mountaineering accident. And other people would be like, Oh, how ghastly.'

'I guess the fact you're imagining being celebrated in death means you don't really want to die.'

Glenda makes a face. 'Good one,' she says.

Bastian returns to looking out the window.

'Is your relationship with Rebecca over, then?' she asks him.

'I think so.'

'I'm sorry.'

'It's fine. Really, it's been over for a while.'

Bastian escorts Glenda all the way to her parents' house.

'You're so kind for doing this,' she says.

'To be honest, you probably owe me some sort of blood debt now.'

Glenda can't bring herself to laugh. Maybe deep down she believes that she does. She says, 'You're coming in, yeah?'

He shakes his head. 'I'm off to Wakefield.'

Glenda pulls out her phone, touches the screen with her thumb a few times, then sends him a message with an attachment of the address and the phone number he needs.

They hug. It's a proper hug, the kind where you feel the warmth of the other person's body.

Glenda goes inside the house, ducking her head though it in no way reaches the lintel. She turns and waves, then shuts the door behind her. Bastian sees a light being turned on in the hall.

Bastian makes his way back to the station and searches for a train that will take him to where he needs to go. He buys a cup of tea at the AMT stand. There's a lot of waiting around. A lot of time to think. He sits on a bench and wraps his hands around the hot paper cup until it begins to scald.

He is making his way to Laura's house.

He doesn't want to just turn up, so he sits at the station and composes a message to her. He will let her know that he's in the area, and ask if he can come and see her. If she's free. If she wants to.

He'll go over to Wakefield and sit and read his book, he'll have a coffee. He might go to the Hepworth Gallery. An exhibition currently on there was advertised to him on his phone that morning. It is a combination of sculpture and sound installations, which ties in with Bastian's interests in jazz and hi-fi equipment. And if Laura gets back to him, he'll go over and have a proper chat.

The brief time Bastian and Laura spent together ended abruptly. The abrupt ending was prompted by a conversation about how Laura funded her studies. Although Laura's mother was unable to work, Laura received no college bursary for complex reasons involving a wage-earning but absent father, and the length of time for which her mum had been off work. Her fees were covered by her loan and her loan also made some provision for maintenance costs, but it did not cover all her expenses. Having a regular job during term time was forbidden, as the university felt that having a job would detract from study. Laura found work in the holidays, but in these months her half-brothers were also off school and it made more sense for the family financially if Laura helped out with the childcare.

Laura mentioned to Bastian in passing that she had a profile on a website called Oxbridge Escorts, and that she had been paid to go on dates with rich men. Bastian was horrified.

They were sitting in Bastian's college room with the windows wide open. Bastian's room overlooked the river and the splashes from punts and shouts from punters rose with the midday heat. It was a lazy morning of coffee and sex. Bastian then went out for a couple of croissants and more coffee. There was a kettle and cafetière on the desk in his rooms, but Laura said she wanted froth, so Bastian walked out of the college, through its neo-Gothic gatehouse and across a wide street to a coffee shop where baristas created the appropriate froth with jugs of hot milk and a nozzle that spouted steam.

Bastian carried two cappuccinos in one hand and a brown bag containing two croissants in the other. The butter leaked from the pastry and made little greasy windows in the paper. As he walked back through the college he felt happy, possibly happier that he had felt in years. Happier than he has felt ever.

Laura was sitting naked on the bed. She was always easy with her body. She did not worry about her naked body being seen, either by Bastian or being accidentally glimpsed through the window if the light cut the right way and the curtain slipped, or if she leaned against the windowsill to pick up her phone or a glass of water. She didn't mind taking up space. She would happily sprawl across a sofa or a double bed with her arms stretched wide and her legs apart. Bastian was intrigued by how comfortable she seemed in her body and how comfortable she made herself in the available space.

Laura's laptop was open in front of her. The Oxbridge Escort profile page was up on the screen. Bastian asked her what it was and she explained.

'Like, as in an escort escort?'

'As in an escort escort.'

'So you go on dates with men for money?'

Laura shrugged her shoulders.

'I don't know what to say,' said Bastian.

'Then don't say anything,' said Laura. 'Look, I'm only on the website now because I'm deleting my profile.'

'But you've been doing it before? If you're deleting it now, then. What? How long have you been doing it?'

'A couple of years on and off.'

'I – what? I don't know what to say.'

'So you keep saying.'

'Well, how did you think I'd respond?'

'I didn't think you'd find out. You came back sooner than I was expecting. When you got back I didn't want to – I don't know – slam my laptop shut or anything weird like that. It's just, something I do. Did. Have done. It's no big deal.'

Bastian was still holding the coffees and the brown paper bag. Laura reached out for her drink, and Bastian handed it over automatically. She was now sitting up on the bed with her legs crossed. She had pulled the duvet up around her and she held the coffee cup between both hands. She pulled off the plastic lid and brought it up to her mouth to lick off the milky foam.

'Look, it is what it is. It's something I did for a couple of years, and may do again in the future, but I don't want to do it at the moment because, well, call me old-fashioned but I don't want to go on dates with other men right now.'

'There is nothing old-fashioned about this.'

'Actually, it's the most old-fashioned profession in the world.'

'Wait a second. You mean, you did actually sleep with them? It wasn't just dates. You are actually a prostitute? Great. That's great.'

'Don't be a dick.'

Laura got up. She started moving round the room, pulling

her things together. She found a pair of knickers on the floor and put them on. She pulled her bra over her head, then the slip-on dress she'd been wearing the night before. She found her wash bag and started to stuff it inside her rucksack. Bastian was too shocked to stop her, or to say much else. He paced around the room a bit, he tried to drink some of his coffee but by that point it was cold.

She kept shaking her head and calling him a prick. She had gone red and wasn't meeting his eye. She left and he was too stunned to do anything about it.

Service Station

Agatha sits in the back seat of the Rolls Royce with Fedor the borzoi, his long head resting on her lap. She draws her hands through his fur, teasing out knots with her fingertips. Anastasia is sitting in the front with Roster. There is a barrier that divides the front from the back, so Agatha and Fedor are cut off from their travelling companions.

Agatha doesn't mind. It gives her a rest from the maternal affection she's been receiving these last few months. Since her mother came to stay she has offered her opinion on every aspect of Agatha's life. A couple of days ago, the tension boiled over.

Anastasia saw the photo of Precious. Her daughter is sent material from all the London galleries; she's a patron of many. Anastasia was riffling through the post and came across the brochure. She recognised the woman on the front as Precious, from the images provided to Agatha by a private security firm she employed. Anastasia flicked through the brochure, and recognised another of the pictures, presented as a thumbnail at the back. She went to the gallery by herself one morning to see the full image, to make sure she hadn't made a mistake. She asked the attendant if he knew the name of the man in the picture, and he sneered at her, as if she'd just asked him whether Caravaggio was still alive.

'I don't think it's listed. They're all characters from the neighbourhood in which the artist immersed herself.'

Anastasia knew exactly who the man was, she just wanted to make sure. She went back home to Agatha with a selection of postcards from the exhibition. She stole the postcards so she wouldn't have to queue at the counter, slipping them into the pocket of her long trench coat.

She showed the faces to her daughter. Agatha recognised Precious but not the man.

'Why are you showing me this?'

Anastasia thrust the postcard closer to her daughter's face. 'Not the black girl. The man. Look at him,' she implored. 'He used to work for your father. He's just what we need.'

'In what sense is he just what we need?'

'He was a legend back in the day. The hardest man north of the river, and that was only because the gangs in the south wouldn't come up this way to test themselves against him.'

'Amazing,' Agatha said dryly. She was in her bathroom, flossing her teeth. Anastasia went to sit on the edge of the bath.

'None of your legal methods are working, Agy. It's taking far too long. If you want any of those new flats built this decade, you need the whores out quickly.'

Agatha continued to pull the thin white tape from the plastic reel. She cut it to size, then threaded it between two incisors. She looked at her mother in the mirror but didn't reply.

'Did you hear what I said? It's not working. Nothing is happening!'

Agatha pulled the thread back and forth several times, then repeated the procedure. She remained calm while her mother's temper swelled.

'You're a bloody idiot!' shouted Anastasia. She threw the exhibition postcards at her daughter, and stormed out of the bathroom, slamming the door behind her.

It was good to be leaving London. The city felt restless, potentially dangerous, and there had been a couple of strange encounters. The first was with an aggressive canvasser who came to Agatha's door. The second was with a disgusting-looking tramp who accosted her near her house and kept going on at her about some ancient artefact he'd found, and would she like to buy it off him. The man was obviously crazy.

Agatha has travelled this route many times before. Roster used to drive her from London to her school in North Yorkshire. Now she comes this way to visit her horses, to watch them race, and to stay in her country house.

There's shooting on the estate but it is not something in which she takes an interest. Landowning neighbours have begged her to keep the gamekeepers on. They offered to help manage the staff, run the shooting, and maintain the moorland to prevent it turning to scrub.

Agatha has no interest in shooting pheasant, nor does she have any interest in allowing rich men from London and Dubai to tramp through her woods and over her moors, firing shot at the sky.

She dismissed the majority of the grounds staff as soon as she took possession of the property. There were complaints from the local community and obnoxious articles in the village gazette. Obviously she didn't bother to read these, and ultimately it was her choice and nobody could do a thing about it.

While she is here, she will see her eldest sister. Valerie Howard has lived on the land all her life. She was born to Donald and his teenage sweetheart in 1936 and raised by her mother and grandparents in the village while her father made his fortune in the city. She never left. She never married. She worked on the smallholding, milking cows and collecting eggs. When her father bought Bythwaite Hall in the 1960s – bought from the family he'd poached from as a lad – Donald installed his first daughter in the gatehouse, told her to look after the place, paid her a cursory stipend. She has been there ever since.

Valerie has lived off the land all her life. She hates the fucking land. She hates the dirt that gets under her fingernails and into her clothes and hair. She hates the weeds that strangle the crops. She hates the foxes that come in the night for her hens. She hates the hens that get themselves caught, that pick up infections, that peck their own eggs to a gritty pulp before she gets a chance to collect them. She hates the cows that stand there all day looking at her with those blank, accusatory eyes, or that moan into the night after she slaughters their calves. She hates the flies and the wasps and the aphids and the bees and the beetles and the birds and the rats and the mice and all the dirt that won't come out.

She repeats these sentiments to Agatha every time they meet, like a veteran soldier reliving the trauma of war. And she does all she can to destroy the land. Pesticides are her friends. She embraces toxins. If she had her way the whole estate would be concrete and animal traps and barbed wire fences.

She makes Agatha laugh. Last time Agatha was up at Bythwaite Hall, the two sisters walked the perimeter of the estate. Valerie has been doing this every year since before Agatha was born, and now that Agatha owns the property, they do it together. It is the closest thing Agatha has to a family tradition. The walk is just under fifteen miles and it takes the whole day, over moors clad with heather, through copses of oak and ash and hazel. In places, the scent of wild garlic is so strong Agatha has to cover her mouth and nose with her sleeve. In other places, the air is so fresh, she feels as if she could live off just one breath for the rest of her life.

They take lunch with them. Valerie prepares a selection of old-fashioned sandwiches, with fillings like corned beef or salmon paste and cucumber, which Agatha finds herself enjoying despite herself. They eat them while sitting on a dry-stone wall or a tree stump. Valerie calls this walk *The Beating of the Bounds*. Last time they did it Agatha asked Valerie where the phrase came from, and Valerie simply took hold of her long walking stick, made from a branch of yew with a cleft at the top for her to rest her thumb in, and started thrashing at the vegetation at each side of the path.

Valerie walks with her ancient bitch Border terrier, Bunny, and last time, Agatha was able to introduce her to Fedor, who was at that point still quite puppyish. The old bitch will now be able to walk clean underneath the body of the long dog without so much as bowing her grizzled head. Last time, she spent a couple of minutes humouring the puppy's playful advances, then spent the rest of the fifteen miles entirely ignoring him. Fedor kept bending his front legs and lowering his head to the ground, wagging his tail, then letting out a couple of plaintive, high-pitched yelps. After a while he gave up, and while his old cousin trotted after her mistress, tucking herself into the path, nose almost pressed against Valerie's rubber boots, Fedor bounded off, ranging across the heather, jogging between tussocks and shrubs, jumping over muddy puddles, then stooping to bury his nose in interesting scents.

Agatha led the way. The path was thin and the grasses on either side were high and uneven, and rigid with frost. The sisters could only walk in single file. Valerie was slower than she had been before.

'Valerie, how old are you?' Agatha asked.

'It's rude to ask a lady her age. Didn't your mother teach you that?'

Instead, Agatha did the calculations in her head. 'You must be at least eighty.'

'I suppose I must be.'

'You are very fit for someone of that age.'

'I suppose I am.'

They continued to walk. Valerie then asked Agatha if she was still embroiled in 'that spot of bother with the mucky lasses'.

Agatha explained that she was, but that she was working with the police to sort something out. They would probably make some arrests soon.

Valerie dug her stick into the ground and leant down on it, then turned round to face her young sister. 'There were once an infestation up at big house. Bees, it were. You were still a baby and without father, I was only one around to look after place. I saw them coming in and out through eves so I went in to have a look. There were thousands of them. Do you know what I did?'

'What?'

'I got one of them smoke canisters they put in hulls of warships to clear rats off. I put it in hall and pulled out pin, then legged it. There were so much smoke. You've never seen like. Thick clouds of smoke. Grey, but so grey it were almost blue. It came pouring out of everywhere. It came out through gaps in window frames, out from cracks beneath doors. It came pouring out through tiny holes in brick and plasterwork. Out through chimneys. Out through roof. It was like big house were bleeding. Bleeding its guts out like a pig. It were a sight to see. And it did for the bees. I used to go in to sweep place every spring, and I were still finding them carcasses ten years later.'

Valerie pulled her stick out of the ground and continued to walk, beating at the debris around the path as she went.

Of all the sisters, Valerie is the one who most resembles Agatha, even though she is now old. None of the other sisters look like her at all. In Agatha's opinion, at least.

Agatha cannot know how much she looks like her father. She never met him. People say she looks like her mother. It is a compliment: her mother is an exceptionally beautiful woman. Agatha is beautiful too, but not as breathtakingly beautiful as Anastasia, and whatever it is in her that has diminished her mother's perfection must come from her father. She isn't sure what this essence of him is, but it is certainly something that Agatha and Valerie share.

The only point of reference Agatha has for how her father looked is photographs, gaudy paintings, and her own appearance and that of her sisters. Although it might seem as if the photographs or paintings would offer the most accurate, faithful, true-to-life portrait of the man, this is not the case at all, for the photographs and paintings are not alive. They do not move, they do not breathe, they do not make a sound, they do not smell like him, they do not reveal character, mannerisms, gait. The best approximation Agatha can make for the father she never met comes as a composite of herself and his other children. Agatha and these five other women each carry a portion of his whole.

The journey from central London to Ryedale is mostly on motorways and dual carriageways. Agatha suffers from motion sickness so is unable to read in the car, but she listens to an audiobook about the Thirty Years War. At the halfway point of the journey they pull in at a motorway service station so Fedor can stretch his legs.

Agatha generally prefers to stay in the car during these breaks to avoid the fat, lumpy people who trudge from the car park to the fast-food restaurants. They spill coffee and sugary drinks on the floors and tables and their children shout and scream. They can't use the toilet without strewing paper all over the floor or pissing on the toilet seat. The thought of these communal lavatories makes her feel ill. All those ugly, dirty, stupid creatures pissing and shitting and menstruating in the cubicles next to her.

On this occasion she's not permitted to remain in the car. Anastasia wants to buy a new lipstick. She opens the back door of the car and drags Agatha out, insisting she help her choose. Agatha tries to persuade her to wait until they are back in London so she can go to Selfridges or Harvey Nichols or a Mayfair boutique, but Anastasia apparently wants the lipstick immediately. Agatha goes with her into the service station and finds a make-up concession inside a small branch of Tesco. Her mother is such a child.

They stand together for several minutes, passing shades to each other, arguing over hues, smudging testers on to the backs of their hands.

'You are absolutely not buying a glittery one. Absolutely not.'

'You're not the boss of me.'

They try more testers and smear more colours on the backs

of their hands. They hold the lipsticks against their faces and look into the square mirror at the side of the concession to check if the colour complements their skin tones.

'Let's get one for you too,' Anastasia suggests.

'I'm not going to buy my make-up from a stand at a motorway service station.'

'Oh but it's good enough for me, is it?' There's hurt in her voice, hurt that's been building from these last few months of cold dismissal from her daughter.

'No, it's not. That's why I suggested you wait. And if you can't wait until we're back in London then at least let's pop into somewhere in Ripon or Helmsley. They will stock some better brands.'

'Yes, yes, they all stock those brands that look the same. You want to dress me up like some horsey aristocrat. Well, I'm sorry, Agatha, but that just isn't me. I like lipstick with blue glitter and if you have a problem with that, well it's tough.'

There's no reasoning with her. She's so sensitive these days.

'You can wear whatever you like when you're picking up men on the French Riviera but excuse me if I don't want to turn up in the owners' enclosure with a mother who looks like a prostitute.'

Anastasia carefully places the lipstick back on to the stand, turns to her daughter and slaps her hard across the face.

That's another thing about her mother: she watches too much daytime TV.

Anastasia is wearing several rings on each finger. They caught Agatha's skin and there's a small amount of blood on her upper lip.

A middle-aged woman in a blue uniform is stacking sandwiches into a nearby fridge. She stops mid-motion, turns towards the scene. Her eyes are open wide.

'What the fuck you looking at, you dumb bitch?'

The shop worker scurries away to the side of the shop, quickly types a code into the keypad on a locked door and disappears behind it.

'I cannot believe you just did that,' says Agatha quietly.

Anastasia rummages in her handbag and pulls out a fresh tissue. She moves it towards her daughter's face to wipe away the blood. Agatha takes a step back.

'You will never touch me again.'

'Oh please. Oh please. That was nothing. If that was the worst you've had, then you've led a very easy life indeed, my dear.'

'Maybe so. But I won't be treated with so little respect.'

'How would you like me to treat you? Would you like me to bow and curtsey; treat you like a little princess because you've got your money now? And where did that money come from? Did you earn it? Did you fight for it? Was it your skin and sweat and blood that secured it? No. It was mine. All mine. Oh, my sweet naive precious little princess. If you only knew the things I had to do to give you this life. The things I've done. The things I've seen done. The things that have been done to me. But no. You believe it, don't you? You really believe it? You believe that you have these luxuries because of your own superiority.'

'The business has gone from strength to strength under my management. You would see if you ever bothered to study the figures. But you wouldn't understand even if you did look. You can't read. You certainly can't count. You know nothing of finance and business. And it wasn't you who built this fortune; it was my father. And it's clear that though I never met the man, I take after him rather than after you. He built an empire from scratch. All you've ever done is find rich and powerful men to cling on to. And that's a skill, is it? That's a skill? That's something I should admire you for, be proud of, emulate? You think I'm embarrassed of you? Well then, yes. Yes I am. Of course I am. How could I not be? You're nothing but a whore. A whore, a whore, a whore.'

The blood above Agatha's lip is beginning to dry. She takes the paper tissue from Anastasia's hand and uses it to dab the cut.

Anastasia's face settles into an expression Agatha can't quite read. She might be about to apologise or she might be about to spit in her daughter's face. After a short pause, she says, 'Your position is under attack on a number of different fronts. Your sisters are still trying to prove that either you or Donski's last will is illegitimate. That band of hookers have kicked up a huge fuss. The newspapers have become involved – the left-wing press because you're rich and because of your political donations; the right-wing press because the roots of your business are sordid, and also because you're a woman and a foreigner in their eyes. You need your friends at this moment. You need your mother.'

'I have everything under control. When I need help, it will come from well-educated, qualified, trained professionals, whose services I will pay for. You don't know anything about it.'

'I don't know anything about it? I have been defending your fortune your whole life. I've been fighting your half-sisters since the moment I popped you out. I used to go to arbitration with your mouth clamped around my tit. I know what they're like. Don't underestimate them. They would rather see everything crumble than allow the estate to remain under your control. You can use your lawyers and your politicians and your policemen and your business speak all you like, but do not forget how this fortune was won – because that is what they will use against you.'

Agatha doesn't answer immediately. A family with small children comes into the shop. They busy themselves at the refrigerators, selecting and reselecting combinations of sandwiches, wraps, fizzy drinks and packets of crisps that fit the shop's meal deal. They're oblivious to the scene on the next aisle. The dad is wearing a checked shirt and faded blue jeans. He becomes more and more irritated by his wife and two elder children who keep changing their minds and squabbling over the last BLT. The mother intervenes with suggestions of sharing but this is poorly received. Only the youngest child, a girl of about five, stands back from her family and watches Anastasia and Agatha as they argue.

The little girl sees the face of the older woman crumple in anger then relax in despair. She sees the colour of her cheeks range from red to white to red. She sees tears build at the corners of her eyes then boil over and drip down her face. The older woman says the work 'fucking' a lot. The little girl knows this word because her older sister whispers it to her between mouthfuls at the dinner table then giggles then whispers it again behind her hand then giggles. She sees the older woman turn and leave the shop with a lipstick clenched in one hand and her handbag in the other. The younger woman, whom the little girl cannot fathom as a daughter because daughters are little children like her, stands still.

Agatha goes to the till and waits for the checkout assistant to re-emerge. She pays in cash for the lipstick her mother has taken, sliding loose change over the counter one coin at a time.

Set in Silver

'I was an idiot for trusting that bitch. But whatever. Damage done. Lesson learned. I've moved on.' Precious has not moved on. 'The thing that fucks me off, though, is that it was so blatantly obvious something like this was going to happen. I should have spotted it a mile off.'

'If she was a bloke you would have,' says Tabitha. 'We're constantly on the lookout for dodgy blokes – men who pay you for one thing then demand another, men who don't pay what they've agreed to pay, men who pretend to be all charming then are complete jerks. We're wise to that. But with a woman it's a whole other game.'

Tabitha is standing by the kitchen counter staring at the toaster. It is sitting at a jaunty angle, closer to the edge of the surface than it should be. She pushes it back against the wall. 'Is it just me or is this toaster further forward than it used to be? I shift it back every morning, and it just creeps forwards again over the course of the day.'

Precious ignores her.

'Do you have to move on though?' Candy is sitting by the little table in the corner. The window next to her is open at the bottom, and her arm is dangling out, drooping at the wrist, a lit cigarette in her hand. She keeps leaning towards the opening, taking a drag, exhaling, then rejoining the conversation. 'Isn't there anything you can do about it?'

'Like what?'

'Someone can't just take a photo of you and put it all over the place without your permission.'

'Yes they can. Of course they can. Do you think the

paparazzi ask celebs for permission before selling photos of them arse over tit at 4 a.m.?'

'That's different.'

'How?'

'Precious invited this photographer up to the flat. She posed for her.'

'More fool me,' Precious says. 'If anything, that makes it even less likely I'll be able to do anything about it. God, I'm such an idiot. It's like inviting a known burglar into your home then being surprised when they make off with your jewellery.'

'Fuck her,' says Tabitha. 'Fuck Mona Beardsley. Fuck her to hell.'

Tabitha throws down the pamphlet she is holding. It is a programme for a photography exhibition. The photograph of Precious that Mona took in her bedroom three months before is the image that has been selected to advertise it.

Tabitha had been out for longer than usual that morning. She came back from the shops with a grim expression and thrust the brochure towards Precious. Tabitha had seen a much larger version of the image on a poster by the entrance to the Tube and jogged over to the gallery to see what it was all about.

Young Scarlet is in the room with them. She is leaning over to look at the brochure Tabitha threw on to the floor. She puts on a superior voice and says, 'If it helps, it's a very powerful image.'

Precious looks down too. She sees herself rendered in black and white. There is little contrast between the light and shade, meaning that the whole picture, herself included, has a silvery quality. It appears to shimmer, even though the paper is matte. It looks old, like the photos of people's grandparents she used to see on mantelpieces when she worked at clients' houses, only the subject is different. She is sitting on her bed in her underwear, leaning back with an expression on her face that she doesn't recognise. It is at odds with everything she thinks about herself and feels about her life. She looks scared. She has been captured at a moment of uncharacteristic vulnerability, but this is the version of her that everyone will see. They will look at her and believe they know her. They will be moved by this beautiful, powerful image of a poor, fragile woman, and not realise it is a lie.

Precious recently saw a photo of Agatha Howard. She doesn't own a computer and only uses her phone for contacting friends and family, or the occasional game of Solitaire. Neither does she have a Facebook profile or a Twitter account and she rarely uses email. It wouldn't have occurred to her to stalk an adversary online.

It was Tabitha who had alerted her to the possibility. She had been to the pub with Crystal, and Crystal showed her a picture of Agatha Howard that she had found. Tabitha came home and showed Precious, along with an article from a village newspaper in Yorkshire that connected Agatha Howard to some local job cuts.

'She looks like a right bitch,' Tabitha said.

Precious looked at the photo of Agatha. It had been taken at a high-society function, and she was standing with a man and a woman, and others could be seen behind, milling about holding glasses of champagne.

The men were wearing dinner jackets and shining black shoes. The women were wearing dresses that reached to the floor.

Agatha Howard's dress was black. Black is the most elegant colour but also the most clandestine. It's a colour to hide behind. Agatha Howard's hair was long and blonde. It reached to her chest, and was sleek and precise. She was very beautiful. She had high cheekbones and bright blue eyes, her face was symmetrical and she was tall and slim.

Precious found herself using her fingers to zoom in on the image. She expanded and enlarged parts of Agatha Howard's face and body, and the faces of the people around her, as if

Precious could find clues about her opponent from these close-up sections of skin and black silk; from the way she clutched her champagne flute, to the way she stood with one foot slightly in front of the other.

It was strange to see the face of the person who had caused them all so much grief. Precious couldn't decide whether her first impression of the woman was informed just by the photo or by her knowledge of what the woman had done to them. She looked cold, withdrawn, as if everything around her was dangerous and disgusting, unclean and unkind. Precious and Tabitha were specks of dirt beneath this woman's French-polished fingernail, to be gouged out and flicked away.

'She looks terrified,' says Precious, partly in response to Tabitha's earlier comment.

After this, they tried a couple of times to contact Agatha Howard and arrange a face to face chat. They never received any reply.

Later, after Candy and Young Scarlet have left, Precious gets a call from her eldest son, Marcus. His girlfriend is pregnant again and Precious is eager for updates. She asks him about Nicky's antenatal classes and plans for the birth. They speak about his work situation and the prospect of paternity leave, and they arrange a shopping trip the following weekend so Precious can buy them various essentials ahead of the birth. At first Marcus says she doesn't need to do this, that they can afford to buy these items themselves, but Precious insists and Marcus gives in quickly.

Marcus and his girlfriend already have a daughter, Connie, which is not short for Constance but a standalone name. It is Connie on her birth certificate.

Precious makes a point of spoiling Connie. She wants her to grow up loved, never doubting that she is loved. She wants her to wear warm clothes from expensive shops that last for years rather than months, but which will be replaced regularly anyway. She wants her to go to a posh private school and make friends with posh private-school children and wear a posh little uniform Precious can tease her about when she comes home.

Tabitha has been trying to teach Precious how to knit pullovers and leggings for Connie, but so far the results have been disappointing, and Tabitha has been quickly and efficiently finishing off most of the projects on Precious's behalf, before Precious wraps them in tissue paper and a bow and writes a little note 'Love from Nanna'.

Then Marcus says, 'I saw you had another interview in the paper.'

Precious stops speaking immediately. She thought neither of her sons knew of her profession. She thought they believed she still worked in a beauty salon. She was careful in those interviews. She wore a mask and did not give away personal details, except her first name. The thought of Ashley and Marcus knowing their mother is a prostitute makes her feel ill. She feels no shame for her own sake but young men can have a strange sense of honour that extends to all their female relatives. It is one thing to feel at ease about her choices in life but another to be easy about them when around her sons.

She says, 'What interview?'

'The one in the weekend supplement, about all the evictions. You look lovely in the photos. Behind the mask, that is.'

Precious says nothing. Tabitha is in the kitchen, emptying the dishwasher. Precious can hear the clink of cutlery and crockery in one ear, and her own silence in the other.

Marcus continues, 'You're getting quite a following. The things you've said about property ownership and renting and gentrification and all that have really hit a nerve. You're a major hashtag.'

'I know,' she says.

'How many interviews is this now? I've counted twelve.'

'Fifteen, including the radio ones. I was on BBC Radio London and LBC.'

'I should be keeping a scrapbook, for the grandchildren.'

'Marcus—'

'I think it's great what you're doing, Mum. You've got a real talent for this kind of thing. You should've gone into politics or something.'

Precious is silent again.

'Anyway, Nicky's making lunch, I should go and help her. But I'll see you next weekend, yeah? And maybe talk in the week.'

'Okay,' says Precious.

'I love you, Mum.'

'I love you, Marcus.'

Precious presses the red dot on her iPhone to hang up the call. Tabitha comes through from the kitchen with a dust-cloth and a bottle of furniture polish. She notices the grave look on her friend's face.

'You all right, love?'

'Yeah,' replies Precious, unconvincingly. She puts the phone face down on the sofa and gets up. She goes through to the kitchen to pour herself another coffee. She places the filled mug in the microwave. As she waits she leans forward with both hands pressed on to the kitchen counter. She goes back into the other room before the microwave has finished. She says, 'You know that thing we were talking about the other night?'

Tabitha is at the table, brushing crumbs from its surface into her hand. She turns towards Precious and makes a noise of recognition.

'I'm thinking of going for it. I mean, what have I got to lose? Other than, for example, my self-respect.'

Tabitha sprays the furniture polish on to the table and scrapes the white foam across the wooden surface with the cloth. 'You won't embarrass yourself,' she says. 'How could you? You're so good at this stuff.'

Tabitha takes a handful of crumbs to the kitchen and deposits them in the bin. Then she brings through a couple of glossy holiday brochures that were on the countertop. She and Precious have been idly contemplating a European city break.

'Budapest or Bucharest?'

Precious does not respond. She has sat back down on the sofa and is swirling the dark steaming coffee in her mug, waiting for it to cool.

'It turns out Marcus knows all about what I do for a living,' Precious says.

Tabitha nods. 'I thought he probably did, love. He's not daft. Ashley too?'

Precious shrugs. 'I didn't ask about that. I assume so. To be honest, that would explain why he hasn't been answering my calls recently. Marcus was okay with it though.'

Tabitha comes to sit next to Precious. The sofa springs squeak as she settles herself. 'Marcus has got that nice girlfriend. She probably set him right on it. Ashley is a bit younger, more hot-headed. He'll care more about what his friends might think, but he'll come round.'

'Do your family know?'

'What family?'

Precious nods.

'They weren't my family long before I went on the game though,' says Tabitha. 'It's different with you. You've had a different life.'

Precious takes Tabitha's hand. 'If I'm going to stand, I'm not sure there'll be any time for either Budapest or Bucharest. It'll be campaigning round the clock from the sound of it. That all right by you?'

'That's all right by me.'

Birds of Paradise

Filming is behind schedule. Tempers flare. Systems of account-ability and delegation break down. Budgets are stretched. The set is a mass of cables and switches and lights and cameras and actions and glass and metal and plastic and rubber and silicon chips and electrical pulses and duct tape and health and safety notices and Perspex and full technicolour and folding chairs and building facades with no backs and boxes with no contents and books with no words and fine powder the shade of any conceivable skin tone and powder of every other shade that shimmers and sparkles and is painted on to ladies' eyelids so their faces flash like birds of paradise. There are blunt swords and hollow war hammers and dogs and horses, and digital devices that pretend to be analogue and electronic devices that pretend to be mechanical, and blue and green screens and sensor dots all over people's faces and hands and ice buckets of champagne and healthy options in the canteen and a gym for keeping fit and an on-set masseuse and a ban on mobile phones, and gossiping in the hallways and – for other people – lots of admin, and – for Lorenzo – lots of self-enforced networking, lots of making the most of things, lots of giving it everything, and then sometimes lots of hiding in dressing rooms, lots of slipping away to the local village for a solitary pint, lots of reminding himself of why he wanted this in the first place, lots of smiling and nodding and 'Yes please' and 'Fine, thank you' and false laughter he hopes sounds real.

Lorenzo isn't due on set until 2 p.m. and is sitting in a little rented cottage on the edge of a small village called Coomby, which is somewhere in Yorkshire. The studios are at the other end of the village, housed within a series of converted aircraft hangars on an old RAF base. There's a scrubbed wooden table and a wood-burning stove. He feels like he's on holiday, only his days are filled with sitting about in a converted aircraft hangar with no natural light.

Lorenzo spends the morning flicking through yesterday's *Financial Times*, which he picked up from the green room the day before after the other broadsheets had been taken. He scans the paper, its pink pages blushing with wealth. It is possible to buy shares in Manchester United. What an odd thought.

The hanging around isn't all bad. Lorenzo has made friends with some of the other actors. Clive and Andy have small parts as the guards of the brothel which Lorenzo's character is meant to run. There is Jenina, with whom he also shares scenes. She's playing an old prostitute who is now more of an administrator. He's also friendly with the women who play the many and various whores, but most of them keep themselves to themselves. They stand naked in the background of scenes, lounging around or pretending to perform sex acts. They have facilities in a different part of the building and are only brought into the filming area at the last minute and are taken away again at the end.

There is also Eddie Kettering. Eddie Kettering is a star. He has a leading role. He is a hero, a love interest, a talent, a body, a face, a sensation, a phenomenon. Lorenzo has a couple of scenes with him. Yesterday they had lunch together in the canteen.

'Big day tomorrow,' said Eddie as he slid into the seat opposite Lorenzo with his lunch on a tray.

Lorenzo nodded.

'You ever done any sex scenes before?' Eddie asked. He spoke with an affected East London accent, though Lorenzo and everyone else knows he went to Harrow.

'Not like this one. When I played Othello, there was a sort of sex scene with Desdemona, but it was – you know – more abstract, kind of behind some net curtain things. And then those net curtains were used as her handkerchief later on when Othello finds the handkerchief.

'Oh right,' said Eddie. 'Hot.'

Lorenzo laughed blankly. 'Yeah,' he said.

'They're okay,' said Eddie. 'Sex scenes, I mean. I've done a few. It depends on how fit the girl is, and not for the reasons you might think. I mean, first off, there's nothing sexy at all about doing a sex scene, and actually you probably want to be doing one with someone on the less hot side in case of accidental boners. But also, if you're doing one with a super-hot girl, it'll go on for ages. All of the techies and producers come along and find ways to make it last for as long as possible so they can get a proper look.'

Eddie acted as though he was telling a joke, so Lorenzo responded with a laugh.

'Fuck only knows what today will be like. I've never done an orgy before. Not on film anyway.' Eddie didn't actually wink but the look he gave Lorenzo had a similar meaning. 'It's not with any big-name girls though,' Eddie continued. 'Just with a bunch of extras. I bet the crew will still want to make it last though. You're just watching on, aren't you? Your character, I mean.'

'Um yeah, I think that's the idea.'

'Love it. What a pervert!' Eddie chuckled to himself. Later in the conversation, however, he did say something of interest to Lorenzo. 'Hey, I had a chat with my agent this morning. The showrunners are already thinking of commissioning another season. You should get your agent on to that early. I see your character being a real fan favourite. You should have a lot of bargaining power next time around.'

'That'll be good, I guess.'

Lorenzo folds away the newspaper and goes to pour himself another coffee. He hasn't eaten any breakfast. He's trying to lose weight, contrary to the instructions of the show's producer, as it was potentially affecting the continuity and also they wanted Lorenzo's character to be 'a bit chubs'.

Lorenzo goes into the shower and has a wank and a wash then dries and dresses and goes out to the pub in the village. He's meeting Eddie there so they can walk over to the studios together.

It's a short walk. The ground is firm from a week of frosts. He passes a freshly painted postbox and sees that it's embossed with the GR of one of the Georges but he doesn't know which. He likes noticing that kind of thing. There's a wide, open village green and a couple of people have dogs off lead. Lorenzo is a little afraid of dogs and one's a ferocious looking husky, only larger. He crosses the green but gives the dogs a wide berth. The pub is called the Queen's Cushion. A climbing rose covers half the front wall, at this time of year all thorns and dead wood and lofty aspirations and biding its time. The pub has a large porch with a pointed roof and slate floor, and a place for putting muddy wellies. There is no stereo, but a fire crackles a primitive tune.

Lorenzo orders a pint of Black Sheep and pays close attention as the brown liquid splashes to the bottom of the tall glass and collects into a froth. When he was in London he drank lager for speed and ease, but on a day like this and in a pub like this it's only right to have something bolder. The barmaid places the bitter on the counter and takes Lorenzo's coins. The liquid settles slowly and Lorenzo takes his first sip while still at the bar.

'You up here on holiday?' she asks him.

'Actually, I'm here for work.'

'Only I've seen you a few times now and I thought it was getting to be a long holiday.' She chuckles to herself, though Lorenzo didn't realise she was making a joke.

'Ah, no, I'll be here for a little while yet. I'm in a cottage up the hill.'

'Oh, aye,' she says.

She doesn't ask him about his work. He's been led to believe people in the North are extremely friendly but so far he hasn't

230

found that to be the case. It's not that they're cold. They just say what's needed to be said and leave it at that.

Lorenzo leaves the bar and goes to sit by the fire. He looks around at the pictures on the walls. They are, for the most part, drawings, watercolours, and prints of hunting scenes. Fox hunting, game-bird shooting. There's a corkboard with notices pinned to it advertising a local yoga class, an amateur production of Ibsen's *Public Enemy*, and an anti-fracking campaign group, also called 'Public Enemy'. Another notice advertises a new fitness scheme in which people from cities come out to the countryside in the evenings and weekends and work on farms instead of going to the gym. They can shift bales of hay or do scything or heavy lifting, and they pay the farmer rather than the other way around. There's an app for it. Lorenzo takes a photo and sends it to Glenda. She'll see the absurdity. He's missed her these last couple of months. He wonders what she'll think about the show when she sees it. She was so eager for him to go for the audition and then afterwards, for him to take the part, but she hadn't read the script. She didn't know about the kinds of things he was required to act out. A couple of days ago he had to film a scene in which his character held down a prostitute, someone who was new to the brothel, while she was raped by two men. The character, although she had no lines, was meant to be fourteen, but for legal reasons was played by a young-looking eighteen-year-old. While filming, the director kept instructing Lorenzo to hold the girl's wrists tighter, tighter. 'We have to believe that she can't get away. You're holding her so loosely she could easily escape.' Lorenzo had queried the direction on the grounds that he didn't want to hurt the girl. 'Oh god, I'm fine,' she said, happily. 'Go for it.'

A couple of weeks ago, Lorenzo attended a preliminary press conference about the show. There was already a lot of hype surrounding it and some early trailers. At the press conference one of the show's creators was asked about the violence: the graphic portrayals of violence, physical and sexual. The journalist asking the question then added an explanatory comment which contained the phrase 'the current climate'. The show's creator, who was called Nick and had been the silent man at Lorenzo's audition, responded that he saw the project as 'fundamentally feminist'. When asked what he meant by that, he responded with the assertion that if we accept sexual violence is an epidemic within society, that it happens everywhere all the time, then we have a duty as artists and writers to show it in all its horror, and that if artists and writers don't show it in all its horror then they were doing a disservice to the victims of sexual violence, and in fact if they 'cut away' the implication was that there was something shameful about being the victim of violence. In other words, we have a duty to bear witness.

Lorenzo was sitting at the end of the long table. The famous actors and producers were towards the middle. As Nick said these things Lorenzo turned in his seat and paid close attention to his facial expressions and body language. He was pleased with himself, there was no doubt about that. Lorenzo thought it unlikely that Nick was motivated to create this TV show out of a desire to address sexual violence in society.

The content of the TV show was making Lorenzo confront all sorts of things about himself he hadn't thought about in years.

Lorenzo had a girlfriend at school. He was handsome and popular and he had a vulnerability about him that drew girls closer to him. He had lots of offers. The girl who became his girlfriend was one of his best friends. Her name was Anabel, and soon after her sixteenth birthday, when they were both in Year 11, she told Lorenzo that she was in love with him. She watched a lot of BBC adaptations of Jane Austen novels so, although they were young, she declared her feelings in overblown terms. The proposition had not occurred to Lorenzo at the time but it was a natural enough progression. They already spent much of their time together. People around them were getting boyfriends and girlfriends and, although

Lorenzo never spent much time thinking about girls, when Anabel made the suggestion, he realised that if he were to have a girlfriend, as he probably should at some point, he would want it to be someone like Anabel. At first, very little changed. But soon, when he went round to her house after school, instead of watching TV or getting on with homework, they sat on the couch kissing.

Lorenzo has always enjoyed kissing and regrets its relegation in adult life to foreplay. He and Anabel began their relationship with nothing but kissing, and hours were spent rolling around with each other.

Lorenzo generally got an erection during these episodes and after a while Anabel began to reach down and hold his penis, first over his clothes and then beneath them. He followed her lead and reached down and touched her between her legs, where it was hot and wet. He found coarse hair and neat folds of soft skin. He most enjoyed the feel of her breasts. She had truly wonderful breasts, even then, and certainly now. Lorenzo and Anabel are still friends. He fondled her breasts with both hands and gently squeezed her nipples, which made her moan and sigh. He remembers liking this.

After they had been boyfriend and girlfriend officially for six months, and celebrated a six-month 'anniversary' with a trip to the local Odeon, Anabel mentioned to Lorenzo that her parents were away for the weekend and would he like to stay over? He said that he would, knowing what was implied and expected.

They began in the usual way. Music from the hi-fi cut through the silence and dulled any embarrassing sounds. Anabel suggested they investigate a rack of wine bottles her parents kept in the cupboard beneath the stairs. They chose a bottle of red at random, though Lorenzo pretended to recognise the label. They drank several glasses each and danced before starting to kiss. They took off each other's clothes and stood fully naked before one another for the first time. Anabel looked different fully naked. Lorenzo had seen naked sections, but never all of it together. Instead of being a series of female body parts, she was a whole creature. This changed everything, though he could not say why. He realised it must be the same with him. He was no longer the parts of his body she has touched while kissing him; those parts which were male. He was all of the other parts as well.

He felt suddenly shy: all stomach and lungs and bladder. As he lost his nerve, she became determined. He could not tell if she was moved by sexual desire or by a desire to get the job done. It seemed to him it was the latter. He knew her well and this was her homework face. She pulled him towards the bed and then pulled him on top of her. In their kissing she always made the first move but this time she lay back, still in charge, but somehow instructing him with her posture to take the lead. He was the man, he realised. He knew men were supposed to take the active role, but he felt weak and small and childish. He managed to get on top of his old friend and put his dick where he was supposed to put it. He pushed and was met with more resistance than he expected. Anabel's face still expressed determination, but beneath the determination Lorenzo saw fear and pain. He pushed again and she actually cried out, but not in pleasure. He wanted to ask her if he was hurting her or if she would like him to stop but he knew that if he did those things he would really lose his nerve and his dick would go all limp along with the rest of his body.

He reminded himself that sex was supposed to be the best thing in the world. There were tears in Anabel's eyes. He reminded himself that this was what Anabel wanted. He pushed again. Something inside her snapped. He found himself further inside her than he expected, which is strange because he had assumed he had been fully in previously. He was so shocked he pulled out, and she screamed again but said through tears and a clenched jaw, 'No, no, keep going, I like it.'

Lorenzo didn't like it. He didn't like it at all. There was

blood on the sheets. He had heard some kind of vague rumour about blood, though he had not anticipated quite as much. He looked down and saw blood on the condom hanging from his now-limp dick. He pulled it off in horror and threw it on to the bed. He felt certain what he had done was illegal. His friend was bleeding and crying and it was his fault. He had just assaulted her, surely. If that was not assault, then what was? Lorenzo made his excuses and rushed to the bathroom, shaking. He was desperate not to cause offence and was terrified that his response would have done so. Teenage girls always thought everything was their fault.

When Anabel came to find him she was dressed. She brought his clothes too, folded neatly. He had showered in her bathroom and wrapped himself in a fresh towel. He changed back into his clothes. They went downstairs to drink orange squash. Anabel ended up comforting Lorenzo rather than the other way around, which seemed absurd to Lorenzo even at the time.

There was no need to break up with her. When they returned to school on Monday it was clear that their relationship was over. A couple of months afterwards Anabel started going out with a boy from a different school whom she met at an orchestra club. Lorenzo was fairly sure they started having full sex almost immediately. He and Anabel remained friends but did not speak of the encounter again, although it crystallised Lorenzo's own understanding of desire. He found Anabel and many other women physically appealing. He still does. He likes the way they look and feel, but desire is not about whether a body is drawn in curved or straight lines, but about the exchange of power. With Anabel he was expected to subjugate. This seemed to be what she wanted or thought she wanted, or a mode into which they both couldn't help but slip.

Eddie Kettering arrives late to the pub and doesn't have time to get a drink before they head off. The barmaid glares at him as he sits down next to Lorenzo without buying anything, and when Lorenzo says goodbye to her on the way out she doesn't look up.

Outside, Lorenzo raises his hood against the cold. It is the shortest day of the year and though early afternoon, the bare hedgerows and fence posts on the horizon are tempting grey night. On the walk, they chat about their Christmas plans, and Christmases they remember from childhood. When they arrive at the studio, they go to their separate dressing rooms. Lorenzo sits in front of a mirror while a make-up artist smears pastes across his cheeks and eyelids. Then he dresses in gaudy silk robes and goes out on to set where an assistant director is explaining the purpose of the scene.

'Basically this is the point at which our hero – that's you, Eddie – starts to realise the battalion he's been placed with is full of absolute bastards. They're all in the brothel going at it and smashing up the joint, and our pimp – that's you, Lorenzo – is stood there, like, with dollar signs in his eyes basically, and our hero is, like, Wait a second, this isn't right. This is the turning point when he decides to go it alone. So, you know, important stuff.'

Lorenzo gets into position. Eddie Kettering gets into position. The soldiers get into position. The extras playing the prostitutes get into position. The scene begins.

Tuck Shop

Laura and Bastian sit together on the swing seat in the garden. The hinges are rusted and squeak when pressure is applied. The garden is overgrown. There are brown patches where the dog has urinated. Laura owns a plump Staffordshire bull terrier cross, called Flora, who has a prominent underbite. On the patio, there is moss, pieces of broken concrete. The plastic garden furniture seems to have rotted, causing Bastian to wonder whether a new strain of bacteria has developed in this garden that can devour hydrocarbons, which can be cultivated and nurtured and spread across the oceans to save the turtles, albatrosses, sea horses and prawns from discarded water bottles and microplastics.

'Did you feel this way two years ago?' asks Laura.

Bastian thinks about her question. 'Yes,' he says. 'But I wouldn't have known to give it that name. I wouldn't have known what name to give it.'

Laura nods slowly, reflectively.

Then Bastian asks, 'How did you feel about that time?'

Laura looks at him and also thinks about the question.

'A lot of it is a blur,' she says. 'My main thoughts and memories about the time we spent together are associated with how it finished. I guess I felt pretty bitter about it all.'

'Bitter?'

'Well, yeah. I'm over it now, but it hurt. It really hurt.'

'Why hurt?' Bastian turns to Laura and the swing seat clunks and screeches.

'Are you serious?' She can tell from his expression that he is. 'You dumping me and just going back to your girlfriend. That hurt.'

'That's not how it happened.'

'Yes it is.'

'No. I mean, I got back together with Rebecca but I didn't dump you.'

'Oh, I'm sorry, are we still together? I didn't realise.'

They sit in silence. Bastian's fingers find a rip in the swing-seat cushion, and he begins to fret the synthetic lining. He never realised Laura wanted anything more. She had always seemed so confident, so in control of what she wanted and when. What he said was his true reflection on events, but it now seems his interpretation was skewed.

He had arrived at Laura's house just after lunchtime. It was she who opened the door, which he'd been hoping for. He knew she lived with her mum and younger siblings and was dreading the process of introducing himself to them before he'd had a chance to see Laura and explain his arrival.

After a while, Laura says, 'You know, Bastian, it is possible not to depend totally on the approval of other people but also to care. I wanted you. And when you went back to her it hurt.'

One of Laura's little brothers comes out of the house with a football under his arm, which is so large compared to his skinny frame he looks like an ant carrying a bulky item of booty. The boy shuffles forward awkwardly.

'What is it?' Laura asks him.

'Ryan and me have got football practice.'

'Ryan and I,' Laura corrects.

'Ryan and I have got football practice, only Simon's mum can't come pick us up because they're in Tenerife.'

'So what do you want me to do about it?'

'Will you take us in the car?'

The boy drops the football and takes hold of his T-shirt, pulling it away from his body and wringing it through his hands. He holds his weight on one foot and then the other. His eyes skip between his sister and Bastian and the ground and the sky.

Laura sighs dramatically. It's a sigh that adults reserve for children.

'Why didn't you tell me about this sooner?'

'Forgot.'

'When did Simon's mum tell you they were going to be away?'

'Don't know.'

'Oh, for goodness sake, Curtis.'

Laura gets up from the swing seat and it falls back and creaks loudly. Bastian plants his feet firmly on the ground to steady it.

'You coming?' Laura says to him.

Bastian would have been happy to go anywhere with Laura but tries not to seem overly enthusiastic. He gets up and follows Laura and Curtis back into the house and waits while the boys rush around collecting their things while Laura shouts instructions at them and looks at her watch pointedly and goes out to the car to start the engine and honk the horn aggressively.

Bastian enjoys seeing this side of her. He sits in the front seat with her and the boys sit in the back with their mess of shin pads and socks and water bottles and goalie gloves.

They drive to the sports ground and the lads go off to join their football training while Bastian and Laura stand together on the sidelines talking.

Laura works for a charitable trust that funds food banks, homeless shelters and support services across the north, but she's currently looking for a new job.

'Whatever you do,' she says, 'don't go and work for a charity. Believe me. In general, they treat their employees like shit.'

'I was thinking of doing some volunteering,' says Bastian. 'I've recently been feeling this need to be a better person, but Glenda says volunteering denigrates the value of labour and that charities prop up capitalism.'

'Fuck Glenda. I mean, she's probably right, as per usual, but do what you want.' Laura laughs.

'Are you set on staying up this way?' Bastian asks.

'I've not got much choice. Someone's got to look after my mum and the kids. But also, I guess I feel a kind of weird commitment to the area. Most people who get Cambridge degrees – first class, by the way – fuck off to London afterwards. But, I don't know, I like it up here.'

'No, I get that. I sometimes fantasise about moving to Cornwall,' says Bastian.

'Why Cornwall?'

'It's my favourite place in the world, probably. I used to go there for the summer when I was a child, back when my mum and dad were still together. Mum used to spend all day painting the sea and the moors and lanes, and I had this, Enid Blyton-esque childhood.'

'Lots of tongue sandwiches and tinned peaches?'

Bastian raises an eyebrow.

'That was my main take-away point from all the Enid Blyton I read as a child,' Laura explains. 'The elaborate picnics. I didn't really understand the concept of eating tongue, so I guess it stuck in my head.'

'I don't think I ever ate tongue.'

The lads finish their stretching and begin a dribbling exercise. The coach is in his early fifties with a red face and a gravelly voice. He issues instructions with encouragement, and jokes and laughs with the boys. Though clearly past his prime, he runs around with them and kicks the ball back to the lads when they overrun it. The football pitch is peppered with molehills like small explosions of feral interference. The white lines need repainting, and the nets between the goalposts hang loose.

'So Rebecca kicked you out, and you decided to get on the train and come and see me?'

When Laura phrases it like that, it sounds bad. Bastian tries to think of a way of explaining that he and Rebecca were unhappy together for a long time; that he regretted things ending with Laura almost from the moment it happened. He felt the need to explain to her that his biggest failing was being totally passive; of sleepwalking through his own life. He hadn't ended things with Rebecca and come to find Laura sooner not because he lacked the desire, but because he lacked the ambition.

Laura waits for Bastian to respond but when he doesn't, she speaks again. 'To be totally honest with you, Bastian, it's slim pickings up here. I haven't had good sex since I moved back home and for whatever reason, despite myself, I just well fancy you. So, although I know in this situation I should be outraged and that I should feel, I don't know, used or disposable or something. Despite that, I am absolutely going to have sex with you as soon as we can get a moment to ourselves. If this makes me weak or a bad feminist or what-ever, never mind.'

After that, the atmosphere changes between them. Bastian becomes suddenly and inconveniently aroused, only there's still another forty-five minutes of football training to watch, and even when they get back to Laura's house it will be full of children and dogs.

But he's thinking about her body. Her strength. The way she pushed back against him as they used to kiss. The way she gripped his arms with her hands; the way she stretched out her long legs when he was inside her, and linked them behind his back, and he felt her thighs against his hips. And the way, when she was on top of him, she rested her weight on his chest with a single hand, and rocked back and forth, and how his breathing came to work with and against her rocking. When Laura wanted something from him, she asked. When he wanted something from her, he asked, and he knew that she would give him a straight answer.

She doesn't think there's anything special about him. Bastian has been led to believe by any book he's ever read and any film he's ever seen that it is good for the person you love to think you're totally one hundred per cent remarkable. All fictional characters seem to very much enjoy being told that they're wonderful and beautiful and intelligent and brave –

the most wonderful and beautiful and intelligent and brave people that have ever existed in the history of the world. But Laura doesn't seem to think Bastian is any of these things, except perhaps beautiful, and that's okay. That's exactly what he wants.

He's average. He's mediocre. He doesn't think these things about himself because he lacks confidence or because he has low self-esteem. He thinks them because they're true.

At school, Bastian and his friends were told that they would rule the world. That wasn't even hyperbole. They were told that they would literally rule the world. The world of business; the world of politics; the world of culture; theatre, film, television. At the time he just thought: fine. But that was before he realised what ruling the world would mean, before he had a chance to decide upon the kind of world he wanted, and the life he wanted within it.

Bastian's eyes follow the line of the football as it's kicked from boot to boot.

'Are you coming?' Laura calls from a few metres away. She's turned and is walking towards the sports centre. 'Tuck shop, yeah?'

Bastian hasn't heard anyone use the phrase 'tuck shop' for years. Bastian jogs after Laura. She doesn't lead him to a tuck shop. They go into an empty changing room at the end of a corridor. Laura pushes Bastian gently against the wall and kisses him, and as she kisses him she lifts her knee so that her foot strokes against his calf and she leans into him with her pelvis and he feels himself go hard, slowly then quickly.

He enjoys the loss of control, of the response his body has to her touch. His mind can just shut down now, and for this he's grateful. There's no point in having a mind anyway, or in personhood at all. As she kisses him and reaches down to unbuckle his jeans, he leans back against the wall, dissolves into it. I am nothing, he realises. I am nobody.

Anastasia

Following their argument at the motorway service station, mother and daughter part company. Anastasia finds Roster waiting by the car. She tells him she'll be making her own way back to London. He doesn't object. He has known her for a long time and knows there is no point arguing.

Anastasia makes her way towards the lorry park to find a likely looking driver. She knows what to look out for – how to find a target, and how to work him. She has played this game before.

It doesn't take long. He looks lonely and eager. He is heading to London and says she can join him. She climbs up into the passenger seat, checking as she does that the interior door handles are still intact and that none of the locks have been tampered with. While he goes off to pay for his diesel, she looks behind and beneath the seats for anything suspicious: rope, cable ties, weapons. All she finds are a packet of tissues and a half-eaten box of Cadbury's Milk Tray. The driver doesn't come across as a psychopathic murderer but you can never be too careful.

The journey south involves a lot of listening. Anastasia has travelled on many long journeys and has listened to lots of talking men. The driver speaks about the roads and the state of the haulage industry. Anastasia is in fact deeply interested in all aspects of business and industry. She is fascinated by the making of things and the ways in which those things get from one place to another and are then transformed from one thing to another thing. That said, she doesn't let the lorry driver know that she finds his conversation interesting. She knows from experience that it can be dangerous to bolster a strange man's sense of self-worth. Almost as dangerous as undercutting it.

Also, he keeps forgetting her name. 'Anna, is it?'

'Anastasia,' she corrects him.

Anastasia isn't her real name. She adopted it when she came to London. Nobody could pronounce her real name but 'Anastasia' was the kind of name these people thought she should have so she gave them what they wanted. Her old name was ugly when pronounced by the English; she did everything she could to forget it.

The journey back to London goes more quickly. Perhaps it's because Anastasia is agitated. She passes the same pylons, the same motorway bridges, the same road signs, albeit reversed. They drive through a thick cloud of fog that has descended since the morning. The fog gets stickier as the city gets closer, as if attracted by its mass.

Anastasia would do anything for her daughter. It is an inescapable, uncomfortable fact. She supposes it is a connection that was established at birth, only Anastasia can barely remember her daughter's birth. She reads about birthing choices that women make these days, in glossy magazines. When she was pregnant she had never heard of birthing choices. She had never realised there were any choices she could make. She was seventeen years old, in a foreign country, under the protection of a man who was old enough to be her grandfather. When she felt the contractions, she was rushed to the nearest hospital. The rest of the process must have been vivid at the time, but it is now a series of facts; not a story but an itemised list. The labour lasted eight hours. Eventually the doctors performed an emergency C-section. Agatha weighed 5lbs 9oz.

Anastasia was left with neither sensory nor visual memories of the events, and they exist for her now as if they happened to someone else. When she thinks about it, it is like looking at the scene through a steamed-up window, slowly wiping away lines with an index finger.

Anastasia presses her index finger against the steamed-up window of the lorry. As she looks out, she begins to form a plan. Who from the old crowd does she still know in London? Which of the men she came over with from Russia still lives there? She thinks about Vlad. When she first met him he was fresh from the KGB, only not the section that dealt with intelligence and espionage, the section that dealt with enforcement. He'd seen the inside of soundproofed torture facilities and knew how to use the equipment there. And there is Mikhail, his heavy. Both are now respectable businessmen and live in Belgravia. They deal in imports and exports and stocks and shares. They are unlikely to want anything to do with this, for the same reason that her daughter wants nothing to do with this.

She had met other hard men through Donski. He came from a criminal background and had always kept a foot on that side of the fence, even after he'd become old and bought property. As the driver speaks, she makes a list in her head of some of the old crowd, judging who she is most likely to be able to find and who will be willing to do the job that needs to be done.

It doesn't take her long to make a decision about whom to approach.

Anastasia is dropped off on the busy Euston Road and walks through Bloomsbury to Soho.

It is nearly Christmas, and the city is full. There are only a few days until the high street closes, so shopping has become frenzied. There is no time for browsing, only purchasing, and the pace of pedestrians has quickened. The lights have been up for weeks and flash with festive messages that only make sense when it's dark. In the dark, they shine brightly and cover the street in beads of colour. During the day, they look awkward, out of place, the tangle of wires resembling bare hedgerows against a cold white sky.

In London, Robert Kerr lies back on his sofa with a can of beer listening to BBC Radio 3. It is incredible how his tastes have changed over the decades. He can't think of any reason for it. When he was a lad he listened to rock and roll. When he joined the gangs he listened to punk. Now he listens to Brahms, Mendelssohn, Schumann, Thomas Tallis, Ralph Vaughan Williams.

This is what people always said would happen but he hadn't believed them. This is what adults tell teenagers.

'Just give it a few years,' they say. 'You won't be able to stand that rubbish.'

That part isn't true. He still enjoys all the music he used to enjoy, just not as much as he did.

A couple of years ago he watched a BBC Four documentary about sound. It talked about hearing. Teenagers' ears are much more sensitive, it said. That's why those high-pitched hummy things outside shops work. Young people can't stand the buzzing so they don't stand around on street corners drinking cider any more. Or something like that.

Actually, Robert can't remember if the government ever actually introduced those high-pitch hummy things or whether it was just a policy that was mooted to curb the rise of the hoodies, such as ASBOs or hugs, and he had just assumed it had happened and got one possible future that existed in the past confused with the actual future that actually happened in the past.

Anyway, the kinds of sounds that come out of a distorted guitar amp are – sonically speaking – a lot more complex than the sounds that come out of a piano. So – sonically speaking – punk music and heavy-metal music are actually lots more complicated than classical music.

Robert pulls himself into a sitting position and finishes the beer. It has become warm and tastes indistinct. Cold beer has all sorts of flavours, even cheap cold lager, but warm beer just tastes warm.

He crushes the can in his right hand and gets up from the sofa. He walks to the other side of the room and throws the can into the bin, then picks up his electric guitar which is sitting on a stand in the corner. It's a 1962 Fender Telecaster in traditional butterscotch, though the nitro is now worn thin. It is probably worth a mint these days. He plugs it into his amp and starts to hash out some chords. He turns up the volume. He looks over to the clock on the wall to reassure himself that his neighbours are at work, then laughs at himself for being so un-punk these days that he gives a fuck.

He is trying to distract himself from thinking about Cheryl. Even he has enough self-awareness to recognise that.

'We think she's been trafficked, forced into prostitution.' That's what the policeman said. The top policeman who came in to question him in the interrogation room, the man he sees on the telly and on campaign posters all over the city. They thought Robert was involved. He wasn't. But when they let him out, he got to thinking: the Archbishop's cellar is beneath the brothel, and that's where Cheryl lived. Robert tries to imagine the women he knows there mixed up in that kind of thing. He can't. It doesn't seem like them at all. That Karl, and his new associates, on the other hand . . .

There's a knock at the door. He opens the door and sees a woman he hasn't seen for nearly thirty years.

'Can I come in?' Anastasia asks.

Robert steps back to allow Don's girl inside, only she is not a girl any more and Don is dead.

Anastasia looks around Robert's flat. It has hardly changed at all in nearly thirty years. She sees the same brown sofa, the same table and chairs in the corner, probably been used twice since she was last here, and only twice before that.

A new-looking television with an enormous screen has been placed on the sideboard. The picture is of footballers warming up before a match, but the sound has been muted.

There are unopened letters on the sideboard too, and a stack of takeaway menus.

'I don't have visitors very often,' says Robert. 'Never. And of all the people I thought it might be when I heard the knock,

I think you might have been at the bottom of the list. You or your late husband, back from the dead.'

'It's been a long time,' Anastasia agrees.

The weekend bag Anastasia was taking with her to Bythwaite Hall is slung over her shoulder. She lets it drop to the floor, and she places her small handbag on the table.

'I remember decorating it,' she says. 'Well, I remember choosing colours and materials. It was very fashionable in here when it was first fitted out.'

'Oh aye,' says Robert. 'It was always wasted on me. I've never had an eye for that sort of thing.'

'I never did ask Donski why he gave you the flat. Loyal service?'

'Something like that.'

Anastasia guessed at the time that Robert Kerr was one of her husband's heavies; one of the men who sorted out problems that required a particular kind of sorting.

He offers Anastasia a drink. He hesitates at first. It has been so long since he has had guests, he has forgotten how these things are done, but he sees her eyes move around the flat and eventually to the kitchen and he asks her if she fancies a cup of tea. He has some old teabags in a cupboard, but no milk.

She accepts, more because it's an automatic response than out of any desire for refreshment.

Robert fumbles with the kettle. He maintains a basic level of cleanliness in the flat. He wipes surfaces and occasionally hoovers, but it is only him living here and there seems little point going above and beyond. The kettle is covered in fingerprints and is full of lime-scale. He fills it with water and switches it on, and a couple of minutes later he hands Anastasia a mug of just-boiled water poured over a teabag, which floats on the gently steaming surface.

'My daughter pays you a monthly allowance, yes?'

'If it's your daughter who is in charge of your late husband's estate, then yes, your daughter pays me a monthly stipend.'

Anastasia takes this in. The evasion, then the admission. He is sensitive about receiving this money, she can tell. It is natural for him to be sensitive about it. He needs the money but, equally, it connects him to a past which he would, perhaps, rather not be connected to. They all share this same heritage; the funds its legacy produces. With interest.

Up at the Big House

An old-time rails bookie stands between Agatha and the object of her desire. She is in the members' enclosure with the other owners, trainers, and well-to-do people. The racecourse is stratified according to price but not only according to price. There are cheap sections and expensive sections, but to enter the members' enclosure you have to be invited. Gambling outlets are forbidden so exclusive bookmakers set up stalls along the rails and lean over to serve the affluent customers within.

Agatha is placing a bet at one of these outlets when she sees a young man across the paddock wrestling a spooked colt. He is tall, with a slight but athletic build – the kind boys have in adolescence before they go on to be powerfully built men: soft muscles tucked inside a skin that hasn't yet hardened and grown coarse.

Agatha watches the races from an upper level with a group of acquaintances who have heard something of her net worth. She courts their advances and drinks their expensive champagne. The waiter has put liqueur in the bottom of her flute. It isn't cassis but something similarly fruity. What a bloody stupid thing to do with first-class brut. Another waiter arrives with a tray of canapes, and Agatha tries a few. They are all disgusting. The racecourse obviously employs a chef with a higher opinion of himself than is merited.

Agatha's horse is running in the second-to-last race. His name is Albert's Rule, but she doesn't know why. She let Roster pick the name, and in explanation he mentioned something mysterious about a man he used to know. The horse was a birthday present to him, though he prefers betting on the dogs. Roster has gone to watch the races from the main stand, but before they parted ways in the car park, Agatha secretly tucked an expensive cigar into his jacket pocket. He'll find it when he reaches for his wallet. He likes to smoke when he wins a bet, which is often.

Albert's Rule refuses the starting stalls. The jockey tries all the usual tricks but he won't budge and the referee disqualifies him. What a fucking embarrassment. Agatha has had a lot to drink by this point and she says this out loud. 'What a fucking embarrassment.' She isn't joking but her comment is taken as such by the assembled crowd. They laugh sycophantically.

Agatha has had enough. She leaves abruptly without saying goodbye to anyone. She pushes her way through the crowds on the lower levels and on the terraces outside the enclosure. People are making their way to bookies to place their bets on the last race of the day. She steps over discarded plastic pint glasses and dropped betting slips. Moments ago these pieces of paper contained a world of possible futures, clenched feverishly in expectant fists. Now they are as worthless as Weimar banknotes.

She has half a mind to shout at somebody about Albert's Rule. His shoddy performance was surely the fault of the handler or the jockey or trainer. If she can find any of them she will let them know how she feels. She goes over to the stables. Instead she sees the young lad from earlier.

He is wearing a matching Adidas set of soft jersey joggers and sweater which subtly hug his figure. He has broad shoulders and a skinny waist and strong but slim arms and legs. His neck is lean and long and his Adam's apple protrudes just above his collar. His lips are full and red in the cold, and his cheeks are flushed with exertion.

The horses in the stable are still pumped with adrenalin from their races. They neigh and stamp and dance about in their stalls. The lad is leaning over one of the open half-stalls to reach in and check something on the inside of the door.

Agatha approaches but does not speak. It takes him a while to register her presence. Then he turns around.

'You all right there, love?'

'Fine, thank you.'

He blinks rapidly and smiles. She can tell that he finds her attractive, and also that he is shy.

'Do you work with Thomas Waugh?' Thomas Waugh is the name of the racehorse trainer she employs.

'That I do.'

'He trains several of mine. Albert's Rule was running today.'

The lad's face relaxes at the mention of a horse he knows.

'He's a lovely lad. I take him out on the gallops every morning. He handles like a dream. None of us expected what happened up at the start just now. It's not like him.'

'Yes, well, it was very disappointing, to say the least. But, look, when do you finish up here? I'd like someone to come to the Hall and inspect the stables. I currently don't have any animals at the house itself but I'd like to. Only, the facilities need to be safe. Perhaps you could cast an eye over it.'

'Oh. Er, I guess I could do that for you. Wouldn't you rather it were Mr Waugh?'

'You'll do fine.' Agatha waits.

He says, 'Oh, you mean now?'

'Yes, that would be best.'

'Ah, okay. Well, I'll just ask Mr Waugh.'

'I've already seen him. He said it was fine and that you'd be a good person for the task, that you just needed to finish up a couple of your jobs and then you'd be free to come with me.'

'Right then. Well then. I'll just sort out these last two stalls.'

'I'll wait in my car. It's the Rolls Royce in the members' car park. The blue one. Not the hideous gold one.'

'Okay.'

The flirtation is subtle but effective. He asks for fifteen minutes to finish his work, and Agatha goes and waits by the car. He seems flustered but the decision has been made.

Agatha sends Roster a message, and he arrives in the car park soon after she does. He makes no response to the news they will be waiting for an additional passenger but tucks his copy of the *Racing Post* inside his coat and climbs into the driver's seat. Agatha gets in the back and arranges a cashmere blanket over her knees. The car has been sitting cold, so needs warming. Roster starts the engine, turns up the heating and opens all the vents. He also presses the electric lighter, which is set into the driver's console, and pulls the cigar from his pocket. Agatha watches from the back seat as the node begins to glow, as Roster releases it from its socket and holds the hot tip to the end of the cigar. The dried leaves kindle. Roster wets his lips and sucks on the other end, pulling the first rush of air through the chamber and drawing smoke into his lungs. When he exhales, the car is filled with a thick smog that rises and hangs around his head.

Agatha doesn't mind. He isn't a regular smoker but has enjoyed the occasional cigar for as long as she can remember. She likes the smell, and the way Roster breathes it in and blows it out. When she was a child he used to entertain her with smoke rings, or by exhaling through his long nose.

'You won, then?'

'Two out of the six. I placed in all but one. Up on the day.'

'Congratulations.'

When the lad arrives, Agatha opens the back door, then shuffles across to let him sit next to her. Roster turns on the radio to give them privacy.

Roster finds first gear. The wheels grip the gravel and begin to roll. It is a twenty-minute drive back to Bythwaite Hall, along narrow roads then winding lanes. The hedgerows are frozen bare. The fields were ploughed after the harvest, before the soil became too stiff and turgid, and the lines of orderly furrows have frozen hard, preserved until spring.

They reach the gatehouse, which sits at the edge of the grounds. The lights are on, meaning her sister is at home. Roster took Fedor to Valerie before they left for the races, but Agatha hasn't been to see her yet.

There is a long driveway, edged with beech. Bythwaite Hall

can be seen at the end: a Tudor manor, with a large Victorian extension, and a vast climbing hydrangea.

The car stops by the front door. As Agatha steps out, Roster opens his window and whispers, 'poor chap'. Agatha ignores him. She climbs the steps and the lad follows her in. His rubber-soled boots are still wet from stepping on frosty grass. They squeak on the stone floor. Agatha looks down at his feet as he shuffles, awkwardly.

'It's probably best to take those off,' she says.

He does as he's told and places the boots side-by-side next to the doormat. Agatha offers him a drink.

'A glass of water would be great, thanks.'

'I was going to have something stronger. A whisky?'

'That sounds nice. I'll have whatever you're having.'

Agatha leads him into a sitting room and guides him to a chair. Then she goes over to the drinks cabinet and pours Balvenie from a decanter into heavy tumblers. She holds one out for him, and he gets up again, comes over to her and takes it, then sits back down.

The lad looks around. The walls of Bythwaite Hall are lined with portraits of the previous owners. Before her father bought it, the manor had been in the same family since the fifteenth century. There are hunting scenes with lusty men, muskets and spaniels. There are gilded portraits with neo-classical backdrops, presenting their subjects as paragons of learning; men with torrents of borrowed curls. Then there are vases, coats of armour, coats of arms, hunting trophies.

She can't remember the name of the family who owned the estate. They won the land by making good choices during the Wars of the Roses. Before that, who knows what they'd been. Mercenaries, butchers, peasants. They must have felt very smug by the end, Agatha supposes. They must have thought it would all last for ever. She imagines their descendants living in three-bedroom semis on the outskirts of shitty towns. She imagines them driving Vauxhall Astras and buying lottery tickets in the hope of better times.

She looks over at the lad, as out of place as her, or them.

Why is it she can only feel attraction towards men like this? Younger, less powerful, less experienced. She needs to catch them before they become confidently aware of their place in society.

'How old are you?' Agatha asks.

'Eighteen.'

Good, she thinks. *Old enough*. The last thing she needs is trouble of that kind.

The lad drinks his whisky in a single gulp. The alcohol makes his eyes water. Clearly, his only experience of spirits comes from drinking shots on a Friday night.

'Would you like some more?' Agatha asks. She sips her own whisky delicately.

'Er, yeah.'

She pours again, and he consumes it in the same manner.

'How are you feeling?' Agatha asks.

'All right, thanks. Only, I've been working in the yard all day and I feel a bit minging. Is there anywhere I can get a quick shower? Sorry to ask.'

'It's fine. I'll run you a bath.'

As Agatha and the lad climb the wide staircase upstairs, the last of the natural light is dragged from the Hall and spread to a different part of the world. The place is eerie in the dark. The stairs and wooden floorboards creak as they're trodden, and Agatha can hear the lad breathe loudly and deeply.

The light in the bathroom is bright and reflects against the white tiles. In the centre of the room, there is a bath standing on brass lion's feet. She releases water from the taps and it splashes on the pit of the basin. The sound rings around the room, bouncing off the hard surfaces. Agatha goes to the cupboard and pulls out some expensive bath oils, and she drips them into the running water.

'I've never used owt like that before,' says the lad.

She smiles. There's a chair at the side of the room, facing

the bath. Agatha sits on the chair. The lad stands by the heated towel rail.

'Do you know why I brought you here?' Agatha asks.

'I've got a couple of ideas. I'm not sure it's got owt to do with stables.'

'You're not wrong.'

'I was thinking, maybe, you wanted to get to know me better.' He's not looking at her as he says this but at the running water coming from the taps.

She crosses a leg over the other. 'Do you find me attractive?' she asks.

He seems startled by the question. 'Yeah, obviously. You're like a model.'

Agatha smiles, and feigns bashfulness. She could have been a model, and maybe would have been if it wasn't such a demeaning profession.

Agatha takes a deep breath. The lad is sporting a stupid grin. He seems pleased with himself. She can't decide whether she finds this obnoxious or alluring. 'The bath's ready. Are you going to get in?'

'Sure.' He begins to take off his clothes. He pulls off his socks and tosses them aside. Then he lifts his sweatshirt over his head, and then his T-shirt. He is tensing his muscles and pulling in his waist, to show his body at its best. She likes this. She likes that he's trying to please her.

He loops his thumbs over the elastic of his joggers and pulls them down. He steps out of them and kicks them over to the corner of the bathroom where the rest of his clothes are now piled. He is wearing a pair of old, off-white boxer shorts. He pauses before taking them off. He pulls at the front to make himself more comfortable, then apparently realises that the pants are his only remaining item of clothing, but also that he has agreed to get into the bath, and that obviously he can't back out now, and obviously he wants to fuck this hot woman because what lad wouldn't, and what kind of lad would he be if he didn't?

He pulls the boxers down and stands naked in front of her.

His body is exactly as she hoped it would be.

His stupid grin re-emerges.

She realises she finds it obnoxious and alluring, and alluring because it is obnoxious, and obnoxious because it is alluring.

He steps over the rim of the bath and drops his foot into the water. There is no grace in his movement, but Agatha isn't looking for grace.

The lad washes himself. For the most part his method is practical, efficient, but on occasions he remembers why he's been brought here and he affects a sensual air, leaning back or stretching or flexing muscles in a way he obviously thinks is seductive. Agatha would have found it embarrassing if he wasn't so physically attractive, and if she wasn't so truly turned on.

He gets out of the bath and steps into a towel she holds out for him.

Agatha leads him into her bedroom, which is connected to the bathroom by a short corridor with clothes rails on either side. She instructs him to climb on to the bed. He does. She takes hold of his wrists and draws them above his head, then proceeds to fasten them to the bedposts with a pair of leather belts.

'Kinky,' he says, mundanely.

She takes a handkerchief from the bedside table and stuffs it inside his mouth so he cannot speak. Then she takes another and uses it to blindfold him.

'I won't hurt you,' she says. 'It is simply that I do not like to be touched, or spoken to or looked at. So, here is what is going to happen. I am going to go down on you. Then I am going to climb on top of you and fuck you, then I am going to leave. You won't see me again. Roster will come in and untie you and show you out.'

Agatha slowly undresses and folds her clothes on to a chair at the side of the room. She returns to the bed and places her left hand on his chest. She runs her hand down his body. It is fresh and new and beautiful.

Coup d'état

Soho is a word with no etymology. It sprang to life through declaration, like um . . . or oy!

The Archbishop is the same.

It is said he was born in a little hut in the woods, long before the trees were cleared for pasture, long before the pasture was cleared for houses, long before the houses were divided into flats. The Archbishop has stories of the first speculators who built tenements on the Lammas Land, where the poor folk hung laundry, and grazed their animals come August. It was said he started out as a gravedigger and was seen to hang around the churchyard. 'There are bodies beneath the ground. There are bodies all around.' He points. 'There. There. There.' He speaks of the plague as if he remembers it. He tells them how they thought animals spread disease so they slaughtered them. The bodies of dogs and cats were piled high; food for the rats they used to chase away. His topics of conversation change as quickly as his moods. 'Lord Nelson was here the last night he ever spent on dry land. Came up to Soho to visit his coffin maker. I knew him personally, of course. I could have been with him on that ship.' The Archbishop tells people he went to the same parties as the real-life Casanova and that he remembered the square of land they now call Soho Square when it was trampled by hundreds of aristocrats, who drank and danced until the sun grew hot and the wine and beer and sweat grew stale. The Archbishop tells all who will listen that Casanova stole all his stories of seduction from him because he was too dignified to write them down. He was once a town crier, or so he says. He was once a roaming troubadour, or so he says. He posed for

Joshua Reynolds. He posed for Francis Bacon. He gave Karl Marx all his best ideas and had long drinking sessions with him in his flat on Dean Street. He has been known to go out on to the street and flag down passers-by. He takes people on tours, from the Pillars of Hercules on Greek Street to the statue of Anteros in Piccadilly Circus. 'He is the god of requited love,' the Archbishop tells all who will listen. 'The brother of Eros. Eros creates a desire that is unfilled; Anteros gives us the antidote.'

The Archbishop sits in his cellar, where he always sits, where he has always sat. Over the centuries the buildings around have been torn down and rebuilt, but this one has endured. The cellars are original, dug into the earth with bare rock for floor, bricks and timbers propping up the walls. He is a hoarder. He has filled his space with artefacts. He has kept every pair of shoes he has ever owned. They are laid out next to each other in chronological order, the toes and heels scuffed, the laces snapped, the soles worn away. He has collected items dropped on the street: single gloves, umbrellas, tasteful, minimalist business cards, sunglasses, receipts, maps, bottle tops, curious coins, foreign banknotes. He has brought them back to his cellar and arranged them like precious artefacts in a museum, displayed on shelves and tabletops with little labels relating their provenance. He has a nail from the nail bomb that was let off in the Admiral Duncan pub on 30 April 1999. He has snail shells, discarded by the restaurant above. He has boxes of dead media. There are vinyl records, CDs, old 78s, film negatives in small, medium and large formats, plate-glass prints. And he has books, collected from the bookshops and newsagents that have shut their doors. They are stacked in boxes in no logical order: poetry abuts porn.

Some of his disciples are around him. Paul Daniels comes in.

The man they call Paul Daniels is fuming. His rage has been building for months. He has always been an emotional man, with whirling, tumultuous thoughts. His schemes and ideas in these last months have gathered a kind of physical presence he can almost touch. It is as if, with Debbie McGee gone, his thoughts and feelings have taken on her weight; the place she used to occupy. Only they are louder and more aggressive than his woman ever was. They tug and pull at him and obscure his senses.

Paul Daniels stands in front of the Archbishop and lifts a long index finger in his direction.

'I have come to claim my crown.'

The Archbishop gets up to face his challenger. He shakes his garments. He draws himself up to his full height. Usually frail, he now looks strong. 'The crown is on my head. And that is where it will stay.'

'It's mine,' Paul Daniels protests. 'I found it. I pulled it from the earth. It yielded to me.'

'I am the lord of this manor. I am the ocean to which all rivers lead. If gold is found, I shall have it.'

'You're a thief. You would have nothing if it wasn't for us.'

There are murmurs of accord from the gathered crowd, but when the Archbishop spins around as if to confront those whose voices he heard, they lower their eyes.

The man they call Paul Daniels speaks again. 'You've had your time. We want change.' It is unclear whether he speaks for anyone else in the room, but Paul Daniels, at least, lunges forward and pushes the old man to the ground. The Archbishop puts one hand out to break his fall and the other up to his head to hold on to the crown. He hits the earth. A crunch of brittle bones breaking rings out through the cellar. A shelf is knocked, and decades of tat come tumbling down.

Paul Daniels reaches down for the crown, but the Archbishop is not yet defeated. He kicks out with both legs and brings his adversary to the ground with him. They grapple. Hands are pressed to throats; fingers are pressed into eyes. The man they call Paul Daniels uses his teeth. The man they call the

Archbishop makes the most of his long, sharp fingernails. Blood is drawn. Paul Daniels is above his adversary, bearing down. He pulls the crown from the prelate's head but sacrifices his position to do so. The Archbishop grabs at the magician's throat and squeezes. Then Paul Daniels pulls back, spluttering, but rolling on the floor. The Archbishop has the advantage.

At first, the crowd stands to watch the men wrestle. Then they begin to drift away. The Archbishop and Paul Daniels are left to the room, and the crown, and the battle which shows no signs of concluding.

Last Night Stand

Precious will never get used to the long nights. When she moved to London, it wasn't the damp that shocked her, or the cold. She was expecting those things. Those are the things everyone warns you about on this island. It was the dark. When she used to visit with her family as a girl, it was always in summer. When she moved here, she arrived in May, when everything was bright and fresh. But then the light left. She couldn't believe it when November came. She didn't initially notice there was less daytime, and then she saw that she was going to work in the dark and coming home in the dark too. And then December came and it was even worse.

Precious is standing by the window, looking out on to the street. It is dark. It is the shortest day. It is the longest night. The streetlights are glowing. Some of the bulbs are the old yellow type that have shone against the Soho night for decades, once novel, now dated. Others have been replaced with bright white LEDs. Precious dislikes the new colour. It makes visible that which should, at night, remain invisible. It illuminates the city's wrinkles, like an ageing starlet betrayed by an unexpected camera flash. The pavement shines. Puddles reflect the light, each droplet a tiny star.

Some men across the street are unloading a drum kit from the back of a white van and carrying it to a bar at the end of the road. One of the men stacks a couple of cymbals precariously on top of the kick drum and lifts them all into the air. She watches as the cymbals begin to slide and hears the jarring scrape of the brass against the rim of the drum. The man spots them falling and reaches out to catch one, dropping the kick drum on to his foot. He manages to halt the cymbal's descent, but the other, the larger of the two, hits the pavement with a sharp edge, rolls off the kerb with a clatter, and along the road in a decreasing spiral, the ringing sound becoming higher and higher in pitch.

Later, when she remembers her last night in Soho, this is the image she will recall.

Men in uniforms arrive in the middle of the night. Precious isn't working. She finished a couple of hours ago and is watching a true-crime series on Netflix. She's engrossed by the real-life events, the ordinary people caught up in the debacle, the slow unfolding of the mystery, the injustices at the heart of the case. She ordered a food delivery and it has just arrived. The skinny lad stands outside her door in cycling shorts and a light-blue waterproof jacket. He's rummaging in his bag for her vegetable biryani. She is already on her phone, giving his service a five-star review, deciding how much to tip. It is important to support people like him, she thinks. It must be a difficult life. She would tip a waiter in a restaurant at least ten per cent of the total bill, if not closer to fifteen, so why not this boy. He rushes around the city in the middle of the night to scratch a living, and he is younger than her sons.

When she first hears the banging, it sounds very far away. It is a noisy neighbourhood and anyone who lives in Soho must quickly learn to organise sounds into layers of import-ance and proximity. The sound is that of metal banging against wood and is most likely someone throwing beer barrels into a cellar, or empty crates out into the street. Precious is not even fully aware of the commotion. It is something her brain easily blocks out. Then there is shouting. Again, this could be anything at all: drunks being kicked out of a club; someone getting into a fight in the next street.

The boy pulls out a plastic bag containing her food and holds it out to her. Precious puts her phone back into her pocket, smiles at the boy, and takes hold of the bag.

'Fuck these fucking fuckers,' says Tabitha between her teeth.

263

She rushes over to the door and slams it in the lad's face. As it swings shut, Precious catches a last glimpse of his puzzled expression, hand still stretched out in front of him. He has no idea what is going on. Precious doesn't know either.

'It's a fucking raid, the fucking bastards,' Tabitha explains. She begins to dash around the bedroom, gathering items that might serve them well in any number of given circumstances, then changing her mind about what those circumstances might be and dropping the items on to the floor. 'They are not getting their hands on you. They are not getting their hands on you. My god, if there's one thing I hate on this earth it's the fucking pigs.' Tabitha takes hold of the bedpost and tries to drag it. The bed is too heavy so she abandons the attempt and rushes over to the wardrobe, which is closer to the door. She shoves it with all the strength she can muster and it tumbles to the floor, blocking the entrance. Then she takes other items of furniture and begins to pile them on top of the wardrobe. She takes the drawers out of the bedside table then picks it up and places it on top, then adds the drawers themselves with their heavy contents. She has apparently forgotten about her bad shoulder. As she rearranges the room, Tabitha herself is transformed. As she builds the barricade, the years appear to fall off her. All of the energy she has ever possessed in her long life comes rushing back, from the past into the present, as if a collection of younger selves has gathered and come to the aid of their senior version.

Then Precious begins to hear the noise for what it is. The banging is coming from the bottom of the building, way down at street level. There is a slow, repetitive thud, again and again, and then there is the sound of ripping and splintering, as a way is forced through the thick wooden door.

Now the shouting comes from within the building itself, and she hears dogs beginning to bark. Two, maybe three. Big dogs with deep barks mean strong jaws, long teeth.

Precious stands, transfixed. She doesn't know what to do. She feels suddenly incompetent, something she's never felt in her life before. It's as if all she has in this world are the clothes she's wearing and the plastic bag containing the box of biryani she's holding in her hands. Everything she's able to reach out and touch feels suddenly very close. Anything she can't reach out and touch feels very far away. The rest of the world, outside these walls, is remote. She hears the shouting from downstairs. Shouting and screaming.

Precious runs to the window and looks out.

The men behind the masks aren't men. They are a natural disaster: a hurricane, a flood. There's no reasoning with them. They cannot operate any of their human faculties. They are robots, cyborgs, automata. Tabitha once told Precious a story about her past, when she was still living in Leeds. The police picked a bunch of prostitutes up off the street then took them back to the cells and raped them. Precious knows not all policemen are the same. But, in those masks, they all look the same.

Tabitha is pulling at her arm; pulling at her jumper. Tabitha knows what to do. Tabitha's seen it all. She's been there, done that.

'Come on, Precious, come on. I won't lose you. I won't fucking lose you.'

Tabitha is crying. Precious has never seen Tabitha cry.

'I'm not going to prison and neither are you. Come the fuck on.'

Tabitha takes hold of Precious and steers her towards the fire escape. They step out on to it together and at Tabitha's insistence they begin to climb. Both women are in their dressing gowns. Precious owns two dressing gowns. One is made of silk. It is black with red trim and reaches to the middle of her thigh. She wears this when entertaining clients. The other is made of a purple fleecy material and reaches below her knees. She wears this one when she is with Tabitha or alone. Thankfully, this evening she is wearing the purple dressing gown. As Precious follows Tabitha up the steps to the roof she begins to shiver. She pulls the dressing gown tighter around her body. Her feet are bare save for some flimsy slippers that cover her toes but leave her heels exposed. The cold wind wraps her ankles.

From the building they have left, Precious can hear banging and shouting and furniture being thrown.

They get to the top of the fire escape and step out on to the flat roof. Up high, the wind is even stronger and colder. It blows through their dressing gowns and pyjamas. Precious takes small comfort in the garden. She is standing with her rose plant, her herbs, the evergreens, but comes to the sad realisation that this is quite possibly the last time she will see any of them. She hopes they won't be destroyed. It wouldn't matter to anyone else; they are only plants. But she put them there herself, and she has cared for them for years. She can see a slug on the rose right now, the cheeky bastard. It seems to be feasting on the leaf mulch she placed at the base, but it will soon make its way up the woody stem and begin feasting on the plant itself.

Precious moves towards the edge of the roof and looks down. She can see people being dragged out of the building. Some of the girls were working. She can see naked bodies being thrown on to the street. Girls in underwear, shivering as they are shoved into police vans. Men too, cowering in the cold beneath the stark lamplight.

She can see the dogs now, as well as hear them. Huge German Shepherds and Dobermans, up on their hind legs, pulling on their leads furiously, jaws gnashing.

She has known dogs. That sort only have love for their handlers and they will perform whatever task is asked of them. Right now they are being held back, but they are pulling with all their strength to be free, and if any of those police officers let go of the rope, they would be on their victims, tearing them apart.

'Why did they bring the dogs?' Precious mutters.

It was a vaguely rhetorical question but Tabitha responds anyway. 'They'll be searching for drugs, or firearms.'

266

Precious looks down again. Some of the Archbishop's disciples have begun to come out of the cellar. She doesn't know if the police even went down there or whether the vagrants just came crawling out on hearing the commotion, like worms at the sound of stamping feet. They hear the thumping, think it might be something good, then come up to the surface to see, only to get stamped on or run over or pulled from the earth by hungry blackbirds and fed to a nest of squawking chicks.

The police scoop them up as soon as they appear. The lot of them are funnelled into the back of a windowless van. She sees them, thin and pasty, hunched over, dejected. The doors of the van are shut behind them, and then the vehicle begins to drive away.

They never did find that Cheryl Lavery, she reflects.

Tabitha comes to join Precious at the edge of the roof. She has carried the handheld megaphone from the street protest up to the roof with her. She hands it to Precious.

'Call for help,' insists Tabitha. 'Say something.'

'It's three in the morning, hun. We'll wake the neighbours.'

'That's the idea.'

'Who is going to help us?' She points. 'The police are down there.'

Tabitha snatches the megaphone. 'I'll do it, then.' She switches on the device and begins to shout through it, calling out for help, denouncing the police, screaming out injustices past, present and future. The batteries give in after about forty-five seconds and the grainy, electronically enhanced voice fades to a hoarse, human rasp, battling the billowing wind.

Precious begins to laugh. Tabitha looks at her friend. Her face is cross at first then she smiles, then she laughs too. The women laugh together.

'God knows what I thought was going to happen,' says Tabitha. She throws her head back and laughs again. Precious draws her in for a cuddle, then notices something. 'Look,' she says. 'There are some people staring at us from that hotel window.' A light has flicked on in the building across the street, and a man and a woman are peering out nervously from behind a thick set of curtains. The woman has a phone pressed against her face.

'She's calling the police, look. From where she is she can't see the police down on the ground. She must think we're up to no good.'

'Do you think she's calling the police so they come and help us or so they come and arrest us?'

'Hard to say.'

There is now also a crowd of people gathering on the street. Some are pointing upwards. Some are shrieking and shouting things Precious and Tabitha can't hear.

'They think we're going to jump,' Tabitha observes. 'Are we going to jump?'

'No we are not,' Precious replies, incredulous. 'I don't feel suicidal at this moment in time. Do you?'

'Not one bit. I have an unquenchable lust for life.'

'Well then.'

'It's just I thought this was going to be a much more effective and dramatic last stand than it has in fact been.'

Last Night Stand: Part II

A few streets away, Robert Kerr has been unable to sleep. He is slumped on his couch in pants and an old T-shirt, a brown beer bottle in one hand, the TV remote in the other. He is watching a football match broadcast live from Chile. Small figures run around on a sandy pitch, their movements narrated in a language he can't understand.

Roster and Anastasia will surely kick him out of the flat, but he doesn't know when. They'll be stopping his money too. He has no pension, no other source of income, and he has nowhere else to go. He told Anastasia to fuck herself, and he's glad he did. He always liked her, but he wasn't in a million years going to do what she wanted him to do just because he used to carry a flame for her.

They won't pay him any more, though. Anastasia made that clear, and Roster made that clear too, months ago. People like that expect you to be loyal for ever. But Robert has other loyalties. He isn't in that world any more, and he doesn't want to be.

He would go and ask Lorenzo for advice, but he's still away somewhere working on a film. And Robert isn't sure Lorenzo is that fond of him any more. He regrets the confession he made.

He sits up. He'll phone the lad in the morning or send him a text. He's not going to let that friendship slip away from him, as everything else has slipped away. He will make it right.

Maybe he will move out to the suburbs like Lorenzo's parents. They are somewhere by the sea. He might move back to Scotland. He won't know anyone any more, but at least he'll be able to get to the Ibrox. But how will he live? He hasn't done an honest day's work in decades. And he's retirement age as it is. Perhaps he will be able to draw a state pension. These are all concerns now.

He turns off the telly. He can't follow the action. The flat is quiet now, unusually so. He can't hear any of the regular hubbub that continues in this neighbourhood all day and night, and he finds it unsettling. Robert is afraid of silence like other people are afraid of the dark, and has spent his life avoiding it, moving in large crowds, living in the busiest parts of busy cities. When silence falls he goes out to find a racket – the clinking of glasses or the hum of traffic. When the world is quiet, he is alone in his own head, and that's a place as dark as any night.

He needs noise.

He gets out of bed and finds items of clothing in his wardrobe, then puts on a pair of sturdy boots, wraps himself in a thick coat, and goes down to the street. Only a few places will be open at this time of night, but he'll find somewhere.

Then he hears the voice. There is a voice shouting out over the rooftops. It is far away, but it seems to carry eerily, as if the person is speaking directly to him. He begins to walk towards it, taking alleys and backstreets. As he walks, he begins to hear other voices. There are men shouting. There are women screaming. He begins to run, but not away from the panic. He runs towards it.

Last Night Stand: Part III

There is a wall behind Tabitha and, without looking, she puts her hand back to lean against it. She screams. She tries to pull her hand away but it is stuck. She screams again.

Precious rushes forward.

Tabitha screws up her face in a grimace and lets out a deep breath through her teeth. She turns and looks down at her hand, lets out a brief 'oh god' and then looks away and shuts her eyes.

Precious now sees what her friend has done. The low walls of the roof are covered with spikes, to keep away birds and burglars. As she leaned back, Tabitha skewered her hand on one of these spikes. It has pierced her hand through the centre of the palm and has come out through the other side.

'Oh my god,' says Precious. And then she realises that panicking won't be of any help to anyone. 'Don't worry, love,' she says, in the calmest, most reassuring voice she can muster. 'It'll be okay. I'll get help.'

'Don't leave me here. Just get it out of me. Just get it out, and I'll come down with you.'

'I don't know if that's a good idea. It might make it worse.'

'Just get it out of me!'

'Okay, okay.' Precious relents. She steps forward and takes a closer look. There isn't as much blood as she expected, but she realises that more will come once the hand is freed. She pulls the cord from her dressing gown out of its loops, to use as a bandage. The fabric isn't thick but it is long and she will be able to wrap it around Tabitha's hand several times.

There isn't enough light to see the wound clearly. Precious asks Tabitha if she is able to hold her phone torch with her other hand, so that Precious can investigate further. Tabitha holds up the phone and switches on the light and a beam of white descends to Tabitha's hand and the sharp metal spike cutting through it. Tabitha's skin looks pale, even paler than usual, partly because of her injury, partly because of the bright white light from the LED. The blood that has emerged looks as if it is already beginning to clot. It is turning the colour of the rust on the metal spike and it is even taking on its texture, like a cuttlefish flushing the colour of the seabed.

Precious places her fingers beneath her friend's hand, and pushes upwards, gently at first then harder until Tabitha's hand is free.

Tabitha inhales sharply but she does not scream again.

As predicted, the blood begins to flow in earnest. Precious recalls some of her medical training and wraps the belt of her dressing gown tightly around Tabitha's hand, securing it with a knot. She instructs Tabitha to keep her hand raised, to lessen the flow of blood. The older woman does this at first but soon finds that she is too tired to hold her hand up. Precious carefully takes hold of Tabitha's wrist and raises it up herself. The pair stand on top of the building with their arms raised in this manner, as if celebrating a sporting victory.

'Fuck this building,' says Tabitha. 'Fuck this place.'

The friends look at each other, and without saying a word, there is an understanding. There is no way out. Whatever they thought they were going to do when Tabitha barricaded the door of their flat and they came up to the roof, it is impossible now. Tabitha needs medical attention. The only way to get it quickly is to submit themselves to the police.

They stand for a few minutes huddling together against the wind, drawing their night clothes closer to their bodies. Tabitha bemoans her lack of cigarettes, and for once Precious agrees that at this precise moment there would be nothing better.

'Don't be annoyed right now,' says Tabitha. 'But I've got a confession. I did actually hide some up here. They're under that plant pot.' She nods in the direction of a large terracotta planter.

'I could kiss you.' Precious helps her friend on to the garden bench and lifts the pot to reveal a half-full packet of tobacco, some papers, filters and a plastic lighter. She joins Tabitha on the bench and begins to roll two cigarettes.

They hear men shouting downstairs. It is almost comic. The voices are deep, artificially deep, as if the situation has elicited the deepest frequencies in the human range. There is stamping and bashing, as if all the men are chasing each other around the building, up the stairs, down the stairs, through doors, in and out of rooms and cupboards, as if in a vast pantomime, an animated cartoon.

'You know something, Precious. I think this last year, while we've been having all this grief with the landlords, I'm not sure I ever actually thought we'd have to leave. I just thought it would all sort itself out somehow, and we would end up getting to stay on, and everything would go back to normal.'

'That's funny,' replies Precious. 'I thought the exact opposite. I never for a minute thought we had any hope.'

'Why did you fight so hard, then?'

Precious shrugs her shoulders and pulls her lower lip back and forth between her teeth. 'I suppose I didn't want us to go without a fight. I thought it was important to stick up for ourselves, whatever the outcome. And I'm glad we did, even though I'm not sure it's made any real difference in the grand scheme of things. But it's made a difference to me – a difference to all of us who were involved. And it was worth it for that.'

They will leave their home together and they will not come back. It is inevitable. It was always inevitable.

Precious hears someone calling her name. She hears it again, but the person, whoever they are, isn't calling from the side of the street where the crowd have gathered and where the police are shovelling their friends and customers into the backs of vans and police cars. She hears the voice from the other side, from the alley behind the building, where the restaurants keep their bins; the entrance that she and Tabitha use when coming up to their flat.

'Hang on a second.' Precious lifts herself up off the bench and goes over to see who is calling. Down on the ground she sees a large man. His face is turned up towards her, but it is dark on that side, and although the moon is bright, a cloud has just cut across it, and she can't make out who it is at all. The man calls again and she recognises the voice. She had never heard a Glaswegian accent before she met Robert.

'Robert! What on earth are you doing?'

'I'm coming up!'

'For god's sake. How? You going to King-Kong it up the side of the building?'

'Yes,' he shouts. 'Yes I am. I'm coming to get you.'

Precious can hear the ruckus within more clearly. There is shouting and banging. She can make out the sounds of someone being arrested. The police officer is reading them their rights, and the arrestee is shouting obscenities. She can't quite hear enough of the voice to recognise it. It might be Candy. Then again it might be Hazel.

'Go back home, Robert. You'll hurt yourself.'

'I'm not going home without you. I'm going to get you out of here. I'll fight them all off if I have to.'

'Don't be ridiculous, you'll do your back in.'

Despite their protestations, Robert begins to climb. First he raises himself up on to the bins, and then reaches for a drainpipe. It is a proper old metal drainpipe. Robert is a heavy man, but the drainpipe is securely attached to the wall, and it holds his weight. He grips with both hands, and puts his feet on the ridges, then climbs like a great silverback up the trunk of a tree.

When he nears the top, Precious reaches out a hand for him and he takes it, and she helps him up on to the roof. He stops for a moment to look around, panting heavily.

'Nice garden you've got up here,' he says.

'Yeah, it's not bad, is it?'

Robert spots Tabitha and nods in her direction, and she smiles back, weakly. Spotting the paleness of her face, he says, 'You all right, love?'

'Not really,' she says. She shows him her hand, and the blood that has dripped down her arm, having now dried hard. Precious explains what happened, then says, 'We'll have to go back down.'

'Bugger that,' says Robert.

'We have to. We need to get her hand seen to. We're just up here having a last sit and cig and then we'll go down.'

'No. You can't. They'll get you both on some bullshit pimping charges.'

'We'll fight it, obviously. But what's the alternative?'

'Come down the back way,' he suggests. 'Down the way I've just come. Then leg it.'

'With this hand?'

'Well, I'll help. Or else I'll create a diversion. I'll go down there and draw out as many of them coppers as I can, and you can slip past me. I'll take on the whole bloody Met if I have to.'

'They'd kill you, you crazy fool.'

'Please let me do this for you,' says Robert, seriously. 'What am I for, if not for this?'

Precious considers, then looks over the side of the building at the drainpipe. 'There might be a way down for us, if you help, Robert, and if, together, we carry Tabitha. Are you up for it, Tabitha?'

'You know me, Precious, love. I'll do anything.' She winks at Robert.

Robert blushes.

Precious takes Tabitha by one arm, and Robert raises the other. Precious is unsure whether any of this will work, but perhaps if Robert goes first, there will be a way to lower Tabitha down.

'Stop,' says Tabitha.

Precious thinks she must be accidentally hurting her. 'I'm sorry, love. But we really should hurry.'

'No,' says Tabitha. 'We need to stop.'

Robert already has one foot over the side of the building, ready to take the first step down. 'What is it?' he asks.

'Can you feel it?'

'Feel what?' Precious is beginning to think the loss of blood is affecting her friend's perceptions.

'The tremors,' says Tabitha quietly.

Precious stands very still. So does Robert, though he has less idea what is going on. He is still hunched over, holding his chest, panting heavily. Then Precious feels them too. She feels a trembling in the soles of her feet, through the thin fabric of her slippers. The trembling is subtle, but it gets fiercer. She feels her legs begin to shake. There is a low rumbling, deep within the earth. The pitch is so low, she can hardly hear it. It is something she feels rather than hears. She feels it in her ribs. It creates a funny, hollow feeling in her lungs and it jars with the rhythm of her heartbeat.

Precious looks over at Robert, who has felt nothing. He is looking between her and Tabitha as if the pair of them are speaking in tongues. Tabitha is beginning to move back, towards the intersection between their neighbours' roof and their own. Tabitha uses her good hand to grip the wall, taking care to avoid the contra-avian spikes. She and Precious climb up on to the other roof, and continue to move back, beckoning for Robert to follow.

'Come this way, Robert,' Precious urges. Robert is utterly baffled. He stays where he is. He is clutching at his chest. He still hasn't properly caught his breath from climbing up.

Then the shaking begins in earnest. Tiles fall from the roof. There is a creak as seventeenth-century timbers bend and snap; the trunks of magnificent oak trees that grew in vast forests, that were harvested and bent to the shape of the city – oak trees the like of which don't exist any more, haven't been seen for centuries. The timbers warp, then break in two.

Precious and Tabitha are now on the neighbouring roof. They hold on tightly to a chimney stack and watch as the old building falls away from them, and crumbles. Robert slips out of sight.

Gravy

The pie has a buttery crust that flakes when she digs. The meat is smooth and cut easily with the side of a fork. The best part is the gravy. Agatha has stood by the stove and watched Valerie make it many times. She roasts the meat on the bone, places it on a plate to rest, then puts the roasting tin, still hot, on to the gas hob. She scrapes at the fats with a wooden spoon, loosening the parts that have formed a dark crust. She sprinkles on flour and blends it together with the residue. She adds hot water, stirring all the time. She stirs and stirs and simmers, and the gravy thickens slowly then all at once.

Agatha feels relaxed. Her mind is quiet, focused on the room, the company, the taste and texture of the meal. It isn't a sensation she is used to but it is one she likes. She decides this is how she ought always to function. She will reject anything cerebral. She will always put sensory experience before any other consideration. She will allow her mind to follow her eyes, her ears, her tongue, her nose, her fingertips. Her senses will inform all her decisions.

Roster presumably drove the boy home. Agatha left him in the bedroom and came down to the gatehouse. Valerie will have gone up for the night, but she never locks the door, and keeps a bed made up for Agatha, knowing her youngest sister sometimes likes to sleep down here with her rather than up at the big house on her own. Agatha has always had a room here with Valerie. She uses it less and less these days, feeling the need to sleep in the house she owns, as she should, but she has come down tonight out of a desire to leave the boy alone, and because she was hungry, and suspected Valerie might have something delicious lying around. She found the pie on the hob and has heated a slice.

When the pie is hot through, she takes it over to the kitchen table and begins to eat. Then she hears the floorboards creaking upstairs, the hinges of a door, the flush of a toilet and the turning of a tap on then off. She hears Valerie descend the narrow flight of stairs, then sees her in the doorway in an old burgundy dressing gown that reaches all the way to her ankles. She is wearing thick socks and navy-blue slippers, worn white with age.

'Oh,' notes the old woman. 'It's you.'

'We drove up this morning,' Agatha replies. 'We were at the races. And afterwards I was occupied.'

'You'll sleep here tonight?'

Agatha nods, her mouth full of pie.

'You helped yourself, I see. There's sponge for afters if you want it.'

'Thank you, but this will do fine.'

'Is Reg with you?'

'He had to go out somewhere, but he should be back soon.'

Valerie shuffles into the room and idly dusts crumbs off the kitchen surfaces into the palm of her hand, then deposits them in a bin. She leans back against a counter, puts her hands in the low pockets of her dressing gown and watches as Agatha eats.

'You know,' says Agatha to her eldest sister, 'I might come and live here all the year round. I only have to be in the city for business and I can do much of it remotely.'

Valerie makes a noise at the back of her throat which Agatha takes as agreement.

She goes on, 'I could take a more active role in managing the estate. I wouldn't be taking over from you. You could teach me. If I'm being honest, I have no idea how to run a place like this but I'd like to learn. I think I'd find it fulfilling. We could do it together.'

'It's a big old house,' says Valerie. 'And you'd be in it all alone. I can't imagine Reggie up here all year round. He's a townie through and through. If they cut him open, he'd bleed Thames water.'

Then the door opens, and Roster walks through it. She didn't hear the car on the gravel outside, so is startled when he enters without knocking.

'Radio,' he says. His voice is urgent.

There is an analogue radio in the corner of Valerie's kitchen. Agatha goes over to it, but has a hard time working it. She knows most stations she would need are FM but she doesn't know much beyond that, like what frequencies she needs to tune to. She finds the power switch, flicks it and is met with the crackle of white noise. There are dials on the top, so she swivels them. The white noise fades in and out, shifts pitch, shifts speed. It sounds old-fashioned to her. It is a sound from the past, now a memory; the stuff of junk shops, vintage stores and museums. And what a noise it is. There is nothing like it in the world. It is like the sea on a shingle beach, or the wind on autumn leaves, or a fire cutting through coal, but not like any of those sounds at all.

Agatha is still fiddling with the radio.

'I'll do it,' Roster insists, stepping around her. Valerie goes to wash up Agatha's plate in the sink.

As Roster turns the dial, Radio 4 tunes in and out. They catch loose words.

. . .

. . .

'London . . .'

. . .

'Total collapse . . .'

. . .

Agatha looks at her phone. Nobody has been in touch. The policeman said he would text her to let her know everything had gone according to plan. She looks for the little bars at the top of the screen and sees none. No service. Of course, she would have no service here.

Roster is still fiddling with the old radio, trying to dial in a better signal. The voice of the newsreader is unclear. More snatches of words, incoherent phrases.

He turns to her. 'I heard more in the car,' he says. 'There's been some sort of disaster in central London. A building has completely collapsed. They don't know how many people are trapped beneath.'

'What has that got to do with us?' Valerie asks.

'Valerie, don't be difficult. You know very well that all your father's property is in central London.'

'And you think it is one of ours?'

'It is in the West End. And I caught something about a police raid.'

Agatha looks up at Roster.

'It might not be—' he says.

'Yes it is,' Agatha interrupts, curtly. 'What else could it be?'

Roster concedes the point and begins to move quickly out of Valerie's kitchen. He tells Agatha that he is going back to the big house to collect the rest of her things, then he leaves.

Of course, he is right. They will have to go back now, and drive through the night, but in this moment, Agatha doesn't want to move. She is tired. She is tired of it all: the constant movement, the constant struggle. She wants for things to be easy, for once. She wants to be left alone.

Agatha feels the tears coming before she notices them. She raises a hand and wipes them away, then looks down and sees a smear of black mascara. She lowers her head so her eyes can't be seen, but the tears instead fall to the kitchen table. A couple drop on to the wood and soak in. She catches more with the sleeve of her woollen jumper.

Valerie asks Agatha a question, but Agatha is unable to answer. If she had answered, her voice would have faltered. Valerie turns around to ask again, then sees the tears, then returns to the washing up. 'That's no use to anyone,' she says quietly.

A Vision

Richard Scarcroft is sitting alone in Soho Square. He left the Archbishop's group a couple of weeks ago, which he is now regretting. The weather is getting colder, and it has become difficult to find night-time shelter, or a cosy space to sit during the day. He is wishing he had found the patience to put up with that lot for just a little while longer, at least until after Christmas.

Richard has parked himself on a bench to be up off the cold ground and he has wrapped himself in a blanket and a thin sleeping bag. A couple of disassembled cardboard boxes provide further insulation, and the winter coat he got from the army is at least thick and warm, and his leather boots keep out the damp. He is no longer clean-shaven but has grown a thick beard. It ages him. When he catches sight of himself in shop windows he hardly recognises himself. He looks at least ten years older, maybe more. He looks like his father, or his father's father. There are wiry grey hairs among the smooth brown ones. He wonders whether it is the street that has done this to him or if it is just the natural ageing process. He cradles a paper cup containing hot tea. A cycle courier popped up from behind him earlier and handed it to him with a smile and a couple of words of greeting, and he then got back on to his fixed-gear bike and rode away, gliding as smoothly as a swan in flight, along the paths that intersect Soho Square, out through the open iron gate, towards Oxford Street and out of sight.

Richard holds the cup of tea close to his chest and declines his head so the steam rises and condenses on to his face. He breathes it in like a summer's day, and feels the heat warm the inside of his nose and then all the way to the back of his throat.

He takes a sip too soon. The boiled liquid burns the tip of his tongue but he doesn't care. He will take the burn with him throughout the cold night. He will feel it, numb like a stubbed toe, and taste it, bitter and sweet like cold iron, and be reminded of that cup of tea. It is proof.

The interaction with the cycle courier has also left a mark, like a warm thumbprint in cold clay. An act of kindness, a smile, a nod, some eye contact, the recognition of Richard as a fellow human being.

Richard hears the screaming but is reluctant to give up his bench and walk towards it. Something tells him it will be trouble. Whenever in his life he has heard a man shout and a woman scream, it has meant something bad is happening. It's not that Richard doesn't care; he just has so little of himself left to give.

Then the rumbling begins. He hears the building collapse – an all-too-familiar sound – but he hears no bomb. Though surely there was a bomb. There must have been a bomb.

This time, he does go. An explosion requires military experience. He has not forgotten.

The gates of the square have been locked, but he scales them easily, and runs to the beginning of the cloud of brown dust, which hangs in the air, illuminated by the streetlights, eerily suspended, as if entirely free from the constraints of time and gravity. He cannot look past it, through it, to see what has actually happened. People are emerging, coughing, spluttering. The first person is a woman in her underwear: a black, lacy bra and knicker set. Her face and hair are covered in a thick layer of the dust, making her look like a petrified Pompeiian. Her hands are bound in front of her in handcuffs. She is running barefoot down the street, and she keeps looking over her shoulder, as if worried she is being followed. Then there is a man. He is entirely naked, and also covered in the dust. Richard thinks he recognises him from somewhere – maybe from the telly. Then there are other people: most fully clothed, some of them look like the usual drunk party people you would see spilling from clubs at this time of night. They are wearing expensive suits and dresses, now ruined. Many of the women are struggling to run in high heels. Some take them off. Some of them fall over, then pick themselves up and keep running.

Richard tries to flag someone down to find out what is going on. He spots a woman who is fully naked, her hands also bound. She is running at full pelt towards him.

'Are you okay?' he shouts in her direction. He doesn't expect her to stop. She seems totally unfazed by her nakedness.

To his surprise, she does stop and speaks to him. He asks her what has happened.

'Earthquake, or something. I've no idea. Some massive hole just appeared in the ground, and the building went right in. I just ran. I don't think there was any of us lot still in there, but maybe some police. Fuck knows.' Then she runs off.

Richard continues. The dust is beginning to settle. As he closes in on the scene, he sees police standing around. Nobody seems to be doing anything at all helpful. Everyone and everything is covered in the dust. The old brothel is in ruins. It was one of the old Soho buildings that was always a bit crooked. Now Richard can see doors, and bedposts, and timber beams poking up out of the wreckage. Beyond the wreckage, there is a gaping hole.

Then he sees her, walking up through the dust, illuminated from behind. He recognises her instantly although is startled by the sight. Her face has been on posters across the capital and she has been at the centre of his thoughts too. He never really spoke to her much, never really knew her, never really knew if she was in any sense knowable. The face he saw on the posters – fresh, happy, identifiable – was different from the face he knew in real life – gaunt, frail, invisible. The face he sees now, just there emerging from the dust, is similar to the idealised version from the publicity campaign. She looks renewed. Her skin is bright and shining. Her hair has been washed and brushed, she is standing straight and tall, as if she has grown into her own representation.

Spring

Spectral Dust

Lorenzo stands on his tiptoes. There is a gap in the hoardings above his eye level and if he straightens his back and raises himself up on to the balls of his feet, he can see through to the crater. He catches sight of some ancient-looking timbers sticking up from the churned ground like the ribs of a beached whale, black now from years of smog, and a small yellow digger propped up on its chains at the edge of the recess, the teeth of its bucket set into the soil. The air still feels thick with dust, three months later. Lorenzo doesn't know if it's really there, or if it's just that he can feel it because of all the stories he's heard. Apparently, the fug took weeks to settle. When the building fell, a cloud surged high into the air and hung defiantly, as if it had phantasmal agency, lingering as a grim warning; a spectre of the building that had stood on that spot for centuries.

Like everyone else, he first saw the images of the collapse the morning after it happened. Camera crews from all the major news channels set themselves up on the street outside the exclusion zone and streamed live footage of the rescue efforts. Lorenzo watched on his phone from his rented cottage near the film studio as fire crews and paramedics rushed around in protective clothing, their faces obscured by the breathing apparatus it was necessary for them to wear. The news channels sent their main anchors to the scene and they delivered the rest of the day's news while on location, panning back to the Soho street when there were pressing updates.

Lorenzo's mum phoned him from her new house in Essex as soon as she heard the news on the radio. Lorenzo wasn't able to get away – the producers had a long list of shots they needed to get done before cast and crew departed for Christmas – so his mum said she'd pop to town and check on the flat. The flat wasn't particularly close to the site of the sinkhole, but it made sense that one of them went to check on the place, just in case. Maria also had lots of friends still in the area and was anxious to make sure they weren't hurt.

Lorenzo and Maria continued to exchange texts while she was on the train to Liverpool Street, and she kept sending him links to the video clips from the scene and other updates, even though he had access to exactly the same online media sources as she did. She texted him again when she arrived at her old flat:

Flat fine. Bit messy. X

Lorenzo received this while waiting at the side of the set between takes, and he put his phone away in irritation. The flat was fine. It was perfectly clean. He had left in a bit of a hurry and hadn't sorted out the sitting room as well as he maybe should have, but it wasn't as if he'd left dirty dishes in the kitchen before making the journey north. The next time he checked his phone, he saw that his mum had sent another text:

It looks like a warzone.

Lorenzo assumed this was from the scene itself. When he got a minute to himself, he gave her a call. She told him there was dust across the whole district, and the closer you got to the old walk-up, the harder it was to breathe. It was all over the pavement, on lampposts, windowsills, on top of postboxes, benches, vans, cars and in the air. A huge cloud of brown-grey dust just hung there, as if it was solid. It didn't fall to the ground as quickly as she expected.

Lorenzo went straight to his parents' house in Essex for Christmas. He changed trains in London on Christmas Eve, getting off at King's Cross, taking the Circle Line to Liverpool Street, and then getting the train on to Clacton-on-Sea. It would have been easy enough to stop off in Soho, but he didn't. At the time, he told himself it was because the rail network, and

London itself, was so busy, and if he missed any of his connections he might not be able to get to his parents' house for Christmas at all, which would have been upsetting. He thinks now that it was because he wasn't ready to see it. He hadn't had the news about Robert then, but he feared the worst without being able to articulate why. He always suspected Robert spent time at the walk-ups, and it seemed more than likely after what he'd told Lorenzo about his past.

Lorenzo returned to London a couple of days ago. The last week of filming was frantic. Everyone on set was stressed, tired, overworked, and even people who were otherwise perfectly friendly went around shouting at each other. The show wrapped a month late. Lorenzo had intended to go on holiday afterwards, and had booked flights to Majorca, but was forced to cancel them once the necessity of staying on at the studio became apparent.

The first couple of days being back in London, Lorenzo mooched around his flat. Everything looked and felt and smelt different. His mum had obviously forgotten to shut one of the windows before she left and a pigeon had wandered in and laid a single egg in his underpants drawer. He found it when he went around vacuuming the carpets and dusting the surfaces. At first it seemed so surreal he couldn't quite make out what it was. It sat there, the size of a walnut and the colour of full-fat milk, so simple and perfect. For a second it looked to him like a brand-new creation, as if he'd made a miraculous discovery: a divine teardrop, frozen solid on descent. After the surprise passed, he saw it for what it was and had to laugh, at the thought of his own confusion, at the thought of the pigeon herself waddling in here, full of egg, gently squatting over his socks and boxer shorts, laying then leaving. He wondered if the pigeon had tried to incubate her creation at all or whether it was just a hit and run.

This evening marks the first time he has returned to the Aphra Behn since being back. It has changed. The Behn used to be a traditional pub. The colour palette was brown and burgundy, and the walls were covered in wood panelling that matched the bar and the furniture: oak polished with a dark walnut tinted varnish. The walls were decorated with old prints and ornate mirrors advertising defunct breweries. The area directly around the bar had wooden floorboards, likewise tinted and polished, but further back, where there were low tables and chairs there had been a fitted carpet, happily threadbare enough to obscure what had been a particularly vile pattern.

Now, there are exposed brick walls and the place is decorated with slogans, inscribed on framed posters, around the borders of the new menus, on metal plates hung on the wall above the bar. There are motivational slogans, weird puns, fake antique advertising posters to replace the real antique advertising posters. The TV in the top corner above the bar has doubled in size and next to it is a list of live sports events that will be showing over the next few weeks.

It isn't Lorenzo's kind of place any more. He stops outside and looks in through the window. There's no sign of Sheila. She would usually be here, guarding the door, leaning against the cracked paint of the exterior walls. The cracked paint of the exterior walls is no longer cracked, or rather it is no longer there. It has been covered with a new colour. It used to be a postbox red. It is now somewhere between grey and navy. It is stylish and joyless; elegant in a deliberately masculine sort of way.

He feels sad, kind of hollow. He has lived in this neighbourhood his whole life and has been coming to the Aphra Behn since he was first able to pass for eighteen. He steps inside. The worn, stone step is still the same. It still has its little sunken pocket in the middle that is just the right size to accommodate his foot.

Lorenzo doesn't recognise either of the bar staff but they seem broadly in keeping with those here before. He is about to order a pint of something cold and generic when he notices the taps have changed and, accordingly, the beers too.

Lorenzo thinks of Glenda. She moved back home to her parents' house a couple of months ago, just before Christmas. She seems happier. She has sent him photos of dinners her mum has cooked and loaves of bread her dad has baked. Glenda's mum is a notoriously good cook and Glenda's dad is a notoriously good baker. Lorenzo hopes she has put on a bit of weight. He will be seeing her tonight. She is visiting and staying with her friend Bastian in his new flat. Bastian's girlfriend, Laura, will be there too. They are all going out for dinner at a fashionable restaurant Lorenzo has chosen.

Lorenzo's phone vibrates. It is lying face down on the table so he turns it over. He has received a text from Eddie Kettering, only when Eddie Kettering put his number in Lorenzo's phone, he entered it under the name Dikie Detergent, which is an anagram of Eddie Kettering. This is what has flashed up.

Lorenzo opens the message.

Hey. You back in London yet?

Lorenzo ignores him and turns his phone back over. He doesn't want to see Eddie but he realises that if he has a couple more pints, he'll probably end up replying anyway and meeting up with him and possibly having sex. In the last couple of months of filming, Lorenzo and Eddie had a casual thing going that neither of them, Lorenzo least of all, had any desire to give a name to. They simply sometimes went to each other's dressing rooms and had fast, fumbled sex. There was no discussion or analysis, which is how Lorenzo wanted it to remain. Eddie is hot, but Lorenzo finds him irritating and juvenile and has no wish to form an emotional attachment. Besides, Eddie is engaged to a stylish socialite called Miranda Billing. Lorenzo concedes that there might be some kind of moral issue here that he might have to think about at some point, but it isn't a pressing matter and much more Eddie's problem than his.

On a more positive note, Eddie had actually given Lorenzo some good ideas. On one occasion, they were hanging out on set and Lorenzo made an idle comment about being disillusioned with acting, largely because of the parts he found himself being put forward for. Eddie suggested that he start writing his own material – plays or screenplays.

Lorenzo has brought a notebook with him to the pub. He gets it out of his satchel along with a couple of pens and a pair of headphones. He puts the headphones on and plugs the cable into his phone, then scrolls through his music until he arrives at some slow, soothing electronica. Next, Lorenzo opens the notebook. It is more expensive that it needs to be, but Lorenzo appreciates quality paper: he appreciates quality in most things. Details matter. He clicks his ballpoint pen and puts it to the page. He will write a play. He wants it to be subtle, sophisticated, cerebral. He doesn't want it to be gaudy or melodramatic. Big ideas, big themes, but told through small, everyday interactions.

He begins. He sips lager and sits back in his chair to think. He pays closer attention to the music coming through his headphones. He watches the new pub patrons, and wonders about their lives. He feels irritated by how much the Behn has changed, and resolves never to come here again, although he knows he probably will, that he'll learn to put up with the changes and then he will forget about them, and forget how the pub used to be and forget about the people who used to come here. He practises his signature a couple of times, then writes out all the letters of the alphabet in upper and lower case. He draws a series of concentric circles. He sips his lager. He fiddles with his phone. He admires his elegant stationery.

Later in the afternoon, he gets up and puts his writing materials back in his satchel. He notices that his ballpoint pen has gone through the page and left a cobweb of scratched graffiti on the veneer tabletop. Feeling quietly satisfied by this result, and not at all guilty for defacing the new furniture, Lorenzo leaves, and wanders slowly back to his flat.

Hanging Carcasses

She stands among hanging carcasses. Each pig has its own meat hook and is wrapped in plastic. The heads have been removed and taken to a different part of the kitchen, where they will be boiled and stripped and turned into sausages and terrines. Beneath the plastic, the pigs appear white, pallid. Their legs are splayed. The posture looks uncomfortable but then she remembers the pigs are dead. She is to chop them into sections, trim the skin and sinew. A few still have their heads attached. These animals are to be spit-roasted. It is one of Cheryl's jobs to take the long, thin spit and thrust it the length of the animal.

Cheryl is stronger than she looks. Though small and wiry, she is able to carry objects that are up to four times as large as her. She lifts the pigs so easily that the burly men with whom she works feel a kind of strange jealousy, but also a deep-seated revulsion. Cheryl is hyper-productive. Her productivity alarms her colleagues.

'Stop,' her supervisor said to her one day. 'You've butchered too many pigs. We don't need this many.'

She got the job through her social worker. The restaurant is committed to 'turning people's lives around' so they give apprenticeships to people who've just got out of prison, got clean, or have otherwise been down and out. The restaurant sources its meat from the local, pop-up farm that has been set up in Soho Square. It's currently full of pigs that are slaughtered and then brought to this restaurant for butchering.

That's Cheryl's job. She has begun an NVQ in butchery. She is learning to hack and carve and mince. She is learning about the qualities of different cuts, the texture, the cooking time, the price. She is learning how to saw through bone; how to cure. She enjoys using the cleaver best of all. She likes the weight of it in her right hand, and the way the weight shifts as she lifts it up to shoulder height then throws the steel on to the chopping block, right through whatever lies on top.

She and Richard Scarcroft are getting a flat together. The council are helping them. After everything that happened with her disappearance, she's been pushed to the top of the waiting list.

Cheryl finishes with her allotted quota of pig carcasses and goes to another part of the kitchen to help peel potatoes. Strictly speaking, this isn't part of her job, but her social worker is always going on about how good it is to learn new skills.

When Cheryl was underground, she read all about how important it was to have a diverse employment portfolio. Cheryl is a productive member of society now. She keeps telling Richard how to become a productive member of society too, and then he says something back about the capitalist-military machine, and about how they should move to the countryside and grow their own vegetables, and then Cheryl says something back about compound interest, and then the conversation is over.

Cheryl has regular appointments with her social worker, whose name is Miriam. Miriam asks Cheryl questions about her life, about what things were like for her growing up, and about her emotions. She also gives her practical advice, and showed her how to register for a doctor, and how to fill out online forms.

After she came back, the police kept asking her strange questions about where she'd been. They all seemed kind of angry that she had come back, as if it was really important to them all that she stayed missing. In fairness, they had lost many of their colleagues the night she returned, so their upset was understandable. Though Kevin (aka Paul Daniels) died too, and the Archbishop, so it's not as if all the losses were on their side. Cheryl had to go and identify the bodies. It was horrible. They were both covered in bruises, and there were cuts everywhere. The Archbishop had had half his face smashed in and all of Kevin's teeth had been knocked out.

One police officer, called Jackie, seemed nice enough, and came to see her afterwards. She brought a box of items that had been found on Kevin's person. 'He had no next of kin,' Jackie explained, 'but I thought a couple of these things might have, I don't know, sentimental value for you, and there would be no harm in seeing if you wanted any of them.' From the box, Jackie pulled old packs of cards, handkerchiefs and magic wands. Cheryl shook her head at the sight of each item, until Jackie pulled out the crown, and Cheryl reached out and took it from her.

'This was mine anyway,' she said.

Jackie smiled. 'I'd assumed it was part of his costume. For when he did his performances.'

'No,' Cheryl replied. 'I found it in the ground.'

'Well, anyway, forensics reckoned it might be over fifty years old. You should see if it was worn by anyone famous. You know, Laurence Olivier or someone. There are so many theatres around here, you never know. That kind of memorabilia can be worth something.'

Packing

Agatha packs her things into a matching set of suitcases. Roster is already waiting by the car, which is parked on the street. Fedor is sitting up on his haunches on the back seat with his long head hanging out the open window. He watches as she comes down the steps with her largest suitcase and runs back up for the second and the third while Roster lifts them into the boot. The sun is bright. There is morning dew on everything that is cold: the iron railings outside Agatha's house, the windowpanes, the chrome hubcaps of the large, expensive cars parked all along the street. There are a few people around – a postman across the road; a man hoisted into the air by an elaborate apparatus to clean the top floor windows of the house a couple of doors along. He spills soapy water from his bucket on to the ground below and the suds forge slow streams across the pavement into the gutter then along the downward tilt to the sewer grate. Once the suitcases are in the boot, Roster shuts it then walks around the car to open one of the rear doors. Agatha slips in beside Fedor. The dog places his head in her lap.

Most of the morning newspapers led with the story. Agatha was given a small amount of forewarning. A couple of investigative journalists asked her to comment, which she declined to do. She tried to phone Michael Warbeck, who has resigned his position in the police and publicly announced his candidacy for mayor. She was told he was unavailable. She tried a second time and was met with the same response. She was too proud to make a third attempt. Her relationship with Warbeck had been strained since the fiasco at the brothel, for which he unfairly blamed her. She, in turn, quite rightly blames him for his poor handling of the raid. The whole escapade was badly planned from the beginning, in her view. And now, because of these headlines, he is refusing to speak to her at all, despite the generous donations she has made to his campaign fund, both in cash and in kind.

Agatha suspects Roster thinks she is overreacting. She tells him so when he climbs into the driver's seat.

'I have no such thoughts. It's not my business to have thoughts of that kind.'

'I know it's not your business but I also happen to know you have them anyway.'

'I do not. I drive you where you need to go, and I don't do anything more than that. If you want to go to the docks, I'll take you to the docks.'

He would also come with her on the yacht, she knew. He had his own cabin, between the skipper's and the rest of the crew, and he had personal items on board at all times, just as she did.

She will give evidence at the public inquiry into the collapse of the building, as has been requested of her. And then she will get out. She will not only leave this decrepit, stewing city, she will leave the country.

Since the collapse, the press has taken an interest in all aspects of her life and business, in a way that is utterly invasive. She is not a public figure, has never sought to be one, and does not deserve the treatment she has received. Reporters have looked into her holdings and her finances; anything they've been able to get their hands on, legitimately or illegitimately, and they have printed stories about her wealth, about her father, about the properties she owns. Anyone with half a brain should realise the incident was an act of god; a sinkhole is an aberration, an uncontrollable geological phenomenon. It can't be her job, as a landlord, to monitor subterranean rumblings. And if anyone could be blamed, it is surely the police, who ran into a seventeenth-century building with battering rams, full body armour and steel-capped boots, with no thought for the integrity of the place. Yet, because a number of those men were killed, nobody feels able to put any of the blame on them, so Agatha has become the villain. Her name has somehow become synonymous with all that is wrong with the city. She has received rape threats from perfect strangers.

Now, the press has unearthed information about illegal immigrants in one of her clubs, and many of the morning papers have led with the story, even though, by rights, the discovery of squatters should be a non-event.

'How the bloody hell was I supposed to know? Am I expected to monitor everything that goes on in those buildings? It's a witch hunt.'

Roster agrees that it is extremely unfair.

Those people had nothing to do with her. All those clubs operated independently. One of the managers had obviously tried to save a bit of money and get in some workers without proper papers.

'Do you think Tobias knew?'

'I have no idea, but that man has always acted in his own interests. If he did know, and he thought there was something he could get out of the telling, then he would have done it.'

'It would explain why he's ditched us, the ungrateful piece of shit. He probably wanted to save his own neck. I wouldn't be surprised to discover he's in it with Warbeck.'

The traffic is heavy. It is the time of day when the back-streets are lined with delivery vans, parked with two wheels up on the pavement. People in overalls carry boxes into restaurants. They run across the road with their hands full and pop out from behind vans.

'They think they can run out into the street without looking and expect other people to fall over themselves to accommodate them,' Agatha says to Roster. 'One of these days, someone is going to plough right into them. It's the road, for god's sake. Roads are for cars.'

Roster honks his horn, then honks it again, then holds his

hand down on the centre of the steering wheel, and the horn rings out in a long, sonorous semibreve.

Her sisters have threatened to turn up to the inquiry today and accost her in person. It's the last thing she needs, especially if the press is there to see it. One of them – Chelsea – gave information about her to a magazine, and Agatha imagines they would all relish the opportunity to stand outside the inquiry making incendiary remarks about her to the cameras and waiting journalists. She pictures them: three sirens, waiting for her as she draws up in her car. She wonders if she will recognise them, whether they will look like her, or like Valerie, or like the painting of the father that still hangs outside her bedroom. When she was a child she thought of her sisters as very ugly – her mother told her they'd had cosmetic surgery back when the procedures were crude. Anastasia described them as 'vacuumed-packed gargoyles'. But perhaps this was all a fabrication. When Valerie speaks about them, they lose their hideous aspect and become unexceptional, almost normal. This frightens Agatha even more: the thought that, when she sees them, she might not know them. They could fall into step beside her, brush against her in the crowd, their eyes meeting her own, and there would be no recognition. Either way, she will try her best to avoid them – go in quickly, give her evidence, leave. She will be on her yacht by evening, then sailing into international waters.

A Choir of Sighs

Precious holds the baby, one hand beneath the child's bottom and another beneath her head. She is three days old and her parents can't decide what to call her. Precious tells them not to rush, the name will come to them in time. 'It's better to get it right than to do it immediately,' she says. 'She'll have that name her whole life.' The baby is met with a choir of sighs each time she opens her eyes or flexes the joints in her tiny hands. Currently, she is asleep. She has a soft round head, a little nose, scrunched-up eyes and a serious mouth that twitches as she sleeps, as if she is sceptical about the content of her dreams. Her thin film of dark hair looks like it is held in place by static electricity.

Precious places the baby in the washing basket among folded bedsheets, fresh from the line, smelling of sunshine. She begins to unbutton her blouse.

Nicky and Marcus have a number of colourful wraps that they are using to wear the baby, and it works best if skin is next to skin.

Precious didn't do this with either of her boys though she had older cousins and extended family members who wore their babies in this way. Nicky tried to show her how to fix the wrap, but Precious stopped her gently, saying, 'I know how to do it. I watched women wrapping babies like that for years.' It was only saying this that she realised she did truly remember. It was as if the image had been tucked away when she left her family behind, and now it comes back, as she takes off her top and bra and puts her baby granddaughter against her chest, wrapping the bright fabric around the pair of them like she's grafting a cutting to a tree.

The baby searches for a nipple, her mouth opening and closing like a cod. 'There's nothing for you there,' Precious croons, 'but I've got something else until your mummy comes out of the bath.'

She sticks out her little finger and the baby begins to chew, surprising Precious, as babies always do, with the strength of her jaws and the little tongue she keeps between them.

With the child settled around her finger, Precious is unable to continue folding the dry laundry into the basket. She leaves the last couple of pillowcases to swing in the breeze and instead potters from one side of the patio to the other, inspecting the plants. Most are in a bad way. She leans over and pulls out weeds with her free hand, snapping the stalks that have died. Precious has encouraged Marcus and Nicky to begin from scratch – to pull everything up, empty out the pots, and buy new bulbs and seedlings from the garden centre, but they haven't taken her advice. She might surprise them and remodel the patio herself. It could be more than this: a little square of life, rather than just a place to hang the washing, and store the rusty gas barbecue they never use.

Being a grandmother suits Precious better than being a mother ever did. There are fewer details, more grand plans. It has more to do with artistry and enthusiasm and less to do with following a strict routine of feeding, burping, changing, washing, sleeping, playing, educating. She wasn't – isn't – a bad mother, but it has never felt like her natural role, rather a part in which she was cast against type. She loves her sons and has done her best for them, but when they were small she found them very tiring and, when they got older, they became more difficult to manage. As teenagers, they got into a lot of trouble at school, and they hung around on street corners with people who were no good at all. It was around this time that they went to live with their paternal grandmother in Crystal Palace. Precious moved in with Tabitha in Soho.

The boys had more space with Ondine – she had a little

semi-detached with a garden and parks nearby, and the change of schools did them good too. They started to apply themselves. Neither of them would have got any qualifications at all if they'd stayed where they were. Precious sent Ondine money so didn't feel too bad about leaving the boys with her. And Ondine bloody well ought to have atoned for bringing up that prick of a son who left Precious with a one-year-old while she was pregnant with their second. Now and again, Precious wonders if the boys had been angry with her; angrier than they had let on at the time. But if she hadn't made that decision, she wouldn't be in the secure financial position she is in now. She definitely wouldn't have been able to give Marcus and Nicky the deposit for this flat, with the same amount stored safely in the bank for when Ashley gets to that stage. Marcus and Nicky don't know anyone of their age who has been able to buy a place of their own – all of their friends will be renting well into their forties. Precious feels a huge amount of pride when they tell her this.

It has been three months since she and Tabitha moved in. Though among family, both women feel uncomfortable. Marcus and Nicky have been accommodating, but the house is small, and having two additional adults in it has made things cramped. Nicky keeps telling them it's fine. 'You do so much around the place, Precious. It's honestly a godsend.' It's true Precious and Tabitha have been making themselves useful. They have been cooking and cleaning and helping with the kids. Precious's elder granddaughter Connie is at the stage of her life when she is learning that her grandmother allows her to get away with more than her parents do, and she is pushing at those boundaries, testing how far they will stretch.

After the incident, Nicky advised Precious and Tabitha to get some counselling. 'You've just experienced something very traumatic. You'll need help to process it all.'

Precious was reluctant, being naturally averse to talking about her feelings, but she agreed to go and see someone who

Nicky recommended. She spoke to him about being up on the roof with Tabitha and Robert, feeling the tremors becoming more and more pronounced, the building moving beneath her feet, the timbers giving way, all her plant pots cascading out of sight.

What she didn't tell the counsellor was how exhilarating she had found the experience. She was worried that it would make her sound callous: people died that night. But, in some ways, it had been spectacular; the most alive she had ever felt.

It wasn't clear what had caused the building to fall into the earth. There was talk of a sinkhole. Other people mentioned the construction of Crossrail, and the subsidence of listed buildings. Precious had argued vociferously that the building had collapsed because dozens of rowdy men in riot gear suddenly ran through it hitting people over the heads, and although it wasn't a particularly convincing argument, it was politically savvy. Precious has to be politically savvy these days. At first all the activists only wanted her to run for the council, but now they're being more ambitious. After the building collapsed, she received even more attention than before, and now her profile has soared.

It is the spring equinox, and bird song has been more noticeable these last few weeks. Precious can hear it now, the sharp, twinkling treble cutting through the low hum of traffic. It is the first day of the public inquiry and she and Tabitha will head over to Westminster in a couple of hours. Some lawyers have become involved (on a pro bono basis) and the press will be there too. Precious has prepared a statement. She runs through it in her head as she holds the baby, keeping her soft skin shielded from the sun.

Nicky comes out on to the patio. She is dressed but her curly hair is wet. She is holding a comb and a bottle of serum. She tilts her head to the side, squeezes a drop of gloopy liquid from the bottle, and rubs it into her hair then uses the comb to tease out tangles.

'You've got the baby wearing down, I see.'

Precious smiles, but the baby hears her mother's voice and gurgles.

'Just let me do my hair,' Nicky says, 'I'll take her from you in a sec.'

Precious holds her little finger next to the baby's mouth, hoping to tempt her for a second time, but now that her mum, and the possibility of milk, is nearby, there is no settling her. The gurgle soon becomes a plaintive cry, and Nicky hurriedly readies herself. Precious unwraps the fabric, and Nicky turns away as her mother-in-law reveals skin.

Precious smiles. 'Sorry, love, I've never been private about my body and I forget that other people are. I didn't mean to embarrass you.'

'No, no, no, it's fine,' Nicky insists, turning back around to make a point, though looking everywhere but at Precious. She takes the child.

'I'm guessing you're more shy about your body,' Precious says as she picks up her bra and slips her arms into each of the loops.

'You could say that. I've always been a bit of a prude. I get nervous when it comes to nudity. Don't know why. I'm one of those women who use the little separate cubicles in the changing room at the swimming pool.'

'Ah, you're one of those! I've always wondered who those cubicles were for.'

'I assume you are fine with getting naked in front of everyone.'

Precious laughs. 'Well, I'm not one of those who parades around, checking out my own arse in the mirror, but yeah, I'm totally fine with stripping off in front of other people.' Then she says, 'It's sort of, you know, part of the job.'

Nicky smiles awkwardly, then looks at Precious, who is now fully clothed. She opens her mouth as if she is about to say something but doesn't.

Precious has enjoyed getting to know Nicky better. The

pair of them have long chats while sitting out here on the patio, or while on walks with Connie, and now with the new baby too. Nicky was never shown how to cook when she was growing up, so Precious has been teaching her these last few months. Tabitha offers contradictory advice from her seat at the kitchen table while she completes the crossword or a number puzzle.

Precious has also been getting to know her sons. Perhaps unconsciously, she has always thought of them as wandering, somewhat wayward, portions of herself, rather than as men in their own right. Now, Marcus is slowly revealing himself to her, and Ashley too, to a lesser extent, when he comes over at the weekend to watch football on his brother's Sky Sports pass. From the sofa, she and Tabitha and Nicky ask deliberately annoying questions while Marcus and Ashley sit on the floor, cross-legged or knees up in front of them with their arms looped around. The pair have sat like this since they were children – as close to the telly as possible.

On the bus to Westminster, there is only room to stand, and Precious holds on to the pole with a hand that becomes clammier, and tighter, as the journey progresses. Through the window she sees London whirling past like a magic lantern. A woman is stacking green mangoes on to the fruit and vegetable shelves outside her shop. A cyclist in pink Lycra is skipping a red light. Up high, an intrepid cat is sunbathing on a flat roof, licking her front paws then rubbing her eyes. The bus crosses the river, and Precious looks out to see white swans and pleasure boats and tourists taking photos.

The bus stop is a little way from the inquiry. A crowd has already gathered outside the building. There are journalists and photographers. Precious recognises some faces from the neighbourhood – shopkeepers and waiters who have come to show their support. A couple of times, she spots a woman who she thinks might be her – tall, glamorous, cold – but she can't be sure. These women have her aspect – from the pictures she's seen – but something about them isn't right. They are too old; too eager.

Then Precious spots a blue Rolls Royce reversing into a parking space.

'That's her,' she says quietly. It is unclear even to her whether she is speaking to the other women or to herself. Tabitha and Nicky follow her gaze.

'Oh right,' says Tabitha.

'Who is it?' Nicky asks.

Precious doesn't answer. She begins to walk in the direction of the blue car, but Tabitha holds out an arm. 'I'm not sure that's a good idea, love. You shouldn't do or say anything without lawyers being around.'

Precious shrugs her off and continues along to the car. She always felt that if she could have had it out with this woman, one to one, it would never have ended the way it did. Precious has a huge amount of faith in the power of human communication; of two people looking each other in the eye and speaking their minds, generously, politely, but clearly.

The driver's door opens and a man steps out. He is old, but not elderly. He moves around the large car, catching her eye, looking her up and down, spotting Tabitha, looking back to Precious. He then pulls at the rear door, swings it open. A huge dog jumps out, and Precious steps back, startled. It is tall and thin, with long, white fur, a pointed face and dark eyes. After the initial shock, she steadies herself, and crouches, then holds out a hand. The dog comes forward and touches his wet nose to her upturned palm.

The Last Laugh

Bastian and Laura are lost.

'Shank, it's called Shank. Not Hunk. Shank.'

'You thought it was called Hunk? Why would it be called Hunk?'

'You know, like a hunk of meat. I thought that was the general vibe.'

Bastian and Laura are trying to find the restaurant, only Bastian has been typing the wrong name into his phone map and has been met with confusing search results.

Bastian tries to visit Laura every weekend. He gets the train on Friday night and another back to London on Sunday afternoon or Monday morning. This is the first time Laura has been down to London to visit him. Her mum has assured her she is able to cope without her. Bastian left his office early to go and meet her at King's Cross.

They are now heading in the right direction. Bastian holds his phone in front of him with his right hand. Laura has slipped her right hand into his left and he grips it tightly, eager to endorse this rare public display of their relationship.

They stop outside the door of a restaurant. It looks to be newly opened. The windows are very clean and it smells of fresh paint. The decor takes its inspiration from an old-fashioned butcher's shop. The waiters are all wearing stripy aprons. They look up at the sign.

'Here we are,' says Laura. 'Hunk.'

Bastian laughs sarcastically. 'It quite clearly says Shank.'

'Oh no,' says Laura. 'I was actually referring to you.'

She gives him a coy smile. He shakes his head but laughs

anyway. Then he pulls her towards him by her coat and kisses her lips.

They have a table reserved, booked in advance by Lorenzo.

They are greeted by one of the waiters in the stripy aprons. He is very tall and muscular. Many of the waiters seem to be tall and muscular. The selling point of the restaurant (according to an online review Bastian read) is that huge pieces of locally sourced meat are cooked publicly. You can see into the kitchens as you eat. There are *parrillas*, which are a kind of Argentine barbecue, and at one side of the kitchen there is a huge, enclosed fire pit where whole animals are roasted on a spit. The waiters have to be strong because they parade around the restaurant carrying the meat.

Glenda and her Lorenzo are already there, sitting at a rectangular table with two place settings at either side. Glenda grins when she sees them, and Lorenzo smiles too. They both get up and come round the table to greet them. Bastian shakes Lorenzo's hand. Then Bastian goes round the table to hug Glenda. He opens his arms and draws her towards him in a tight embrace. She sinks into the hug easily and rests her head on his chest briefly before pulling away. Bastian has only seen Glenda once since she left London, and only for a short time. She looks healthier and happier, and stronger, physically and emotionally.

They all sit down. Bastian and Laura are on one side; Glenda and Lorenzo are on the other. 'We should just get Lorenzo to order for all of us,' suggests Glenda. 'He's been here before and knows what's good. And I find that when you're sharing stuff in a restaurant it gets annoying when everyone has their own suggestions but also everyone is too polite to make any firm decisions, and you end up going round and round.'

Lorenzo orders the suckling pig spit roast. 'It's basically a heart attack on a plate,' he says. His tone makes it clear he considers this to be a good thing.

The furniture in the restaurant is made from chipboard.

Lorenzo says that chipboard is the new exposed brick. The restaurant is lit by bare lightbulbs hung from long electrical cables that have been finished in copper tape.

Bastian and Laura are fascinated by Lorenzo's profession and the actors he's been working with on the TV show. They ask questions about his day-to-day life, what so-and-so and so-and-so are like as people. They offer their opinions on what so-and-so and so-and-so are like in real life even though they've never met them. Bastian mentions somebody he was at school with who's now famous, but none of the others have heard of him. Lorenzo is discreet but makes it clear that he is not totally convinced by the project, and that he's even thinking of looking into a career change.

'What would you be if you weren't an actor?' Glenda asks.

Lorenzo shrugs. 'I'm not sure. The thing about being an actor is that, in theory, you get to be a bunch of different things at the same time. One day you can be a doctor, and the next day you can be a medieval prince, and the day after that you can be an astronaut. You don't have to settle down at any point. But it's also kind of disconcerting, for that very reason. I'm not sure it's good for me. I'm not sure it's good for anyone but, well, some people are addicted to that feeling of endless possibility.'

One of the waiters walks towards them carrying a spit struck through a huge hunk of pork. Some of the pork fat drips on to the floor. The waiter places the meat on a wooden board at the centre of their table and begins to carve it with a long steel knife. The four friends eat in silence, digging their teeth into the roasted flesh, biting down on crackling. They wipe their chins with paper napkins. When they are done, they sit back in their chairs.

During pudding Lorenzo makes his excuses and heads off towards the men's toilets. On his way he takes a left, through a door labelled private, and follows a corridor round to where he supposes the pantry might be.

'Can I help you?' says someone in kitchen whites.

Lorenzo sees no reason to lie. 'I'm looking for Cheryl Lavery.'

The man in kitchen whites looks confused by the request but leads him into a back storeroom where Cheryl is stacking boxes. She is still wiry, dreadfully thin, as he remembered, but she seems healthier. Her skin is smoother, her hair is sleek. She appears at least two decades younger than she used to – younger than Lorenzo, just about.

'Cheryl,' says the man in kitchen whites. 'There's someone here to see you.' He raises his voice at the end as if it is a question, clearly surprised.

Cheryl puts down the box she is holding. It hits the floor with a heavy thud. She turns towards Lorenzo. Her face exhibits confusion, then recognition, then confusion.

'You're that man from the pub,' she says. 'But why are you here?'

He isn't sure he's ever heard her speak before. Her voice is unexpectedly ethereal.

'Did you know a Robert Kerr?'

'Yes,' she says. 'He was kind to me.'

'I was appointed executor of his will. He's left you a little bit of money. This letter, addressed to you, was among his papers.'

Lorenzo pulls out Robert's letter from the inside pocket of his jacket. Cheryl takes the envelope from him and turns it over in her hands, now pale, clean, manicured. She opens it and begins to read, and Lorenzo turns. He gets to the door of the storeroom but then Cheryl says, 'He's not my father.'

Lorenzo turns back but doesn't say anything. He feels disappointed for Robert, but it is too late now anyway.

'My dad's dead,' Cheryl continues. 'My mum told me. He was some kind of businessman. And he was geriatric. Eighty-four or something. He had a heart attack right afterwards, while he was still in bed with my mum.' Then she laughs. 'Knocked up my mum and got killed in the process.

Hahahahaha.' Her laugh is as ethereal as her speech. It echoes around the storeroom, against the boxes and shelves, stacked with glasses and plates. 'He kicked the bucket right on top of her, with his willy still inside.' She laughs and she laughs. Lorenzo turns and leaves, and hears her laughter as he walks back along the corridor, and he even thinks he hears it still when he's back at the table talking to Glenda and Bastian and Laura, though they say they can't hear anything and throw him quizzical looks. But Lorenzo hears it. He hears her laughing and laughing, the sound rising from the basement of the restaurant, hahahahaha, up through steel girders and polished floors, hahahahaha, up through the foundations of the building, hahahahaha up from the belly of the city.

Acknowledgements

Thank you to Leslie Gardner, Darryl Samaraweera, Angus MacDonald and Jon Curzon at Artellus Ltd.

Thank you to everyone at John Murray Press, especially Becky Walsh who has supported me throughout the writing of this book, and Yassine Belkacemi who has looked after me at public events.

Thank you to early readers and good friends: Alastair Bealby, Veronica Bennett, Francesca Bratton, Sarah Cawthorne, Tim Curtis, Jennie England, Cameron Foote, Robin Foote, Marianne Forrest, Caitlin Girdwood, David Girdwood, Lisa Girdwood, Wendy Grace, Sophie Howard, Ian Lea, Celia Moodie, Philippa Morris, Emily Nott, Karl O'Hanlon, Catherine Rogerson-Yarrow, Thomas Rogerson-Yarrow, Nicola Runciman, Helen Spriggs, Alice Taylor, John Weir.

Love and thanks to my family: Caroline Mozley, Harold Mozley, Olivia Johnson, Neil Johnson and Lily Johnson.

Most of all, thank you to Megan, who makes it all worthwhile.